Praise for G. A. Aiken and her novels

"G. A. Aiken is hilarious . . . the humor is
so wry, the characters amusing."
—USAToday.com on *How to Drive a Dragon Crazy*

"A tale filled with Aiken's trademark over-the-top humor,
outrageous situations, and exhilarating action scenes."
—*Publishers Weekly* on *Bring the Heat*

"It is a testament to Aiken's storytelling that a series
that is so over-the-top violent and bloody is also
heartwarming and side-splittingly funny."
—*RT Book Reviews* on the Dragon Kin series

"This tale should definitely please fans of sexy
shape-shifters and epic sagas."
—*Booklist* on *About a Dragon*

"This series is so unapologetic, violent and absolutely
hilarious and has quickly become a PNR favorite of mine."
—Paranormal Haven

"As bawdy, crass, and hilarious as anything I could have
hoped for . . . a chest-thumping, mead-hall-rocking,
enemy-slaying brawl of a good book."
—All Things Urban Fantasy

"A hot-hot series."
—*Library Journal* on the Dragon Kin series

The Dragon Kin series from G. A. Aiken

THE
BLACKSMITH
QUEEN

G. A. AIKEN

KENSINGTON BOOKS
www.kensingtonbooks.com

KENSINGTON BOOKS are published by

Kensington Publishing Corp.
119 West 40th Street
New York, NY 10018

All Kensington titles, imprints, and distributed lines are available at special quantity discounts for bulk purchases for sales promotion, premiums, fund-raising, educational, or institutional use.

Special book excerpts or customized printings can also be created to fit specific needs. For details, write or phone the office of the Kensington Sales Manager: Kensington Publishing Corp., 119 West 40th Street, New York, NY 10018. Attn. Sales Department. Phone: 1-800-221-2647.

Kensington and the K logo Reg. U.S. Pat. & TM Off.

ISBN-13: 978-1-4967-2122-8 (ebook)
ISBN-10: 1-4967-2122-5 (ebook)
Kensington Electronic Edition: September 2019

ISBN-13: 978-1-4967-2120-4
ISBN-10: 1-4967-2120-9
First Kensington Trade Paperback Edition: September 2019

10 9 8 7 6 5 4 3 2 1

Printed in the United States of America

To all the beautiful and amazing horses I got to meet, pet, and nuzzle at the Los Angeles Equestrian Center. All of you gave me a lot to work with as did the owners and trainers I had the privilege to chat with. Thanks to you all.

Acknowledgments

Equine information is easy to find in books, but to actually get to meet the animals and have their movements explained in the context of ancient combat...that is more than just luck. Dean Murray provided me with that information plus years of informative (and fun) discussions on war history (ancient and more recent), horses (from battle steeds to dressage), hand-to-hand combat and martial arts, and sometimes old-time mobsters.

So my heartfelt gratitude goes out to Dean. Because there's truly nothing better than someone who can tell a tale about ancient military operations and always make it entertaining enough to keep the focus of this ADHD gal so that I can use that information days/weeks/years later in my books.

PROLOGUE

The great king had barely taken his last breath before one brother took the head of another.

It happened so fast that I, the Follower of His Word, had no chance to escape. I attempted to run, but the castle halls were quickly filled with battling men and dying women and children. I ended up hiding where I could, but I had to keep moving in order to stay alive.

I could hear the screams of the dying but I was not brave enough to step in. To help. Not with what I already knew.

His Majesty had warned me of this many years before.

"When I die," he'd said, looking at me from his throne, "my sons will tear everything apart. They will destroy everything I've built in their attempt to take my place. But none will be worthy. None."

I don't know the truth of that, but who was I? Just the Follower of His Word. I did not know if any were worthy or if all were. It was not my job to make those decisions.

But I had no idea it would be like this. This . . . fast.

All the youngest boys were immediately killed by their older siblings. Cut down with their protective mothers in their beds. There was no mercy for them.

The older sons quickly faced off against each other but not all of them were true warriors. The weakest met their ends quickly. Those who could fight did their best but in the end, it seemed that only five princes remained: Marius the Wielder of Hate, the Old

King's eldest and most feared; Straton the Devourer; Cyrus the Honored; and the twins—Theodorus and Theotimus—who were too young to have earned epithets but who were already loathed for their viciousness.

At one point, I saw Straton and Cyrus escape the castle grounds; Cyrus taking as many innocents with him as he could in order to save their lives. I tried to get downstairs to join him, but my path was blocked by fighting men.

It was said that Cyrus had taken half of his father's army, those who were loyal to him, and was even now planning his next attack against his brothers while Straton already had an army of mercenaries waiting for their orders. As the day wore on, no one seemed to know where the twins had gone and no one was looking for them, except maybe the remaining brothers. But, despite their battle skills, they were relatively stupid and I was sure that no one had much to worry about. Even if they appeared again at some point, they would easily be wiped out.

That meant the castle and its grounds were currently held by Prince Marius, who had already taken over the rest of his father's army. At this moment I could hear him moving through the castle, killing all those he didn't believe loyal to him and only him or, even worse, those who might have the slightest chance of obtaining the throne through bloodlines.

Not knowing how I would be seen by Marius—I had always been openly loyal to his father and was a distant cousin to Marius—I scrambled into the Old King's room and dove behind one of the giant pillars.

My timing was quick enough, thank the gods! Because another cousin of mine ran into the chamber shortly after me. He was already covered in blood, but Marius followed behind him and took him to the ground by slicing his sword down the man's spine. Our cousin fell to the marble floor and sobbed. Desperately.

"Prince Marius, please! I am your kin! Please!"

Marius said nothing to his begging cousin, simply slammed his blade through his back and directly into his heart, ignoring the fact that the Old King's body was still in his bed.

I covered my mouth, terrified I'd cry out. I was not meant for battle. I was not meant for war. I was simply a chronicler. I took notes of the Old King's life. But each king picked his own chronicler and Marius would not want to have anything that once belonged to his father except his throne and his crown.

Marius finished his work and straightened. I moved farther back around the pillar, praying he wouldn't search the room. But he didn't leave and I knew he was coming. Coming for me.

Then the gods must have heard my prayers because that sweet voice rang out.

"Marius? Where are you?"

"Mother?"

"Oh, there you are!" I peeked around the pillar again and watched Marius's mother enter the Old King's chamber. Maila had been the Old King's lead consort because she'd given birth to his first son. The Old King never married, so Maila was as close as the subjects had to a Dowager Queen. And, unlike the other consorts, she'd lived almost like a queen because when the Old King needed to entertain, it was Maila that he always had by his side. That also meant she had ample gold and jewels and could purchase anything she liked whenever she liked. Her gowns were always the most beautiful and glamorous, her hair artfully done. It also helped that Maila had managed to keep her beauty.

"Mother, what are you doing here? You are supposed to be in the safety of—"

Another cousin ran into the chamber, mace swinging. Maila quickly ducked and Marius blocked the weapon with his sword before slamming his dagger into the man's belly. Again and again, then slitting his throat for good measure.

"Mother, you need to go back to my soldiers. They will protect you."

"I needed to speak to you and it cannot wait. Besides, most of your brothers are either dead or gone. The castle is ours."

"Still, I'd feel better if—"

Another screaming soldier ran into the chamber, sword above his head, ready to strike Prince Marius. The soldier wore the colors of Prince Cyrus and was ready to die for the man he hoped would be king.

Marius raised his weapons again but Maila held up her hand to stop him and, a few seconds later, the soldier stopped in his tracks, his sword still raised above his head. He coughed, blood shooting out of his mouth. Maila gave a small laugh, covering her mouth as the soldier fell forward, dead.

"Mother, what did you do?"

"I poisoned the soldiers' well. Oh, don't look at me that way," she complained. "We both know I could never stay out of this. I've been waiting since your birth for you to ascend to the throne."

"This is my fight."

"Wrong. This is *our* fight. Do you really think all my other sons actually died accidentally? No. I took their lives because it was my right, as their mother, to do so. I couldn't get near your other half brothers because of *their* mothers but I knew when the time came, you'd be able to handle the rest. And here you are doing a brilliant job. So allow me some fun."

The sound of more battling soldiers in the hallway had the prince pulling Maila closer, moving in front of her.

"Just tell me what's going on and make it quick, please."

"A messenger arrived not too long ago. From the Witches of Amhuinn."

I was surprised by that. The Witches of Amhuinn usually stayed in their mountainside fortress, reading their books and keeping their tallies. They didn't dance naked in the moonlight, they didn't sacrifice bulls in the early hours of dawn, they didn't make potions for love or revenge. But despite all that, their declarations had power. Even the Old King respected what they had to say.

And what they had to say must have been important for Maila to leave the safety of wherever her son had placed her.

"What do they want?" the prince asked.

"They have called to the gods and—"

One of the prince's uncles charged into the room, but he was older and didn't move as he once had. Marius took his head and kicked his body to the floor.

"Mother, just get to it!"

"Their seer has seen a queen. A queen to replace the Old King."

I frowned in confusion. In all my years, I couldn't remember the Amhuinn having a "seer." It would have to be someone who'd truly proven themselves since it had always been said the Witches of Amhuinn relied on statistics rather than those who could see into the future.

"What queen?"

"A girl. A farmer's daughter."

"A *peasant?*"

"*I* was a peasant before being sold to your father."

"Then put the bitch in chains and bring her to me. One way or another, I will be the next ruler of these lands."

Maila glanced at the Old King's body in his bed, and I saw no pain, nor pity at his death. "Your half brother, Straton, has already gone after this farmer's daughter."

"Good. Let him kill her. I've got other things to—"

"Don't be like your brothers," Maila snapped at her son. "Short-sighted. Whether peasant or royal, if a girl has been chosen by the Witches of Amhuinn, she will be more readily accepted by the dukes and barons of these lands."

"Why would I need—"

"You need their armies. Cyrus has already taken half your father's men. The rest are loyal to you, but if you hope to win against Cyrus and, more difficult still, Straton, who has been building his mercenary army for years, then you need more men. Men willing to die for you."

"Soooo . . . you want *me* to kill her?"

"No! Dammit, Son! Think! To have a queen at your side, with the blessing of the Witches of Amhuinn. The same sect that put your ancestors on the throne four hundred years ago."

Marius let out a long sigh. "You want me to rescue her from my brother."

"It's too late for that. Protectors have already been sent to her."

"Protectors sent by you?"

"No. These are not friends of ours. But they'll need to take her to the Witches of Amhuinn for the girl to be confirmed in person. We can find her there. Take her and then you marry her. Make her queen."

"I don't want to get married."

"Your father was the only son of his father. You, my dearest, were not that lucky. But having a wife—a queen—does not mean you cannot have your own whores on the side. Your great-grandfather certainly did and your great-grandmother, the queen, always knew her place."

"I don't know—"

"Meet her. She'll be retrieved and brought to you. I'll arrange it all. Once we have her, you can decide if you want to keep her or slit her throat."

Marius blew out a breath and stared at the ceiling. "All right. I'll meet her. But she has to survive Straton first. I'm not ready to face him yet."

"If she can't manage to outmaneuver your half brother," Maila said, stepping over dead family members, "it's not like she'll be a great loss."

"You need to promise me something, though," Marius said to his mother's back.

She faced him. "And what's that, my love?"

"That whoever this peasant is . . . you won't kill her until *I* decide I have no use for her."

"Why would I ever—"

"*Mother.*"

Maila smirked. "I promise. I'll be good." The pair stared at each other until Maila added, "At the very least I'll try."

"Thank you. I've always appreciated your guidance, but now that Father is gone, it's time I make my own decisions."

"Of course."

"So please don't force me to put you away in a nunnery until your sudden and tragic death not too far in the future."

"You'd do that to your own mother?" Maila asked her only remaining son.

Marius stepped close to his mother and gently placed his blood-covered palm against her cheek. "Before you could pray to your chosen gods to save you."

Maila smiled. "You are so very much my son."

They left the chamber, Marius taking his mother back to safety. I took my chance then and crawled through the hidden door under the enormous bed that the Old King had kept secret from all but me.

Once I was on the other side, I slowly closed the door behind me so no one heard my escape. Once I could stand up, I rushed down the narrow, hidden hallway, praying the steel door at the end was not blocked by some burly soldier who'd wonder what I was "up to."

My escape took me several long minutes but once I reached the steel door, I opened it just enough to see if there was anyone in my way. This door led into the forests on the west side of the castle. I searched the trees with my gaze but saw nothing. I eased out and took my time closing the door behind me, afraid to make even the slightest sound. Once I heard the final click, I let out a breath and—

"Leaving us so soon, Keeper?"

I shut my eyes in despair, barely holding back tears as I faced Lady Maila.

"Now, now, don't cry. I'm not here to kill you. I'm here to offer protection from my son." She came from around the tree where she'd been waiting and took my arm. "Things here are about to drastically change and I need my own historian. You can be the Keeper of *My* Word. Won't that be nice?"

What could I say? No? Not to Lady Maila. Not only because of her son but because to challenge Maila was to sign one's own death warrant. And I was not ready to die.

So, instead, I replied, "That would be lovely, my lady."

"Excellent." Together, we headed back to the castle. "And you can now call me Dowager Queen. It's quite fitting, don't you think?"

"Yes, my lady."

"And just wait until you meet my son's future queen. She's like no one you've met before."

I hoped the Dowager Queen was correct. Because that poor girl, whoever she may be, would have to be quite special if she was to have any chance of surviving this mother and son.

CHAPTER 1

The massive head of the hammer landed hard on the ground, startling the men who had strung him up.

He could see her—barely—as he hung there. He tried to warn her. To tell her to get away. These were soldiers for hire. They had no loyalty to anyone but themselves and the one paying them.

They had stumbled upon him sleeping by this same tree and before he knew it, they'd decided they wanted his meager things and the three horses he'd been traveling with and, Oh! Wouldn't it be fun to see him swing?

Well . . . no. No, it was not fun to swing.

Still. He didn't want this very large woman to risk her own life to save his. Men like this were even more cruel to women than they were to lone men sleeping under trees.

She'd swung her big hammer up and over her head and, when the massive head had hit the ground, she'd stood there a moment. Chin down. Her muscles tense under her sleeveless, black leather tunic.

After that brief moment, she lifted just her gaze and growled, "Cut him loose."

One of the soldiers laughed. "Look what we have here, lads! A big-armed slut looking for—"

That hammer was up and swinging before the soldier could finish his statement, sending him flying into another nearby tree. Bones cracked and blood shot out of the soldier's mouth.

Swords were drawn and they surrounded her.

"Bad decision, woman," another soldier said.

"No," she replied. "Bad decision coming to *my* town and killing a boy."

Wait one moment. He wasn't dead yet! Of course, that was mostly because the soldiers had taken their time dragging him off the ground so that he'd die slow. They'd literally said, "Let's watch him die slow, lads!"

One soldier swung his blade at the woman and she easily parried the move with that astoundingly large hammer before ramming the head into the man's chest. He fell back, his chest caved in, his gasps for breath painful to hear.

He wanted to watch more, begging the gods to protect this brave but foolish woman, but his gaze began to dim. He was choking to death.

No! He wasn't going to die. He was going to fight!

Making the decision, he worked harder to get fingers between the rope and his throat in the hope of loosening it. As he struggled, he looked out toward a nearby hill, and saw the herd of wild horses he'd spotted the night before. At the time, he'd thought the three horses he'd been tending would blend in with the herd. He'd even stripped them of their saddles and bridles and hidden them right outside the forest. But that hadn't worked out as he'd hoped.

Now, those wild horses were charging over the hill in what seemed to be a panicked run, barreling down toward them. But as they moved over that hill, for a split second, Samuel thought he saw . . . people? Running amongst the horses? *Over* the horses?

Or he was becoming delusional. That was possible too.

Because he was dying. And he would die if he didn't get the noose off.

Knowing he was running out of time, Samuel fought harder. Struggled to get the rope from around his neck.

Most of the men moved away to avoid the oncoming herd. But one attacked the woman. That's when a gray stallion charged between them. When the stallion passed the pair, its back hooves kicked out, catching the man in the head and caving in his skull.

The woman took her chance. She pulled a blade from her belt and hit where the rope had been tied off.

Samuel slammed to the ground, choking and gasping, his fingers now able to dig under the rope; to pull it up and over his head.

A leather-gloved hand appeared in front of his watery gaze.

"Get up, lad!" the woman ordered. "Get up, get up, get up!"

Grasping her hand, Samuel let her pull him to his feet. That was when he realized the horses were running past them. But none had crashed into them. It seemed they were purposely avoiding Samuel and the woman while they trampled the other men.

The woman was looking at Samuel, her gaze on his throat, when suddenly her entire expression changed and she lifted that hammer with the head bigger than Samuel's skull. He took a quick step back just as she turned, swinging her weapon up at the same time.

The metal head slammed into a sword, and the tall, massively built man holding the weapon stared down at her through a mass of thick dark hair.

"That hammer is ridiculous," the man said.

"I love my hammer," the woman replied. "I made it myself." She pulled her weapon away from his sword. "You're Amichai. Aren't you?"

Which explained to Samuel the mighty mane of hair and the leather kilt.

"Perhaps introductions later," the Amichai replied. "You should be more worried about what's behind you." He moved his gaze to Samuel. "Down, boy."

It was barely an order, muttered low, but Samuel immediately followed, dropping to his knees. Just as he did, something whipped past his head. He heard a grunt and a snapping sound. A body fell down beside him and Samuel cringed. He couldn't help it because the woman's hammer slammed on a soldier's face, crashing into it. Blood, skin, bone, and brain exploded out, briefly blinding Samuel.

A hand gripped his upper arm and hauled him to his feet again.

"Behind me, boy," his female rescuer said, pushing him back until he hit a tree trunk.

Samuel wiped the gore from his eyes in time to witness one of the soldiers swing his sword at the woman's head. She jerked to the side and used her hammer to parry the blow, then followed up with a punch to the head that sent the man stumbling to his knees. Not that Samuel was surprised. The shoulders on that woman. By the gods!

The Amichai who had stepped in to help now fought other soldiers. But he was not alone. Like most people from his part of the world, he traveled with others. Two men and a woman. Also tall, also powerfully built, and all of them heavily armed. Based on that description alone, they could have been from anywhere, but the leather kilts, tattoos of their tribes, and what his father always called "their mighty manes of hair" made it clear they were from the Amichai Mountains. The expanse of mountainous territories ruled over by powerful, unfriendly tribes. The Old King's territory butted right up against the base of the Amichai range but he'd never dared challenge the tribes head-on. No one had. They were considered brutal barbarians. Mad killers who ate their own and sacrificed babies to their dead and their demon gods.

Samuel didn't know if all that was true, but at the moment he dearly hoped not. Because they and the big-shouldered woman were the only things keeping him alive.

Reaching for his own sword, Samuel abruptly remembered that it had been snatched from him before the soldiers had strung him up.

"What's your name?" the woman asked, battering the soldier on the ground with her hammer. His face caved in; his chest cracked open.

"Ssss . . . Sssss . . ." He shook his head; tried again. "Samuel."

"I'm Keeley," she replied, stopping to give him a little smile before another soldier came running at her. She spun the hammer around and rammed it forward, the head battering the soldier in the gut. She quickly raised the weapon, bringing the soldier with it.

Samuel watched her lift the man up and over her head. The muscles in her arms and shoulders rippled with the effort before smashing him back to the ground, the head of her hammer now buried inside the soldier's body.

When she yanked the hammer out, blood and gore spattered Samuel again, but he raised his arm to block his eyes this time.

Samuel had to admit . . . he was tired of getting hit with men's insides.

Lowering his now gore-covered arm, Samuel watched as the people who'd taken it upon themselves to rescue him battled the brutal soldiers. Thankfully—for their own sakes more than his—they were all skilled at close-in battle and had handily taken down the soldiers in due course.

Samuel had just let out a relieved breath when Keeley's head snapped up and she looked toward the nearby road. Just as she did, the Amichai woman crouched down and pressed her hand to the ground.

"More coming!" she called out.

"We should get the boy to safety," one of the tribal males said.

"No time." Keeley stalked across the forest toward the road. "I need an axe," she ordered. "*Now!*"

Another Amichai pulled out a beautiful weapon. An axe that seemed to be one long piece of steel. Keeley held out her hand and he tossed it to her. She caught it easily without even stopping.

"What are you going to do?" one of them asked.

"Block this road." She used the axe to motion behind her. "Over there. Now. Move."

Samuel quickly followed her orders as, to his surprise, did the Amichais. Strange, since he'd been raised to believe they were barbarians that didn't follow the orders of anyone.

Grasping the handle of the axe, Keeley raised the weapon high, her entire body tense, her muscles rippling. Then she brought it down, directly into the base of a large tree. She hit it once . . . twice . . . and the tree came down across the road.

"Gods, she's strong," one of the Amichais muttered behind Samuel.

Keeley moved across the road and attacked another tree. Now there were two very large trees blocking the road, but he could finally see what the others had felt. More mercenaries on horseback, riding hard toward them.

"Impressive," the dark-haired male said, "but I don't know what that's supposed to do. We would have been better off running."

The Amichai was probably right, although Keeley did manage to temporarily stop the riders. The ones in front pulled on the reins of their horses and halted their animals by the trees. The one in the lead laughed when he saw the roadblock.

"What is this?"

Keeley didn't answer. She was too busy carrying the body of one of the soldiers' compatriots toward them.

"You bitch!" one of the soldiers barked. "What have you—"

His question was cut off when that body and its insides hit him and several of the others. She then put two bloody fingers to her lips and whistled long and loud.

"You mad cow," the leader said, pulling his sword from its sheath and—

Samuel stumbled back into the tribal female. He couldn't help himself when a wolf appeared from seemingly nowhere, leaped over the soldier's horse, and took down the leader with his fanged maw around the man's throat.

More wolves came from the trees . . . or the ground . . . Samuel wasn't sure. He really wasn't. They seemed to come from everywhere. They weren't larger than the forest wolves he'd seen in his travels but he'd never met any this bold, this bloodthirsty, or this *mean*.

Then one of those wolves turned toward him and Samuel immediately looked away, desperately chanting a protection spell at the same time. He had to.

Their eyes. Dear gods . . . their eyes!

But before Samuel could truly panic, Keeley came jogging toward him, carrying the axe and her hammer as if they weighed nothing. She tossed the axe back to its owner and said, as she ran past, "Now we run away. Run," she cheerfully pushed. "Everyone run. Quick like bunnies!"

Shocked, confused, and unnerved by the death screams of the soldiers, Samuel and the others ran after Keeley.

Samuel whistled and the three horses he'd been traveling with appeared at the edge of the forest and followed their group, which made Samuel very grateful. He didn't want to go back into that forest to find them and he didn't want to tell his master that he'd lost the horses.

That would be a quick way to lose his head. And after he'd gone through so much to keep it on his shoulders . . .

CHAPTER 2

Keeley Smythe had to admit, she hadn't expected her day to go like this. Not when she'd woken up this morning, forced her siblings out of bed so they could begin their chores while their mum slept until the new baby woke her up with her delightful squalling. Helped her father feed the horses, helped her younger brother turn those horses out into the east fields, and stopped a fistfight between two of her siblings.

All a normal early morning for her on her father's farm. Then, as the two suns rose in the sky, she'd picked up her favorite hammer, kissed her mum and da good-bye, and headed out to her favorite place, the Iorwerth Forests. A vast, dense, treed expanse that Keeley had been exploring since she was a little girl. It was in Iorwerth that she saw her first wild horses. Several herds that had made the forest their home. She would go by every day and spend time watching them. She did it for so long, never bothering any of the animals, that they eventually came to her. The foals first, making their wobbly way over to her spot by a tree. Then the yearlings. Finally the beautiful gray lead mare sauntered over, stared at Keeley for a bit, and then went about her own business. After that, the other horses let Keeley get close, offer them treats or help them when they were hurt. But her best friend, her most favorite was the gray mare's son. A gray stallion that always watched out for her, made her laugh, and warned her when her younger siblings were about to do something they would all regret.

She should have known something was wrong with the day

when she went to make her morning check on the herd and found no animal in sight except for three domesticated horses she didn't recognize. Then she'd heard the raucous laughter of men. Keeley knew that sound rarely meant anything good out in the middle of the woods. And she'd been right—a small unit of soldiers were hanging a boy from a tree for their amusement.

Keeley was very glad she'd stepped in when she had. And was even gladder that the Amichais had come along. Could she have handled that entire unit by herself? Probably. Could she have out-lasted them all? Most likely. Could she have done that and kept all her important bits and pieces? Like her arms, legs, and eyes? Probably not.

So she would forever be grateful to the outsiders who'd come to her aid, which was why she was rushing them through the forest.

They'd just made it into the valley when screams from behind them had Keeley spinning around. One of the soldiers was running out of the forest but he suddenly pitched forward and went down, a wolf on his back.

"Shit," she mumbled to herself.

Two more wolves came out of the forest. One grabbed the calf of the soldier and began to drag him back, inch by slow inch. The wolf that was already on his back swiped at his spine, tearing flesh, sending pieces of bone flying.

The soldier screamed, reached out for Keeley.

"Help me! *Please!*"

Keeley went down on her knees and opened her arms. The black wolf she'd known since she'd found him in the forest—alone, crying, and about to be killed by three religious zealots in the garb of Peace Monks—ran to her. He jumped on her, licked her face, and Keeley dug her fingers into his thick fur and wrestled him to the ground.

She laughed until she heard a sword being drawn. Keeley picked up her hammer and turned on her knees, faced the sound. The black wolf stood next to her, baring his fangs, blood-flecked drool drip-ping down his jaws.

It was the female Amichai who now brandished her sword, gaze locked on the wolves.

"I appreciate that you helped out in the forest," Keeley told the female as she got to her feet, holding her hammer in both hands. "But I won't like it if you insist on threatening my friends."

"Your friends? Those things are your friends?"

"Those *things* saved our lives."

"Those *things* had a meal."

Keeley smirked. "A hearty one, too."

"They were called from some hell pit. Demons. You called *demons* to help you. That doesn't bother you? That they're evil?"

"Evil? What makes you think they're evil?" Keeley asked, truly confused.

She pointed her sword. "Flames. They all have flames instead of eyes! That doesn't bother you?"

"As long as I don't put my hands right on their faces, I—"

"*That's not what I mean!*"

The dark-haired Amichai approached the female. "Give us a moment," he said before pulling the female away.

Keeley shrugged and looked down at the black wolf, his eyes of flame gazing back at her.

"Moody bitch, eh?" she asked and her friend "muffed" in agreement.

Caid of the Scarred Earth Clan looked down at his sister and asked, "What the fuck are you doing?"

"Eyes of flame!"

"I know. I can see them." Hard not to really with their eyes burning bright as the two suns above his head. "But you seem to have forgotten why we're here."

"I forget nothing, Brother. But I do ask what kind of people we are dealing with."

"It doesn't matter. The woman is not our goal. Her sister is. And we can't get to one without the other." That was what they'd been told before they were sent out to protect the future queen of these lands, and after watching the family, Caid knew the truth of it. Because Keeley Smythe might not be the mother or father of her family, but she was the matriarch. And after seeing how she'd handled herself in the forest, Caid knew she was not a woman to be trifled with. So his sister's sudden need to challenge Keeley because of her attachment to demon wolves was beyond him. There seemed to be no animal the woman didn't have a fondness for, and she was not about to let some flames shooting from eye sockets stop her.

By the mighty horse gods of the east, Keeley Smythe wasn't anything like he'd been expecting.

"You'll have to get through the sister before you can get to the girl," they had been warned. "She of the steel and stone."

There were not many women who were blacksmiths in the Hill Lands, but some tried to follow in their fathers' footsteps before finding a mate and settling down to bearing children and hard times. But of the very few he'd met in his years, none—absolutely *none*—had been like her.

She carried that battle hammer with the ridiculously sized head around like it weighed nothing. But he'd seen the damage it—and she—had done. That thing was as heavy as it looked and yet she wielded it effortlessly. Wide shoulders, muscular arms and thighs, and a tattoo of one of the blacksmith guilds made her a woman to be feared. Not dismissed as something in their way.

The witches should have made their warning stronger. Because if this woman decided her sister wasn't going anywhere . . . her sister wasn't going anywhere.

Yet despite the obvious strength of her body and the willingness with which she battered soldiers into the ground for no more reason than to help a boy she didn't seem to know and, perhaps, a little early-morning entertainment, the smile she flashed at the thing standing by her long legs proved that she *liked* this animal. Liked and protected it the way she did the wild horses in the valley and the sheep on her neighbor's nearby farm.

In other words, she wasn't evil. Because those who were evil didn't care about anyone but themselves. They certainly wouldn't risk their own lives to protect demon wolves with eyes they had to make sure they didn't put their hands near.

"Would you like to come to town with me?"

Caid looked over his shoulder at the blacksmith. The wolves were gone, as was the soldier, although they could still hear his screams from the forest, hysterically begging for death.

She smiled at him. "I'll take you to my shop. You can have some food, something to drink. Relax for a bit before you get back on the road. Wouldn't that be nice?"

With a nod, Caid agreed. "We'd appreciate that."

"Well, I do owe you a lot. You protected me and my young friend here . . ." She glanced at the boy. "Samuel? Right?"

"Yes. Samuel," the boy replied.

"Let's go, lad. We need to get something on that neck of yours."

Hefting the head of her hammer on her shoulder and holding the steel handle in her hand, she started off, speaking to them over her shoulder.

"I think you'll all like my town. It's a lovely place."

"Come on," Caid said to his sister, motioning to Farlan and Cadell. "We're going with her."

"And we're just going to ignore the demon dogs she's friends with?"

"Demon wolves and yes." He turned his sister around by her shoulders and pushed.

"I'm in charge," she reminded him.

"And our father always says if you have to remind your team of that . . ."

"I'm Keeley by the way," Keeley told her new friends. She walked backward so she could speak directly to them.

"I'm Laila." The female Amichai pointed at the dark-haired Amichai. "This is my brother Caid." She pointed at a shorter but wider blond male. "This is Farlan." She gestured at the male with light-brown hair and an extremely scarred jaw. "And this is Cadell."

Facing forward, Keeley said, "Welcome to all of you."

"So we're just going to pretend those wolves don't exist?" Laila asked.

"That's *exactly* what we're going to do!" Keeley joyfully replied. She'd just survived a battle and she felt pretty good about herself. Why ruin it all by fighting a woman she barely knew?

"Are you a witch of the dark gods?"

"Me? A witch?" Keeley had to laugh. "I have one loyalty aside from my family and it's steel. That's where my heart and love are."

The female suddenly cut in front of Keeley, blocking her from going farther.

"Then how did you call those things to you?"

"*Laila,*" her brother warned, but she merely held her hand up to him.

"I found a puppy once. I helped it."

"I'll ask again. The eyes didn't bother you?"

"Your eyes don't bother me. Why should his?" When the female's gaze narrowed and her head tilted to the side, Keeley added—because she still didn't want to fight—"The world is filled with all kinds. Can't go around ignoring the suffering of others simply because someone looks different from what I've seen before. All I know is he didn't bite me. He didn't try to rip my arms or legs off or go for my throat. So I helped. Just like I helped Samuel. Just like I'm trying to help you."

"I do appreciate that," Laila admitted, "but still—"

"Life is too short to go around hating things I know nothing about. My ignorance doesn't mean others should suffer. Now, I'm going to my shop. You can come with me and Samuel, or you can stay here, worrying about animals you won't see again." Keeley stepped close, lowered her voice so only Laila could hear her. "Or, you and your lot can keep following me around like you've been doing for the last few days and *I* can continue to pretend I don't see you. Something I've been doing because nothing you've done makes me believe you mean any harm to my kin. So it's up to you what you want to do from here since it seems that you are in charge of this little *herd* of yours." Keeley raised a brow. "Understand, Amichai?"

It took a moment for the female to respond. She'd been busy gawking at Keeley with her mouth open. Finally, she tossed her head, hair flipping away from her eyes, and said, "I understand. Perfectly."

"Good. I'm glad. Come along, Samuel!" Keeley called out.

Then, with a wink and a smile—the one that annoyed her mother to no end—Keeley continued on once more. And this time . . . no one stopped her.

Laila gawked at Keeley Smythe as she walked off with Samuel and the boy's three horses. Eventually, her brother came up to her.

"What was that about?" he asked.

"She knows who we are."

"Why do you look so shocked? *Everyone* knows who we are. The kilts usually give it away."

"Let me rephrase. She knows *what* we are."

That did make her brother pause. "What makes you think that?"

She looked at Caid. "She called us a herd."

"Huh."

Cadell and Farlan joined them.

"Is something wrong?" Cadell asked.

"The sister knows what we are," Caid replied.

"Should we kill her?" Farlan asked. When Laila closed her eyes in frustration and let out a little growl, he added, "What? That's a valid question."

"No, it's not!" she snapped. "We can't kill the sister. And we are definitely *not* killing her because she knows. Before this is all said and done, I'm sure a *lot* of humans will know. Should we kill them all, Farlan?"

"If they cause us problems . . ."

Sucking her tongue against her teeth in disgust, Laila followed the blacksmith. "Talk to him, Caid!"

"Talk to me about what?"

"The fact that you're being an ass."

"According to you, I'm always an ass."

"This is true." Caid put his arm around Farlan's big shoulders. "And if you harm the blacksmith in any way, I'll take your cock off and give it to me cousin to make jewelry with. Understand?"

Farlan rolled his eyes but nodded. "Fine. I understand."

"Excellent!" Caid pushed his comrade on. The less talkative Cadell walked alongside him, his smile irritating his friend.

Caid, sensing he was being watched, looked into the forest. It was deep and dark in there even though it was late morning now, but he could see all those burning eyes staring at him. Studying him. It was then that he felt the blacksmith might be wrong. They would be seeing those wolves again, and Caid was not looking forward to that moment at all.

CHAPTER 3

Caid stood in the middle of Keeley Smythe's "shop" as she called it and, for once, he marveled at what he saw.

They'd been following her for about five days before meeting her face-to-face during that minor battle, but they'd never gone *into* her forge. They just wanted to get an idea of who she was and what her family was like.

Her "shop" was not just a forge. She'd apparently purchased the two pitches behind hers and had hired masons to come in and erect a proper building. The first part was a typical forge, with a large hole in the ceiling to allow the smoke to go out. But behind that was the "shop" part, where she sold all manner of steel weapons and then, behind that, was where she brought in the horses for reshoeing.

There were two horses already waiting for her when she arrived, and they were clearly happy when they saw her, affectionately nudging her with their big bodies and resting their giant heads on her shoulder.

But this wasn't a one-woman business. Keeley Smythe had workers. Men and a few boys, who worked the forge. The boys were all in training, but the older men were blacksmiths in their own right. Perhaps they'd found working for themselves too expensive and working for the Old King too dangerous. More than one blacksmith had ended up on the wrong side of the Old King's rages. Or the rages of his sons.

After she assisted the two horses, Keeley returned to Caid and the others. "Let's get you some food and water. Samuel, there's a place out back for you to clean up. Wash your neck," she said, pushing him toward a back door. "I'll put some healing ointment on it after."

Once Samuel was through the door, an older woman emerged from another room. Yawning and scratching her head, she wore nothing but a plain shirt and, stepping from the doorway, she took a nice, long stretch, arms over her head, her body going up on her toes. Tragically, she wore no undergarments and the stretch allowed the shirt to rise until they were all given a lovely view of her crotch.

"Good gods, woman!" one of the blacksmiths complained. "Put some bloody clothes on!"

Caid had never heard a man tell a woman to put *on* clothes before, so he sensed she did this sort of thing often.

Smirking, Keeley pointed at the woman. "This is my cousin. Keran. She lives here."

"It's only temporary."

"It's been temporary for five seasons."

Keran finally had her eyes open and she looked over their group with cold eyes. That's when Caid noticed all the scars. Some on her face. Many on her neck. Quite a few on her legs and arms and more than seemed reasonable on what he could see of her torso when she took another quick stretch—much to the annoyance of the workers. But underneath all those scars were muscles. Hard, trained muscles.

What cleared everything up for him was the tattoo she bore on the side of her neck. Like her cousin, she wore the tattoo of a guild. Unlike her cousin, though, it was not a worker's guild, but a fighter's. Which meant that in her younger days, she'd get in a pit and fight others. Sometimes with weapons. Sometimes with bare hands. And always to the death.

He'd honestly never met a fighter with a little bit of gray at the temples. They never managed to live that long.

"Perhaps you would be kind enough," Keeley teased her cousin, giggling as she spoke, "to put some clothes on before my workers are overwhelmed with your beautiful self."

Keran patted Keeley on the shoulder. "I know how hard it is for them." She turned, but then stopped; blew out a very large breath. "There is something I forgot, Cousin. In my room . . ."

"Ewwww. I don't want to know about that."

For a moment, the fighter appeared confused, but shook her head. "No, lady idiot. You have a visitor. She got here just a few minutes before you did."

Frowning, Keeley stepped around her cousin, but after peering into the room her seemingly always smiling face suddenly had a thunderstorm of an expression. One even Caid would never want to confront.

"What are you doing here?" Keeley demanded, stepping back.

A woman walked out of the backroom. Prim and proper and covered from neck to feet in thick white robes that made her look a tad . . . chunky. White gloves on her hands. A small white cap sat on the back of her head, barely covering her shorn, dark blond hair. She was a nun. Caid didn't know which sect she belonged to, though. She wore no markings on her clothes.

She lifted her hands up, palms open. "Before you say anything," the nun began, "let me just explain . . ."

Laila yawned and the nun saw her for the first time . . . then the rest of them. Her gaze moved over their unit as she slowly lowered her hands. Caid blinked in surprise. Those were not the eyes of a godly nun. Not the way she'd just sized them up.

"Who are your friends?" the nun asked, attempting a smile.

Keeley sneered. "Are you fucking kidding me?"

Startled, the nun looked back at Keeley. "What?"

"You come here, asking questions about *my* friends, and you think I owe you an explanation?"

"It was an innocent question."

"There's nothing innocent about you . . . *sister.*"

"All these years," the nun said softly, shaking her head, "and you are still *an annoying cow!*"

Caid blinked in surprise at the way that sentence went from soft to yelling.

Keran pushed her way between the two and shoved them apart. "Cut it out." Both women opened their mouths to argue, but

THE BLACKSMITH QUEEN • 25

Keran quickly added, "I'll get fully naked right here! Tits and bush for the world to see!"

They closed their mouths, turned away from each other.

"Good," Keran said. "Now I'm going to put on some clothes. You two play nice until I get back or I'll start the punching. Understand?"

She wisely didn't wait for an answer, but as soon as she had disappeared into her room, closing the door behind her, the nun said, "I can't believe you still haven't changed."

"Why should *I* change? I didn't desert my family. That would be you. And for what? To supplicate yourself before some god so you can take care of everyone *but* your kin?"

"It's always so simple for you, isn't it?"

"It is. Family is all. Something you still haven't learned and don't care about."

Sisters. They were sisters. Caid knew that now. They didn't look at all alike, but only siblings could bring out the worst in each other this way.

"Don't tell me what I care about, Keeley," the nun snarled. "You have no idea what I care about! What matters to me!"

"I don't care what matters to you! Get the fuck out of my shop!"

"I'll leave when I'm damn well ready. I don't answer to you! *Not anymore!*"

The back-room door opened and a now-dressed Keran stepped out. "How are we all doing?" she asked, grinning. "Everyone having fun?" When no one answered, she suggested, "Why don't I get food for everyone. You lot look hungry. Fresh bread. Some cheese from Marcy's pitch, eh? Doesn't that sound lovely?"

"I have work to do," Keeley barked before storming away.

"I'll take that as a yes," Keran said, heading toward the front exit.

The nun, though, didn't move. She was too busy watching her sister through narrowed eyes . . . until Samuel came through the door that led out to the back of the shop, freshly washed. At the sight of him, the nun's entire body tensed and her eyes grew wide. But the boy completely panicked, spinning around and attempting to flee out the door he'd just come in. First, though, he ran into the doorframe, backed up, shook off his dizziness, and then ran out, slamming the door behind him.

The nun let out a deep, pained sigh, her eyes briefly closing before she returned to Keran's room.

"Did you see that?" Laila asked him.

"How could I miss it?" Caid asked. "I was standing right here."

"Think the nun fucked the boy?" she whispered, giggling.

"That boy," Caid told her with great confidence, "has fucked no one. Except maybe himself."

Keeley focused on working some iron pommels because she needed to hammer away and steel needed much more finesse. Thankfully all the mercenaries making their way into her shop these days needed swords for their battles. Keeley had been making a small fortune off the upcoming war between the royal brothers and, at times like this, work helped her deal with her rare bouts of rage. She lost herself in the smithing so that her mind could focus on something other than the fact that her younger sister, born only a few years after her, had the bloody nerve to stand before her in that ridiculous outfit and act all pious and gods-infused. Bitch was lucky Keeley didn't punch her right in the nose! And the fact that she didn't point out how chunky being a gods-damn nun had made her showed the strength of Keeley's will. Because those white robes weren't hiding anything! Except her feet. Why did she need to hide her bloody feet? She not only had to give up sex to be a nun but her feet as well?

What religion insisted on covering its worshippers to that extent? Why was that necessary?

Why had her sister given up everything to join those religious fanatics? That's how Keeley thought of the sects found throughout the land. They ruled the lives of their members and Keeley did not like that at all. The gods she chose to worship didn't make her dress in any specific way. They didn't ask her to give up her life for them. A few nonlethal sacrifices for the start of the planting season and to bless her most important weapons, and her gods seemed more than happy.

What she *didn't* have to do was give up her entire family! *That* her gods never asked of her.

And Gemma had been raised the same way, their mother hoping the sisters would work the forge together. A true family business. It was a nice dream but not one that Keeley ever expected her sister to realize since she'd never loved blacksmithing the way Keeley always had. Keeley believed that people, when they could, should do what they loved. She *loved* working with steel, just as their father loved working his farm. Why would she ask Gemma to do something—anything—she didn't love?

Yet locking herself away in some nunnery and giving up all freedom to appease some random god . . . ? That was something Keeley would never understand. Her sister deserved better.

But, after she'd turned sixteen, Gemma had suddenly disappeared one night before the winter frost, leaving nothing but a note for their parents to find.

That was more than a decade ago, and none of them had seen her since. It was true, their parents had received a few letters here and there through the years, letting them know Gemma was safe and had left of her own free will. But no messages for Keeley or their other siblings. As if Gemma expected them to forget she'd ever been a part of the family. As if she wasn't blood. Their blood.

Keeley just didn't understand what could have kept Gemma from her own for all that time. Keeley couldn't imagine that sitting around all day—or kneeling—to pray to a god that might or might not answer could ever replace being with family.

But now Gemma was back! Gliding into Keeley's shop with her pristine white robes and gloved hands, acting like they were old acquaintances rather than sisters.

She was so busy seething, Keeley had no idea how long she'd worked on that last pommel, letting her anger and annoyance at the current situation flow into her work. Usually, working was just how she enjoyed her day, but at the moment . . . it was keeping her from putting her sister in a headlock and squeezing until she'd put some sense back into her.

When she finally stopped, her hair drenched, her arms and hands dirty, she stepped back from the forge and into one of the Amichais.

Keeley faced the one called Caid. Well . . . she faced his thick neck. She had to tilt her head back a bit to meet his eyes, which was strange for her. She was tall, like her mother, and there were few men who could match her height except for her father. "It was the fact he could look me in the eyes and not the tits that sold me on your da," her mother liked to say.

"Something wrong?" she asked when Caid just stared down at her with what appeared to be a dangerous scowl. But that could be just the way he looked at everyone.

It was hard to tell, but she had yet to see a hint of a smile on his face or anything resembling happiness. Even when Keran got Caid and his cohorts' food, he just appeared *angry* at his bread and cheese. As if the meal had threatened him in some way.

What Keeley found secretly funny was looking at Caid's angry face beneath all that hair. A literal *mane* of brown and gray hair with some thin streaks of white, although she doubted any of those colors had anything to do with his age. She could also see his sharp cheekbones, wide nose, and deep-set brown eyes; but she refused to find someone so eternally pissed off attractive. Life was too short to be that angry.

"The boy's gone," Caid finally announced.

Keeley frowned. "What boy?"

"The one you risked your life for."

It did take her a minute to realize who he was talking about, but she blamed Gemma for that too. The little cow had distracted her.

"Why did he leave?" She raised a brow. "Did you say something to him?"

"I said nothing to him," he replied flatly. "I had nothing to say."

"Did you frighten him with your glare?"

His scowl became decidedly worse. "What?"

"Your glare. I'm sure that nice young boy found your glare ter-rifying. I'm used to it," she said, pointing at herself. "I get glared at all the time. Insecure males mostly. But that boy has been through enough today and he doesn't need your . . ."

"Glaring?"

Keeley fought her urge to laugh. There was something about this Amichai that entertained her; she just wasn't sure what it could be. "Yes. Exactly. You probably terrified him."

"I didn't."

"Then why did he leave?"

"He saw your sister and—"

"My sister?"

"The current expression on your face," he said, "makes me feel like your sister may be currently unsafe. Like I should warn her to run away."

"Too late!" Keeley spun away from Caid, marched through her shop, and stormed over to her sister, who was sitting and sipping tea.

Calmly, Keeley leaned down and said, "*What did you do to that boy?*"

Keeley's bellow startled Caid and everyone else in his unit; his sister quickly sidestepped away from the two women. Not that he blamed her. The blacksmith was frightening when angry. Especially since he was guessing that Keeley wasn't angry very often. Even after she'd fought for her life and the life of the boy against those soldiers, she had nothing but a smile and a laugh for them all.

But when she screamed into her sister's face . . .

Caid would never do that to his sister. Not because he was above that sort of behavior but because Laila was a puncher. Despite being the youngest of them all, she'd been a fighter since birth.

But sister fighting sister was a different and decidedly more dangerous thing.

Then again . . . one of the sisters in this current dispute *was* a nun.

Still holding her mouthful of tea, Gemma gazed up at her sister, eyes narrowed. Caid briefly thought she was going to spit her tea directly at Keeley, but instead, after a moment, she swallowed. With dainty precision, she placed her cup of tea down on the wood table beside her.

Lowering her gaze, she seemed to center herself, letting out a small breath before she abruptly slammed both her hands against her sister, sending her big-shouldered sibling sliding back several feet.

Shocked, Caid quickly moved between the two women just as Keeley came charging back.

Caid had to use both hands to keep her from attacking her sister, and he could sense the nun now standing behind him. Once the pair couldn't get to each other, the screaming began. Caid hated screaming. Not the words. He could not care less what the sisters were saying to each other. For him it was just the sound. If one was not in danger, one should not be screaming. But it seemed the Smythe sisters had never heard that before. Because they were yelling now and he was not happy about it.

While Caid and Farlan did their best to keep the two females from killing each other, the workers stood around, gawking, and his sister and Cadell stood back, waiting for the fighting to stop because they didn't like screaming either.

There was one who did seem to be enjoying herself . . . Keran the cousin. She sat on a windowsill, a leg hanging down and swinging while she ate an apple and laughed but did not help. She was not helping.

Caid continued to push back against Keeley, whose intense strength was really beginning to impress him. He glanced over at his sister, about to ask for her help, when he noticed one of the older workers standing behind her . . . and staring at the long bare legs stretching from underneath her leather kilt. The man leered and, after making sure his boss was truly busy with the nun, he stretched out his arm and began to snake his hand under Laila's kilt.

Despite all that was going on, Caid couldn't help but smirk when his sister's gaze moved from the fighting siblings to a spot across the room. Before the worker could even touch her, she had sensed him. With a slight tilt of her head, her eyes spotted him behind her.

Laila folded her arms over her chest and did what Caid had known she would.

Keran adored her family.

Well . . . not all of it. Her own mother and siblings she had no patience for because they didn't understand her and had never tried. It was her choices that bothered them. But what did they expect? For her to go into a forge every day, pick up a hammer, and work with steel? Just the thought . . .

In her early years, the boredom would have destroyed her.

It wasn't her fault either. That she had not only the love of a good fight, but the skill to win. Her own mother had said she "came out of my womb swinging! Nearly knocked out poor Nelly, the midwife who was helping with the birth."

So Keran had gone off one day and entered the fighting guild. Unlike the stonemasons and blacksmiths, she didn't have to start off as an apprentice, working for nothing and tolerating the general abuse of the elders. Instead, she just started fighting those who were her age, her size. Eventually, she moved up the ranks until she was known throughout the lands.

But, also unlike stonemasons and blacksmiths, eventually all fighters had to stop. If they wanted to live. She was more than forty springs and had gone out on top. She could have returned to the guild and instructed the younger fighters but . . . that wasn't her. She had no desire to teach others.

Keran also could have gone home, but . . . for what? Her family had no use for her. And she didn't plan to spend the rest of her days listening to her siblings and their youngsters chastising her about her choices. So Keran had come to see her aunt. Also a blacksmith, but she'd always been kind and Keran had liked her young cousins.

It still had shocked her, though, the way they'd welcomed her. Without question. Without judgment. And Keeley . . . sweet Keeley had given Keran a job. "Stay at the forge," she'd said over some ale at the local pub. "Keep an eye on things when I'm not around."

"I can swing a hammer, Cousin, but only to break someone's jaw," she'd reminded her.

"Really? I can crush a man's entire face with one hammer swing." She'd grinned, showing those adorable dimples. "I have enough blacksmiths working for me. All men, by the way, which should keep you highly entertained."

"I do have an appetite." She'd studied her cousin. "You sure you don't mind?"

"You're family!" Keeley had exclaimed. "We always make room for family. It's just about finding what you're good at. And keeping those bastards in line when I'm not around . . . that, my cousin, sounds exactly like what you would be good at."

And she was. As always, her cousin had been right.

Still, sweet Keeley had one weakness. Her only weakness. Her siblings. All the younger ones, she kept in line just by being herself. But the second oldest . . . dear, pious Gemma? She'd always refused to fall in line.

Which made seeing her in her holy garb, covering herself completely as if even the wind touching her was a sin against the higher ones, more entertaining to Keran more than she could say. Because she knew how Keeley would react.

Exactly the way she was reacting now. Like a crazed banshee exploding from all her rage.

How dare her sister not do *exactly* what she'd told her to do!

Ahhhh. The women in her family. They were amazing. And insane. Because you needed to be both if you wanted to survive this world the way they did. Making their own choices and rules and ignoring all the men who tried to tell them no.

Even better, though, was that Keeley hadn't returned from the forest alone. She'd brought friends! Amichai friends!

Keran had met Amichais before, but they weren't a friendly people. Not that she blamed them. Those in the Hill Lands didn't like those from the mountains and made that clear by their treatment. So the Amichais wisely kept to themselves, sticking to the wooded areas and bigger cities—where they could mostly be ignored—in their kilts, chainmail shirts, and heavy armaments.

She still wanted to keep an eye on the Amichais since she had no idea why they would help her cousin and that skittish boy. There was just one problem: She was unable to see out of the corner of her left eye. Not since that brutal battle with a man three times her size; Keran woke up three days afterward with the winner's gold purse and a blood-filled eye that didn't clear up for weeks.

So it wasn't her sight that told her something had happened off to her left. It was the sounds: a man's cry of pain and the destruction of the wall separating her room from the rest of the shop.

Keran was off the windowsill and facing the rest of the Amichais in seconds. But they were just standing there, while one of the workers was writhing on the floor of her bedroom, holding his chest with one arm . . . and sobbing.

She jutted her chin at the female Amichai—since she seemed to be in charge—and asked, "What happened to him?"

"He tripped."

Keran smirked. "Into your ass?"

Keeley stood beside her now. "What are you talking about?"

"This one is a bit of a grabber," Keran told her cousin with a shrug, "and I think he was rude to one of your friends here."

"If you knew that about him before this, why haven't you dealt with it?"

"I did," she said, rubbing her nose. "I twisted his arm and shoulder until they splintered like kindling; once he healed up, he came back to work. I thought he'd learned his lesson."

Keeley let out a long sigh, her gaze locked on Keran. "Why did I put you in charge when I'm away?" she finally asked.

"I have *no* idea," Keran admitted.

Keeley knew what she'd seen over her sister's shoulder. Even though they were arguing, there was no way to miss how Laila's lower half had changed just before she sent Rob flying through a wall.

Thankfully, though, Gemma hadn't seen it. Who knew what her religious fervor would make of what Keeley had seen? Keeley already knew what the Amichai were and she didn't care. Her sister, though . . . she was no longer the girl Keeley had once known. She knew she couldn't trust Gemma. Not with her new friends. But she knew who *could* be trusted with their safety.

"I'm going home," Keeley abruptly announced, motioning to her workers to toss the grabby idiot out of her establishment. He could find work somewhere else. She turned to the Amichais. "And you lot are coming with me. You'll get some rest and figure out what you want to do in the morning."

Laila nodded. "That would be—"

Gemma caught Keeley's upper arm and yanked her toward the door.

"Give us a moment," she politely asked the Amichais before dragging Keeley into the street.

"What are you doing?" her sister demanded once they were outside.

"Remembering how I was raised," Keeley spit back. "I see people who need help . . . and I'm helping them. That's what we do."

"You're spouting Da's goat shit right now? In this moment?"

Keeley shook her head. "What the fuck are you talking about? What moment?"

"We can't bring strangers home."

"I'm assuming you're coming home. *You're* practically a stranger."

"You are such a—" Gemma clenched her jaw and closed her eyes. "Can't you see the danger all around you?"

Daniel the shoemaker walked up to them and abruptly put a baby lamb in Keeley's arms. "For your mum. Tell her I'll get her the baby goat in another week or two."

They stared at the lamb bleating in Keeley's arms as Daniel returned to his shop.

"Yes, Sister, the danger is *everywhere*."

"Keeley—"

"The Amichais saved my life and the life of that boy you scared away. They didn't have to. They could have left me to fend for myself, but they didn't. So the least *I* can do is offer them supper and a safe place to stay for the night."

"You can put them up in the pub."

"Old Stump isn't going to let Amichais into his pub and you know it."

Keeley could tell her sister was attempting to think of more arguments to dissuade her but she didn't want to hear them. She didn't want to hear anything. So she used her elbow to push open the door to the shop and leaned in.

"You, lot!" she bellowed. "Let's go!"

The Amichais walked out and Keeley motioned to her cousin. "You too."

"Why me?"

"Because you're family," she lied. Not that Keran wasn't family. She was. But that wasn't why she was bringing her home this night. No, it was because she was the best fighter Keeley knew and if her sister turned out to be right, she wanted the extra defense. But she wouldn't say any of that in front of Gemma. Not now. Not ever.

Keran walked out of the shop and closed the door behind her. The three kin stared at one another for a long few seconds before Keeley lifted the baby lamb a bit and said, "By the way, we're not sacrificing this one for your gods. In case you were wondering."

"I wasn't wondering actually, but feel free to *fuck off,*" Gemma shot back before stomping off after their guests.

Keran glanced at her. "You know, I could be wrong but . . . it seems that nuns have changed since my day."

CHAPTER 4

"**I**t's like she expects me to forget what she's done! But I'll not forget. I'll never forget!"

It took some time, but Caid was starting to think that this woman was talking to *him*.

Maybe she wasn't.

He looked around at the others. Laila was chatting up the nun, trying to find out what she was doing here. He knew his sister's way of thinking and in Laila's mind it would seem strange that the nun should suddenly appear when she'd been gone for so long. But Caid also got the feeling the nun was chatting up Laila in the hopes of finding out what *they* were doing here. Unlike Keeley, though, he didn't think this one or the cousin knew what they were.

He glanced behind him and there were Farlan and Cadell. For some unknown reason, Keeley had suddenly handed them each a sword from her shop. "I just finished these yesterday," she'd said before they began to walk through town. "They're a bit nicer than what you have and will serve you both well."

She'd been right too. The swords she'd given them were definitely superior to what they had, which was why they were both busy examining their new weapons and discussing them rather than chatting with the blacksmith who'd created them.

And then there was Keran. The cousin. She was bringing up the rear . . . and seemed to be talking to herself because no one was around her. Whatever conversation she was having, though, she seemed to be enjoying it.

So what did all that mean?

He glanced down and to his left. Aye. Keeley was talking to *him*.

"What are your thoughts?" she asked, a baby lamb draped over her neck like a fur cape.

"I . . . I honestly don't know because I didn't know you were talking to me."

"Who else would I be talking to?"

"Anyone?" Caid gestured to the world around them. "Literally *anyone*."

"But I like talking to you."

"I haven't been listening."

She shrugged. "That's never stopped me before." She studied him a moment before asking, "Does no one talk to you?"

"Not willingly."

"Why? You're very pleasant."

"No," he insisted. "I'm not. Ask *anyone*. My own sister will tell you . . . *not* pleasant."

"Are you not pleasant on purpose?"

"If I'm pleasant, people will talk to me." He leaned in a bit. "Understand?"

"Of course! Some people . . . they never know when to shut up. But what can you do?" she went on. "Life is full of talkers. People who can't help themselves. As a blacksmith, though, I *have* to talk."

"Do you?"

"Oh, yes. I need to know exactly what people want, when they want it, how they want it. And often they won't say unless you ask them specific questions."

"Sooooo, you're saying there's no way to get you to stop talking to me?"

"Well . . . I'm not speaking to my sister. Ever. *Again*," she emphasized. "And when Keran talks to herself, that's not a conversation you ever want to interrupt. But you're here, so . . . No. There's not."

Suddenly, and without warning, she linked her arm with his and leaned into his side as they continued to walk to her parents' farm. The baby lamb even rested its head against Caid's shoulder, like it belonged there.

"But isn't this lovely?" she asked.

"Is it?"

"It's been a beautiful day and it's turning into a beautiful evening. You'll get a hot meal and some good wine and a roof over your head for the night. What could there possibly be for you to complain about?"

"You *talking* to me?"

"You might as well get used to it, Amichai. Because if you think *I* talk a lot . . . wait until you meet me da."

Keeley handed the baby lamb off to Keran and then threw herself into her father's outstretched arms, letting him lift her off her feet in a big hug. She knew at some time he would become too old to do that, but until that time came, she was going to enjoy the way her father welcomed her home.

"How was your day, my little Keeley?"

"Interesting." She leaned in and whispered in her father's ear, "Amichais, Da."

"What?" He quickly lowered her and turned to face the Amichais standing behind them. "By the gods," her father sighed. "True Amichais. It's been decades."

Grinning, her father grabbed each Amichai's hand and shook it. The Amichais didn't shake hands, so they only seemed confused and slightly offended.

"True Amichais on my farm! What a blessing from the gods! Names," he ordered. "Names."

"I'm Laila." She pointed at her brother. "Caid. Farlan. Cadell."

"Nice to meet ya, lads. I'm Angus."

"Good morrow, Uncle!" Keran greeted in passing as she headed toward the house with the baby lamb over her shoulder.

"Keran, girl. Ale's in the cupboard," he added, stepping away from the Amichais. "And who is your friend here?" he asked, turning toward his second oldest daughter.

Keeley heard his quick intake of breath when he recognized Gemma.

"My dearest girl," he said, arms wide open as he moved toward her, but Gemma quickly caught his hands, not allowing him to hug her.

Keeley could see the startled pain on their father's face and she wanted to beat her sister into the ground for hurting him.

"Father. It's so good to see you."

He nodded, holding in tears. Unlike their mother, their father tended to cry a lot.

"I see you joined an order," he noted, sniffling.

"I did."

"Well . . . we're all very proud of you."

"Despite how chunky a life of piety has made you," Keeley remarked, walking between her sister and father so that Gemma could no longer hold his hand.

"And you have shoulders like a man!" Gemma shot back.

Keeley spun around, ready to slap her sister and those ridiculous white robes into their neighbor's farm several leagues away but her father stopped her.

"None of that, you two." He nodded at Gemma. "Your mum will want to see you. Go." When she walked off, he focused on Keeley. "And Big Bart is having problems with his back again. Go fix it."

"Is he really or are you just saying that to make me stop fighting Gemma? Because I'll never stop fighting Gemma!"

"Be a girl, Keeley. Try. For me. Because if you two don't get along, I'll have to hear about it from your mum. I don't want to hear it from your mum. Understand?"

"Yes, sir."

He leaned down, kissed her forehead. "That's my girl."

Keeley started off toward the stables but said to her father, "Da, could you take care of our guests for me? They helped me today, so I owe them."

"Of course! It'll be my pleasure."

"I've told them a lot about you, and Caid, there,"—she pointed—"he has been dying to talk to you. To hear *all* your stories!"

Her father clapped his big hands together. "And I'll be more than happy to tell him *everything*."

Unable to help herself, Keeley looked over her shoulder at Caid. The Amichai was glowering at her through that shaggy hair he refused to push off his face and she struggled not to laugh at him. He was so annoyed, and she knew her father would only make it worse.

* * *

Keeley's father watched her and the others walk toward the farmhouse at the bottom of the hill. When they were a good bit away, the man looked back at Caid.

"Have they been bickering all the way back from Keeley's shop?"

Laila answered for him. "Aye."

He chuckled. "My girls. They can't help themselves." He faced Laila. "They'll get over it. Gemma's just like her mum, and she never holds a grudge. At least not forever."

Angus jerked his head toward several buildings. "Let me show you where you'll be sleeping tonight."

"Wait," Laila said, holding up her hand. "You're just going to let us stay here? Without asking us any questions?"

The man's grin was wide and exactly the same as his eldest daughter's.

"Really?" His grin grew even wider. "You want me to ask ya questions?" Arms crossed over his massive chest, he stepped closer to Laila. "You want me to ask what Amichais are doing this far south? Why one of the protector clans sent out a *battle* unit to come here? Or maybe you want me to ask why you've been lurking in the forest surrounding me farm? You want me to ask you about all that?"

Laila didn't answer; she was too busy gawking at the human with her mouth open. Again. Father and daughter knew how to surprise.

Keeley's father chuckled. "Yeah. That's what I thought. Come on then," he said, heading down the hill. "I'd let you stay in the house but we have a lot of brats and they can be noisy."

He glanced back at them as he walked. "But you lot don't mind the stables, do you?"

Then Angus laughed. Long and loud, enjoying himself immensely.

Keeley watched her mother hug Gemma until the babe clasped to her breast began to whine.

"Want me to take her?" Keeley offered, reaching for the child, but her mother pushed her hands away.

"No. I have her."

Their mother sat down in her rocking chair, her gaze locked on

Gemma. An intense stare that had Keeley looking back and forth between the pair.

Keeley wasn't jealous. Gemma would say she was just jealous, but she wasn't jealous. She was annoyed! The two of them pretending to speak to each other without words. Just long looks. *So* annoying!

"So you can hug Mum, but you can't hug Da?"

"Oh, piss off!"

"That's it!" their mother snapped before they could get into it again. "I'll not have my two eldest daughters squabbling like their younger siblings."

Keeley pulled out a chair from the kitchen table and sat down. Another long look passed between her sister and mother, and then her mother said, "Why don't you go check on the children, Keeley?"

"Because I'm a babysitter now?"

"Keeley!"

Keeley stood and stomped out the back door, making sure to slam it closed.

"That was unnecessary!" her mother yelled after her.

With a sniff, Keeley continued on into the surrounding field where her sisters and brothers were playing. Three of the older ones, two girls and a boy, watched over the much younger pack of wild animals. Screaming, laughing, and pouncing on one another like jungle cats, the offspring of Keeley's parents continued to grow happy, healthy, and strong. Just as Keeley had.

One of the children spotted Keeley, screamed louder than she had before, and charged over. In seconds, Keeley was tackled and taken to the ground by nine brats that she loved dearly.

Laughing, she hugged and tickled and kissed each one until they became bored and ran off again. Except for one: Endelyon, and she had plans to work with Keeley one day as a fellow blacksmith, which was why Keeley pulled out a tiny steel hammer from her travel bag and handed it to the child.

"Yay!" Endelyon cheered. "My own hammer!"

"Now don't go attacking your—"

"*By this hammer I rule!*" she screamed before charging after her older siblings.

"I said no attacking!"

"Always give a child a hammer," a voice said from behind a tree, "that she can kill her siblings with."

Getting to her feet, Keeley grinned and walked around the tree.

As she expected, her sister Beatrix sat with her back against the trunk. She wore a bright yellow dress, the skirt spread out around her, along with many books and parchment scrolls.

Keeley relaxed her shoulder against the tree. "We have visitors. If you don't want to talk to them, you may want to avoid dinner."

"Gladly."

"I'll bring something out for you." She dug into her bag and pulled out a thick book, handing it over to her sister. "Here."

Beatrix took the book, glanced at it. "You and your precious philosophies."

"You're the only person in the family who likes to talk about philosophy, so yes. I keep getting you books on the subject. That way we can discuss."

"Yet my philosophies never change."

"I wouldn't know," Keeley admitted. "You've never told me what they are."

Beatrix gave one of her small smiles. "Anything else?"

"Yes. A few letters." She handed those to her sister as well, but instead of reading them, Beatrix merely tucked them away in a small pocket sewn into her gown. She never opened the many letters she received in front of anyone. But she'd always been a private person. Something Keeley respected.

"So, who are our guests?" Beatrix asked.

"Centaurs."

Beatrix gave a small chuckle, shook her head. "Listening to Da's tales again?"

"Something like that." Still leaning against the tree, Keeley folded her arms over her chest. "Gemma's back."

"Gemma who?" she asked, dipping her quill in ink and writing on a piece of parchment.

"Our sister."

Beatrix's hand paused over the parchment but, after a second or two, began to move again. "I see. What brings her here?"

"I don't know. Guilt, maybe?"

"Doubt it." She glanced up at Keeley. "Perhaps one of her gods sent her."

"She is a nun now."

Beatrix let out a surprised laugh. "Really? Did they also sew up her pussy? Because I can't imagine her no longer using it."

"Stop."

"Oh, are we still pretending?"

"She's still *family*."

"And she's still Mother's favorite," Beatrix said. "I'm sure she'll be fine."

Beatrix got to her knees, piled her books and papers together in her arms, and got to her feet. Her beautiful yellow dress swirling around her.

"New dress?"

"It's not as expensive as it looks."

"I didn't say anything."

"But you were thinking it."

Keeley watched her younger sister walk away.

"Where are you going?"

"Away." She glanced at Keeley over her shoulder. "I'll be in the feed shed, where it doesn't smell like shit."

"Dinner—"

"I'll eat later."

"Then there was the time I met elves," Keeley's father went on. "Not a friendly lot. Downright rude. But I liked them anyway."

"Is there anyone you don't like?" Caid finally had to ask the man.

"No."

Caid didn't know how to respond to that, but he didn't have to. Keeley entered the stable.

"Everything all right?" her father asked.

"Yes. Gemma and Mum are doing just fine."

"Keeley."

"I mean, why should Mum give me a little more respect as I actually have stayed to help care for the family."

"*Keeley*."

"Especially when Gemma has just run off and become the whore to a god—"

"Keeley!"

Keeley blinked. "Yes?"

"Big Bart," her father said.

Keeley stomped down the line of stalls until she reached an extra-large one. She opened it, went inside, and a few minutes later, came back out with a limping horse. A horse that met the name "Big Bart" head-on.

She had Big Bart stand in front of his stall and she took some time to stroke his hair and muzzle. The horse clearly liked her, constantly nuzzling her and trying to get closer. Eventually she held his reins in one hand and began to drag the fingers of her other hand down the animal's spine.

Caid watched while Laila and the others stood beside him.

"What's she doing?" Laila asked.

"I have no idea."

The horse was clearly lame and probably in pain. Humans usually put down a horse as soon as it lost its usefulness, so Caid was surprised to see Keeley tending to the animal as if she had no intention of doing any such thing. If his pain was tolerable, that seemed fair enough. And he could recommend something that would ease the horse's suffering without killing him.

"Did you find it?" her father called out.

"Would you let me do what I do, Father?"

"Oooh," Angus said to Caid. "She's getting cranky."

"I can hear you," Keeley snapped.

Staring at the floor, Keeley continued to move her fingers down the horse's spine until she finally stopped, her head tilting to the side.

Where her fingers rested on the horse's back, Keeley squeezed and the horse began to move all four of his legs; Keeley quickly stepped back, laughing.

She took off the bridle. "Move, would you?" she asked Caid and the others, and they all stepped back.

The horse started running, charging down the center of the stables and out the open double doors.

"What did you do?" Laila asked.

"His spine was just off."

"But . . . what?"

Keeley waved Laila's questions away. "You work with horses as much as I do, you learn to care for them outside of just putting on new shoes."

"Don't listen to her. My Keeley helps all our neighbors' horses. She has a way with them."

"So you're an animal healer?"

"Don't ask me to sew up wounds. But if bones and muscles are giving them trouble . . . I can try to fix them."

"Not just animals, though. She fixes me back all the time," Angus said proudly. "And her mum's."

"If you followed my directions," Keeley chastised, "you wouldn't need me to fix your back all the time. It's the way you pick things up. And you've got to stop playing with the pigs."

"The pigs like me. They're me friends."

"And that's why we haven't had a side of pork in many winters," Keeley muttered.

"You can have pig for dinner . . . just not our pigs."

Keeley opened the back door, but before she could step into the kitchen, her mother and Gemma immediately stopped talking.

She clenched her jaw and, without meaning to, let out a little growl.

Her father patted her shoulder. "Back in the cage, little one," he whispered to her. "Put that anger back in the cage."

Loving her father too much to want to hurt him with any bickering, Keeley took in a deep breath, let it out, and stepped into the kitchen.

"Food smells good, Mum."

"Thank you." Her mother motioned to the pot of bubbling stew sitting over an open fire. "Get that, would ya, luv. I'll get the bread."

Once Keeley had put the large pot onto a nearby wood table so her mother could spoon the food into bowls, she noticed that Gemma was standing by her.

"Need help?" she asked with a sweet smile.

"Sure." She motioned to her sister's white cape. "You may want to take that off."

"I'm fine."

"But you don't want to get a mess on it."

"It's fine," she replied, the smile never wavering.

Keeley faced her sister.

"Why don't you want to take that bloody thing off?" she snapped.

"Why don't you mind your own fucking business!"

Angus cringed before the first shove even happened. He knew it was coming because nothing had changed. His two eldest daughters always bickered. They grew up, it seemed, eternally trapped in mutual headlocks.

But despite their constant arguing and complaining, they still loved each other. That's why Keeley had been so hurt when Gemma, according to her, "just left."

Of course, he also knew *why* Gemma "just left." Because Keeley was the one person in the world who could talk Gemma into staying. Who could stop her from doing what she so deeply wanted to do.

It all made sense to Angus, but not to his two girls.

He waded into what had turned into an embarrassing slap fight, pushing the pair apart.

"That's enough!" he barked. "I'll not have my daughters fighting each other like this."

"Your father's right," Emma said before going to the back door and bellowing for the rest of their brood. Not because she was angry, she just always bellowed at the children or they ignored her.

"You two"—Emma pointed at her eldest daughters—"will not fight in front of those little bastards. Giving 'em ideas. I won't stand for it."

Angus frowned. "Maybe we shouldn't call them little bastards."

"They're little bastards and they know it."

One of the younger girls ran into the house, swinging a brand-new, all-steel hammer, but her mother immediately grabbed hold and yanked it from her pudgy little hands.

"Give me that! And no hitting the Amichais with your fists either," Emma warned. "Or they may just eat you right up!"

"*Mum!*" Keeley and Gemma barked together.

"They're mountain people," Emma whispered. "They do that sort of thing."

Both girls gawked at their mother before Gemma went about getting the rest of the children seated and Keeley went outside to round up their guests.

That's when Emma turned to him and winked.

Reminding him why he would *always* love that woman.

CHAPTER 5

The food was good. The ale even better. But the chatter...?

Caid hadn't known an entire family could talk that much. Now he understood why Keeley talked so much except when she was working at her forge. When she was focused on her work, she only spoke when she needed her apprentices to help her with something. Otherwise, the only sound coming from her was her work hammer bending metal to her will.

But at that dinner table... the talk was never ending. It wasn't just the children either. It was the man and his wife. Did they not speak to each other during the day? Was that why all this discussion at dinner was necessary?

The only one who didn't seem to have anything to say was the nun. Perhaps she was part of a silent sect, but that seemed unlikely as she had been arguing with her older sister all day. More likely it was that she was too busy watching Laila and the rest of them, wondering what they were up to, he guessed.

The meal was winding down, and Caid was staring blindly at the kitchen table, wondering how he could sneak out of here without insulting his hosts, when he felt something climb up his back and stand on his shoulders. Then a little body stretched across his head, arms hanging over his face, and began to snore.

Slowly, Caid turned to Keeley, who sat beside him. She glanced at him, looked back at the younger sibling she'd been chatting with, then... she looked back at him. Her gaze lifted up and her smile was huge. Then came silent laughter.

"Are you going to help me?" he finally asked her.

"But she likes you."

"She threatened me with a nonexistent hammer all through dinner."

"Mum took the hammer. But it would have just been a love tap." When he only continued to stare at her, Keeley finally motioned to one of the older siblings. "Isadora, take her, would you?"

Chuckling, Isadora pulled the snarling toddler off his head.

"Come on," Keeley said before she stood. "Da, we're going to check the perimeter before bed."

Her father waved them off, not breaking his conversation with his mate. A woman, Caid now knew, Angus Farmerson desperately adored. Despite the twelve offspring. Despite the hard work of farm living. Despite the fact his woman had a brutal scar that went from one side of her face to the other. A scar that cut right through her eye, leaving nothing but a white, dead thing that she couldn't see out of. But she didn't seem to care and he didn't seem to notice.

Caid followed Keeley out of the house, across the farm, and into the woods. They continued to walk until they reached a lake.

A herd of wild horses were relaxing by the water. Some grazing. Some sleeping. But none of them bolted at the sight of Keeley.

She stopped at the lake's edge, staring out into the darkness.

They just stood there for several minutes until Caid finally asked, "What are we doing?"

"Hear it?" she asked.

"Hear what?"

"The silence?" She grinned. "Mum's little bastards, as she calls them, don't come to the lake. She won't let them. She's afraid they'll fall in and drown."

"Did you fall in and almost drown?"

"Once," she admitted. "But it wasn't my fault."

He let her believe that and instead enjoyed the lack of children's voices.

He motioned to the wild horses. "They don't seem bothered by you."

"They're used to me." When he stared at her, she continued. "When I decided I wanted to be a blacksmith, I knew I'd have to work with horses. Shoeing them and such. Da didn't have that many horses then. So I went out and found some horses. I just watched them, trying to see how they lived. Trying to understand them. After a while they didn't seem to mind me."

"I see." He focused on the lake again. "When did you know you wanted to be a blacksmith?"

"Birth."

The Amichai grunted. "That seems . . . early."

"Not for a Smythe woman."

"So your mother . . ."

"The women in my mum's family have been blacksmithing for centuries. We're born to it. Except my grandmother did not forgive her for marrying outside—"

"The family?"

"Ewwww. No! The business. My father's a farmer, you know. The Smythe women usually only marry other blacksmiths. So they can have blacksmith babies. But in my family, I have a brother and sister who want to run the farm. Two sisters who want to join the fighter's guild. Two brothers and a sister who want to be soldiers. A toddler sister who wants to join me at the forge. A baby who hasn't made up her mind yet. And another sister who won't tell me what she wants to do."

"Aren't you forgetting one?"

"Am I?"

"The nun?"

"Ech."

That was when the Amichai did something strange. For him. He laughed.

"I have never met anyone who has such a dramatic reaction to the handmaidens of a god."

"We don't know which god. She hasn't told anyone. She could be worshipping all sorts of evil."

"In her all white, with the no touching? That kind of evil?"

"Color means nothing to me."

"I know. Since eyes of fire don't seem to bother you."

"As I tried to explain to your very judgmental sister, animals are not like humans. It doesn't matter which world—"

"Or netherworld."

She paused briefly to glare at him properly.

"... they come from. Animals are animals. And unless they attack or one is hunting them for food and clothing, they should be left alone to live their lives in the wild."

"Uh-huh."

"And *yes,* that includes wolves that have eyes of fire."

"But your nun sister ... ?"

"She has no excuse!"

"Are you always this inflexible?"

"Actually," she admitted, "I'm a very forgiving person." Keeley rubbed her nose. "But not with her," she finally admitted.

"I see."

Tired of being judged, Keeley turned toward the Amichai, and asked, "Why are you here?"

He stared at her but didn't reply.

"I know you've been following me and lurking around the farm. I want to know what's going on."

"Why?"

"In case I have to kill you," Keeley replied with total honesty, "I'd rather not get too attached."

"Fair enough. But we haven't been lurking around your farm," he corrected. "It was more of a sneaking."

Keeley narrowed her eyes on the Amichai. "You do know I'm carrying my hammer?"

"How could I miss it? The head is so huge."

"I like my huge head." She stopped, realizing how that sounded.

"There are things you and your family need to know. But it should come from my sister."

"She's too busy trying to get information out of *my* sister while my sister does the same thing to her. So I'm asking *you*. What's going on?"

Caid looked off and she could tell from the expression on his face he was debating how much shit he'd have to eat when his sister found out he'd told her everything. But before she could push him or he could decide to speak on his own, the gray stallion from the wild herd ambled out of the darkness, moved up behind Caid, and rammed his head into the Amichai's back.

Caid slowly looked over his shoulder at the horse. "*Really?*" he demanded.

"He likes me," she told him. "Always keeps an eye out for me. You probably shouldn't annoy him."

"I annoy everyone."

"I like a man who knows himself."

Caid stared at her for a long moment, then said, "My sister says you already know I'm not a man."

"Well, at least half of you is," she said on a little snort.

"Why didn't you say anything to the others?"

"Not yet. Especially me mum. She'd probably start hacking at you all with her big cleaver."

"That seems excessive."

"My mum's not good with being startled. Or people with hooves."

"You don't seem to mind people with hooves."

Keeley smiled. "Of course not. Your people saved my father's life. Without your tribe I wouldn't have siblings. You lot brought him back to me and me mum. He told me everything when I was a little girl. About the Amichais. About the different tribes. About the mountains and how beautiful they are."

"And he told your mother?"

"Oh, gods, no!" she said on a big laugh. "My mother would have thought he was insane. She already thinks he's a little insane. Assumes it's all because of the few times he got his head split open when he was a soldier."

"He didn't tell your mother, but he told you?"

"He tried to tell her but . . . you see, we're a lot alike, me and me da. And we don't scare easy."

"But your mother . . . ?"

"Doesn't scare at all," she said quickly. "She can be startled, but she'll not be scared. Please don't ever forget that. For your own sake."

"Noted."

"So are you going to tell me?" she pushed, the stallion now standing behind her and resting his large head on her shoulder. "Why are you and your friends here? What do you want?"

Caid took a few steps toward the lake but he didn't step in. He simply stared out over it before announcing, "The Old King is dead."

"I know. That's why I've been making so much money lately. Mercenaries. It's fabulous."

"What about the future king?"

"What about him?"

"Do you not care who it might be?"

She couldn't help but chuckle. "Why should I care? They're all bad. They're all cruel and greedy and I hope the hells welcome them and their royal cohorts when they die, because they'll not get their due justice on this plain. But I'm not sure what my philosophy on the royals has to do with anything."

"There has been a prophesy," he said, turning to face her. "A prophesy about the next ruler."

"And . . . ?"

"And the prophesy doesn't call for a king. It calls for a queen. And the witches have named your sister."

"*The nun?*" she snarled. Because Keeley would just *bet* that her nun sister would love that!

"No, no," he said quickly. "Your other younger sister. Beatrix."

"Oh," Keeley replied, surprised. "I see." She thought a moment. "Yeah. Beatrix might like that."

Caid stared at her for so long, he lost track of time. And it could have continued for much longer except that Keeley finally said, "Is something wrong?"

"I tell you that your sister has been prophesized to be the next queen and your response is, 'she might like that'?"

"Well, she might. It's hard to tell with her." She stepped closer and whispered, "I wouldn't say she's shy, but she's definitely not chatty. She only tells you what she wants to tell you. But," she added, a little louder, "she does like pretty dresses. And I'm sure she'd have no problem wearing a crown."

Again, Caid could only stare, because he didn't know what to make of such a response.

But then something happened. He saw it. On her face. Keeley started to think.

"Wait . . . the Old King's sons. Do they know?"

"We're not sure. But once they do—"

"They'll come for her."

Keeley suddenly paced away from Caid, and the stallion that had been standing behind her sidestepped out of her way. The horse shook his head and let out a snort, which set off the rest of his herd. Some ran away. Some stayed put, but their hooves hit the ground and they snorted their discomfort.

This was the Keeley his sister had been warned about by the witches. The one who would tear the world apart to protect her kin.

"I'll have to talk to my parents. They're not going to like this, but they're not unreasonable."

"Your sister wasn't at dinner tonight."

"No."

"Why?"

She stopped pacing, shrugged. "My sister was not in the mood to entertain strangers. No offense."

"Was that it?" Because Caid understood. He didn't like entertaining anyone either, much less strangers.

"She's also not a fan of Gemma."

"Because she's a nun?" Caid asked, only slightly joking.

Keeley did manage to smile. "Shockingly, no. They've never gotten along, sadly."

"For any particular reason?"

"I would say they have different views, but Beatrix keeps her views to herself. So they've never liked each other."

"Do you like Beatrix?"

"She's my sister!"

Caid frowned at that response. "I'm afraid that's not really an answer."

"We're family. I love her."

"I love my brother Quinn. I haven't figured out if I like him, though. I love my sister, too, but I also like her because she doesn't annoy me nearly as much as anyone else."

"I do like Beatrix. She just doesn't share much of herself with anyone. People who are introspective are like that sometimes. I don't fault her for it."

"But Gemma does fault her?"

"I don't think so. She just doesn't like her. And the feeling is mutual. But family is all. That's what my father taught me. That's what he taught each of us. But does it matter? Siblings don't always get along."

"I know," Caid replied.

"But there's a reason the witches have chosen her. Isn't there?"

"We'd like to find that out. Laila would like to leave tomorrow with Beatrix, but I know she'll understand if that's not possible. No more than three days from now, though. Do you think you can manage that with your family?"

"Wait . . . you want to take my sister? Where?"

"To the Witches of Amhuinn. Once they meet Beatrix, they will confirm her future rule or deny it. We're not a part of that. We're only here to protect her."

"But why? She won't be your queen."

Caid admitted the truth. "The Old King kept the truce between our lands. His sons will not. Everyone knows that."

"If my sister goes with you . . . I go."

He'd had a feeling that would be coming.

"But it will be up to my parents to decide if she goes anywhere."

Caid nodded. "I'll let Laila know."

He turned to walk back to the stables, but Keeley's voice stopped him.

"Before you go . . ."

"Yes?"

"I want to see you."

Caid faced her again, knowing exactly what she'd meant. "No. You don't."

"I do." She grinned. "I promise not to judge."

"It's not your judging that concerns me. All humans judge. But you don't understand. I come from a protection clan. We do not work with gods or make spells. We protect our lands and our people. Meaning we don't look like the other centaurs. We're predators. Hunters. We kill and destroy."

"I can't tell if you're trying to scare me or seduce me." She shrugged. "Whatever. I want to see."

* * *

The Amichai stared at her for a long time. So long, she feared he might have had a seizure.

"Are you all right?" she finally asked when the silence went on and on.

His gaze was locked on a spot behind her head and she wasn't sure he was going to answer until he said, "I'm fine. Just . . . thinking about your response."

Caid shook his head, took several steps back. "I'm . . . I'm . . . walking away from you now."

"Will your sister show me?"

"Stop talking to me," he ordered as he walked away. "And stop staring at my ass."

"Just wondering how it looks with four legs."

He stopped. Faced her. "What?"

"You know," she admitted, "that sounded less . . . strange, in my head."

"Did it? Really?"

CHAPTER 6

Gemma stared out the small front window at her father and sister. They'd been talking for long minutes this early morning as the suns just began to rise in the distance.

Her mother came to stand beside her, her youngest babe attached to her breast once again.

"Wonder what they're talking about," Gemma said, watching the pair closely.

"I'm sure they're plotting our deaths."

Gemma gasped and faced her mother, but she just laughed. "I'm joking! Does your god not allow joking?" she asked.

"Now you sound like Keeley."

"Your sister is stubborn and opinioned. Just like you. You two must learn to work together. This is especially important to *me*," her mother went on, "because I don't want to have to hear your father complain that his beautiful daughters don't get along. Gods, the whining."

Gemma knew her mother was right, but still . . .

"You could tell her the truth," her mother softly suggested. "Instead of all this lying."

"I was going to. But then she brought her friends."

"They seem nice enough."

"Mum."

"I hope it's not that they're Amichais that bothers you so much, my love. I expect better of you."

"Amichais that come out of nowhere? Right to our door? You don't think that's strange?"

"I think all sorts of things are strange. Because they are strange. But strange doesn't automatically mean evil and wrong."

Gemma heard someone on the narrow steps that led to the upstairs bedrooms. She looked over her shoulder and finally saw Beatrix for the first time.

She wore a pale pink dress that must have cost her parents more money than they should have ever spent on one garment. She held several books in her hands and her dark hair was artfully braided and curled as it fell down her back.

"Sister," Beatrix said.

Gemma nodded, not feeling in the mood to do more. She hadn't slept all night, staying up to keep an eye on things. And when she was short on sleep, she could be quite cranky.

Without another word, Beatrix walked out the back door to find a tree to sit under where she could read. That's all she did. Sit on the ground in her beautiful dresses and read, taking brief breaks for food and drink. Sometimes a nap. It was what she did before Gemma had left and it seemed that her lifestyle had not changed.

"Stop glaring."

"I can't believe you never forced her to do anything," Gemma complained to her mother. "Keeley and I were up every day, before sunrise, helping Da in the stables and out in the fields."

"Your sister's business is doing so well these days that on occasion we have stable hands and fieldworkers. So we don't need to make your sisters and brothers do anything. And that's what Beatrix does . . . nothing."

"Shouldn't you have made her do something? Anything?"

Her mother didn't reply, but Gemma wasn't exactly sure why. She didn't see any shame on her mother's face. Or resentment at Gemma's chastisement. Her expression was carefully . . . blank.

Knowing not to push, Gemma instead asked, "Think Da likes Keeley more than me?"

Her mother rolled her eyes. "I can't believe you are still asking that question. *Why are you still asking that question?* Do you think your sister is asking your father that stupid question?"

* * *

"I think Mum likes Gemma better than me."

"I'm not listening to this insanity again," her father said, before kissing her forehead.

They'd had a long talk this morning and had decided on a course of action regarding Beatrix. Angus just had to convince his wife. A task that Keeley was grateful her father had insisted on doing. She'd been fearful she'd have to do it.

"Now, I'm going to get my day started," he said, his big hand on her shoulder. "You help your mum and talk to the Amichais. You seem to have a nice rapport with them."

"Yes, sir."

"And stop worrying," he said with a smile. "This will all work out." He leaned in and whispered, "Just imagine. Us lot . . . royals!"

They both laughed and Keeley kissed her father's cheek before sending him on his way. He was humming as he walked off because he was a man who loved his work. He loved his farm. There weren't a lot of people in the world who were just happy with their lives as they were, but her father wanted nothing more from life than what he had.

Then again . . . neither did Keeley. Of course, if she was going to leave for a few weeks to protect her sister—or, at the very least, bring her home when it turned out she was not going to be any-one's queen, something both Keeley and her father were starting to believe—she'd need to get things organized at her shop.

"Good morning, Sister," Gemma said from behind her, making Keeley jump.

"Stop sneaking up on me!" she snapped.

"I wasn't. I was just greeting you and attempting to be nice. I guess I shouldn't have bothered."

"Oh, stop with the pity."

Gemma moved in front of her. "Pity? I never asked for your pity."

"Then what do you want? Why are you even here?"

"What I do and why I do it is up to me," Gemma said, stepping closer. "So perhaps you should mind your own business."

"Ooooh," Keeley mocked. "Listen to the fancy talk you've learned from your nuns. I'm surprised they let you speak at all!"

"Oy!" Keran barked at them from the far side of the house. "Are you two going to keep this bickering up? Can't speak for your parents, but *I'm* tired of hearing it."

"Where did you come from?" Keeley asked. She hadn't seen her cousin since dinner.

Keran pointed back toward the house and began to speak but abruptly stopped. She stood there, staring at Keeley and Gemma.

"What's wrong with you?"

"I'm . . ." She held up a finger. "I'm . . ."

"Are you having some sort of spasm?" Gemma demanded.

Keran stared at them for another moment, then she turned her head, opened her mouth, and unleashed everything that she had eaten or drunk in the last twenty-four hours.

"Ohhhh!" Keeley and Gemma cried out, quickly moving farther away from their cousin.

When she finished unloading her insides onto the ground, Keran nodded.

"Gods, I needed to do that."

"But did you have to do it *there?*" Keeley asked.

"At least I didn't do it on the children."

"Oh, that's nice."

Keran laughed and walked over to the well. She pulled up the water bucket . . . and poured the entire thing over her head.

Once she was soaked and more awake, she returned to them and gazed into their faces for a moment before asking, "So . . . are we going to discuss your sister being future queen or pretend it's not happening?"

For two people who didn't look that much alike and seemed to have nothing in common except their parents, Keeley and Gemma did have moments that reminded Keran that they were, in fact, sisters.

Like now. Both of them gawked at her, eyes wide, then simultaneously went into full-blown panicked lying.

"What are you talking about?"

"You're insane."

"There's nothing going on."

"What did you hear?"

"Have you been snooping again?"

"There's nothing going on!"

They abruptly stopped yelling and looked at each other, both leaning back. One sizing up the other and vice versa.

At the same moment, they both asked, "You know?" Then, "How do you know?" Which led to, "Who told you?"

Keran snorted and scratched a scar on her scalp. She had a lot of scars.

"You two," she complained. "Who cares how you found out? Does any of that matter? I think our real concern should be Beatrix being queen."

When the pair only stared at her, Keran let out a very long sigh. "So we're going to play this game now, are we? You can't seriously be thinking—"

"With the right advisors—"

"Oh, Keeley, come on! I know she's family and all but you can't be serious." Keran motioned to Gemma. "And what about you, nun? Are you just going to stand there and let this happen?"

"She's our sister."

"What are you talking about? You don't even like her!"

"That's not the point," Keeley cut in. "She's family. Our family."

"*Your* family," Gemma muttered.

"I know she's family," Keran shot back. "But that doesn't mean—"

Gemma suddenly raised her gloved hand, cutting Keran's next words off.

"Can you hear it?" she asked.

"Hear what?"

"I can hear it," Keeley said, stepping forward. "Someone's screaming . . ."

On horseback, he charged over the hill that led to the farm. He held the reins of two other horses, bringing them along with him as he screamed in warning. It took a second for Keran to remember him.

"*They're coming!*" Samuel desperately bellowed. "*They're coming!*"

Keeley saw the boy she'd rescued come over that hill and heard the words he was screaming . . . and she knew. She just knew.

"They're coming for Beatrix."

"They'll burn this farm down and kill everyone." Gemma said

out loud what the three of them already knew. It was the way of the Old Kings. They left no witnesses to what they'd done, and Keeley doubted his remaining sons would be any different.

"Gemma, the children."

Gemma didn't even speak, just ran to the house.

"Keran. Go to the stables," Keeley ordered her cousin, motioning with both her arms for the boy to head to the stables as well. She didn't want him riding over the main field in front of the house. "Let the Amichais know what's happening and let the horses out."

"You're worried about the horses?"

"We'll need those horses to get everyone out of here, and if they're trapped in a burning stable—"

"You're right, you're right," Keran said, charging off toward the stable.

Keeley reached down and grabbed hold of the steel handle of her hammer. She hefted it onto her shoulder and started to walk across the field. Ready to challenge anyone who came over that hill to attack her family. If nothing else, she hoped to give the children enough time to get away.

But a panicked screech came from the trees on her right and she started running, taking her hammer off her shoulder and carrying it by her side.

She entered the small forest, already knowing what had made that sound, her heart dying a little in her chest. As she passed a large boulder, she saw the wild gray stallion stumble, three arrows protruding from his beautiful neck.

Keeley ran to her friend, reaching him as he dropped to the ground. He landed on his side, the sounds of his suffering tearing through her.

She fell to her knees beside him, dropping her hammer so she could place her hands on his head.

"No, no, no, no," she chanted, tears filling her eyes.

She examined the wounds to see if pulling out the arrows would help. But even through her tears she knew it was hopeless.

"I'm so sorry," she whispered in his ear.

Kissing his head one more time, Keeley grabbed hold of the ends of two arrows and, after taking a deep breath, she shoved them all the way in and through the stallion's neck. He thrashed a bit more while Keeley used her body to hold him down, but he soon stopped.

Sobbing, she rested her head against her friend's body one last time. She knew she had to move. She knew death was coming for her family. Even now she could hear the hooves of warhorses all around, riding toward her family's farm.

She didn't have time to wallow in her grief. Especially now . . . with four strangers standing behind her.

Keeley reached for her hammer with a blood-covered hand.

"Now, now, brave girl. None of that," a male voice said. "Hate to shoot you down before we even have a look at ya."

She didn't bother to grab her hammer, but she did wipe the gray stallion's blood on the head, marking it for revenge, before she got to her feet and faced the men.

They wore surcoats of bright blue, with a jungle cat and swords emblazoned in even brighter gold on the front. One of them held a bow, an arrow already nocked.

"You must be the oldest," a soldier with short brown hair said. But before Keeley could respond, he quickly added, "Didn't mean that like it sounded. Just assuming you're the oldest daughter. The one he didn't want."

"Which brother is paying you?" Keeley asked, wiping her still-wet eyes with the backs of her hands.

"Straton."

"The Devourer." She smirked. "Of course."

Gemma pushed her sisters and brothers toward the back door. The older ones helping the younger. Her mother was behind her, the youngest babe still attached to her breast. But her mother could do with one arm what many couldn't do with two.

"Everyone out!" she ordered. "Move!"

Gemma yanked the door open just as the front door was kicked in. Her mother facing the intruders.

"Take care of them, Gemma," she said, before pulling her youngest off her breast and tossing her to one of the older girls. "Go!"

Gemma pushed her screaming siblings out the door and didn't look back.

* * *

Keran ran through the stables, unbolting the latches and swinging the gates open. With a yell, she set the horses running out the doors at the front, back, and sides of the building.

She stopped at the last stall, expecting to see the Amichais still there but they were gone. Not even their travel bags remained. She'd been hoping the warriors would help them fight, at least until the children were safe.

Disappointed, Keran ran back toward the front. She passed the boy who'd given them warning.

"You!" she barked at him. "Come with—"

The fist slammed into her face as soon as she'd made it out of the stables, flipping her head-over-ass into the dirt.

With her children out of the house, Emma faced the men who'd stormed into her home. She didn't bother fixing her clothes. Her right breast was exposed, milk still dripping from where she'd pulled off her hungry baby.

Slowly, making sure she kept their attention, she took a step back. Then another. Attempting to move around the large table where her family ate every day.

One of the men smiled at her. "Don't worry, luv. You'll live long enough to see all your children die."

Gemma started to lead the children straight into the woods behind the house, but she quickly realized troops were coming from that direction. So she turned them west. The lake was big and it would force the troops to go around it to get to the farm.

"Come. Quick," she urged.

"What about Mum?" she heard one of them ask.

"She'll be—"

Gemma stopped, held her arms out to halt the children. Then she motioned them behind her, away from the riders she faced.

"Please," she said to the armed men on horseback. It seemed they'd been sitting there, waiting for them. "They're just children."

"We have our orders."

"I'm begging you, in the name of goodness. Don't do this."

Two men dismounted from their horses and walked toward her. She moved back, hoping they would stop. They didn't.

"Please," she asked again. "Don't do this."

Finally, they did stop, but the way they smiled at her . . .

"You're one of those nuns, isn't that right?" one of them asked.

"Never had a nun before," the other one said.

"Oh, gentlemen," Gemma sighed. "You disappoint me and my gods, greatly."

Angus worked his way through the muck of the pigsty. He knew most were disgusted by such work. Most of his children were, but not him. He loved pigs! They were so friendly and funny. Each with its own personality, its own quirks.

So when they began squealing and running—panicking, actually—he knew something was very wrong.

Busy petting one of the pigs, crouched beside the animal before it took off running with the others, Angus simply looked over his shoulder. A unit of archers watched him, their bows nocked, the arrows aimed at him. And he didn't think they had orders to bring him in alive.

"Oh . . . fuck."

"Did the Devourer tell you to do this?" Keeley asked, gesturing to the body of the gray stallion. "To kill my friend?"

"He made too much noise. It was like he was trying to warn you."

Keeley felt pain wash over her again. "He was. He was trying to warn me. And you killed him. And for what? Because the Devourer told you to kill a girl?"

"He'll be king, you know. And we'll be rich."

"If you wanted to be rich, lads, you shouldn't have come here." Keeley gave a small shrug. "Actually, the last thing you should have ever done . . . was come here."

Emma now stood on the far side of the table, staring at the men who'd invaded her home.

"You can keep moving away from us," one of the soldiers said. "But it will only be worse for you when we catch you."

"I'm not running," she told them. "Me old gran would turn in her grave if she ever knew I'd run from worthless cunts like you."

That's when they charged. So she gripped the end of the table and lifted, shoved, and flipped it, using the strength she still had from her blacksmith days. Her power sent it across the room, slamming into the men and knocking them to the ground.

Angus dove into one of the cast-iron pig troughs his wife had made for him their first year on the farm. He landed, grabbed the sides, and rolled it over on top of him. Arrows hit the trough and bounced off. He waited for the ping of the last one hitting and then he pitched the trough at the archers.

Hearing it strike its mark, then the barks and gasps of men's pain, he jumped to his feet and, with a scream of soldier's rage, Angus Farmerson ran full force into his enemies.

Feet repeatedly struck Keran, hitting her in the sides and legs and back, but she kept her head protected as best she could by curling into a ball.

She heard a male roar and felt bodies land beside her. Lifting her head a bit, she saw that Samuel had thrown himself at two of the men. Now they were down to four.

Four she could handle.

The kicks to her body continued but she waited until one reached her right shoulder, striking and striking again. When the foot pulled back for another kick, she reached out, grabbed it behind the ankle, and yanked.

The man fell and Keran quickly rolled over him. She got to her feet, clearly surprising the men as they stopped their attacks to gawk.

She grinned. From her first time in the pit she'd been beaten nearly every day, by men and women mightier and meaner than this lot.

Lifting her foot, she rammed it into the face of the man she'd climbed over, enjoying the sound of the crunch and the gurgling that followed.

"All right, lads," she said, pushing a slightly battered Samuel behind her. "Who's first?"

* * *

Emma ran to the table and yanked free one of the two short swords she'd strapped to the bottom of it.

The soldiers were just attempting to get out from under it, so she stepped on the wood, pressing it down to pin them there—at least for a few more seconds—and swung her weapon. She cut the throat of one, hacked off the arm and part of the scalp of another.

The last had gotten to his feet. Emma spun and swung her weapon again. The steel blade she'd created herself years ago imbedded itself in his skin, and fresh blood spurted out, hitting her across the face and bare breast.

She wrenched the sword out and he dropped to his knees, staring up at her as his life's blood flowed down his surcoat.

He would die soon and she turned to go out the back door, to her children. But she stopped short, realized she couldn't let it go and spun back, gave one more strong swing of her arm. The soldier's head flew across her kitchen, landing on the counter where she'd been kneading bread that morning.

There. Emma always liked when things were complete.

Angus swung the cast-iron trough to the right and into an archer's head. He swung it left, ramming it into the shoulder of another. He sensed someone behind him, turned, and quickly jerked to the side. A blade slid by, just missing his gut, where it had been aimed.

He gave a growl and tossed the trough, making sure it hit another man coming up behind him, and reached out to the one with the sword. Angus's fingers slid around the man's throat and grasped his neck, squeezing until he felt bones break under his fingers like kindling.

Dropping the body in his hands, Angus stared at his family home. He knew his children and wife were somewhere, but he made the excruciating decision not to go to them. Not to help them. Instead, he did what he knew he had to do and ran behind the pigsty.

"Not only did you strike the wrong family," Keeley went on, "but you killed this beautiful animal." She pointed at the gray stallion. "That was a very tragic mistake. For you."

"Your horse, was he?" one of them asked.

"No. But he was *her* son."

The men frowned, temporarily confused, but the one on the far left, sensing something, quickly turned in time to see the front hooves of the gray mare come down onto him, forcing him to the ground and crushing his ribs into his chest.

Keeley grabbed her hammer, spun, and threw. It collided with the face of one soldier, sinking into the flesh and staying there.

She ran toward it, pulled the hammer out before the body could fall. A sword slashed toward her and she fell to the ground, rolling away from the weapon, but quickly jumped back to her feet.

Flipping the hammer around, so the head faced her, she used the handle to strike the soldier in the throat. Then she pressed a metal lever that rested by the head. A narrow blade burst from the handle and tore past soft flesh and out the other side.

Keeley released the lever, letting the blade retract into the handle, flipped the hammer again, and slammed the side of the last soldier's head. He went down to the ground and Keeley followed up with another strike to the front, burying her weapon so deep, she finally hit dirt.

Panting, she yanked her weapon out. She walked to the gray mare, facing her head on. She carefully reached up, pressed her hand to the horse's massive jaw, and rested her head against the mare's nose.

"I'm so sorry for your loss," she whispered.

The mare let out a long sigh that Keeley felt to her bones, but then the mare was scrambling back and Keeley spun around, faced a new group of soldiers running toward her.

"Run!" she ordered the mare as she raised her weapon once more. But the horse stood her ground, refusing to move.

Every time the two men moved closer, Gemma and the children backed up. She did it again and again until her mother finally ran out of the house, a sword in each hand.

"Where have you been?" Gemma demanded, her gaze locked on the two men. The others on horseback stayed by the tree line, in no apparent rush to move things along. They assumed they had all the time in the world to entertain themselves with Gemma's family.

"I couldn't leave until I was done. You know that."

She did. Her mother was nothing if not obsessive. It could be irritating on a day-to-day basis, but at times like these . . . Gemma loved her for it.

Reaching back with one arm, Gemma wiggled her fingers. Her mother placed one of the swords into Gemma's hand and the men, who at this point were only a few feet away, grinned.

"You and your mum going to challenge us, Sister? Do you think that's wise with the child—"

Gemma cut off the head of one soldier, the one that wouldn't shut up. Then she removed the head of the other while he was still trying to pull his sword from its sheath.

She heard the surprised gasps and cries of her siblings and the startled stomping of the mercenaries' horses, but she ignored it all.

Even as the mercenaries yelled at her, even as they readied their attack, she kept her focus and tossed the sword back to her mother.

Gemma crouched down and turned the headless bodies over so that both were chest down. She pressed a hand on the back of each, lowered her body a bit, and kept her gaze focused on the grass beneath them. With a growl, she began the chant.

"Gemma," her mother urged. "Get on with it."

But Gemma blocked her out. She had to. Even as she heard the hooves powering nearer, she kept her focus.

The chant completed, she quickly got to her feet and faced the killers riding toward her.

Closer and closer they got until the headless bodies moved. . . .

The horses reacted before the men riding them, rearing up, and colliding into one another as they attempted to get away; fighting their riders' demands to move forward.

As the mercenaries fought to stay on their mounts, Gemma reached for the collar of her white robe and untied it. Loosening it, she grabbed the two sides and pulled hard, ripping the garment in two.

She stepped out of it, and the first mercenary who managed to get his horse under control saw her . . . and stared. In horror.

After a few seconds, he began screaming. Loud enough that everyone could hear. Everyone would know.

"*War Monk! She's a War Monk! WAR MONK!*"

* * *

The first of the new soldiers came at her, his sword raised. Keeley gripped the end of her hammer with one hand, and the head with the other. She lifted her hammer up. The soldier began to bring the sword down, but then he screamed out, his back arching, his eyes going wide as a blade tore through his chest, and blood splattered Keeley's startled face.

The sword was torn out and the body fell, revealing Caid the Amichai.

He barely glanced at her before he slaughtered the other soldiers who'd come for her. Slashing and stabbing with brutal efficiency. When the soldiers lay dead or dying, he returned to her and the gray mare.

He glanced at the gray stallion. "I'm sorry about your friend."

Keeley nodded. "Are there more?" she asked, pointing to the soldiers at their feet.

"Many more."

"I see. All for my sister?"

"Yes."

"From where?"

"They've sent smaller units to surround your family's farm. But the main force is marching head-on. They'll be coming over that hill."

Keeley hefted the head of her hammer onto her shoulder. "All right then."

She started off toward the hill, but Caid's voice followed her.

"I thought you wanted to see."

"Wanted to see what?"

"What I really look like."

Keeley stopped, realizing the gray mare was right beside her. Together they faced Caid.

He still appeared as a human but already she saw that his eyes were different. Glowing gold in the morning suns that had come up over the hill.

Then he began to grow . . . up. His torso lifted tall, stretching a bit, even widening. And beneath his torso, his legs went from human to horse. Even his kilt turned into a horse's bridle seconds before two more legs appeared as that part of his body stretched and grew massive. Bigger than any warhorse she'd ever seen.

The gray mare pawed the ground with one hoof and her head swung hard, her long hair hitting Keeley in the face. But it didn't stop her from seeing.

His body stopped growing, finally. But then, from the sides of his head . . . antlers. Not massive ones to herald he was a male, but big and strong enough to be weapons.

His mouth relaxed a bit and she saw white and long powerful fangs.

Caid stared at her with those golden eyes and waited. If he was expecting her to run from him—she didn't have time.

"I have to do something," she told him, starting again toward the hill. "I hope you don't hate me when I'm done."

She patted the gray mare's neck. "And you too, my friend."

Laila and her unit had gotten up before the suns rose. Together, they'd silently made their way to a nearby lake that Caid knew about. There, they'd discussed next moves. Especially if the family decided to fight them on taking Beatrix to the witches.

Her father's original plan had been to just take the young woman, but her mother had stomped that decision into the ground. And Laila had agreed. Morally.

Now, though, as she moved through the crowd of mercenaries on horseback, she realized that to have just grabbed Beatrix would have been a very foolish thing indeed.

Not when the mother stood in front of her children covered in someone else's blood and there were already two headless bodies stretched out in front of her nun daughter. The nun was taking the time to kindly—although stupidly—pray over them. Bad timing, but she was a nun, after all. Maybe she was required to do so by her sect.

The mercenaries began to ride forward and she went along. It was a gift given to her kind by the horse gods. They could blend into any herd of horses without being seen by human eyes. If they were smart. Sometimes her brothers . . . not so smart.

Laila pulled out her bow and quickly nocked three arrows, but before she could use them, the horses surrounding her suddenly reared up and began to panic. Had the nun cast a spell? Did nuns cast spells? Laila had thought all they did was pray and not have sex. And sometimes help the poor.

Confused, she kept her bow at the ready but moved along with the herd. It was when she was jostled to the left that she saw those headless bodies moving. Not the final death throes of men who hadn't realized their heads were no longer attached to their bodies but moving . . . with purpose. Slowly, but surely, getting to their feet.

Then the nun ripped off her white robes and Laila took in a startled breath.

Oh, it had been a very good thing they hadn't taken that girl.

Laila didn't even need to hear the men screaming to know what she was looking at. To fully understand. What the "nun" now wore told her everything she needed to know—and what the woman had been hiding.

The full-length chainmail hauberk with that wide skirt, slit up the front and back for fighting and horse riding. Iron chausses on her legs and chainmail boots with iron spurs. And a black woolen cappa over the chainmail, slit in the front and rear like the hauberk. But on the front and back was a blood-red rune that revealed all.

Gemma Smythe was no chunky nun. She was a War Monk. A knight who'd dedicated her entire life and soul to one of the mighty war gods. Morthwyl, based on her runes. Not only making the woman a trained and very deadly warrior, but one who could also raise the dead to attack their enemies during battle.

The headless bodies pulled their swords from their sheaths and rushed their former compatriots, running toward them at full speed and attacking as soon as they were near. As if they could see them despite the loss of their heads.

They struck the horses nearest first, so that the poor animals dropped and the men on the ground were immediately torn open by the swords of the headless.

The other horses wanted nothing to do with those that were once dead and they immediately backed up and turned away from the running bodies, attempting to charge off but, in their panic, colliding with one another or with the trees.

A few of the soldiers, knowing the War Monk was behind the attack, forced their horses to move forward, their swords pulled.

Gemma yanked a long sword she had sheathed at her side, gripped the handle with both hands, and raised it high over her left shoulder.

Laila released her three arrows, taking out three of the mercenaries in the process. She moved forward, nocking three more arrows, but she was no longer part of the herd. Another scream went out from the mounted men.

"*Centaur!*"

One of them blew a horn that would call to others and Laila quickly spun around, using her now much-bigger ass to knock the horse that had been beside her to the ground. She raised her bow and let the arrows fly, taking out the horn blower in mid-blast and two other men in the process.

She walked backward until she stood beside Gemma. She glanced down at her, nodded her head. "Monk."

Gemma gazed up at her with wide eyes. "Centaur?" She shook her head. "I can't believe Keeley was right."

"She was right about you too," Laila admitted. "You're quite the little liar."

Caid ran after Keeley through the woods, briefly pausing when he heard the screamed "*War Monk!*" coming from off in the distance.

Keeley stopped, too, at that yell, and looked over her shoulder. But then she gave a short head shake and continued running. A few minutes later, "Centaur!" was screamed out, making Caid smirk, and then came the sound of a war horn. Keeley's speed somehow increased as she suddenly veered off.

Caid was right behind her, until she reached a large tree and took a position there. Waiting.

Under his hooves, the earth moved and he knew more soldiers were coming.

Gods, had the princes sent an entire battalion to take down the family? That seemed . . . excessive.

Then again, all he'd heard for the last five minutes were the dying screams of men. None of women and children. So perhaps they knew something Caid and his cohorts did not.

The first of the mounted soldiers came over the ridge and that's when Keeley moved, running out.

Caid went to grab her, but she was already gone. Thankfully, she didn't jump in front of them. She ran out so that she was lined up with the first horse.

She raised her hammer high, pulling it back over her shoulder. Then, with a mighty swing, she brought the weapon down and into ...the side of the closest horse. With a horrid scream, the horse's hooves left the ground and its entire body slammed into the horse next to it. They both went down and the horses behind didn't have time to stop. Instead they stumbled over the pair and fell, forcing others to do the same.

But none of that stopped the rest of the mounted riders. There were more coming over that ridge and riding straight for the house.

Keeley used her hammer to finish off the men whose horses had gone down, but quickly pulled back before any of the soldiers could come for her. She stood by that tree again, staring down the hill. Watching as the soldiers rode into the valley, over the small white fence, and into the first field.

The first group of mounted soldiers made it as far as the middle of that field ... and then were gone. The healthy-looking crop they'd been trampling disappeared completely, the mounted riders and their steeds falling into the camouflaged pit.

Again, those coming in behind couldn't stop in time and half the mounted platoon disappeared into the same hole.

Keeley went up on her toes and yelled out, "Da! Nowwwwwwwwww!"

Caid came around the tree so that he could clearly see what Keeley was calling for. He heard it first. The counterweight, then the snap of the casting arm being released, and over the pigpen a large ball of fire flew into the pit of mounted soldiers.

The pit exploded into flames and the terrified screams of dying men and horses.

"You have a trebuchet?" Caid asked ... because he couldn't think of anything else to say.

"Mum made it. She gets bored when she's pregnant."

"Huh."

"It's very handy." Keeley gave a sad sigh. "But I hate hurting the horses."

She hefted her hammer onto her shoulder. "All right then. Let's go kill the rest so we can get the children to safety."

Gemma had put away her long sword and pulled out her two short swords. She ran at the mercenaries, hacking and slashing her way through them. Laila used her arrows until a few of the men got close. Then she switched to the steel spear she had strapped to her back.

Gemma was just holding these men off until her mother, Beatrix, and the children could slip away. But every time they tried to run, mercenaries moved in front of them. Blocked them.

Getting frustrated but not sure what to do about it, she simply kept fighting. Until Laila suddenly sent out a whistle call.

Gemma didn't know why until Cadell and Farlan rode into view. There was a lot of blood on them, but nothing that had her too worried.

Farlan immediately leaped into the fray, using a large axe to chop away the mercenaries attacking her. He used his back legs to strike at any men or horses behind him. The strength of his kicks knocked the horses back and killed the men outright from blows to their chests or heads.

"Go!" he finally yelled when he was right in front of her. "Now!"

Gemma ran toward her mother and siblings.

Mum was busy fighting off three soldiers on foot with her two swords.

Coming up behind the men, Gemma beheaded one and disemboweled another. Her mother buried one of her blades into the third's belly.

Sheathing her swords, Gemma picked up one of the toddlers who she knew couldn't keep up. She motioned to Beatrix to take the other, which she did but not before she rolled her eyes and sighed a bit.

Gemma struggled to contain her annoyance, knowing this wasn't the time or place.

With the toddler in her arms, she started to run back toward the house. That's when she saw Keran and Samuel.

"Take them!" she ordered, handing the toddler to Samuel and motioning for Beatrix to give him the boy, not wanting to risk her dropping him. "Keran! Watch the younger ones! And move! Everyone move!"

When they all ran toward the house, Gemma returned to the last three men she'd killed. She crouched by them and chanted the song of death, draining the land around her of its essence and putting it into the bodies of these men. They all stood and she pointed at the remaining soldiers battling the centaurs.

The abominations ran toward the fight, their weapons drawn, and Gemma yelled out, "Laila! Get out of there!"

Then, without waiting to see if the centaurs followed her order, Gemma raced after her family.

Keeley battered another man out of her way and took off around the house to get to her family. As she cleared the corner, she ran into more enemies. Startled, she immediately raised her hammer and yelled in rage. So did her enemy.

Then they both stopped.

"Gemma?"

"Oh. It's you." Gemma lowered her sword. "Thank the gods."

Keeley stared at her sister. "You're a War Monk?"

"Is this really the time to discuss it?"

"You're right." Keeley lifted her hammer again to strike her sister down.

"Keeley Smythe!" her mother snapped. "You put that hammer down right this second!"

"She's a necromancer!"

"She's your *sister*," her mother reminded her.

And Keeley knew her mother was right. Despite whatever had set her sister on this path, they were still blood. And family was all.

"Fine." Keeley lowered the hammer. "Sorry," she bit out.

Gemma hissed and pushed past her.

But before Keeley could rip her judgey little head off, her mother grabbed her by the back of the neck and whispered against her ear, "She's your sister, you love her, and nothing will come between you two. Understand?" When Keeley didn't answer quick enough, her mother squeezed. "*Understand?*"

"Yes."

Her mother followed after the rest, but before Keeley could move, Beatrix caught her arm.

"What's going on?" her sister demanded.

"Beatrix—"

"Now," she pushed.

"Fine. You're the future queen."

"Ahhh. I see," Beatrix replied, her expression never changing. That reaction bothered Keeley but she didn't have time to figure out why. "And the men attacking here today . . . ?"

"Mercenaries of Straton the Devourer."

"Not the oldest, then?"

A strange question, but . . . "No. I saw the crest. It's the Devourer."

"Huh. Interesting."

Was it?

Keeley took her sister's hand. "Don't worry. You know I won't let anything happen to you."

Beatrix studied Keeley's hand, then looked up into her face. She gave a small smile. "Of course you won't."

"Are you sure about this, Da?" Keeley asked her father, her hand pressed against his back.

Caid wanted to give them more privacy but he stayed close. For their safety.

"I'm sure. But I can't do it myself."

"Don't worry about that." Keeley kissed her father's cheek. "Go help Mum get on the horse. You know she hates riding."

Angus grunted and walked away from the small farmhouse he'd bought with every penny of the money he'd saved during his time as a soldier. A house his entire family had been living in for years. Once he'd disappeared behind the stables, Keeley glanced at her War Monk sister.

"I can do it," Caid offered.

"No," Keeley replied. "This is up to us."

She nocked an arrow, aimed the weapon, and waited.

Her sister placed her thumb and forefinger on the arrowhead and softly spoke a spell. A flame flared and Gemma stepped back to her sister's side. Keeley's gaze stayed on her the entire time until she said, "That's completely normal."

Gemma's jaw tensed and she snarled, "If what you're asking is whether I am pure evil, I'm not. But should that change at any time"—she locked a vicious glare on Keeley—"trust me when I say that *you* will be the first to know."

Caid cringed a bit, worried that at some point he'd be preventing one of these sisters from killing the other.

Keeley let the arrow fly and it went through the open door of the house. Their father had doused the lower floor in ale and the entire thing was covered in flames in less than a minute. He'd already set fire to all the crops and released the animals. Only the horses that hadn't run too far from the stables would continue to be used by the family.

Gemma stormed away from her sister and Keeley handed the bow back to him.

"Thanks for that."

"Of course."

"I don't know if there will be enough horses for all of us," she said as they walked toward the stables. "Mind if I catch a ride?"

Caid stopped walking, faced her. "Really?"

She blinked up at him. "I'm . . . I'm sorry. I was just joking."

"That's the kind of joke that makes some of my people very angry. Especially my sister. Don't let her easy ways fool you. She has a bit of a temper."

"I didn't mean anything by it. It's just . . . my heart is breaking because I know my father's heart is breaking. And there's nothing I can do to help him."

Realizing that she wasn't mocking him or being cruel, Caid immediately felt bad. This was why he rarely dealt with people. Most greatly annoyed him and he wasn't very good at hiding that annoyance. But Keeley, much like her father, didn't annoy him much at all. There was something so earnest about her. So open. She didn't seem to hide anything from anyone.

"I don't know your family well," Caid carefully told her, "but I truly think the only thing your father cares about is that his children and wife are alive and well."

Keeley nodded. "I'm sure you're right."

They began walking toward the stables again.

"Who taught you to fight like that?" he asked, suddenly irritated by the abrupt silence between them. "Your mother or father?"

"Both. My father was a soldier. For the Old King's armies. Many years ago. He always said, 'I know what soldiers do when they have free rein. I don't want that for my daughters.' And my mother was a firm believer that it's a poor blacksmith who doesn't know how to wield her own weapons."

"Well, they did a fine job with you and your sister."

"My parents taught Gemma how to wield weapons but that other shit...? She learned that from someone else." Keeley rubbed her forehead but all she did was smear the blood around. "Do you know anything about War Monks?"

Caid opened his mouth, closed it, opened it again...let out a long breath.

Keeley raised her hands. "Forget I asked."

"No, it's not that bad. It's just—"

"No. Don't even bother. We both heard the screams of those mercenaries. Cold-blooded men who kill for sport and gold and yet my much-shorter sister sent them into a panic. I think that says all I need to know."

They neared the others, who were already mounted and ready to go. The smallest children being held by a sibling or parent.

"Where are we going?" she asked him.

"That's up to you. We need to take your family someplace safe."

"But I thought—"

"The children can't come."

Keeley stopped. "I will *not* leave Beatrix. Do you understand?"

"Of course. But you don't want your brothers and sisters around the Witches of Amhuinn. It's simply not wise."

"That's fine."

"But we should move. In case more of Straton's men come."

Keeley started walking again but she was suddenly nudged forward; the gray mare stood behind her.

She petted the head of her friend, whispered to her. "You poor thing. I don't want to leave you."

"I don't think you're supposed to."

Keeley frowned. "What are you talking about?"

"She wants revenge. Not just on the ones who killed her son, but on those who destroyed her life. She thinks you can give that to her." Caid glanced at the mare. "She's offering her services. As your war mount."

Keeley looked over her shoulder at Beatrix. Her sister sat side-saddle on a small mare. Back straight, brown hair reaching past her hips, already looking the part of a royal. She wasn't exactly what Caid would call "pretty." And there was something off about her. Something he felt was missing.

It didn't matter, though, did it? She'd been chosen for a reason and, once she had the witches' blessing, then war would come. There was no way around it. Not with the Old King's sons fighting for that crown.

Keeley placed her hands on the gray mare's massive jaw and lifted her head. "Ride with me into battle and I will do my best to give you the revenge you seek. Fair enough?"

The mare trotted over to the rest of the family, stopping in front of Keeley's father.

Confused, Keeley looked up at him.

"Get your saddle," Caid told her. "She's waiting for you."

Straton stared over the edge of the pit where a good number of his hired men and their horses had been burned alive.

"What kind of people are these?" his general demanded.

"Clearly not the kind we were expecting," Straton remarked as he stepped away from the pit, unable to stand the smell another second.

"I thought these were farmers," the general snapped at one of his men.

"They are." Straton looked around at what remained of the family's farm. "What annoys me is that I can't even burn this place down out of spite. They've already done that."

His general came to his side. "Prince Straton, I promise—"

"I don't want to hear it," Straton cut in. "Just find them. Now."

"Yes, my lord."

"What if they split up?" another soldier asked.

"Track the *girl*," he spit out. "We can kill her family at a later time. I need that girl dead. Don't come back until she is."

CHAPTER 7

The family traveled for three solid days, with Angus leading the way. Caid and his unit stayed in their natural forms and shadowed the family as they moved along.

The plan, as far as Caid knew from his sister, was to take the family someplace they deemed safe and then to take Beatrix to the witches for the confirmation.

Once she was consecrated as queen, the next steps would be decided by Beatrix herself. Until then, Laila was in charge. But she was letting the family believe otherwise. The situation was already tense. The first night had been hard, with the youngest children scared and crying. The older ones bickering and nervous, worried they were about to be attacked.

They weren't. But Caid was sure they were being tracked. The second night, though, Caid and Farlan handled the two trackers the Devourer had sent out, burying their bodies deep so the next set of trackers wouldn't be able to find them.

By the third night, they arrived at their destination: a castle complete with moat that was high on a hill with the sea at its back.

"You have royal friends?" Caid asked Keeley, who'd been surprisingly quiet the entire trip unless she was attempting to soothe her young siblings.

She laughed. The first he'd heard from her in days. "Hardly."

Angus rode until he reached the moat; the metal gate was closed against any intruders.

"Oy!" he called up to the towers. "Archibald!"

They waited but no one came. Not surprising to Caid. Who knew where inside that castle this Archibald was? He could be asleep in his bed or the kitchens in the back of the castle.

"We could be here all night," his sister complained to him.

She was right. They could easily be here all night. Longer if this Archibald was actually dead.

Angus glanced at his wife and, after a sigh, yelled out, "I know you see us, you bastard! Just open the fucking gate!"

He came out of the darkness. A giant of a man. Bigger than Angus, it seemed. Long red hair in a braid that hung over his massive shoulder, a steel helm with horns on his very large head, and what Caid could only call insane blue eyes gazing down at them.

"Good gods," Laila muttered.

"Why should I let you in, you fucking bastard!"

"Because you owe me!"

"*I owe you shit!*"

Keeley and Gemma both rolled their eyes, and their heads fell back in irritation. For once, they looked alike; but they didn't know it.

"You open this fucking gate, or I'll *tear it down with my bare hands!*"

"*Just try, you arrogant cunt!*"

"*That is it!*" Emma bellowed. Her horse took her close to her husband. "Both of you stop this! Please!" She looked up at the giant man. "Hello, Archibald."

"My dear sweet Emma?" The large man's voice changed, and Caid cringed at the neediness in it. "Is that you?"

"Of course."

"It's been so long."

"Oh, please," Angus growled out.

Emma punched his shoulder before replying to Archibald, "Could you open the gate? For me? Please?"

"What about *him?*" Archibald snarled. "Am I safe?"

"No!" Angus snapped.

"Yes!" Emma said over her husband. "You have *my* word."

Archibald took his time, but finally replied, "Fine."

When he disappeared into the darkness again, Emma turned in her saddle to say to her husband, "Could you *please* stop being a horse's ass?"

"He started it. He always starts it."

"I don't care who started what. I just want our children safe. Remember them? Your little bastards?"

"Of course I remember—"

"Then give me your word."

"But—"

"Angus, I swear by all that is unholy—"

"Fine." He cracked his neck and shoulders. "I will do my best not to remind him what a worthless cunt he is."

"That's all I ask."

The drawbridge was slowly lowered and Caid couldn't help but ask Keeley, "Is Archibald a royal?"

"Hardly," she repeated.

"Then who is he?"

"Our uncle. My father's brother."

"They seem very angry at each other."

"They are. They both wanted the same thing, but only one could get it."

"Your mother?" he asked softly.

"No," Keeley answered. "The family axe."

"The . . . the *family* axe?"

"Uncle Archie got the axe. *Then* my father got my mother. And they've never let each other forget it."

The drawbridge landed and the family rode across it, heading into the courtyard.

Caid and Laila held back a bit, making sure there was no one behind them. When they felt it was safe enough, they followed.

As they walked across, Caid said to his sister, "You know, the longer we know this family—"

"Yes. It's true. Our kin is not *nearly* as insane as our father insists we are."

Before her mother could dismount from her horse, Uncle Archie was there—his fierce helm tossed aside—wrapping his hands around her waist and lifting her down.

"My sweet, sweet Emma," he growled, pulling her into his arms.

Keeley jumped off the gray mare and ran—literally *ran*—to her father's side and grabbed his arm. Gemma grabbed the other, and it was only the raw strength of a blacksmith and a knight that kept him from beating their uncle to death.

Once Uncle Archie got their mum onto the ground, he moved his hand to her waist and led her toward the castle door.

"Come, my sweet Emma," Archie urged. "I have a lovely *axe* to show you."

That set their father into a tailspin of even more rage, but Keeley fought hard to keep him under control.

"Please, Da," she begged. "We need him."

"No, we don't. I'll kill him and this place will be ours as long as we like!"

"Daddy, that's a horrible thing to say." Gemma placed her hands on his chest and pushed their father back a few feet. "You need to find a way to get along with Uncle Archie."

"I'd rather set us both on fire!"

"That's enough, Da!" Keeley stood beside Gemma. "You two are brothers. You shouldn't be doing all this ridiculous bickering over nothing."

"She's absolutely right, Daddy."

Her father stared at her, stared at her sister, and then said, "Are you two fucking kidding me?"

Caid walked into the castle. It was the kind of place humans liked to live in. Made of stone with high ceilings but no matter how high they were, it didn't change the fact that they were still trapped inside. Trapped like rats in a hole in the wall.

That was not for centaurs. They had tents. Some had yurts. They all had roofs, but they had roofs they could walk away from anytime they wanted. Anytime they needed. He couldn't imagine living in one place without ever moving. Without ever venturing out far and wide.

But for what they needed right now . . . this place would do.

"Here it is," Archibald was saying, pointing out an old, battered tree axe that was pinned to the stone wall above the big fireplace. "The family axe."

Laila came from behind the big stairs that led to the upper floors. "There's no one here," she whispered.

Caid looked down at his sister.

"No one. I think he lives in this place alone."

"That actually could work for us."

"That's exactly what I was thinking."

Keeley walked inside, stood next to him. "Is he showing her that stupid axe?"

"Seems so."

Gemma walked into the castle with their father. She had her arm looped through his, but his face was red and his hands curled into big fists. He seemed ready to snap and Caid would bet gold his brother knew that.

The War Monk had on her white robes again, making her look like the pious little nun that she wasn't.

"Uncle?" she called out.

"Niece." He looked Gemma over. "You've gotten chunky."

The War Monk's eyes narrowed on her uncle but she controlled her annoyance and forced a smile. "I'm sure, after all these years, you and my dear father can put aside your differences. Move on to a new relationship appropriate to such wonderful men."

Archibald smirked. "Need my help, do you?" Now his brutal blue gaze examined his brother. "I knew you could never take care of your family."

And that was it. Angus Farmerson pulled away from his daughter, leaped onto the big wooden table in the middle of the room, and launched himself at his brother.

Laila sighed. "I guess we should stop them."

"Do we really have to get in the middle of this?"

Caid was in no mood to get between two human males fighting over a gods-damn axe.

But his sister didn't even have a chance to insist—and she would have—because Keeley was moving. Yet it wasn't the two men she got between. That was her mother and sister. They struggled to pull the males apart. Keeley, however . . . she grabbed that weak, worthless axe off the wall and dropped it on the floor. Then she unslung her hammer from the sling she had strapped to her back, gripped the steel handle with both hands, raised it high above her head—gorgeous muscles rippling—and swung it down. Once. Twice. Three times. Destroying the wood handle.

That stopped everyone.

"Keeley! What have you done?" Angus cried.

"Mad cow! How could you?" Archibald yelled.

Keeley picked up the pieces of the family axe and tossed them into the fireplace, followed by the iron head.

She faced her shocked father and uncle. "Are we now done with this never-ending *bullshit?*" she ended on a bellow. "Our family is in danger and you two are fighting over a ridiculous axe!" She gestured to Emma. "And Mum!"

"Oy!"

"*We,*" she said, leaning down and speaking directly to the two men, "have more important things to discuss than your years-old horseshit! So get your old asses off the ground, put some smiles on your faces so as not to scare the children, and maybe . . . *maybe!* . . . I will be nice enough to make you two mad bastards a new bloody axe!"

Grudgingly, but most likely afraid *not* to follow her orders, the brothers stood.

"A *steel* axe?" Archibald softly asked.

"From handle to head," Keeley sweetly replied, now that she'd gotten her way, "as long as you two don't keep pissing me off."

The brothers gave each other another good glare before nodding in agreement.

"Good." She motioned to Gemma. "Bring everyone in."

As Gemma silently returned to the courtyard to gather the children, as well as Samuel, Farlan, and Cadell, Laila leaned into Caid's side and teased, "I think we may have found the queen's general."

"I have to admit, Sister," Caid said in all seriousness, "I was thinking the same thing."

Keeley put her baby sister into the bed, noting the hammer still gripped in her little fist. She pulled the fur over her sleeping form and started to stand, but Endelyon proved she wasn't asleep when she grabbed Keeley's wrist. So strong already. Keeley was proud.

"Don't go," Endelyon whispered.

"I'll stay with you until you fall asleep," she promised.

"No. Don't go. Don't go away."

Keeley sat on the edge of the bed and leaned in so she could see her sister's face in the candlelight.

"What are you talking about?"

"I'm scared."

"Don't be. Mum and Da won't let anything happen to you. They'll protect you."

"Not protect *you*."

Keeley suddenly understood what the nearly four-year-old was trying to say.

"Are you scared for me?"

Endelyon nodded.

Keeley leaned across her sister, resting her elbow on the other end of the narrow bed so they could whisper to each other as they liked to do early in the morning before Keeley had to go to work.

"What are you worried about?"

Endelyon took a good grip on a lock of Keeley's hair. "B—" she began, but then her gaze moved to something behind Keeley.

Looking over her shoulder, Keeley saw Beatrix standing in the doorway. She gave a short jerk of her head, motioning toward the stairs. Keeley held up a finger before turning back to Endelyon.

"Talk to me," she gently pushed. "Tell me what's bothering you."

Her sister held her little hammer out.

Keeley grinned. "I made that for you. It's your protection. I have my own," she said, reaching down and lifting her favorite weapon.

Her sister giggled, reaching for the hammer. But the head was still covered in blood and her sister was too young for that, so Keeley put it back on the floor.

"One day, you're going to make your own mighty hammer," Keeley told her. "And then, we'll be blacksmiths together."

"Promise?"

"You bet." She leaned down and kissed her sister on the forehead. "Now get some sleep. Okay?"

"Okay."

"Love you, little bits."

"Love you too."

Keeley kissed her again and then a few more times until the giggling got too much for her younger brother, who threw his wooden sword at Keeley's head.

At some point before he got his first steel one, she'd have to teach him not to do that, but it could wait for another day.

Keeley tucked her siblings in and closed the door on her way into the hall. That's where she found her uncle.

"Sorry, little Keeley." He looked sheepishly at his big feet. "Didn't mean to upset you so."

She crossed her arms and bent her neck back so she could look up at her giant uncle. He was a good five inches taller than her father and her father was a big man. That's why she knew it would be a very bad thing if the fight between the two men went too far. Especially because Uncle Archie was . . . just a little . . . less than sane.

He was a talented stonemason who had, on more than one occasion, gotten himself kicked out of various towns because of the fear that he could "snap" at any time. The royals who hired him always loved his work but couldn't stand to deal with him for any length of time. But over the years, he'd made a good amount of coin and, finally, went off to build the castle they were standing in. All by himself. Like a crazy person would do. She didn't know he'd done such a beautiful job, though. He should be proud. But he was too busy feeling bitter and angry about whatever horseshit had gone on with his brother years earlier.

"You're lucky I didn't use my hammer on you," she told him. "You attacked me da."

"Do you want me to lie and say he didn't deserve it?"

"No. But I need to know my *entire* family is safe while they're here. That includes me da and not just me mum."

He leaned in and whispered, "But if I kill him, I can have her."

Good gods. "Uncle Archie, kill my father . . . and my mother will flay the skin from your very *soul.* And not in a nice way. In the meanest way she can think of."

He glanced off and she could tell he was actually thinking about it. Wondering if it might be worth it.

So Keeley did what she didn't want to do. She hooked the head of her hammer against her uncle's leg and yanked, dropping the older man onto the floor, facedown.

"*Owwww!* You vicious cow!"

She crouched down next to him, pressing her knee against his spine and her hammer against the back of his neck, pushing down just enough... "Now listen up, you mad cock! As my uncle, I adore you. But as my father's brother, I will *kill you* if you hurt him. And gods help you if you manage to kill him. Do you understand what I am saying to you?"

"Yes."

"Say it like you mean it."

"*Yes!*"

"Do I have your word, Uncle Archibald? *Your word?*"

"I give you my word!"

"Good!" She patted his shoulder. "And you will *love* the family axe I make for you. I give you *my* word."

She left him lying facedown on the floor and headed to the stairs. When she reached them, her mother was standing there, grinning.

"That's my girl," her mother whispered as Keeley walked by.

Gemma forced Samuel into a room and made him get some sleep. He felt he should sleep in the stables with the one horse her uncle Archie had and the horses they'd brought from the farm. But why? Because he thought he should suffer as a monk? Except he wasn't just a monk. He was a War Monk. Or would be, once his training was complete. But she really wasn't sure the life of a War Monk was for him. Being an acolyte to one of the other, less violent, gods might be his best bet, but she didn't have the luxury of saying that right now. She needed him. At least until this was over. And the war gods knew he'd served his purpose. His warning of the upcoming attack by the Devourer's mercenaries had given her family the time they'd needed to survive the fight.

And, like any warrior, he needed good rest when he could find it. So if he had access to a bed, he should take it.

Gemma pointed a warning finger at the young man one more time before she finally closed the door and headed toward the stairs.

Despite having had a very good dinner that their mother made from a deer the Amichais had stalked and skinned near the castle,

Gemma was still hungry. Hoping there was some bread and stew left, she went down the stairs and headed to the pantry. She walked past a room with a table and stacks of books. That's where Keeley and Beatrix were deep in very soft conversation.

Her eyes narrowed and she immediately walked into the room, closing the door behind her.

Both her sisters stopped speaking.

"What are we talking about?" she asked.

Beatrix began to reply, but Keeley cut her off. "I think the bigger question, Sister, is why are *you* here? I always thought War Monks moved in packs. Like dogs. Or rats."

Gemma took a moment, using all her training to keep herself calm. She didn't want to become like Uncle Archie and her father. Fighting with Keeley every time they saw each other. They were better than that. Weren't they?

When Gemma didn't answer right away, Keeley went on. "I can't help but notice your timing. We don't see you for more than a decade but then . . . there you are. Suddenly. And dressed as a nun. That was delightful."

"If you're asking whether I knew about the Witches of Amhuinn, I did. Of course I did."

"And?"

"And I think Beatrix is a little young to be queen."

"The Old King was the Old King when he was fifteen seasons. She's twenty-three seasons. She'll be fine."

"Keeley—"

"With the right advisors, she'll be fine."

Gemma crossed her arms over her chest. "I knew you weren't going to be reasonable."

"How is that unreasonable?"

"She can turn it down. Tell the witches no."

Beatrix, leaning her butt against the table, calmly gazed at Gemma. "And why would I do that?"

Gemma finally focused on her younger sister and she desperately fought the urge to start slapping the arrogance out of her. She knew that wouldn't work on Beatrix, but part of her still wanted to try.

"Because you shouldn't be queen. The land will be torn apart—"

"The land will be torn apart anyway. The brothers will ensure that."

"You have no army. You have no allies. You have nothing, Beatrix. All you're doing is putting our family in danger. And for what? So you can wear a crown you couldn't possibly hold on to? Does that make sense to you?"

"What makes sense to me is that our lands need a new leader. I am that leader. If that bothers you . . . I'm sorry. But I will *not* turn this down." She placed her hand on Keeley's shoulder. "We'll leave tomorrow. With the Amichais. You tell Father."

And with that, she and her dark green silk gown swept out of the room.

"*Have you lost your—*"

Gemma jerked back when Keeley slapped her hand over her mouth.

"Shhhh," she hissed, her forefinger held in front of her lips. "Keep your voice down."

Keeley went to the door, making sure to close it quietly. When she was done, she faced Gemma.

"Why can't you be nice?" she asked.

Now Gemma wanted to slap Keeley.

"Because there is no time to be *nice,*" Gemma practically hissed. "There is no time to let her believe, for even a moment, that she should or could be queen."

"Why? Because you don't like her?"

"I wish it were that easy, Keeley. I wish it was just me not liking her so that she could be queen and the rest of us could go on with our lives. But you should know that nothing is that simple. Not in the world we live in."

Keeley studied Gemma for a moment before she asked, "And what if we tell her right now, tonight, that she can't be queen? That our parents forbid it. That you and I forbid it. That no one, not even the Amichais, will escort her anywhere. What do you think happens then?"

Gemma met her sister's gaze, but she couldn't keep it. Not when she already knew the answer to those questions.

"She goes anyway."

Keeley pushed away from the door and went to the table. She slid some books aside and sat down, letting her long legs dangle over the side.

"Of course she goes anyway," she finally said. "She has been waiting for this all her life."

"What are you talking about?"

"While you were off with monks, I was watching our siblings grow up. Like Mum, I can tell you everything about each of them. The ones who'll stay on the farm all their lives. The ones who'll go off to join the military. The ones who will be rich and the ones who will always struggle. And from what I've seen of Beatrix . . . she's been waiting for this since she was born. Since the day Mum held her in her arms and declared to the world, 'This one is a bit plain.'"

Beatrix was a bit plain but it never mattered to the family. Although, now that Gemma thought about it, it clearly mattered to Beatrix. That's why she wore those gowns while living in the middle of a farm with horses and pigs and chickens. The elaborate hairstyles and well-made jewelry. Because she hated that she was plain, while the rest of them barely cared at all how they looked.

"She's been waiting her entire life to be queen, Gemma, and nothing we say or do is going to stop her."

Gemma became impossibly still, nothing on her moving, while her mind turned over the information Keeley had given her. For a moment, it didn't even look like she was breathing.

Then she was coming across the room, her finger pointed at Keeley, until she stood only a few inches from her.

"You don't think she should be queen either . . . do you?"

"She's a spoiled twenty-three-year-old girl who has never left the house she was born in. Of *course* I don't think she should be queen. Princess, perhaps, but not a ruling queen."

"Then why are you—"

"Why argue with her at this stage? It's not going to dissuade her. If anything, it's just going to make her dig her heels in. And, unlike you, I know how stubborn our sister can be."

"You need to stop throwing in my face how long I've been gone."

"You shouldn't have left."

"I have a calling, Sister."

"The gods speak to you?" she asked.

"Sometimes. Yes."

"But Beatrix is the irrational one with dreams of grandeur?"

"Those are two very different things."

"Are they? She believes she can be queen of the Hill Lands and you think you talk to gods. Perhaps be careful before throwing stones from that glass castle."

Gemma waved Keeley's very sound logic away and said, "If you don't think she should be queen, then what are you doing?"

"I will be traveling with her to see those witches."

"Why?" Gemma barked at her. "Why are you feeding this craziness?"

"I'm not letting my sister go alone with the Amichais."

"They saved our lives."

"And I'm grateful. I will always be grateful. But she's still family. And we protect family. I'm not letting her go anywhere by herself." Keeley pushed her hair off her face but was annoyed when it slipped forward again. "Especially because I know she'll need me when this all settles down."

"What do you mean?"

"Once these witches meet her, find out about her, they'll change their minds. They'll know she's not the future queen. And Beatrix will be devastated. She'll need at least one of us there to comfort her, and Mum can't go."

"You so sure that's what the witches will say?"

"She's a young woman who has never been more than ten leagues away from the farm she was born in. But, and this is the important part, she is brilliant. I don't mean she's smart. I mean *brilliant*. She'd been able to read when she was still crawling. She could do Mum's books from the forge by the time she was five. She thinks this is all owed to her *because* she's brilliant. You and me . . . ? If someone told us we were going to be queen, we'd say, 'Me? But I'm a peasant. Who's going to make us queen?' But not Beatrix. Beatrix has *always* known." Keeley gazed intently at her sister. "And she's not going to let anyone—especially the two of us—tell her any different."

"If she's so *brilliant,*" Gemma said with great sarcasm, "then why shouldn't she be queen?"

"Because she has no experience with anything. She knows nothing of war or battle or how to get and keep the loyalty of hard men. She has no allies and no royal connections. And none of the Old King's sons will want to marry her to legitimize her that way. She has no friends and, from what I can tell, doesn't want any. I love my sister, but I have no delusions about her, Gemma. She's a good person and will want to do the right thing, but being queen . . ." Keeley frowned. "What's so funny?"

"She's a good person? Seriously?"

"She is to my eyes. Of course, how would you know one way or the other?" Keeley held up her hands. "I'm not going to fight about this with you. I'm going with her tomorrow. And, the gods willing, we'll be back before the next full moon. I don't know if life can go back to normal after that, but at least this upsetting part of our drama will be over."

Keeley jumped off the table and headed toward the door. But Gemma caught hold of her forearm and held her. "Let me go with her tomorrow. You can stay and protect the family with Mum and Da."

"You?" Keeley couldn't help but chuckle a little. "I wouldn't put the Amichais through that. A trip with you two. But, more importantly, you are *not* the one who will be there for her when she finds out the truth. You'll rub it in her face before you comfort her."

"Keeley—"

"I've made up my mind, Gemma. I know what this means to her. To be queen of the Hill Lands. And when that dream crumbles into dust, she'll need someone who actually likes her to be there for her. That, dear sister, is definitely not you."

"I'm not letting you go off with strangers!" Angus raged, pacing like a caged bear. "You're my daughter! It's my job to protect you."

"I can care for myself," Beatrix softly argued. "Besides, I won't be alone. I'll have Keeley with me."

"And me," Gemma suddenly piped up.

"*Like hells you will!*"

"Da!"

Beatrix's flat gaze had locked onto Gemma. "I didn't ask *you* to come with me."

Gemma clapped her hands together and cheered, "Then this is a fun surprise!"

Caid cleared his throat to stop from laughing. The way she'd said that and the look her younger sister had given her revealed a brutal battle of wills. A battle their parents were completely unaware of as Angus continued to rage.

"*None of you are going anywhere!*" Angus bellowed. "You'll stay here where you're safe! With me! And your mum."

"If you want my opinion . . ." began Archibald, who stood against a far wall.

"Gemma," Keeley said, without even looking at her sister. And Gemma pulled a small blade from her sword belt and threw it in her uncle's direction. She didn't hit him, but she landed the blade in a spot quite close to his head.

Caid was impressed. The older man didn't flinch, but he did put up his hands, palms out, and said, "I'll mind me own."

So he wasn't always irrational. That was good to know.

Angus's wife put her arm around his shoulders. "Are you done?"

Angus did look exhausted. He was breathing heavily, big shoulders heaving, concern etched into his face. "I can't lose me girls, Em. I can't."

"And you won't." She kissed his forehead and moved so she stood in the middle of the hall. "This is what we're going to do and none of you are going to argue with me."

"Well—" Laila began but a raised finger stopped her.

"None of you," the older woman insisted.

"You two"—Emma pointed at Caid and Laila—"are going to take our Beatrix to the Witches of Amhuinn. Get everything confirmed and solidified. We'll make all our big decisions then. Keeley, Gemma, and Keran will travel with you."

"Mum—"

"Mother—"

There went that terse finger again and both immediately fell silent. "The two centaurs, Fartness and Cud-filled—"

"Farlan and Cadell," Laila corrected.

"—will stay here and protect the family."

"My lady—" Laila began.

"I am no lady, centaur. I still have bits of brain and blood stuck under me tits because I have not had the time nor inclination to bathe, due to our travels. So don't attempt your soft words with me."

"Fine," Laila shot back. "Farlan and Cadell are here to protect the future queen. Not her less-than-noble siblings."

"You want the queen, lady pony, you protect the family. We're a unit. I won't have our youngest dragged across the lands, but I won't leave them defenseless either."

"You lot are hardly defenseless."

"Without Keeley and Gemma? We're practically naked. So, these are your choices. We all go . . . a slow, plodding way to travel with children. Or you leave those two hearty stallions to my tender care and you make great haste to the Witches of Amhuinn. Which is it?"

Laila had no choice. Not now. Not with the Devourer's men still searching for Beatrix.

"Farlan and Cadell will stay here."

"Good." She returned to her husband's side, putting her arms around him. "Now all of you might as well get as much sleep as you can. Tomorrow will be a hard, long day."

"I'm still worried about you," Keeley said. "What if the Devourer's men come here?"

"So little faith in me, niece?" Archibald asked.

"If they come," he said, leading Keeley and Caid deep into the bowels under his home, "I will get the family out this way."

"Including my father?" Keeley asked.

"If I must."

"You must, Uncle."

He stopped walking, forcing Keeley to stop behind him. He looked at her over his shoulder. "You should have been my daughter, you know. All of you should have been mine."

"That's such a strange thing to say! Why would you say that to me?"

"Because you should know that your father stole your mother from me."

"How did he do that?"

"He just did!"

"Maybe between the two of you, he just seemed less insane."

"She might have said something like that." He started down the stairs again. "But we both know the truth. That we were meant to be together."

"If you two had gotten together, *I* would not be here."

"That's not true."

"I may look like my mother, Uncle, but I am my father's child. More than any of my siblings. So unless you are wishing me away . . ."

"No. Of course not."

They finally reached the last of the stairs.

"This is steep," Caid noted.

"It is." Keeley took the torch from her uncle and held it high, moving a bit down the hallway. "This leads out?"

"It does. Right next to the Wenlan Docks. We can get a boat there if needed."

"Good. Bring Mum and Da down here tomorrow. Let them see where they'll be going. They'll want to get the older children comfortable with coming down here as well. Especially since they'll be carrying the little ones." She raised the torch higher. "Make sure all these torches are lit all day, every day. You'll never know when you'll need to make a run for it."

"Any other orders? Maybe you want me to dance for the children."

Keeley reached up and pressed her palm to her uncle's cheek, replying in all seriousness. "All I ask is that you keep my family safe."

"For you and your mum . . . anything."

Caid watched Archibald make his way back up the stairs until Keeley tapped his arm and motioned in the opposite direction.

They started trekking down the long tunnels.

"Making sure he's being truthful about where this ends up?" he asked as he followed her.

"I don't think we need to go the entire way, but I want to make sure it doesn't end after a few feet either."

"He built all this by himself?"

"I hope so."

"Why do you hope so?"

"My uncle is paranoid. If he involved some poor sod to help him build the castle, trust me when I say that poor sod is also *buried* somewhere under all this."

Caid winced. "Sure it's a good idea letting your family stay here?"

"We have little choice. Besides, my uncle may be a mad bastard, but he's also a mad fighter. Like one of those berserkers of old. He'll throw himself in front of an entire army if it means protecting my mother and her offspring."

"And your father?"

"Will need to watch his back. But hopefully we won't leave him here too long." She continued on for a bit in silence, but Caid could tell she had more questions.

"How does this process work?" she asked.

"Process?"

"The witches." She stopped, faced Caid. "They won't hurt my sister, will they?"

"They just want to see her. Make sure their prophesy is correct. Consult the gods, or whatever they do."

She frowned. "And if it's not? If they decide she's not queen. Will Beatrix be in danger from them?"

"Your bigger problem will always be the Old King's sons."

"That doesn't really answer my question."

"Your sister will be safe until she's either crowned and has an army at her back or the brothers know she's no longer their worry."

"And how will we ensure her safety?"

"We'll figure it out. We won't desert you. Not after all this."

Keeley seemed to accept that answer and began moving down the tunnel again.

"Can I ask you a question?"

"Of course," Keeley said easily, glancing back at him with a smile.

"When we were attacked at your parents' farm . . . where were your wolves?"

"My wolves?"

Caid simply raised an eyebrow and Keeley nodded. "Oh. My friends."

"I thought for sure you'd call them to your side."

"They're my friends," she explained, briefly stopping to light a torch affixed to the wall. "But I don't actually have control over them. I know they won't attack me, but I can't say the same for my family. I won't risk my siblings."

Caid didn't mention that she'd happily risked him and his unit, plus poor Samuel, but what was the point? Laila could handle anything, unlike the babe still feeding at her mum's breast or the toddlers who liked to play with the piglets.

"Can I ask *you* a question?" Keeley gave him that smile again and Caid immediately stopped walking.

"No. You can't ride me."

Keeley spun around to face him, forcing Caid to jerk his head back so the torch in her hand didn't burn his face off.

"Oh, please!" she begged. "Just a little ride? Down this tunnel will be fine!"

"*No.* I am not a pony."

"Of course you're not! You're a mighty stallion."

"That's not going to work with me either." Arms crossed over his chest, he leaned in and said, "And tell your father to stop asking Cadell for the same thing. He's getting cranky. And when Cadell gets cranky . . ."

"I'm very hurt," she complained.

Caid turned her around by her shoulders and gave her a little push so that she'd keep moving. "No, you're not. But if you keep asking, you might be more hurt than you or your father would like."

Instead of being frightened by his stern tone, Keeley simply laughed and continued on.

Laila stood on the second-floor landing, her arms resting on the banister, and her gaze focused on the floor. She was thinking of their upcoming travels, debating strategies and all the different ways they could get to their destination. There were at least three routes they could use to reach the Witches of Amhuinn, but none of them seemed safe enough.

Since all of them were less than safe, she focused on deciding which would be the fastest.

"There you are," Laila heard from behind her.

Young Beatrix held out a scroll. Unrolling it, Laila looked it over.

"A map?"

"Yes." Beatrix pointed. "After some research, I think this way is the safest and fastest."

"What about—"

"It's true," she cut in. "Duke Sangor's territory is along this route, but he moves his entire household to the outer reaches of his lands from the autumn to winter seasons, which means, at most, we'll only have to worry about a few guards getting in our way. My sisters can handle them while we keep moving."

"Uh-huh."

Beatrix finally looked Laila in the eyes. "I see," she said. "My eldest sister has convinced you that I'm just a young girl with no sense."

"Your sister never said—"

"I am young. That is true. But I'm very logical and I'm not about to put myself at risk, now am I?"

But she was willing to put both her eldest sisters in danger if it meant she could get through Sangor's territories safely.

"Look over the map," she insisted. "I'm sure you'll agree with me. But if not, that's fine too. I just ask you to keep an open mind." She did something that she probably thought was a smile, but actually looked more like a grimace.

As soon as Beatrix went back to her room and the door closed behind her, Gemma came out of her own room and quickly made her way to Laila's side.

"What did my sister want?"

"She gave me this map. She suggests we travel this way."

Gemma snatched the map from Laila's hand and studied it closely.

"Sangor's territory," Gemma muttered. She looked off, eyes narrowing. "He moves his household to his eastern territories in the fall and winter months. That will mean only a few of the guards will be around to protect the main house."

"That's what your sister said."

Shaking her head, Gemma asked, "Why does she know that?"

"I don't know. She's your sister."

"I am well aware that she's my . . ." Gemma frowned, her focus no longer on Laila. "Now what's that about?"

Laila looked over the railing to see her brother and Keeley enter from a back hallway. Keeley seemed to have returned to her chatty, comfortable self. Something Laila thought her brother found annoying. And yet, he didn't appear annoyed. He didn't exactly seem happy either, but not annoyed.

And he always looked annoyed. She couldn't think of a time when her brother *didn't* look annoyed. Just like their father.

"You know, I can't . . . I can't think about this right now." Laila stepped back from the railing. "It's just too much."

"More than too much." Gemma handed the map back to Laila. "I'm going to bed."

"You seem more worried than I'd expect a War Monk to be," Laila said before Gemma could disappear into her room. "Is that because you're worried about the Devourer catching up with us? The Devourer finding his way here? Or are you worried about your sister being queen?"

Gemma had her hand on the door handle but glanced back at Laila. "Do I have to pick just one?"

CHAPTER 8

"You have to do it," Keeley told Caid once more.

"I won't. I refuse."

The stubborn centaur had his arms crossed over that massive chest of his and his head turned away from her, but he was in his human form, so she wasn't worried about getting kicked in the head.

"But . . . you can't refuse," she said, confused.

"I won't do it."

Keeley looked back and forth between the centaur and the horse he refused to ride.

"You do understand," she clarified, "that we don't have time to *walk* to our destination, don't you?"

"Yes. So I'll—"

"What? Go as your true self? Even when we pass towns and cities? Does that really make sense to you? We were lucky we made it through the first time, and we didn't pass any towns on the way here." She held the reins close to his face. "We don't have time to argue about this! Get on the fuckin' horse!"

Growling, Caid snatched the reins from her grasp. "I won't use that saddle. Just a blanket."

"Fine. But with you in a kilt, the inside of your thighs will be less than happy over the next few days."

"Then make it a *soft* blanket!"

Keeley quickly made herself busy removing the saddle from Brim. A good, solid gelding that was easy to handle and wouldn't feel the need to compete with a very stallion-like centaur. She kept her head down so Caid wouldn't see her laughing. She knew he wouldn't like it.

His sister came out from the castle and stopped when she saw her brother holding Brim's reins.

"Oh," she said. "We're riding them."

Still laughing, but also fed up, Keeley turned on the female centaur.

"We have no choice! Are you two kidding me?"

"I was just asking!" Laila snapped. "No need to get hysterical."

"I'm not hysterical. I'm just . . . confused! No one's asking you two to eat one! Just fucking ride the thing!"

She pulled the saddle off. "This is Brim," she told Caid. "And that's Frannie," she told Laila. "Good, solid horses that will give you no problems as long as you both don't act like wankers!"

Laila cleared her throat. "Well . . . thank you."

Samuel rushed out of the stables with three more horses.

"What are you doing?" Keeley asked him.

"My horse and Sir Gemma's horses."

"*Sir* Gemma can take one horse." She looked at the three who were currently making her life difficult. "Do any of you understand what we're doing here? We're *not* going into battle," she snapped at Samuel. "And you're not making a moral statement," she informed the siblings. "So cut the shit!"

"Gods bless all of you!" Gemma happily announced from the courtyard steps, and it took all of Keeley's strength not to fling a sword at her. Just on principle.

Instead, she said, "You're bringing one horse. And why are you wearing those stupid white robes again?"

"You want me to travel as a War Monk? We lose the element of surprise."

Now Keeley was just extremely annoyed. By everyone. So she pushed her father's saddle into Samuel's arms. "Let's try this again, shall we?" She pointed at Samuel. "We're not going into battle." Then the centaurs. "You're not making a moral statement." And now her sister. "And we're not *dawdling* our way to the Amhuinn Valley where people will have time to notice that you're a nun, decide to attack, and then shock! 'Oh, no! She's a War Monk! Run for your lives!' What we *are* doing is riding, with purpose, for long hours a day. We will only stop at night. Then start again before the suns rise. We will do this again and again, until we reach the valley. Does everyone understand? Do I need to make it any clearer?"

When no one said anything, Keeley nodded. "Good. I'll go get Beatrix."

"She's not inside," Gemma told her, but only when Keeley was halfway up the courtyard steps.

"Then where is she? Did we lose her already?"

"I'm right here," Beatrix soothed as she swept in through the gates. She wore a lush green velvet gown with a fur cape over her shoulders. Already she seemed . . . royal. Like she was already imagining the crown on her head.

Keeley frowned. "What were you doing out there?"

"Taking a small morning walk. I do it every morning—you know that."

"No one was hunting you before," Gemma coldly reminded her.

"I didn't go far. I would have been able to run back. I just needed to stretch my legs before I get on my horse."

Keeley reached her sister, brushing her hair off her face. "Sure you weren't trying to escape? I'd totally understand," she teased in a whisper.

"Not at all."

"Then why were you—" Before Keeley could finish, she saw the gray mare go up on her hind legs.

Keeley pushed Beatrix behind her and turned to see Samuel stumble back, her saddle in his arms.

"What happened?" she demanded.

"I was just trying to put your saddle on your horse and—"

Keeley rushed to the gray mare's side. The horse came down hard, but thankfully hadn't hit the boy. Putting her hands on the mare's neck, she stroked her muscles and mane.

"Easy," she soothed. "Easy."

With her hands still on the mare, Keeley said, "No one but me is to put a saddle on this horse. Ever. She's here because she wants to be. She's not my horse."

Gemma came close but the gray mare nipped the air near her face and her sister wisely backed away. "Is this one of the wild horses near the farm?"

"It is. She has some unfinished business." Keeley pressed her forehead against the mare's neck. "I'm the only one who'll handle her. If one morning we wake up and she's gone, I'll find another horse. Is everyone clear?"

There was muttered agreement and Keeley accepted that. She didn't have time to explain the relationship she had with the gray mare.

"Samuel," Keeley called out. "Help Beatrix mount her horse, please. You can leave my saddle where you stand."

Samuel, happy not to be crushed under the mare's hooves, ran over to Beatrix's side and walked with her to her horse.

"You do know he's *my* squire?" Gemma asked. "I don't appreciate you giving him orders."

Keeley started to say something to her sister but decided against it. They hadn't even gotten on the road yet and she didn't want to start arguing this early on their trip. Even she didn't have the patience for that.

"I'll let Mum and Da know we're leaving."

Keeley started toward the castle, briefly glancing back. That's when she saw the look on Gemma's face as she turned away from the horses. A glower that was, to say the least, off-putting.

"What?" Keeley asked her sister.

Gemma shook her head. "Nothing."

But Keeley knew her gods-loving sister was lying.

It was an accident really. That Gemma just happened to look over at Beatrix when Keeley mentioned that she was going to get their parents. She'd actually been looking at Samuel, hoping he wasn't going to fall "madly in love" with Beatrix since the boy seemed to fall madly in love with any woman who showed him the slightest interest. So she saw what no one else saw.

An eye roll. As if the idea of saying good-bye to their parents was a waste of Beatrix's precious time.

It was a small gesture—and one all of her siblings had made before, even herself—but Gemma knew there was something different about this eye roll. Something . . . meaner. If nothing else, Gemma knew she didn't like it. She also knew there was no point in telling Keeley about it. Not yet anyway.

When their parents came out of the castle with the children and Uncle Archie, their father was already crying.

"Father," Gemma soothed, "we're coming back."

"I know. I know." He wrapped her in one of his big hugs, something she'd missed greatly during her years of training and battle. "But I'll still miss me girls until I see you again."

"Don't worry, Daddy." She squeezed him hard. "We'll watch out for each other."

"I know you will." He kissed her on the cheek and whispered, "And don't let Keeley make you so mad all the time."

"I'll try," she whispered back.

Giggling, they stepped away from each other.

Her mother was next, those strong arms of hers nearly crushing Gemma's ribs.

"Don't forget what we talked about," her mother whispered against her ear.

"I won't, Mum."

Emma stepped back. "Love you, sweets."

Gemma joined Keeley in saying good-bye to all the children. Beatrix just waved from the back of her horse, although she did lean down and kiss both her parents on their cheeks.

Once they were all mounted and ready, the centaurs rode off first, clearly uncomfortable with the idea of *riding* horses but doing it anyway. Keeley rode beside Beatrix. And Gemma brought up the rear with Samuel.

But as they neared the drawbridge, Keeley suddenly yelled out, "Hold!"

They all did, and Keeley looked over her shoulder. "*Keran!*" she barked out, annoyed. "Get your ass out here!" That's when Gemma realized they'd forgotten their cousin.

When there was no immediate answer, their mother bellowed, "Keran Smythe! You answer right this second!"

"I'm here," a voice from behind the stables announced. "I'm here."

Keran stumbled out into the courtyard, pulling her horse behind her. They waited while she put the saddle on the large beast and took some supplies from Archibald.

She started to mount her horse but abruptly stopped, went over to the side of the stables, and threw up against the building.

All the children screamed or retched or both, then ran back into the castle. Gemma's father and uncle lowered their heads so they could laugh in peace and her mother just shook her head in disgust, her lip angrily curled.

"I'm all right," Keran announced as she stumbled back to her horse. "I'm all right." She mounted and got comfortable in the saddle. "Let's go," she said, weaving a bit in her seat before she settled in again.

"Really?" Gemma had to ask her sister.

"At least we know she can fight," Keeley said before motioning to the centaurs. "Let's go."

They set off again, and as soon as they crossed the drawbridge, Archibald pulled it up and closed the gates behind them.

They rode hard for four days, stopping only when the suns went down, and moving again before the suns rose the next morning.

They skirted towns and cities as best they could, taking the route that Beatrix had suggested from the beginning. They even went through Duke Sangor's lands without meeting one guard or soldier.

On the fifth day, Caid woke up before anyone else. Samuel was on watch but he'd fallen asleep in the tree he'd been perched in. Caid knew he should yell at the boy, but he seemed to be having enough trouble managing his role as a future War Monk. It wasn't for everyone.

Gemma, however, seemed to have chosen her life perfectly.

Thankfully, they were moving so much during the day and so exhausted when they finally camped for the night that fighting among the three sisters was kept to a minimum. Although Caid did notice how closely Gemma watched her younger sister.

Caid wasn't sure how he felt about that until one morning when he was standing behind a large tree to take his morning piss and saw Beatrix making her way back to camp. She moved silently and picked up her step when she saw that the sky was lightening, announcing that the suns were beginning to rise.

She passed right by the tree he was standing behind and he was tempted to jump out and startle her, but he really just wanted to know what she was up to. Because he could sense she was up to something.

Just as Caid finished his business and came around the tree, the rest of the party began to awaken and Beatrix was standing among them.

"What are you doing up?" Keeley asked as she got to her feet.

Beatrix gave that small smile and replied, "Just taking my morning walk."

"Well, don't go far when you do that." Keeley passed her sister and tugged on a strand of her long hair. "All right?"

"Of course."

Caid watched Keeley head toward a nearby stream and he followed, crouching beside her as she used handfuls of the clear rushing water to wet her hair and face and a rag to scrub her neck.

"I saw your sister coming back to camp before everyone woke."

Keeley took several gulps of the water before asking, "What is going on with you and Gemma?"

"Pardon?"

"Both of you keep watching where Beatrix goes. I'm not sure what you two are worried about."

"Gemma's seen her go off on her own too?"

"Just once. Our second day on the road. But she always takes a morning walk. When we were home, she'd take her walk and then spend the rest of the day reading or going into town to shop at the dressmaker."

"Keeley—"

"She's a creature of habit. Stop worrying."

It might have sounded as though Keeley was arguing with Caid, but he knew she was actually arguing with herself.

"I just want to make sure she's safe," he lied.

Keeley let out a breath, placed her hand on his forearm. "Sorry. I'm being snappy. I don't mean to be."

"It's fine. We're all tired. Good news is we should arrive in the valley by tomorrow."

"Thank the gods. I've never traveled so far or so long before. My back is getting a tad cranky."

Caid stood and held his hand out for Keeley. She looked at it and he explained, "I thought I'd help since your back is bothering you."

"Oh. That's nice."

He rolled his eyes, but she only giggled and slipped her hand into his. He pulled her up and tried to take his hand back, but Keeley didn't seem in the mood to release him.

"Let's hold hands for a little while," she teased.

"Woman, give me my hand."

She laughed harder. "You are so easy to irritate." She tossed his hand away. "Has anyone told you that?"

"*Everyone* has told me that. You're not so special."

"Awwwww," she said, stepping away, "we both know you're lying about that."

The valley came into view and Keeley had to halt the gray mare so she could gaze in wonder.

She really hadn't known what to expect. Ever since she was a child, she'd heard about the Witches of Amhuinn and the valley they lived in. She'd heard they lived in caves so she was expecting . . . caves. What she didn't expect was that the side of the entire mountain at the end of the valley had been carved into some sort of castle. Not like her uncle's, which was mostly tower, but an actual castle. Like something the king himself would have.

"By the gods," she breathed out. "That's . . . astounding."

"It is," Caid agreed. "I never tire of coming here."

"I can understand why."

Beatrix rode her horse up to Caid's side, her gaze moving over the travel party before she asked, "What are we doing?"

Gemma motioned to the witches' home. "Beautiful, isn't it?"

"Oh, it's lovely," she replied. Then she immediately ordered, "All right. Let's go."

She rode down the hill while the others followed. But Keeley waited a bit, watching her sister ride off. It took her a moment to realize that Caid was still beside her.

"Your sister isn't one for taking a moment to enjoy the beauty of things, is she?"

"My sister finds beauty in books."

"I understand that. My brother is the same way."

"Is that why he didn't come with you and Laila?"

"No. He didn't come because he didn't give a flying fuck who the next ruler was because they're all bad. According to him," Caid added.

Keeley laughed. Her first since the day before. The closer they got to the Amhuinn Mountains, the sadder she felt. She missed her family. She missed her shop. She missed the wild horse herd. She missed just being able to take hammer to steel. Even though they'd burned their family home to the ground, it could be rebuilt. But even without the farm, just being with her kin would make her feel better. The gentle bickering of her parents. The screams and laughter of her siblings. She needed to feel that love again. The love of family.

"It's going to be all right, you know," Caid said.

"What is?"

"All of this."

"What if they don't want her?" Keeley finally asked.

"Don't want her?"

"As queen. What if they change their minds?"

Caid raised an eyebrow. "Are you going to *help* them change their minds?"

"What?" Keeley quickly shook her head. "No! No, no. I would never do that."

"But you think she shouldn't be queen?"

Keeley twisted her lips and tightened her grip on her reins. "Forget it."

"Keeley, it's all right. It's good to question. It's good not to take things at face value."

"She's my sister. I love her. I should want her to be queen."

"No one doubts you love your sister."

"But I'm a horrible person, yes?"

"*No.* That is not what I was about to say."

"But I should *want* her to be queen. She's so smart and, yes, she's young, but what she doesn't know she can easily learn. With her intelligence, she could be an amazing ruler. I should be helping her obtain her goals, not hoping the witches choose someone else."

"You do know that most people would want their sister to be queen, but only so others would be forced to call them 'm'lady' or 'm'lord' or so they could have unlimited access to the Old King's gold and jewels."

"I wouldn't mind having some jewels," Keeley admitted. "I've always wanted to make my father a copy of his old battle sword from when he was a soldier. Only I'd include a jeweled hilt." She grinned, nodded at Caid. "The mistake a lot of people make is that they want the entire hilt to be covered in jewels. In battle, that will do nothing but hurt your hand. But if it's done correctly, you can display a jeweled sword on your wall or pull it down and destroy an entire army in case of attack. My da would love that."

Keeley took a moment to think about her dream sword and that's when she noticed that the centaur who never smiled had a grin so wide, she barely recognized him.

They stared at each other until she asked, "That isn't what you meant . . . is it?"

Laughing, he rode off and Keeley followed.

CHAPTER 9

As they rode up to the front gates of the mountain fortress of the Amhuinn Witches, armed and armored guards glowered at them from behind full steel helms; their eyes a bright and extremely unnatural green.

In unison, the ends of steel poleaxes were slammed into the ground and then crossed, blocking their entrance.

Laila clicked her tongue against her teeth and her horse walked her closer to the guards. "We've brought the future queen to see your mistresses," she announced.

The guards didn't answer, but Keeley didn't even know if they *could* answer.

Laila dismounted and handed the reins to a terrified-looking Samuel. She glanced around at the horses and, without warning, the animals all moved back or simply away.

With a toss of her blond and brown hair, Laila shifted into her centaur form. Once the antlers appeared at the top of her head, she pawed the ground with one hoof, leaned forward a bit, and roared in the faces of the guards.

Still the guards didn't answer, but they did move. Quickly. Pulling back their poleaxes and stepping aside.

It had been a few years since Caid had been inside the mountain fortress of the Witches of Amhuinn. But nothing had changed. He knew that as soon as they walked into the main stone hall with their horses, and a young witch quickly approached with a scroll clipped to a piece of flat, polished wood gripped in one hand and a quill in the other.

"Yes?" she asked, gazing at them over the half spectacles she wore.

Laila, not bothering to shift back to her human form, gave a short bow of her head before she said, "I am Laila of the Scarred Earth Clan and Only Daughter of the Clan Chief. As requested by the Witch Queen, I have brought Beatrix of the Farm—"

"Actually," Keeley interrupted, "it's Beatrix Smythe."

"No, it's not," Gemma debated. "It's Farmerson."

"In our family, we take our mother's name."

"Only if you plan to be a blacksmith, and I think we all know that Beatrix has no intention of doing that."

"*You* go by Smythe and you're not a blacksmith."

"I can make a sword and I know the Old Songs."

"Ooooh," Keeley mocked, wiggling her fingers. "You know the Old Songs. I'm so impressed."

Beatrix, still sitting sidesaddle on her horse, snapped her fingers in the direction of her sisters. The sound startled both women into silence but their expressions told Caid much. While Keeley looked moderately impressed, Gemma appeared ready to snatch her younger sister off her horse by her hair and beat her soundly.

"Beatrix of the Farm is just fine," Beatrix announced.

The witch nodded and quickly scanned the scroll she had in her hands. Then she dipped her quill into the pot attached to the piece of wood and checked something off on it.

"Now, please, leave your horses here." She motioned to a young man nearby. "He'll take your horses to the stables inside our fortress and—"

When the man tried to take the reins of the gray mare, the horse reared and backed up.

"Sorry," Keeley apologized. "She stays with me."

"Fine," the witch replied crisply before adding, "Take the others." She looked everyone over. "You may keep your weapons. Caid of the Scarred Earth Clan, feel free to be yourself."

For some unknown reason, that offer had Keeley turning to him with a giant, happy smile on her face and her eyes wide. Kind of like a happily startled farm dog. She looked so ridiculous, he had no option but to chuckle and tell the witch, "I'm fine, thank you."

"Excellent. Right this way," she said, before turning on her heel and moving off.

"You don't want to be yourself?" Keeley whispered to him.

Caid placed his hand against her back and gently pushed her ahead, ignoring her giggles. As he started to follow, his sister grabbed his arm and pulled him back. Leaning down, she asked, "What is going on with you two?"

"What? Nothing."

"Are you sure? Because you're doing that thing again. With your face."

"What thing?"

"Some might call it a smile. I, however, just wonder if you're having some kind of fit."

Caid yanked his arm away from Laila. "Can we just get this bloody thing over with?"

The witch led them out of the main hall and into another large part of the fortress. The library. The three sisters stopped and stared in wonder at all the books. This was only one of the libraries that the fortress boasted. There were at least five more, with three new ones currently being built deeper into the mountain.

"All these books," Keeley breathed out. "I could spend years here."

"It makes you wonder, doesn't it?" Beatrix asked. "What knowledge these witches hold?"

"Think they'll let us spend some time in here before we go?" Keeley asked.

The young witch tossed "No" over her shoulder as she continued on through the library.

Keeley's smile faded. "That was just rude," she muttered to Caid.

"I know, but these books are ancient and powerful. The witches are wise not to let just anyone read them."

"I'm not just anyone. I'm Keeley Smythe, best blacksmith in the Hill Lands."

"I . . . am not sure that will impress them."

"Typical. No one thinks they need a blacksmith . . . until they do. Then we are the most important thing anyone can think of."

He loved how indignant she was. Because Caid had never known anyone who loved their job as much as Keeley. As if she had no doubt whatsoever that she was doing exactly what she should be doing, and what she was doing was good and right. He didn't know many humans who lived that confidently in their own skin.

Caid had to admit . . . the longer he knew Keeley, the more he liked her. But that wasn't unusual. He liked lots of people.

Oh. Wait. No, he didn't.

"A War Monk?" The Witch Queen blinked at Gemma, her eyes appearing larger because of the thick spectacles she wore. "Are we letting in War Monks now?"

"She's the sister of Beatrix of the Farm, my queen."

"Well . . . all right. But no killing anyone so you can raise them later."

"Not all War Monks do that," Gemma reminded the witch.

"Do you?"

Gemma took in a deep breath. "Yes."

"Then my point is made."

She moved away from Gemma and over to Beatrix. Held out her hand. "Beatrix of the Farm. I am the Witch Queen."

Beatrix took the witch's hand but she held it so loosely—as if she was afraid to touch the other woman—that Gemma had to fight her need to show her sister how one clasps hands in an appropriate greeting.

"Lady," Beatrix began, "I am happy to—"

"Yes, yes," the Witch Queen interrupted. "You're glad to be here and can't wait to discuss the future of the country, blah blah blah. Can we just bypass all that? We have work to do and I really don't like to waste time on unnecessary chit-chat."

The queen returned to her throne, carved directly out of the stone wall, and sat down. She snapped her fingers at one of her assistants and the young witch rushed to her side, holding out a scroll for her mistress to read.

"Call Delora," the queen told another. "Tell her we're waiting for her." She began to read the scroll but still spoke to their travel party. "Delora is our . . . *seer,*" she sneered, her hands lifted, fingers wiggling. "We've never had one before, but times change, or so I've been told. And we do like keeping up with modern things."

The assistant returned to the chamber. "She was sleeping," she announced with obvious disgust.

"It must be nice to have all the time in the world," the queen scoffed. "Amazing how busy the rest of us seem to be."

"Sorry, sorry," Delora said, coming in from behind the throne through another chamber. She had one hand pressed against her lower back and used the other to rub her eyes. "Didn't mean to be late."

Still focused on the scrolls that her assistant put in front of her, the queen pointed at Beatrix. "She's here to be confirmed as queen."

"Of course."

Delora took a few more steps but then stopped, attempted to stretch her spine with both hands on her back.

"Is something wrong?" Keeley asked.

"My back has been screaming the last few weeks. Nothing the healers do is helping."

"Would you like me to try?"

Gemma winced at her sister's offer. She knew it was earnestly made, but she saw the witches in the room suddenly focus on her. If their healers hadn't been able to do anything—they were most likely thinking—how could she?

But it was Beatrix who appeared the most disturbed.

"Maybe Gemma should help instead," Beatrix quickly offered. "I'm sure War Monks are better equipped to help with that sort of thing."

"When she gets hit with an arrow or axe," Gemma replied, "let me know."

"Aren't you the blacksmith sister?" the Witch Queen asked.

"Yes!" Keeley said with that oblivious smile of hers. "But I do this sort of thing for horses."

"Well, if you do it for horses . . ." the queen mocked.

Keeley went to Delora and placed her hands on her back. She moved her fingers down the seer's spine, her gaze focused across the chamber.

"Keeley—" Beatrix began.

"Just give me a few more secondsssss..." Keeley stopped at a spot and dug in three of her fingers. Then she went up to the witch's neck, walked her fingers down her spine until she stopped at a spot between shoulder and neck. She pushed her fingers in again, waited a moment, stepped back.

"How do you feel now?" she asked.

"That's it?" Delora asked. "That's all you're do..." She moved her head, then her shoulders, then her ass. She took a few steps. Smiled. "By the gods, I feel fabulous!" She faced Keeley. "Thank you!"

"Welcome." Keeley shrugged at Beatrix. "See? It didn't take long at all."

Keeley went back to Caid's side and Delora continued to walk around in circles and move her shoulders.

Five, four, three, two—

"Can we just finish this?" Beatrix snapped, fed up that her future as a queen should be held up for even a moment because of someone else's discomfort.

"Delora," the Witch Queen barked, "stop shaking your ass and just do this thing already."

"Calm down. All of you. So emotional."

Delora stood in front of Beatrix. "Your hands, dear."

Beatrix placed her hands in Delora's. Gemma was expecting some moaning and swaying as she'd seen other seers do. But Delora's technique was much more... straightforward. And blunt.

She scrutinized Beatrix's face for a very long moment. When she finally pulled away, she casually announced, "Yes, Beatrix. You *will* be queen."

Gemma watched as a small smile formed at the corner of Beatrix's mouth, and that's when Gemma felt a real sense of panic. A real sense that all she'd hoped for was about to—

"Of course," Delora added, "so will *she*." And she pointed at Keeley.

As one, they all looked back at Keeley. Even the witches looked away from their precious scrolls to focus on Gemma's elder sister. When the silence went on and on, Keeley—who'd been staring at the floor, probably sad at the prospect of losing her younger sister to a life of royal privilege—lifted her head and saw everyone gawking at her. When that went on for more than a second or two, she quickly looked behind her, didn't see anyone, looked at them all again, then behind her once more. And this look felt more than just confused but desperate. Like she was praying there was someone—anyone—behind her.

Keeley pointed at herself. "You're not speaking to me."

"Of course I am."

The Witch Queen pushed away the scroll in front of her. "The blacksmith? Are you sure?"

Delora scowled. "Are you questioning me?"

"Always."

"I'm not wrong."

"But I don't want to be queen," Keeley argued. "I want to go back to my shop. I have orders to fill!"

The Witch Queen waved that objection away and added, "Well, that won't be happening anyway."

"Why?"

"I guess you haven't heard. Your shop has been destroyed by the Devourer and all the men who worked there have been killed."

Her hands over her mouth, eyes wide in horror, Keeley gawked at the queen.

"They're all dead?" Gemma asked.

"I believe the younger boys you had working there as apprentices were able to escape. But that's because the men protected them; they died in the process. The Devourer burned down the entire town, but based on the tally I received of deaths, most of the residents were able to escape."

Because of her size, it was often easy to forget how fast Keeley could be. Especially when she was angry. And she was angry now.

That's why, when Keeley was suddenly running toward the Witch Queen, her hammer out, Gemma didn't even think about stopping her sister. It didn't even occur to her. It might have occurred to Keran, but she was half-asleep, leaning against a wall. Oblivious as always.

But just as Keeley got close to the throne, Caid swooped in behind her and wrapped his arms around her, picking her up off the ground. He held her and took her back across the chamber.

"You bitch!" Keeley hissed at the Witch Queen. "You talk of people's deaths and the destruction of their lives as if it's nothing!"

The Witch Queen stood. "I have done no such thing! I was simply being direct. Explaining how you can't go back to your old life, no matter how much you may want to."

Keeley pulled herself out of Caid's arms but she didn't advance on the queen again.

"I don't care if my old life is gone. I will *not* be queen."

"Woman, I have no idea if you're supposed to be queen or not. Delora is our seer. So your decision to be queen may not be your own. It may be the will of the gods."

"Don't give me that will of the gods bullshit!"

Laila quickly stepped in front of the Witch Queen. "My lady, is there somewhere our party can talk? In private."

She gestured to one of her assistants. "Take them to my privy chambers."

One of the witches motioned to Laila and scurried off to the back. Laila motioned to the rest of them. Gemma had to wake up Keran and push her behind everyone else. She was about to follow until she saw that Beatrix was still standing in front of the queen but her focus was on Delora.

"Beatrix?" Gemma called out. "Are you coming?"

"Of course." Lifting the skirt of her gown, she swept past Gemma and followed the others to the Witch Queen's privy chamber.

CHAPTER 10

"I'm going to kill everyone in this place!"

Caid grabbed the hammer that Keeley was swinging around and, for a few brief—but terrifying—seconds, they played tug-of-war with the damn thing until he was finally able to get it away from her.

"*You need to calm down!*"

"What if it's true? What if the town's been burned to the ground? What if it's our fault?"

"Our fault?" Gemma asked. "Don't you mean *her* fault?" She pointed at Beatrix. "She who would be queen?"

"How can you blame her? She knew nothing about any of this."

"How do you know?" Gemma demanded. "You don't know what she's been up to!"

"You sound ridiculous!"

"Our entire town is destroyed and, once again, you're only worried about poor Beatrix!"

"*Our* town? Bitch, you haven't even been here in more than a decade!"

Gemma pushed past a now-human Laila so she could scream right in her sister's face. "*Are you going to keep throwing that at me? It's still my town! I still care!*"

"*You don't care about anyone but yourself!*" Keeley screeched, shoving her sister hard.

Gemma kept her feet, so she was able to come right back and

shove Keeley. Then they took hold and were trying to drag each other to the ground.

Caid caught Keeley around the waist and pulled while Laila attempted to grab Gemma, but that got her a defensive elbow to the face, breaking her nose.

His sister's head snapped back. "Owwwwww!"

Keran stepped in then, pushing her hands between the battling sisters and shoving them apart.

"*That's it!*" she bellowed.

The sisters began to point at each other and screech, but Caid had no idea who was saying what. Keran didn't let all the screeching and hysterics bother her. She just grabbed each woman by her collar and yanked the two close. She began whispering to them, and whatever she said managed to calm them down. Then she jerked her head toward a corner and Caid saw Beatrix standing there. Alone, quiet, and very pale. She had her hands tucked into a fur muff, the hood of her cape over her head.

Noticing what Caid assumed was her sister's devastation, Keeley pulled away from Gemma and Keran and went to Beatrix.

"Come," she coaxed, gently taking Beatrix by the arm and leading her out of the chamber they were in.

Relieved not to have to get between a War Monk and a pissed-off blacksmith, Caid now focused on his own sister.

Her nose was still bleeding and there were growing bruises around her eyes.

When Caid placed his fingers around her nose to feel the damage, his sister whispered, "We need to talk."

Together, they exited the chamber and headed down the passage. They passed the chamber that Keeley and Beatrix were in, the pair against the far wall, speaking softly to each other. They continued on until they found another empty chamber and stepped inside. Thankfully, all these passages and chambers were well lit with torches affixed to the wall, so while they spoke, Caid could put his sister's nose back where it belonged.

"What is happening?" Laila asked.

"I wish I knew."

"Do you think that witch is toying with them? Ow!"

"Sorry. Sorry. She's done some damage to your nose."

"Do what you must."

"And I doubt the witches are toying with anyone. They're not exactly known for having a playful way with people."

"But both sisters can't be queen."

"I know that. And so does Keeley. Honestly, though, she doesn't even want to be queen."

His sister pulled her head back so she could look him in the eyes. "Come now, Caid. Who wouldn't want to be queen?"

And Caid answered honestly, "Keeley Smythe. Or have you not been paying attention this entire trip?"

"I don't care what any of these bitches say, Sister. I have no intention of being queen."

"I know that," Beatrix replied softly. "I really do."

"But why would they say that? Are they hoping to turn us against each other?" Keeley shook her head. "That's foolish. That would never happen. We're family."

"Of course."

Keeley began pacing around the chamber. "So what now? How do we confirm you as queen and move on from here?"

"What do you mean?"

"I mean, how do we make you queen so you can destroy the Devourer for what he's done and then build our town back? All the people we've ever known have lost their homes. Their businesses. Their entire lives were there. And he's destroyed it all. Because of us. As queen, *you* can fix that."

Beatrix flashed a small but sweet smile. "Gods, Sister. You really do care, don't you?"

"Of course." Keeley stopped pacing and stood in front of Beatrix. "Just tell me what you want me to do. Tell me what you *need* from me. So we can fix this and help those who are innocent. It's the right thing to do. You see that, yes?"

"I see it."

"Good. Now"—Keeley clapped her hands together—"I say we go back to the throne room and talk to the witches and . . . and . . . and . . ."

Keeley stopped talking. Her mind felt wiped clean and for a moment, she forgot what they'd been discussing. She forgot where she was. She forgot who she was. She forgot everything.

But she forgot only for a moment. Then it came rushing back and she finally looked away from her sister's face and down at her hand, which was wrapped around the bloody knife handle sticking out of Keeley's lower gut.

"I know you won't understand," Beatrix calmly explained. "It wasn't supposed to be you. Not once Gemma showed up. I was so glad when she came home. The timing was perfect. Then that idiot Delora . . . she just ruined it all and I had no choice. But for me to get what I want, it had to be done."

Keeley clung to the hope that this was just an accident, that her sister had stabbed her accidentally. Perhaps she'd just meant to threaten her with that blade and she'd stumbled or panicked.

But, as if to prove her wrong, as if to make sure Keeley understood exactly what was happening, Beatrix didn't release the weapon. No. Instead, she pulled it across Keeley's belly, attempting to disembowel her. If she was as strong as Mum or Gemma, Keeley's guts would be pouring out onto the floor.

Keeley, however, was able to wrap her hands around the wound, keeping everything inside her body as she slid against the wall and down to the floor.

Beatrix tucked her blood-covered hand back into her fur muff and gave Keeley another one of those small, sweet smiles.

"I am sorry," she said again, but Keeley didn't really think she was. Because there was no sorrow in her face. No pain in her eyes. Actually . . . there was nothing in those eyes. And Keeley finally understood, there had never been *anything* in those eyes. All these years she'd been searching for a sign of . . . something. When she didn't find it, she simply assumed she wasn't looking the right way. But now she knew. There was nothing there. Nothing.

Sitting on the floor, Keeley watched her younger sister, whom she'd always protected, always cared for, calmly exit the chamber. She headed back toward the throne room, leaving Keeley and the rest of her early life behind.

CHAPTER 11

Caid had just pushed his sister's broken nose back into place when he sensed something was wrong. It was the prey animal that lived deep in his soul; always restless, always anxious. Always knowing when danger was close by.

He released his sister and walked into the passageway. He saw Beatrix's fur cape disappear around a corner, which meant she was not heading back to the throne room. He began to follow her. Protecting her was still his job until they got her onto her throne, but something . . .

"What's wrong?" Laila asked as she rushed to his side, her eyes tearing from the pain he'd caused fixing her nose.

He didn't answer his sister. His sense of dread was so overwhelming, he couldn't. Instead, he simply turned toward the chamber he'd seen Keeley and Beatrix in.

"What's wrong?" his sister asked again.

Caid ignored her, walking past her to the chamber entrance. Keeley was on the floor, her back against the wall, her legs bent at the knees, her hands covering her stomach, and a pool of blood leaking out around her.

She looked up at him with those dark eyes. She didn't say anything. She didn't have to.

"Laila!" he cried out, now running to Keeley's side and landing on his knees next to her hip.

"By the gods," his sister gasped behind him. She crouched on Keeley's other side, moved the blacksmith's knees, and they both froze at the sight of the knife handle sticking out of her stomach and the blood that poured over her hands. "I'll get help," Laila said before she ran off yelling for assistance of the witches.

Caid was afraid to touch Keeley. Afraid to take out the knife. Afraid it would kill her instantly. For once, he didn't know what to do.

A few seconds after his sister had run out, her voice still demanding help, Gemma ran into the chamber with Keran right behind her.

"Holy fuck," Keran barked out. "What the fuck happened?"

Caid shook his head. "I don't know."

"Where's Beatrix? Caid!" He looked at Gemma. "Where is Beatrix?"

"I don't know," he said again. "I saw her leave, I think."

"Was she being dragged? Was someone with her?"

He shook his head. "I don't think so."

Gemma gazed into his eyes but before she could ask anything else, the witches rushed into the chamber and pushed Caid and the others away so they had access to Keeley.

As Caid went to get up, Keeley's blood-covered hand grasped his and he saw the panic in her eyes; watched tears slide down her face and into her hair.

"Centaur, move!" a witch ordered him. "Move!"

Their hands were pulled apart and Caid was pushed across the room by firm, confident hands.

"Please, my lord centaur, let us care for her."

Laila took him by the arm, dragged him into the passageway. Gemma came out a few moments later, rushing past the witches hurrying in.

"Samuel!" she called out, motioning to her squire.

"What's happened?" the boy asked, confused by all the witches moving in a panic. He seemed to be spinning in circles as he came down the passageway, trying to see why all the witches were running around him. "Keeley's horse was going mad in the throne room and then she just took off! Now everyone is running. But no one will tell me anything."

When he was close enough to hear her without screaming, Gemma ordered, "Find Beatrix."

"What? She's with you, isn't she?" His eyes widened. "Gods, was she kidnapped?"

"I don't know. Just find her." Samuel started to go, but Gemma pulled him back. "If she's alone when you find her . . . follow her. Don't let her see you, though. Stay in the shadows."

"I don't understand. Why would she be alone? Why would you want me to—" He glanced into the chamber. It took him a moment, but when he realized that it was Keeley on the floor, bleeding, he started to run toward her. But Gemma quickly pulled him back.

"Go! Find Beatrix. She went—" Gemma looked at Caid over her shoulder.

He pointed toward the passage where he'd seen her cape disappear.

"And bring her back, yes?" Samuel asked.

"No. Just find out where she's going if she's alone."

"*If* she's alone—"

"Go, Samuel! Please."

The boy ran and Keran called to Gemma. "We're moving her!"

Caid pulled away from his sister and stalked back into the chamber.

"I'll take her," he said, crouching down beside Keeley.

"Someone should hold her legs," a witch said. "We're taking her to the healing chamber."

Laila held Keeley's legs and nodded at Caid.

Together, brother and sister lifted the blacksmith and followed the witches deeper into the mountainside.

After about ten minutes, the passageway Beatrix had taken split into two opposite directions and Samuel had no idea which way to go. He did not want to return to Gemma and tell her he'd lost her sister. Especially if she'd been taken by the Devourer or one of his minions.

As he stood in the middle of the two passageways, looking back and forth, he saw Keeley's horse coming out of the left tunnel, running up to him.

Samuel reared back. The horse had already tried to pound him into the ground with her front hooves more than once since they'd started this trip. And he had no desire to be found by Gemma as nothing more than a pulpy residue left on the cave floor.

But the horse didn't attack. She stopped, and when Samuel moved forward a bit, she backed up. By the third time, he understood she wanted him to follow, so he did. Running after her as she galloped down passageways and tunnels and through empty but—thankfully—lit chambers. They traveled down and down until they arrived at an opening that had no lighting and led into the far side of the valley.

Samuel stepped in front of the mare but stayed close to the wall and the darkness in case there was someone ready to take Beatrix and put her into chains.

But that's not what he saw. He saw a very calm Beatrix simply . . . waiting. She was not in chains and she was not sobbing in despair. She was just . . . standing there.

Then, at one point, she pulled one of her hands out of her fur muff and scratched her face. Samuel gasped in shock. The blood on her hand. Her hand was soaked in blood and she didn't seem bothered by it at all.

Confused, disturbed, and attempting to rationalize what he was seeing, he started to turn away but Keeley's horse bumped him with her muzzle. Samuel looked back and saw a carriage with four horses coming through some trees. The carriage stopped in front of Beatrix and the driver dismounted. He opened the carriage door and dropped a small set of stairs. Holding her hand, the driver assisted her into the carriage. The stairs were returned, the door closed, and the driver went back to his seat. With a lash, he sent the horses turning around so they could head back the way they'd come. When the carriage was facing away from him, Samuel saw the crest on the back of the vehicle.

"What the *fuck*," he muttered to the gray mare behind him, "did I just see?"

CHAPTER 12

Once Keeley was in a proper bed in the witches' healing chamber, Gemma was sure that her sister was dead. So much blood had been lost and she didn't seem to respond to anything. But the witches kept working, making Gemma and Keran leave Keeley and wait in the passageway outside.

Eventually, a panting, sweating Samuel returned, with Keeley's gray mare behind him, refusing to be led away when several of the witches tried.

When the witches were reassured by the centaurs that the horse would not be allowed into the healing chamber itself, Gemma led her squire down the passageway.

"All right, tell me. Did you find Beatrix?"

"Yes. She was alone."

"Are you sure?" Keran pushed and that's when Gemma realized her cousin had followed.

"She was definitely alone."

"Where is she now?" Gemma asked.

"She left the fortress through a tunnel."

"A cave tunnel?"

"Yes. She seemed to know exactly where she was going. It led her straight into the valley where a carriage met her soon after she arrived."

Gemma and Keran exchanged glances.

"A carriage? Are you sure?"

Few people in the Hill Lands had carriages. Except, of course, for the—

"It was a royal carriage," Samuel replied. "And the crest on the back was the crest of Prince Marius."

"Prince Marius . . . ?" That didn't make sense to Gemma. Why would her extremely smart sister ever get in a carriage with one of the Old King's sons? They would just kill her, wouldn't they? As the Devourer had already tried to do.

"That makes no sense," Keran said, shaking her head.

Samuel had been Gemma's squire for nearly two years and she'd learned to read his silences because he was often scared to death to tell her things.

"What else?" she finally asked him. "What aren't you telling me?"

He let out a shaky breath and focused on the ground.

"Samuel, spit it out!" she snapped.

"She had blood on her hands."

Gemma blinked. "She was wounded?"

"No. I . . . I don't think so. And she was very calm. And patient."

"Patient? You mean she was waiting for that carriage?"

"I think so."

"Wait," Keran cut in, "what are two saying?"

Gemma knew what she was saying but she didn't have time to inform Keran because the healing witches began barking orders at one another, some ran out of the chamber, and others ran in.

Pushing past Samuel, Gemma tried to enter the chamber to see what was wrong. What might be happening with her sister. But several witches pushed her out.

"We do not need your kind of help, War Monk," one of them said. "You can wait outside."

Not willing to risk her sister's chances of survival, Gemma respected the witches' demand and returned to the passageway. And that's where all of them waited.

The carriage pulled to a stop where Marius waited with several of his men. He glanced up at the suns again to gauge the time and wished his mother would hurry up. Most people he wouldn't waste his precious time waiting for, but when it came to his mother . . .

She had proven herself to him in ways others had not. And not merely by being his mother. Marius didn't believe in automatically giving respect to someone just because she had expelled him from her body as a million other women had done through time.

No, his respect came from the brilliant guidance his mother had given him over the years. With that, she had earned his loyalty. But still . . . he had more important things to do right now than meet some woman his mother would like to see him marry.

The driver opened the carriage door and lowered the steps. Maila stepped down and immediately moved to him, kissing him on both cheeks.

"Come along, my dear," she said. "Don't keep my son waiting."

The small woman, bundled up in a fur cape, stepped down from the carriage. She pulled the hood of her cape back to reveal her face, and the men beside him gave polite coughs or began to shuffle their feet. All of them looked down or away.

She wasn't hideous, but she wasn't worthy of a king either.

Speaking from the side of his mouth, Marius said to his mother, "She's a little plain, isn't she?"

His mother sighed. "Marius—"

"It's all right," the woman said. "I don't get insulted."

With a straight back and a confident walk, she came to stand in front of Marius.

"So you're . . ."

"Beatrix."

Marius stared at the muff she had her hands stuffed in. "Is that blood on your fur?"

She glanced down, cursed. "I've been trying to get that out."

"Were you injured?"

Maila took Marius's arm. "Let's go inside and—"

"I don't mind answering," Beatrix said. "I killed my sister. This is her blood."

With a smile, she entered his tent.

Marius locked his gaze on his mother.

"Really?" he asked.

"I promise there's a reason. A good one!"

"Uh-huh."

* * *

Beatrix studied her fur muff. Studied the blood on it. Her sister's blood. It was strange . . . she felt nothing. She'd thought she'd feel exhilaration. She'd taken her first human life, and she'd always read that such a thing was exciting. But no. It wasn't nearly as exciting as she'd dreamed.

Then again, her sister had not cried out. She had not fought back. She had done nothing.

Not like those cats. The barn cats they used to have. Her father and Keeley had blamed the demon wolves from the woods for the cats' deaths, but it had been Beatrix. Because she wanted to see what it was like to take a life. She'd been three at the time and the little cats had put up such a fight. Even the kittens.

Gemma had seen the scratches on Beatrix's arms. Tried to blame her for the cats' deaths, but Keeley wouldn't hear it. She always protected her. It was a shame she'd had to kill her.

Especially because that hadn't been the plan. It was Gemma she should have left bleeding out on the floor. The one greeting their ancestors. But gods-damn Keeley wanting to help everyone with their back problems had created this dilemma as much as anything else.

And now having the War Monk still living after seeing what she could do in battle was . . . troubling. But it was too late for regrets.

Now she was in the thick of it. And Beatrix had to admit . . . this *was* exhilarating.

Prince Marius walked into his tent along with his men and his mother.

"Explain to me, woman, why I shouldn't kill you right now."

"I don't know why you're upset, my king. I thought it was common among royals to kill their siblings. Besides, wouldn't killing me now just be kind of boring when I could be your queen instead?" Beatrix asked, examining the maps stretched out over the wood table in the middle of the tent.

"I don't want to be rude, Lady Beatrix, but you are *not* pretty enough to be my queen. Or anyone else's."

"Marius!" Maila gasped.

"It's all right. I'm not pretty at all," Beatrix admitted. "I know that. And words about it don't hurt me. Besides, I've compensated for my lack of beauty with something more important."

"Intelligence?" he asked, mocking.

"Ruthlessness." Beatrix pointed at one of Marius's generals. "Did you know that he's been communicating with your brother? The Devourer?"

"Lying whore!" the general yelled.

Beatrix put her finger to her lips and whispered, "Shhh." Her gaze moved back to the prince. "But he is not your worry. He just wants to keep his options open should you fail. I, personally, admire that kind of planning."

Marius sighed. "Mother, I don't think this is going to work out. . . ."

Maila shook her head because she had no idea what was going on. She thought she did, all smug and ready in the carriage, but the Old King's whore was nothing more than a means to an end. Just like killing Keeley had been.

"Your real concern," Beatrix went on, "are those two." She pointed at two of his other generals.

"She is mad," one of them said, laughing.

Beatrix pulled out the parchment she had tucked into her dress and began to read, "My dearest Lord Cyrus, as we wait for your word on our next move, I can tell you with assurance that your brother's army grows weaker by the day. There are many among them we can turn to our side without much effort—"

"Who wrote that?" Marius demanded.

Beatrix held the parchment up for the prince to see. "Do you not recognize the seal, my lord?"

"That's a lie!" the young general yelled out. "You did this, witch!"

"I am no witch. I am no royal. I'm just a farmer's daughter with nothing to do but find out information. And keep it . . . until I need it." She shook the letter. "This is a year old. And it's not the only one I have . . . from each of them."

Marius pulled his sword. "You cunts!"

"No, my prince! She lies . . . you cannot . . . you cannot . . ." The young general looked at each of them. "What are you all staring at?"

The prince pointed with his weapon. "You bleed."

The young general touched the blood that poured down his

chin, not realizing that the blood also came from his eyes, his nose, his ears.

"What have you done?" the older general, also bleeding from every orifice, asked Beatrix.

"I've killed you. Had your chainmail poisoned . . . so I never had to raise a finger."

The older general took a step. "You vile cu—"

He dropped. Before he could finish and his partner fell on top of him. Both dead. Their blood still pouring out of them.

The prince faced her again, his sword still out, aimed at her.

Beatrix smiled. "My lord . . . can we speak alone?"

The chorus of "no" was loud and came even from his mother, but Marius waved them off.

"I'll be fine."

"My son—"

"You brought her, Mother. Now let me talk to her."

The Dowager Queen and remaining generals left the tent.

Beatrix dropped into a chair and gestured to another on the other side of the table. The prince put his sword back in its sheath and sat.

"I know I'm not what you were hoping for."

"You're right there. A beautiful woman of royal blood with a dowry and her father's soldiers would be what I'd expect."

"No worries about the soldiers . . . your dukes and lords will give you all the soldiers you request. And we both know you'd get tired of any woman who graced your bed more than once."

"True. But what can you provide that others cannot?"

"The world."

One eyebrow went up. "The world?"

"While other little girls played with dolls and learned to tend house, I've been planning to get everything there is to be taken. While you and your brothers bicker over your father's puny territories, you could be advancing into the mountains."

"For what?"

"Slaves. Warriors. Dwarves. Elves." She gave a little smile. "Centaurs. Do you have any idea how much those creatures would sell for?"

"Centaurs? And what would all this gold made from enslaved centaurs be for?"

"To take your kingdom where even your father never dreamed."

"Where's that?"

"The Dark Lands."

He briefly went pale, his gaze locked on her. "Woman, are you mad?"

"Don't tell me you're frightened."

"They have dragons there."

"Probably not that many. And I've done lots of research. Those things can be killed."

"And then there's that human queen. The crazy one?"

"The more insane, the easier to destroy. Her people are probably *dying* for her to be burned in a cleansing fire." She leaned in, resting her elbows on the table. "The Dark Lands are there for the taking."

"And you're the one who's going to help me with that?"

"The gods talk to me. Tell me what's possible."

"So you're a seer then?"

Beatrix waved his words away. "Hardly. I can't see the future. Or the past. I have just been blessed to see the possibilities. Of what could be."

Prince Marius glanced off, silent. Then he shook his head.

She pressed her hands flat against the wood table. "The Witches of Amhuinn were playing games. They confirmed I would be queen. Then they said my sister would be too." Beatrix let out what she knew to be a sad-sounding sigh. "My sister believed them. She took me to one of the chambers. To talk, she said. But she attacked me. I grabbed a blade . . . next thing I knew . . . she was dead on the floor."

"You really didn't think your sister would want to be queen?"

"Every woman wants to be queen, my lord. But we're family . . . family is all." She brushed at nonexistent tears. "Honestly, though, I think it was the witches who killed her. They toyed with her until she was crazed. I truly think for their own cruel amusement." She tapped the table with her index finger. "How many others are they going to tell this tale? First my sister . . . then who? One of your dukes with a large army? A king in a nearby land?" Beatrix raised her gaze to Marius. "Or maybe that mad bitch in the Dark Lands."

He stood, walked to his tent opening but he didn't leave, simply clasped his hands behind his back.

"And what do *you* suggest we do, Lady Beatrix," he asked, "for such an affront . . . to a future queen?"

"The only thing we can do, my king." She dropped back into her chair. "Destroy the obstinate little cunts before they have a chance to do any more damage."

Spying some biscuits across the table, Beatrix reached for the plate and added, "It would also be nice if we can take as many of their books as possible."

Marius slowly turned his head to look at Beatrix over his shoulder.

"I'm an avid reader," she admitted before taking a bite of a delicious biscuit.

CHAPTER 13

For hours the witches tended Keeley; younger witches following orders, often running in and out of the chamber while the older, more powerful witches cut into Keeley, sewed organs, and closed her, only to open her up again. All while chanting ancient healing spells and calling on their gods.

Gemma silently called out to Morthwyl. Well, at first, she chanted softly but when Keran asked, "Are you going to bring Keeley back to life so her corpse can kill Beatrix?" she stopped and did it silently. But war gods were moody, at best, and didn't always come when called. They often demanded a sacrifice or, even better, a battle to get their attention and rewards.

Hours turned to days. Two days specifically. And Gemma was moments from giving up all hope.

She looked across the passageway and watched the two centaurs. They were still in their human forms and sat close to each other on the floor. When Caid sadly laid his head on his sister's shoulder and she stroked his hair, Gemma began to wonder how attached the centaur had become to her sister. But Keeley had that way, didn't she? With people. With animals. And, like their father, with centaurs.

Finally an elderly witch walked out of the chamber. She wiped her bloody hands with a white linen cloth and stopped in front of Gemma and Keran.

"Your sister lives," she announced with no preamble. "The gods must have heard our prayers."

"More like she's too pissed at whoever did this to her to die," Keran said.

"Whatever it is, so far it's working."

"So far?" Gemma asked.

"Your sister was nearly disemboweled. She's lucky to be breathing at all."

"So what do we do now?" Keran asked.

"We wait for my sister." Gemma got to her feet. "The next move will be hers."

"As you like." The witch glanced around. "Now I'm going to check on your sister one more time and get some sleep. You lot should too. If she wakes up"—and Gemma felt that "if" like a knife to *her* gut—"it won't be for quite a while."

After the elderly witch returned to the healing chamber, Gemma motioned to the rest of them to follow her. They went to another chamber and she faced the centaurs.

"I understand if you have to leave. As I told you, based on what Samuel witnessed, Beatrix is off . . . somewhere. Doing something. I honestly don't know what. Not yet."

"Do you really think she's with Marius?"

Gemma shrugged at Caid's question. "I know Samuel wouldn't tell me something that wasn't true. I can't say the same for Beatrix."

Laila's nose crinkled a bit before she said, "You don't really think that your younger sister actually had anything to do with Keeley's . . ." She shook her head. "She couldn't have. Wee thing like that."

"I wish I had an answer for you. I wish I could tell you 'no' and have no doubts when I said it. But I truly can't."

Gemma had been so distrustful of Laila when she'd first seen the Amichais at Keeley's shop. But now, looking in those earnest, big, brown eyes, she realized that over time, she'd come to trust Laila and Caid in a way that she never had with Beatrix, her own blood. She'd never trusted her sister, and that had been one of the biggest issues between Gemma and Keeley when they were younger. Because as far as Keeley was concerned, family was family.

"We're not leaving," Caid suddenly announced. "I will not leave your sister until—"

Screams from the healing chamber cut the rest of Caid's words off.

Gemma and Caid were the first in the passageway when the elderly witch came at them and shoved Gemma with way more strength than Gemma would have thought possible.

"What have you done, War Monk?" the witch demanded, her voice filled with rage.

"*Me?* I haven't done anything!"

"Liar!"

"What are you talking about?"

The witch gripped Gemma's arm with bone-breaking strength and yanked her back until they reached the healing chamber. The witch pulled her right up to the entrance and demanded, "*This! What have you done?*"

There were eight of them. Seven surrounded Keeley's bed but one . . . one stood directly on her bed, at Keeley's feet, and snarled at them, warning away anyone who might be a danger to Gemma's sister.

"I did not call them. We worship the gods, not demons."

"Then where did they come from?"

Keran stepped in beside Gemma, took a look, and casually announced, "Oh! Those are Keeley's friends."

Gemma cringed, then glared at her idiot cousin.

"What?" Keran asked. "Are we lying about that? Because Keeley would never lie about that. And look . . . they're here to protect her. That's nice, isn't it?"

"Are all your sisters evil?" the witch asked Gemma.

"Keeley is not evil! She just happens to love animals." Gemma looked at the beasts snarling in warning from across the chamber. "Even animals with eyes of pure fire, drool of blood, that have clearly been birthed from one of earth's many hell pits. . . ."

To say the Witches of Amhuinn were not happy about having demon wolves in their sacred space would be a gross understatement. But Caid was more than happy to see the creatures. Because once Keeley's bitch sister found out that she hadn't killed her—and unlike everyone else, he was *sure* it was Beatrix who had done this to Keeley—she'd send someone to finish the job. He planned to stand guard over her for as long as necessary, but he wouldn't resent the extra assistance.

"Our queen will know about this," the healer witch warned before storming away, but the centaurs had a healthy amount of influence with the witches and he was not above using it if he must.

"I'll take first watch," Caid said, stepping into the chamber. Gemma grabbed his arm and yanked him back seconds before one of the wolves could bite his entire face off.

"Are you mad? They'll kill you!"

"I'm not leaving her alone."

"No one says you have to leave her. Just stay out here."

But he didn't want to do that. He wanted to be near her so that she knew she wasn't alone.

The gray mare walked into the healing chamber, stepping between Caid and the wolves. The beasts snarled at her, bared their fangs, but she went up on her hind legs and came back down hard. She tossed her head, pawed the ground.

The wolf on Keeley's bed motioned to the wolves on each side. The animals moved back and the gray mare looked at Caid.

Caid walked into the chamber, and the wolves made no move to attack. He grabbed a wooden chair from against the wall and pulled it close to the bed near Keeley's head. That's where he sat, resting his elbows on his knees and gazing down into her pale face.

The wolves encircled the bed again, with Caid now on the inside. He had no intention of leaving. He could sleep here. Wait for her to awake.

Because he had to believe she would awake.

CHAPTER 14

Gemma snapped awake when she felt something drip on her cheek . . . and that's when she came face-to-face with the lead demon wolf. He stood over her, his bloody drool drizzling from his massive jaws.

She thought he was there to kill her. To take off her face since he'd just missed Caid's. But then he began to pace and whine. After several seconds of that, he trotted out.

Gemma scrambled to her feet and ran into the passageway and back to Keeley's healing chamber. Her sister was still alive, but unconscious. The centaur was sitting in the wood chair but his arms were resting on the bed, his head lying very close to Keeley's. He was asleep but so close to her sister, Gemma was sure if Keeley hiccupped, he'd be awake and reacting. The wolf had settled back on Keeley's bed, by her feet, but he gazed at Gemma.

He was trying to tell her something but she didn't know what. She didn't speak demon. At least not yet.

Still, Gemma couldn't just walk away. She crouched at the end of the bed and looked deep into the balls of flame that were the wolf's eyes, trying to see something. Anything that would tell her what she needed to know.

But as she crouched there, moving her head a bit to one side and a bit to the other, attempting to decipher whatever the flames were telling her, a voice beside her asked, "What are you doing?"

She didn't look away from the wolf, afraid she'd miss something, but told Keran, "He's trying to tell me something."

"The *dog* is trying to tell you something?"

"Wolf. The *wolf* is trying to tell me something."

"Okay." Keran grabbed her arm and yanked her to her feet. "Come with me."

Together they exited the healing chamber and Keran led her to an empty tunnel.

Once ensconced deep inside, Keran said, "I know you're upset about your sister. *I'm* upset about your sister. But it's not like you to sit around, staring at dangerous demon beasts, waiting for them to tell you things. That seems like something your uncle Archie would do. You don't want to be like your uncle Archie, now do you?"

"It's not like me?" Gemma asked, her exhausted mind desperately trying to grab something in Keran's words. She just wasn't sure what.

"It *wasn't* like you. There was that period you were away." Keran frowned. "Has being a monk made you mad? *Are* you like your uncle Archie?"

"No. Because you're right. That's not like me. Because you know me. You *know* me."

Keran no longer frowned; now she just appeared panicked. "What is happening, Cousin?"

"You know me, but do you feel you know Beatrix? Do any of us know Beatrix?"

"What are you going on about?"

"Do you think Beatrix would hurt Keeley? Do you think she *did* hurt Keeley?"

"I don't know." Keran stretched her neck as if all the tension in the world had lodged in the muscles there. "I mean, it doesn't seem like her."

"What does she seem like to you?"

"That was filled with sarcasm," Keran shot back.

"I wasn't being sarcastic. I'm asking. What does she seem like to *you?*"

"Oh. Well. Uh . . . she seems . . . um . . ." Keran glanced off. "She . . . uh . . . loves to . . . uh . . . read. And she, uh, seems to be a thinker. I don't think she likes . . ." Keran now looked at the ceiling. "I actually don't know what she doesn't like. Or what she does like.

Except books. She really likes books. Then again, Keeley likes books. When she wasn't working with iron or rescuing demon dogs—"

"Wolves."

"Whatever. She was reading."

"But what are Beatrix's feelings on politics? Society? The gods?"

"Uhhhh . . ."

"How does she feel about slavery? Torture? The royals?"

Keran could only shrug.

"But," Gemma went on, "if I asked you about Keeley . . ."

Keran suddenly laughed and began rattling off, "She hates slavery and slavers and strongly believes they should be wiped out. She feels torturers should be tortured. And that the royals are as useless as your gods."

"Doesn't that bother you?"

"I don't have religious preferences."

"Not that—" Gemma bit off her insult. "Doesn't it bother you that you know so much about Keeley and almost nothing about Beatrix?"

"I spend tons of time with Keeley. Beatrix is always reading or getting dresses made in town. So it's not surprising I don't know much about her."

"So what are you saying?"

"I'm saying you can't use my lack of knowledge to prove Beatrix killed her own sister." Keran grimaced. "I mean . . . *tried* to kill her."

"Fine. What do you know about me?"

"I don't know shit about you. No offense," she added.

"What about the baby?"

"Oh, gods! You have a baby?"

"No! Mum's baby!"

"Oh. That baby. And that's easy. Nothing. Your mum won't let me take care of her."

"Why not?"

She shrugged. "The first time I had her in my arms, I dropped her."

"Keran!"

"She was fine! They bounce at that age."

"No, they don't!"

"It doesn't matter. What I do know is that I know *nothing* about the baby." Keran suddenly raised her forefinger and added, "But when I roll my eyes back in my head, she does laugh."

"Why do you keep making my point for me?"

"All right, fine!" Keran snapped. "I'll admit that I have no idea what makes Beatrix laugh. Or cry. Or rage. To be honest, I don't think she's ever been *any* of those things. That still doesn't mean—"

"That she tried to kill her own sister?"

"You can think what you want, Gemma. But without proof . . ."

"I need to find out the truth."

"How? Beatrix is gone. We don't know when Keeley will wake up."

Neither said "if" but Gemma knew it was implied.

"Maybe you should talk to the witches," Keran suggested.

"Yes, I'm sure they'll be gagging to tell me everything they know."

"Were you being sarcastic that time?"

"Definitely." Gemma scratched her jaw. "The Witches of Amhuinn haven't exactly been friendly. I doubt they'll spill their guts to me. And why should I ask them anything anyway?"

"Because it all started with them. Besides, you're a monk."

"So?"

"Aren't you trained in interrogating witches?" Keran shrugged. "Just do that."

The Witch Queen—Belinda to those who'd died many decades before—went over her tally of numbers again to make sure she'd gotten the math right. Nothing annoyed her more than when she was off by a point or two. It was sloppy and Belinda did not like sloppy.

Satisfied her numbers were correct, she started to sign off on the paperwork when the War Monk suddenly appeared before her, slapped her hands on the arms of Belinda's throne, and threatened, "Tell me what you know, witch, or *I shall burn you at the stake!*"

Belinda didn't have time to ask "What the unholy fuck did you just say to me?" before the monk's cousin was there, grabbing the woman's arm and dragging her kin off a few feet.

"What are you doing?" the cousin demanded.

"What you told me to. You said interrogate her as I'd been trained. That's how monks interrogate witches."

"Or you could *ask* her your questions like a normal person. That's always an option."

"I guess . . . although this seems faster."

"Does it really?"

The monk rolled her eyes. "Fine. I'll ask her nicely."

"Again with the sarcasm."

The monk stood once more before Belinda's throne.

"I have a question," she said with a forced smile.

"Yes?"

"How did you decide that my sister would be queen?"

"That's actually a bit difficult to answer."

The cousin suddenly appeared behind the monk. She was a good bit taller and towered over her the way the monk's sister did. "Why is that difficult to answer?"

"Because in the past, when we were involved in choosing kings and queens, we did *not* do it the way your sister was chosen."

"Chosen?" the monk repeated. "You mean by the gods?"

"No. That's not how I mean. We are the Witches of Amhuinn. Our gods expect us to do the work."

"The work? You mean, like, sacrifices?"

"Of course not. Barbarians make sacrifices. Our gods are math, science, and logic."

"Are those just words you're using?" the cousin asked. "Or actual gods?"

"Both." Belinda leaned back on her throne. "Our order has been requested to choose a ruler about a dozen times over the past three thousand years or so."

"Who requested it this time?"

"No one."

The War Monk frowned. "What do you mean 'no one'?"

"It means what you think it means. But we didn't need anyone to request anything. It was obvious that the Old King would die, his many sons would slaughter one another until only the strongest remained, which was exactly what happened. The oldest three each have an army and definite plans of being the new Old King. Now the twins also remain, but they're weak and will probably be eliminated before the true Brothers' War comes to pass. Finally, when it's all said and done, one son will be left standing. That one will be the *new* Old King. In other words, we were not needed to predict this eventual outcome."

"If no one requested that you choose the new queen, then why did you choose my sister?"

"That was Delora. She said the gods had given her a name. The name of your sister."

"I thought you said your gods expected you to do the work."

The Witch Queen nodded. "They do. But she *swears* she's a seer."

"If you had no faith in her, then why did you give my sister's name to the royal counsel?"

"*I* didn't. Because I didn't care what Delora saw, didn't see, or thought she saw."

"So Delora informed the counsel?"

"No. She informed the Dowager Queen before the Old King even died."

"I thought the Old King had no wife. Only consorts."

"That's true. But there is one of his consorts who is brave enough to claim the Dowager Queen title, and that is Maila of the North."

"Maila?" the cousin asked, moving around the War Monk.

"Yes. Maila. The mother of Prince Marius."

Laila entered the healing chamber and started toward the bed. One of the demon wolves raised its head and snarled but she pointed a finger at him and warned, "Uh-uh."

The beast rested his massive head on his paws and Laila moved to her brother's side. She brushed her hand across his forehead and his eyes opened.

"Hungry?" she asked. But before he could answer, a high-pitched scream rang out through the chambers and tunnels.

Laila pulled her sword and moved to the foot of the bed, taking a battle stance. The demon wolves, now on their feet, all growling, stood on either side of her.

Witches poured out of the other chambers, rushing around,

panicked. Another scream and, a few seconds later, Gemma stormed by, her fingers gripped tight in the hair of the witch Delora. The War Monk yanked the witch through the passageway, heading toward the throne room.

"Oh, shit." Laila pointed at her brother, stopping him just as he was about to run after Gemma. "Stay here with Keeley!"

She followed Gemma instead, nearly colliding with Keran in the passageway.

"What's going on?"

"As my mother would say," the fighter snarled, "we've found rats in the pantry."

Laila didn't know what that meant but she went with Keran to the throne room.

As soon as Gemma passed through the entrance, she threw Delora to the floor. This was the War Monk Laila had seen when the farm was attacked. A warrior who felt her family was threatened and acted accordingly.

"*What did my sister promise you, whore?*" Gemma bellowed at Delora, her angry voice ringing out against the cave walls.

"Nothing!"

"Don't lie to me!"

The witch, on her knees, held her arms out to the rest of her order. "My sisters . . . my queen, help me. Don't let this War Mo—"

"Tsst!" the Witch Queen hissed, her gaze never lifting from the scroll she had before her, her quill scratch-scratching urgently against the parchment.

Delora's watery eyes narrowed in anger. "What are you doing?"

"I am"—*scratch, scratch*—"busy calculating"—*scratch, scratch*—"the odds of"—*scratch, scratch*—"your being a treacherous cow."

The queen finished, leaning back and announcing, "Look at that. The odds are *huge* in favor of your being treacherous."

Delora stood. "You'd believe—"

"Numbers? Over you? Always. Numbers *never* lie."

"The calculations could be wrong."

Coming out of her seat, the queen roared, "*My calculations?*"

But several of the younger witches jumped in front of her. One of them begged, "Please! My queen."

The Witch Queen sat back into her throne. "Be glad your sisters have such coolheaded natures."

Gemma leaned in behind Delora and growled, "Too bad I don't."

"You don't frighten me, War Monk," Delora said to the pacing Gemma.

"Because you think you have my baby sister's loyalty?" Gemma slipped her arm around Delora's neck, letting it hang there casually like they were old friends. "The loyalty of a woman who stabbed her own sister? Does that seem . . . *wise* to you?"

"Basic logic." The queen sighed. "Like math, that is not one of her best subjects."

"Why is she even here?" Laila finally had to ask. "Our chieftain has always told us we go to the Witches of Amhuinn for knowledge. But she's stupid."

"I am right here!" Delora barked. "A little respect!"

Gemma tightened her arm around Delora's throat and said softly, "Shut. Up."

"She's a legacy." The queen pointed at Delora. "Her mother . . . one of the best witches I ever knew. Math, science, logic, history. They all fell at her feet, determined to be her possession. She was brilliant enough to be—"

"Witch Queen," Delora snapped.

"True." The sitting Witch Queen smirked. "Sadly, she had one great weakness. She insisted on mating with stupid men. Not the Warlocks of Godomor. Not the Monks of Spikenhammer library. Not even the War Monks . . . no offense."

"A little offense taken," Gemma admitted.

"I mean, at least you lot have enough knowledge to raise the dead. That's impressive. Disgusting but impressive. But Delora's mother . . ."

"Beware what you say, crone," Delora hissed.

"She kept. Fucking. Idiots. For years she only bred boys and we just sent them away. The smarter ones went to the Warlocks of Godomor and the stupider ones, we didn't care. But then she had Delora," she said on another long, painful sigh. "As per our laws, we had to keep her. So sad. While our other legacies soared in every subject, for dear, sweet Delora, schooling was nothing but a struggle. Math . . . a struggle. Science . . . a *painful* struggle. Basic logic . . . nothing! Then, one day, she announced that she had been blessed by the gods and was a seer."

"Were her predictions right?" Laila asked.

"Mostly. From what we could tell."

"How did you manage that, I wonder?" Gemma asked, pulling Delora in tighter and pressing her jaw against the top of the witch's head.

Then . . . slowly . . . Gemma's expression began to change as realization dawned.

"Were all her predictions . . . royalty based?" the War Monk asked.

The Witch Queen gazed at Gemma for a very long moment before she finally said, "As a matter of fact . . . yes. Yes, they were. Something that the other royals and the Old King truly appreciated."

Gemma began to laugh and Delora yanked herself away.

"Keeley was always right about her," Gemma said amidst her laughter. "Beatrix is fucking brilliant." She put her hands to her head. "She planned all of this!"

"You don't know that, Gemma," Keran argued.

"I do know that. I feel it. Not using premonition, either. Just logic. It's what she's always wanted."

"To be queen?"

"To be in *power*. And she used you two idiots"—Gemma pointed at Delora—"you and the Dowager Queen to get it. And you let her!" she finished on a laugh.

"No offense to you and your family," the Witch Queen kindly noted, "but none of you have royal blood. We checked both your lines when Delora made her prediction and there's"—she shrugged—"nothing."

"Beatrix promised Maila something. And Maila, in turn, promised *her* something."

They all focused on Delora and the Witch Queen smiled. "My job. She promised her my job."

"I should be Witch Queen," Delora insisted, which got nothing but brutal laughter from her witch sisters.

"But why kill Keeley?" Laila asked over the laughter. "I mean, your sister lives, Gemma, but that was clearly not the plan."

"I don't know. To prove Beatrix's loyalty to Prince Marius?" Gemma studied Delora. "They'd consider Keeley a threat if they thought she might become queen and push the current royal family out. Especially if Beatrix promised she would *never* do that herself."

Now they were all studying Delora and saw the panic on her face. The fear. Then, her expression changed. False bravado spread around her like a blanket, and her grin was wide as she looked straight into Gemma's eyes.

That's when Gemma told the Witch Queen, "Gods, you're absolutely right. The bitch has absolutely *no* logic."

"None." The queen tossed up her hands in defeat. "I can forgive a lack of skill with science or math, but ye gads, the lowest animals have common sense. *Crows* have logic. Rats. But you," she said to Delora, "nothing but empty space."

"What are you talking about?" Delora demanded.

Gemma shook her head. "Do you really think my sister will put you on this throne?"

"Especially when she doesn't plan for there to be any throne," the queen tossed in.

"What do you mean?"

Leaning forward in her seat, the Witch Queen growled at Delora, "She needs you dead, stupid girl. She needs all of us dead."

"She can't risk the truth getting out."

"I would never tell," she whispered. "I promised Maila I would never tell."

"But you'd always know, ya dumb cow!" Keran practically cheered.

"And you'd be able to hold it over her," Gemma reminded her, "as long as you live."

"And that, *Sister,* is something that a future queen cannot have."

Delora began to debate, attempting to convince herself, Laila assumed, but Gemma's head lifted and she held up a finger to quiet everyone. Her gaze moved to the high ceiling of the throne room. Everyone fell silent . . . waiting.

Laila's sensitive ears heard it soon after. The whistling. And she was running back to her brother when Gemma screamed out, "*Move!*"

The first fireballs crashed through the ceiling, turning everything around them into flame and destruction.

Gemma pulled a few witches out of the way and stomped out the burning gown of another.

"Go!" she yelled at Samuel. "Get to my sister! Take Keran with you!"

She ran to the throne, but the Witch Queen was already moving, with several of her assistants beside her.

"You know what to do," the Witch Queen ordered. "Don't delay. The doorway will only be open for five minutes."

Gemma grabbed the Witch Queen's arm and pulled her around. "Come with us! We'll protect you!"

The queen laughed and pressed her hand against Gemma's cheek. "You are not what I expected, War Monk. But you need not worry for us. We are leaving this place until all things are settled."

"This world?"

The Witch Queen's confused frown embarrassed Gemma even as the fire around her spread.

"*No,* woman. We are going to the Northlands. Far away from here. Witches there will protect us and our books and papers until we can come back. They are warriors, a lot like you. We'll be safe with them." A large book was pushed into the queen's arms. "I must flee, Monk. But there is something you must remember. Keeley isn't dead. And we will not be here to agree or disagree about who was named queen."

"Delora was just lying about Keeley."

"She was lying about Beatrix as well." The queen reached up and placed her hand on Gemma's shoulder. "I'm guessing your sister is using Marius's forces to attack our fortress. A fortress that has stood here for more than four thousand years without incident. Beatrix is a dangerous woman. She will take down anyone who gets in her way. But your sister Keeley . . ."

"Is just a blacksmith."

"Don't underestimate her. You've already made that mistake with Beatrix. And see where we are now?"

"The door is open, my queen!" a voice yelled from one of the nearby tunnels, while the sounds of wind battered the walls as fireballs battered the building. "Please! Come!"

"Good luck to you, War Monk."

"And to you, Witch Queen."

Delora attempted to push by the queen, trying to run down the hall where the doorway had been opened. But the Witch Queen caught the bitch by the collar of her dress and yanked Delora back, tossing her to the ground.

"Where do you think you're going, traitor?" the queen asked.

"You can't leave me!"

"You can die here with your collaborators," she tossed over her shoulder, waving as she walked off.

"Noooo!" Delora cried out. She scrambled to her feet and again tried to enter the tunnel. But Gemma wasn't about to let that happen.

She grabbed Delora by her hair and yanked her around. With a quick swipe of her eating dagger, she slit the witch's throat from ear to ear.

Gagging, Delora dropped to her knees, her hands around her throat, attempting to stanch the blood. But within seconds, she was facedown on the floor and unmoving.

Gemma pressed her hand against the witch's back and chanted the song of death.

The corpse stood again and Gemma pointed at the doorway. "Go. Kill the enemy," she said, knowing the bitch wouldn't make it far. But she still deserved this end.

Gemma rushed back to the healing chambers, but by the time she arrived, her unconscious sister was already on a pallet and the pallet was attached to a work harness that Caid and Laila had somehow gotten on the wild horse. The demon wolves surrounded the horse and Keeley.

"Where are we going?" Gemma asked, moving past her cousin, Samuel, and the horse, so that she'd be ahead of them all.

"Amichai lands," Laila replied. "We're not that far."

"All right. Stay behind me. Be ready for anything. Kill anyone who gets in our way."

"*Or,*" Laila quickly suggested, "we can try to survive this by sneaking out a back way that I know."

Gemma shrugged. "If you insist on going with logic . . ."

Smirking, Laila took the lead. With a dramatic shake of her fine mass of hair, she shifted to centaur. The tips of her antlers nearly touched the stone ceiling. They were not as big as her brother's . . . but they still made a dramatic statement.

Gemma pulled out her two short swords and adjusted her shoulders, ready for battle.

"Wait!" Keran abruptly called out as she ran back into the healing chamber.

"We need to move, Cousin!"

Keran returned but she now held Keeley's hammer.

"She'd have killed us all if we'd left this behind," she said with a smile.

And her cousin had a point.

CHAPTER 15

The journey was long, but Caid barely noticed.

He ate, but only when his sister put food in his hand. He slept, but like a prey animal. More awake than asleep, waiting for an attack at any time.

Caid walked on the left side of Keeley's pallet, hyperaware of any strange sounds or changes in bird flight patterns. Anything that was out of the ordinary. Because at this point in their journey, there was no cover. There were no trees to hide their progress or tunnels to escape through. They were out in the open until they hit Amichai territory.

As they moved along, though, he kept expecting Keeley to wake up. Kept expecting her to raise her arm to shield her eyes from the two suns. Or simply ask where she was or where her family was. Maybe ask for some water. Anything that would tell him she was getting better. Anything that would tell him she would live.

But when they finally stepped onto Amichai soil, there was still nothing from Keeley. No sign that would give him hope.

A situation that made him sad for many reasons, but especially because he would have loved for her to see that which so few humans had seen. Her father being one of those few.

Many believed that the Amichais lived *on* the mountains, but that was wrong. The Amichai Mountain range actually encircled hundreds of thousands of leagues, land ranging from vast forest to open plains to hill-riddled grasslands. There were lakes and rivers throughout that ensured clean water and a good supply of prey animals for food.

The importance and beauty of these lands was why the dwarves, elves, and centaurs worked so hard to keep them closed off from most humans. Between humans' constant need for war and their insistence on destroying all they touched so they could "rebuild," the Amichais knew it would take little time for mankind to destroy all they loved.

But Keeley was different. She would love it here and Caid knew—in his hard, spiteful heart—she would take it upon herself to protect the creatures of this land as she protected the wild horses near her home and a boy stranger she'd never met before.

Just seeing her expression as they stood on the ridge that led down into the centaur valleys would have made his bleak day shine.

Sadly, she didn't wake in time to see or comment on any of that.

She also had nothing to say when Caid's hooves touched centaur tribal lands and their travel party was immediately greeted by armed centaurs drawing down on them with their bows and nocked arrows.

If it had been Caid's clan, he wouldn't have been too concerned. Unfortunately, it was the Clan of the Red Rivers. Another protector clan like the Scarred Earth, except these centaurs were a smaller breed and instead of antlers, they had curled horns. Although smaller than Caid's people, they were still extremely dangerous and often thought that Scarred Earth didn't do enough to protect the tribal lands—like kill any human on sight. Even before interlopers reached the mountain range.

Even worse, this battle unit was being led by the young son of the clan's leader. Diarmad constantly expressed his belief that his father should be the chieftain, ruler of all the centaur clans.

Of course, for that to happen, Caid's mother would have to step down. She had no intention of doing that, and the other chief leaders wanted her to stay in power. So, Diarmad and his kin did what they could to cause problems. Something Caid and Laila usually tolerated in order to keep the peace. But this was the wrong moment to point arrows at Caid's sister.

And that wasn't because Caid was, to say the least, a little tense these days.

"Diarmad," Laila called out to the centaur male she used to beat up when they were yearlings.

"Laila. Happy to see that you and your brother have returned. Alive."

Yes. Of course he was. "Thank you. Now if you'll just—"

Diarmad held up his hand, then used his forefinger to point. "What is *that?*" he asked.

Laila glanced in the direction he pointed and found the burning eyes of Keeley's demon wolves staring back at her.

"Pets," his sister replied, forcing Caid to briefly lower his head to stop himself from laughing.

"And that?"

Now Laila didn't look, simply answered, "That's my friend Gemma."

"You're friends with a human War Monk?"

"Someone has to be. All that piety makes a being lonely."

"Laila, you know I can't allow any of these . . . *things* in our camp."

"You can and you will because they are part of the queen's entourage."

"The queen? Last we heard the *queen* was with Prince Marius."

"The Witches of Amhuinn confirmed *two* queens. The one we do not want is with Marius. The one we definitely want is here and she needs a healer."

Smirking, Diarmad began, "You'll have to wait here until I—"

"No, no." Laila moved until she stood right in front of Diarmad. She towered over him and her swishing tail told Caid she was quickly losing her patience. "I'm not playing this game with you. The queen needs a healer and my friends need food and water. I will not let you waste our time with your bullshit. So fucking move."

Caid looked toward his sister, saw that Diarmad's team had all their bows now aimed at her. Not wise. Not wise at all.

Not because of Laila. Not even because of Caid. Neither of them had any doubt that Diarmad would *never* risk his life or the lives of his clan by killing either of them. Instead, he was doing what their kind sometimes did. Starting shit to prove how strong and in control he was, even though he'd be thoughtful and rational when he backed down.

But he was so busy doing all that, he wasn't really paying attention to what was moving up behind him and his oblivious battle unit.

Light gold eyes locked on Diarmad through white and blond hair. Taller than Caid and equally wide, Caid's brother Quinn broke into a run at the last minute, a sword in his hand. He leaped up, all his legs off the ground, the sword now over his head, both hands on the hilt. And with a roar of anger, he brought that weapon down on Diarmad's hind quarter.

Laila took several steps back; Caid and the rest of their party moved in turn like one well-trained military unit.

Diarmad fell to his front right knee, letting out his own roar that had birds scattering from the nearby trees and rocks. He tried to crawl away, but Quinn wasn't done. He was never done. Not until he'd made his point.

Pulling back his arm, fist cocked, Quinn rammed it forward and *into* the wound he'd opened upon Diarmad.

Laila's entire body cringed at the action, because both of them knew Quinn was wrapping his fingers around Diarmad's femur . . . and tugging.

"Stop it, Quinn," Laila finally barked over Diarmad's desperate screams; his Red River kin were becoming restless and angry.

"Not until he understands," Quinn said, his voice disturbingly calm. "Because no one aims arrows at *my* sister. I should tear this leg off just for that alone." Then he tugged again.

"*Quinn!*" Laila bellowed when Diarmad screamed out once more.

Quinn leaned in and softly said against Diarmad's ear, "You're so lucky my sister is kind and forgiving. But keep in mind, dear Diarmad . . . *that I am not!*" he finished on a chilling bellow.

He yanked his hand out, blood splattering. "Take him to the healers. But not Petra"—the strongest healer in the camp—"Laila needs her for her friend."

Diarmad's fellow centaurs helped him back to their camp and Quinn pulled their sister into a big hug, his blood-covered hand leaving prints on the back of her chainmail shirt.

"I'm so glad you're home," he said, kissing the top of her head.

"You have to stop doing that to our people," she admonished him. "It's grotesque."

"It gets my point across. And quickly too. Most importantly, no one threatens one of us without repercussions. You know that."

When Quinn saw that Diarmad and his unit were gone, he looked at the rest of them and asked, "A human War Monk and demon dogs?"

"Wolves," Caid corrected.

"What the fuck are you doing, Laila? Why are you trying to bring crazy into the camp?" Quinn grinned. "Thought that was my job."

Gemma was ready to throw her sister over her shoulder and make a desperate run for it. She'd been fooled by the calm and easy ways of Laila and her brother. But like all beings, human or otherwise, there were many different kinds in any group. Obviously, the centaurs were as dangerous as everyone else. Her father had been a fan, but Gemma wasn't so sure.

Especially when Laila's eldest brother—Quinn, she'd called him—walked down the line of their retinue. He barely glanced at his brother, muttering "asshole" under his breath.

Caid muttered back, "Fucker." But that was about it.

Quinn looked down at the demon wolves growling at him, their bodies tense and trembling with the unspent need to rip the centaur's throat out.

"And why are these things here?" he asked Laila.

"They're friends of the queen."

"Is that supposed to make me feel confident in some way?"

"Don't care if it does, Brother. They're coming with us."

Quinn sighed dramatically and continued to move around the group. He reached the end of the first line, stood at the foot of Keeley's pallet, and gazed down at her prone form.

"Gods, look at those shoulders."

"She's a blacksmith," Caid said.

"A woman blacksmith. How progressive for the humans."

He moved on, reaching Keran. Stopped. Stared. "Keran the Unforgiving . . . yes?"

Keran's grin was wide. It wasn't every day that someone remembered her fight name.

"It is."

"I lost a thousand pieces of gold because of you."

"Foolish to bet against me."

"I know that now."

Quinn passed Samuel, barely glanced at him. "A virgin trainee monk. How odd."

He stopped next to Gemma and said to his sister, "A War Monk. You really brought a War Monk into our territories. Father's going to *love* that."

"She's the queen's sister."

"And probably ready to sacrifice all of us to appease her angry, war-loving gods."

"I don't want to hear it, Quinn. She's as welcome as the dogs."

"Wolves," Caid corrected again.

Quinn, so big in his centaur form, leaned down and whispered to Gemma, "I haven't seen War Monks in an age. Not since I killed three of them when they tried to burn a healer woman as a demon witch."

"That is an unfortunate tale," Gemma replied before rubbing her nose. Once. Twice. Then she sneezed, her head going forward hard so that her forehead collided with Quinn's smug face.

Gemma heard his nose crack, but she didn't think she'd broken it. And he didn't cry out. He simply held his nose as he moved past her, ignoring the blood that poured from it . . . Okay, maybe she had broken it.

"Oh," she said, "sorry about that. Maybe I'm allergic to horse hair."

Caid snorted, quickly turned his head, but Laila laughed out loud, punching Quinn's shoulder when he reached her.

"War Monk she may be," Laila told her brother, "but she's funny."

He motioned toward the camp. "Take your queen to the healer. Tell the guards you have *my* permission."

"Thank you, Brother." She put her hand on his shoulder to lower him a bit and kiss his cheek.

As their little group moved on, Gemma glanced back at the massive and clearly insane Quinn. He was putting his own nose back into place, his light gold eyes watering as he did so. But his gaze was locked on her and did not waver.

"Your brother watches me," Gemma said to Laila. "Is he a vengeful sort?"

"Very!" she tossed back with a smile. "But don't worry. You're with me."

"What does that mean, exactly?"

"That he'll give you ample warning before he has you killed."

"Oh . . . that's . . . lovely."

Beatrix moved through the remnants of the witches' fortress, annoyed but silent.

How did they manage it? All the books were gone. All of them. Not burned by the prince's ridiculous use of fireballs flung at the mountain walls—she had recommended a raid instead, but Marius had refused to risk his substantial troops—they were simply gone.

That frustrated her. She wanted those books. Wanted to absorb their knowledge. But if that wasn't possible, she definitely didn't want the bloody witches to have them. Who knew what they could do with all that information at the ready?

Now she'd have to make a contingency plan.

"There are none here, my lord," one of the officers told Marius.

"They're *all* gone? There are no bodies at all?"

"We've only found a few."

He shook his head. "How is that possible?"

Beatrix wondered the same thing. Those witches with their "math, science, and logic" horseshit. They must have *some* magick skills if they could move so many books and women away from the site of the onslaught so quickly.

Marius glared down at her. "This was a waste of my precious resources. Now we don't even know where the bitches are!"

He stormed off as he liked to do. Like a petulant child. Already she bored of the petty tyrant.

"They'll make themselves known in due course," she said to Maila, who stood nearby. "No need to worry."

Maila motioned to the soldiers lurking close, sending them after Marius.

When they were alone, the Dowager Queen grabbed her arm. Her nails bit through Beatrix's dress and into her flesh. It took all of Beatrix's will not to slash the old bitch's throat.

"Yes, mistress?"

"We had an agreement," she whispered.

"We still do, my lady." Beatrix did not bother lowering her voice.

"What you did to the generals . . . that was not planned. And the situation could have easily turned very badly, very quickly. For both of us."

It was the first time they'd been alone to have this conversation. Beatrix had known it was coming but she wasn't too concerned.

"Not planned but necessary. They were a threat to you." She pulled a folded parchment from a pocket in her dress and handed it to her.

"What is this?"

"Their plans for your death. For some reason, my lady, they felt you were a threat." Beatrix forced a smile. She knew this one to be "sincere."

"It was always about protecting *you*, Dowager Queen," she lied. "Always about protecting you."

She flashed a "friendly" smile and saw Maila's entire body relax.

"So," Maila said, "what is our next move?"

"To get me married to your son . . . and then to secure the lands around the Old King's castle. That will be what Marius's half brothers will attempt to capture once again and we'll have to stop them."

Maila linked her arm with Beatrix's. "And how do you suggest we do that?"

"Don't worry. We won't let those pretenders to the throne even get near your son. He will be the next Old King."

They started back toward the soldiers outside, walking over the smoldering rubble.

"And us?" Maila asked.

"Together we will rule beside him," Beatrix lied.

CHAPTER 16

Gemma waited outside the healer's tent, pacing back and forth for what felt like hours.

As she paced, she knew she was being watched by the centaurs of various clans walking past her, their gazes locked on the blood-red rune on her hauberk. She knew what they feared and she couldn't say that she blamed them. War Monks had a fearsome reputation—and with good reason. But Gemma refused to look down in shame. Refused to pretend she was anything other than what she was. Not when all she really cared about was her sister.

She had attempted to stay in the tent with Keeley but the healer wouldn't allow it. She'd pushed Gemma out with Caid and Laila, Samuel, Keran, and the gray mare. The demon wolves, though, would not be pushed anywhere and they stayed, moving into a silent pile in the corner of the tent, their burning eyes locked on everything the healer did.

Gemma stopped worrying about her sister's safety after that. No one was getting near Keeley while those wolves were near.

Eventually, the healer leaned out of the tent flap and waved at them.

Gemma rushed in but when she stopped, she had a small battle unit of beings crashing into her back, including the gods-damn horse!

The healer turned around and blinked wide when she saw the small crowd.

"I see. She has many friends." The healer's accent was thick, Gemma realized, because she was not originally from the Amichai Mountains. Seeing the white blond hair that she wore in a long braid down her back and hearing that accent, Gemma would guess she was from the Steppes of the Outerplains. How the centaur had made it this far . . . Gemma had no idea.

"Well?" Gemma pushed. "How is she?"

The healer shrugged. "Could be much worse."

"What does that mean?" Caid asked.

"Amhuinn Witches did good job. She should be wake. She should be up, moving."

"But she's not," Laila noted. "Why?"

There went that shrug again. "If I guessed . . ."

"Don't guess, Petra. We don't want guesses."

She took a breath. "She is not in there."

Gemma glanced at Laila, and together they asked, "What the fuck does *that* mean?"

Caid had no idea what Petra Azhischenkov of the True Horse Blood of the Black Sea of Pain and Longing in the Far Reaches of the Steppes of the Outerplains—and yes, dear gods, that was her entire fucking name—was talking about. And not because of her annoying Outerplains accent either. For once, she was making no sense.

"I mean what I say," Petra insisted. "She is not in there. Her body heals, but her soul"—she flittered her fingers into the air—"it is somewhere else."

"Did someone do that to her?" Caid asked.

"No. She did to self."

"So she's in so much pain," Laila reasoned, "that she's taken herself out of her body?"

"No. Amhuinns had many herbs inside her to make pain go 'way. Her problem, less physical, more . . ." She tapped her forefinger against her temple. "My guess, something truly bothers her. But she cannot face it."

Caid could guess what was bothering Keeley, what she couldn't face. Her family meant everything to her.

Gemma walked over to her sister's side, ignoring the warning growls of the wolves, and picked up her sister's hand, held it between both of hers. She leaned down, gazing thoughtfully at Keeley before she screamed, "*Wake up, you ridiculous cow, and face this shit!*"

Keran, scratching her forehead and grimacing, said, "Uhhh . . . Gemma?"

Keeley waved away the loud gnat flying around her and went back to petting her friend.

She loved it here. All green and lush with a lovely stream and big boulders for her to sit on. Why would she ever leave?

"Oy! You! Woman!"

Keeley continued to pet her friend and ignored the male voice barking at her. He'd been barking at her for a while and she kept trying to ignore him, but he was starting to get on her nerves.

A big hand waved in front of her face. Long fingers snapped a few times.

"I know you can hear me!"

Her friend growled and the male voice said, "*That's* not even supposed to be here."

Finally, grudgingly, Keeley looked up—and up—at the being in front of her.

"What do you want?" she asked, not even attempting to be polite. She was in no mood to be polite.

"Why are you still here?" he asked.

"Why do you have eight legs?"

"What?" He looked down at himself. The horse part. "What are you babbling about?"

"You have eight legs."

"So?"

"It's strange. Don't you think it's strange?"

"I'm a centaur god. So no, I don't think it's strange."

"But the centaurs only have four legs, soooo—"

"*Can we stop talking about my legs?*"

Keeley was about to tell him not to yell at her, but her furry friend did it for her. Rolling onto his belly, snarling and snapping at the god; eyes of fire blazing.

The centaur god leaned down from his extremely high position and bellowed, "*You're not even supposed to be here!*"

"Why not?" she asked.

"It's not one of the hells."

"So? He's here for me."

"Your ancestors wait over there," the god pointed out.

"I know. I can hear them. But I am not ready to face them." Keeley bowed her head. "In my shame."

"Oh, for the love of me, stop it! You are not to blame for your sister, idiot woman."

"Then who is? I raised her more than my parents did. They were busy trying to put food on the table. So I took over . . . and *she* is what I created."

"Is that why you sit here? Feeling sorry for yourself? When others wait for you. Wait for your return!"

"Why would they wait for me? I'm a failure."

"Dammit, woman, how could you raise a creature that had no soul to begin with? Your sister was *born* the way she is. A soulless thing with only one ambition. To fill up the emptiness inside her with power. Nothing else will mean anything to her. You were *taught* blacksmithing by your mother and to respect the power of animals by your father. But your love of nature and people . . . that came from within you. From your soul. Your sister will never have that."

"It doesn't matter. I'm dead now."

"*You are not*"—he cleared his throat, stopped bellowing—"You are not dead, woman. That's why you sit here and not with your ancestors. Because you're not dead. You just refuse to go back. So you sit here, on your rock with your pet demon wolf god—"

"Are you a god?" she happily asked her fur-covered friend. "Aren't you the prettiest god ever?"

"—and pretend that you can just stay here forever rather than facing the remainder of your life!"

"What do you want me to do?" Keeley finally asked.

"To face your future and your sister."

"I won't kill my sister. Despite what she's done, she's still family."

"She tried to kill you. If she were slightly stronger or you were a little weaker . . . you'd be dead now."

"She's blood. I won't kill my own blood. Besides"—she sighed out—"I won't say I deserved it, but sometimes I can be difficult. A little hard-headed. Sometimes unreasonable."

"*Wow.*" The god blinked wide. "You really do care about your family. I've had several of my siblings attempt to destroy me and I've never made excuses for them."

"But you are kind of an asshole, so is it really surprising they tried to—"

"You can stop now." He glared down at the wheezing demon wolf god that seemed to be laughing at him. "*Both* of you can stop."

"Are you sure I'm supposed to live?" Keeley wanted to know. "Are you sure you haven't *done* something to me? You and my sister bringing me back, half human and rotting."

"Trust me, woman, when I say that *you* are not my first choice for anything. If you had died, I'd have let you die. It would have meant nothing to me. But," he added, "a wound like yours can take months to truly heal and even longer for you to be at your best. I have sped up that process so that you can hit the ground running. Because Beatrix is not waiting. And whether you kill her or not, you need to realize one thing: She is still a danger to you—"

"I don't care—"

"—and the entire world."

Keeley's breath caught; she stared at him.

"What? You think a woman willing to kill the sister who's always protected her would think twice about destroying whole kingdoms to get what she wants? She is determined, your sister, to rule this world. And she will not let anyone get in her way. Even if she fails, many will die. Many will die anyway, but you could help minimize the number. At the very least, give all those worthless humans something to hope for. Unless," he added, glancing down at the demon wolf god, "it's only your precious animals you care about."

Keeley took in a deep breath and then told the centaur god her true feelings. . . .

"I don't like you. At *all*."

He smirked. "Woman . . . I'm a god. I don't give a fuck." He turned his giant horse-and-human body so he could walk off with his eight legs, but not before he tossed at her, "Of course, Beatrix thinks of herself as a god too. So imagine what her feelings are about *anything*."

CHAPTER 17

Keeley opened her eyes and quickly realized she was in a tent. She wasn't alone either. She could hear someone humming. But she didn't feel unsafe. She didn't feel frightened. Just angry.

She sat up. The woman humming had her back turned to Keeley, busy doing something with herbs at a wooden table. Keeley silently swung her legs over the side of her bed. The demon wolves were in the corner. She held her finger to her lips and they settled down, silent.

Her hammer rested against the bed and Keeley picked it up, stood . . . and walked out of the tent.

Petra turned away from her table with a potion-filled cup that she hoped would help the human woman awake. But when she looked at the bed, that woman was gone.

Her gaze searched the tent but Petra didn't see her patient. She scowled at the demon wolves that had refused to leave while she had tended the human.

After several moments of mutual staring, she asked them, "Did you eat her?"

Quinn was just clearing the tree line near the lake when he saw her. She stood ankle-deep in the water with a ridiculous hammer in her hand, staring out over the water. She only wore a cotton shirt and nothing else. She didn't seem bothered, though, by the cold.

He looked around, expecting to see his brother and sister as well as the woman's own sister and cousin, but she was alone.

With a shrug, Quinn began to move toward her but she abruptly turned and walked out of the lake and over to a large boulder. He watched in fascination as she took the handle of her hammer in both hands, lifted it above her head, and brought it down, again and again, on the boulder. She battered that boulder for several minutes, but what Quinn couldn't believe was that as she did, she broke the bloody thing into pieces with nothing more than that hammer and brute force.

Finally, after the boulder was nothing but rubble, she let out a terrifying scream filled with rage and pain and utter despair.

When the scream faded out over the river, Quinn heard, "Keeley?"

The woman's back straightened but she didn't turn around. She simply pointed her hammer with one hand and asked, "What did you know and when did you know it?"

The War Monk briefly closed her eyes. "I didn't know she was going to try to—"

"What did you know and when did you know it?" the woman asked again, not to be deterred.

"My order found out about her from our seer. A few days before I arrived at your shop. That she would be named queen. None of my leaders told me, though, because they planned to have her killed. One of the elders, a friend, warned me. But . . . she's still my sister, so . . ."

Now Keeley faced her. "You deserted your order for Beatrix?"

"Well, if I'd known she was mad, I guess I would have just let them—"

"Did you tell the boy?"

Gemma's head twitched a bit. "What?"

"Did you tell the boy that he'd be giving up his place in your order by following you?"

"Of course I did. He insisted."

"Good. I'm glad to hear you didn't lie to him."

"What's *that* supposed to mean?"

"He's a loyal boy; he deserves a good life."

"And I don't?"

"I didn't say that."

"But you're thinking it!"

"Oh, am I?"

"I wasn't the one who tried to kill you! *That was your precious fucking Beatrix!*"

"*I am aware that she tried to kill me! I can still feel where she shoved her knife into my gut!*"

She suddenly swung her hammer, now pointing toward him. "And who the fuck is that?"

Gemma leaned over to look past her sister. She sighed. "That's Quinn. Caid's brother."

"His brother?" Keeley looked around. "We're in centaur territory? Why?"

"A lot has happened, Sister. A *lot.*"

Keeley lowered her hammer and her head.

After a brief moment, she looked at her sister and calmly said, "Tell me everything."

Gemma nodded. "Come on. Let's find Laila."

Caid had been gone a total of twenty minutes, if that long. His father had insisted on an update and didn't care that Caid had not left Keeley's side since she'd been wounded. And yet, in those twenty minutes, the gravely wounded Keeley had disappeared and no one had seen her. Petra was convinced the demon wolves had eaten her but Caid had seen them eat . . . they would have left a lot more blood and gore behind.

Then, there she was . . . stalking out of Laila's tent, with that *stupid* hammer clutched in her fist. He'd never been so happy to see such a ridiculous weapon once again gripped in her very-much-alive hand.

"Keeley! Wait!" Laila and Gemma yelled, rushing up behind her.

"With us," Keeley ordered him as she stormed past, while Laila and Gemma continued trying to talk her out of something. But before Caid could move, there was Quinn.

"With us, with us," Quinn mocked, rushing behind the women in his human form.

Caid gritted his teeth. "Fuck."

Worried his brother would make everything worse—because he usually did—Caid shifted to human and followed, but when he saw Keeley heading for the tribal chieftain's tent, he picked up his speed. This was the one place Keeley really should *not* go.

He reached her and attempted to grab her arm, but she slipped through his fingers and was in the tent before he could stop her.

Laila growled; both she and Gemma entered the tent together, with Quinn laughing at Caid as he went in after them all.

"Gods-dammit," Caid muttered before he followed them.

Laila had moved in front of Keeley, her hand pressed to Keeley's chest to prevent her from going any farther.

"What's going on?" the chieftain asked, gaze moving between her children.

"Mother," Laila said, facing Gaira. "I beg your indulgence."

Quinn sat on a nearby table. "Your indulgence is being begged, Mumsie."

Giving that warm smile their mother seemed to reserve for Quinn, she said, "My darling son"—she motioned to his bare legs—"pull down your kilt and close your knees, dear. I don't need the world to see your cock and balls."

"Oh. Sorry."

Laila gestured to Keeley. "This is Keeley Smythe, Mother. The true—"

"Queen. Yes?"

Keeley moved past Laila, no longer waiting for his sister to speak for her. "I'm not queen yet, but I need to be."

"So you can become rich and powerful like the previous Old Kings or so you can kill your sister for what she did to you?"

"I already told that centaur with eight legs that I will *not* kill Beatrix."

"What do you mean you're not going to kill her?" Gemma demanded.

"Eight legs?" his mother asked. "You met a centaur with eight legs? Here?"

"She's our sister," Keeley replied to Gemma first. "I'm not going to kill her and neither are you. And he didn't give me his name," she said to his mother, "he just said he was a god. He was very large, so I believed him."

"Why won't I kill our sister? She deserves to die."

"That's not the point."

"Isn't it?"

"I'm sorry to interrupt," his mother tried again, "but you spoke to Ofydd Naw? Our war god?"

"He didn't give me his name. And killing our sister will just put a curse on this family!"

"Beatrix is a curse!"

"And she's still our sister!"

Caid cringed again when his mother put her hands to her temples. A sure sign she was getting one of her "aching heads" as she called it.

"I'm sorry to interrupt you two bickering ninnies! But am I the only one disturbed that *our* gods are stopping by to say hello to a human?" His mother eyed Keeley coldly. "A human blacksmith," she sneered.

Gemma jumped in front of her sister as Keeley pointed her finger and informed their mother, "Blacksmithing is the most ancient and *noble* art in the world!"

"Keeley," Gemma implored, "let it go."

"You're just lucky *our* mum isn't here. She'd tear your skin off."

"I'm sorry," his mother said, a small smile turning up the corners of her mouth.

Keeley frowned. "Are you?"

"Of course. I shouldn't have insulted you. But in spite of the fact that a god came to you—"

"Gods."

His mother blinked. "Pardon?"

"Gods. I met gods. As in plural."

"You met someone other than Ofydd Naw? Who else?"

Keeley shrugged. "Not sure about the name, but he was a giant version of my wolf friends."

Laila's eyes grew wide. "Your wolf friends . . . ? Do you mean the demon wolves we can't get rid of?"

"They're still wolves."

His mother scratched her cheek. "That's Maelgwn. The other gods use him when someone makes them angry. They'll send him up here to destroy whole cities or entire races of people, depending on how pissed off they are."

Really? Keeley shrugged. "He let me rub his belly."

The entire tent was silent until Gaira looked at Laila with those light eyes and sweetly said, "May I speak to you for a moment, dear?"

"No, thank you," Laila attempted but her mother grabbed her by her hair as she walked by and dragged Laila from the tent.

"What kind of mad human did you bring to our territory?" Gaira demanded, shoving Laila away and shifting to human so she could easily pace in front of her daughter.

"She's not mad. Just different."

Gaira stopped pacing. "She rubbed the belly of a demon god."

"Demon *wolf* god."

"What difference does that make?"

"To her it makes all the difference. As far as she's concerned . . . they're wolves and therefore, they are more animal than evil being."

"Despite the eyes of flame?"

"She just doesn't put her hands near that area . . . so they don't get burned."

Gaira moved in close and reminded her, "You do understand that one day you'll be taking *my* role? As chieftain. You get that, yes? Which means you'll be responsible for *all* these people. Not just the ones who can wield a sword, but the ones who farm, who heal, who make pretty jewelry. You do understand that?"

"Of course I do."

"Then you understand bringing mad human women into their midst is stupid . . . yes?"

"Just talk to her."

"I tried. She bickered with her War Monk—another discussion we'll need to have one day—sister and talked about rubbing the belly of a demon god."

"And Ofydd Naw came to get *her*. To send her back here to battle her own sister. Or did you forget that part, Mum?"

"Don't call me 'Mum.' We're not peasants."

"I know it's hard for you to *not* look down on others, but I've *fought* beside Keeley. I've seen her with her family. I've seen her with her workers. I've seen her challenge the Witches of Amhuinn. Can she win against Beatrix? I really don't know. But I think if we give that bitch Beatrix even the slightest chance, she will destroy *all* of us."

"Tell me what you need, blacksmith," the leader of the centaur clans, Chieftain Gaira, asked Keeley as they walked through her tribal lands together.

"I need an army."

"You'll have to give me a very good reason to assign my warriors to you."

"No, no," Keeley felt the need to insist. "I need an *army*."

"Are you saying my warriors are not good enough for you?"

"No. I'm saying I need a *big* army. Big. Beatrix has access to at least *half* of the Old King's armies. Cyrus the Honored has the other half."

"So what you truly need are allies."

"I do, but I'm nobody."

Gaira stopped, wagged her forefinger at Keeley. "Ah-ah-ah. *Never* say that. You are the true queen prophesized by the Witches of Amhuinn."

"Who are no longer here to verify it."

"They're not dead. Just moved. If you want allies, you need to be that true and prophesized queen. You need to make potential allies promises that you'll one day be able to deliver on."

"That means gold? Because I don't have gold."

Gaira shrugged. "Mhmm. Not all promises mean gold. Sometimes they mean . . . marriage. Perhaps marry a duke or baron with a substantial army?"

Keeley couldn't help but pull her lips back in a grimace.

"I . . . I can't do that."

"Looking for love, are you?"

"It would be nice."

"Well," Gaira went on, "I have another option. It's a little . . . dangerous. And I'm sure my children would disagree with me out of fear for your safety. But it might be an option for *you*. Maybe the only option you actually have if marriage is off the table."

"It is."

Gaira began walking again, and Keeley moved with her.

"Well then, there are more races in the Amichai territories than just centaurs. And at least with one of those races, you might have more in common than you might think. . . ."

Following the Chieftain's train of thought, Keeley froze, gawked at Gaira.

"Do . . . do you mean the Amichai dwarves?"

"As a matter of fact, I do."

When Keeley clasped her hands together and bounced up and down on her toes, Gaira added, "So I guess you've heard of them . . . ?"

Keeley replied to that by squealing and jumping around the chieftain. She couldn't help herself! The Amichai dwarves!

Gaira nodded. "All right then . . ."

Caid stared at his mother. "Why would you tell her that?"

"Why wouldn't I? It's a very good idea."

"It's a mad idea. Mad. The dwarves will crush her bones. The elves will strip her flesh. And the barbarians will make her into soup."

Gaira moved past him, wrapping a scarf around her neck as the evening became cooler. "Stop being so dramatic. None of them are that bad."

"No, they're worse."

"She needs allies."

"*Human allies*. Not dwarves and elves that *loathe* humans."

"The barbarians are mostly human . . . like."

"Mother, be serious."

Gaira turned away from the large mirror she'd been looking into and now gazed at her son.

"Why are you so worried about her?"

"You sent us off to protect the future queen of the Hill Lands. *She's* that future queen."

Gaira raised a brow and moved toward her son. "Are you interested in her?"

"Mother—"

"By the mighty tail of Ofydd Naw, you *are* interested in her." She leaned in and whispered, "Despite those shoulders?"

"*Mum.*"

"Don't call me that."

"Yes, I know. We're not peasants. And she's a strong woman. She has shoulders that go with that strength."

"Hhhmhm. I see."

"Do you? Because I think you entirely misunderstand—"

"Blah, blah, blah! I don't want to hear it! You're just like your father, you know. He used to say I was too skinny for him. But he *loves* my skinny ass."

"I'm leaving." Caid walked toward the tent flap. "And I'll be going with Keeley when she leaves."

"Stop."

Caid let out a breath, faced his mother.

"I did not give you or your sister permission to go anywhere."

"She's going and so am I. Especially if you're sending Keeley into hostile territories."

"You don't know if they'll be hostile to her."

"They're hostile to *everyone*. That's why one lives *inside* the mountains. The other lives high in trees. And who the mighty hells knows where the barbarians live, but we all know to stay away from their lands." Caid threw his hands up. "Are you trying to get her killed?"

"No. I'm trying to get her an army. And she has no time. Marius won't give her any. So she'll have to make do with a smaller army, which means that it will need to be *meaner.*"

Keeley placed her hammer by her bed and took the chalice of wine Laila handed her.

"This will not be easy," Laila said, now handing Gemma a chalice of water.

Gemma sat in a thick wooden chair with her boots and socks off. She was stretching her tired feet.

"I know," Keeley replied, "but I think your mother's right. It's not like I have a lot of choices here. But if I can get the dwarves on my side first, I think I can make all this work."

Laila took the platter of cheese, meat, and bread from the centaur who'd brought it and placed it on a small table by Keeley's bed.

"I'm going with you," Laila said.

"I can't ask you—"

"It's not up for discussion. Besides, who else will keep you two from bickering yourselves to death?"

"I'll be there," Keran offered from a spot in the corner of the tent, her chair turned around, her legs splayed on either side of its back.

"You enjoy their fights," Laila reminded her. "So I don't really see that helping."

"Eh. You have a point."

"You don't even try to disagree," Gemma noted.

"I really don't."

Laila motioned to Keeley's sister and cousin. "We've got tents for you two. Separate ones, so everyone can relax tonight."

"Me own tent?" Keran stood, grinning. "How luxurious!"

Laila was heading toward the tent flap but it was pulled back and her eldest brother walked in. He was in his human form but he was just as imposing as when he was centaur.

Immediately, Laila held up her hands. "Whatever you're planning, Quinn, don't."

Quinn waved his sister off as he came toward Keeley. She reached back, wrapping her hand around her hammer, finding the feel of it reassuring.

He stopped in front of her. "You're going to see the dwarves, elves, and barbarian tribes?"

"That's the plan."

"And this was my mother's brilliant idea?"

"Yes."

He stared at her for an unreasonably long time before he spun around and walked back out.

"What was that?" Keeley asked Laila.

"I have no idea. I stopped trying to figure out my brother a very long time ago."

Caid was heading toward the tent he'd been told Keeley was in when his sister cut in front of him.

"Have you seen Quinn?"

"No. But I've purposely not been looking for him."

"He's acting stranger than usual."

"Quinn is a firm believer in keeping everyone on their hooves by being the most unpredictable horse in the herd."

"It's like having a pet pit dog. You never know when he might snap."

Caid gestured to Keeley's tent. "How's she doing?"

"Amazing. She wakes up from near death and is ready to not only take on her bitch sister and Prince Marius but the entire world." Laila placed her hand on his shoulder. "I'm leaving with her tomorrow."

"It might be a suicide mission."

"So you're not coming, Brother?"

"Don't be stupid." He pushed her aside, ignoring her laugh. "Of course I'm coming."

The demon wolves surrounded Keeley's tent and the gray mare stood inside the circle but outside the tent. He stopped to stroke her muzzle.

"If they make you nervous," he said to her softly, "leave. We'll find you before we go."

Caid ignored the growls as he pulled open the tent flap and stepped inside. At first, he thought it was empty . . . but then the wolves wouldn't be outside protecting it. They wouldn't protect an empty tent. They would follow Keeley wherever she went.

Staying silent, Caid moved through the large tent until he heard the breathing. He followed the sound until he found Keeley on the floor, curled into a corner, panting.

He crouched beside her, pushed her black hair off her face. "Keeley?"

She looked up at him, those dark eyes filled with panicked tears, and said, "Every one of you is going to die, and it'll be my fault. *All* my fault."

CHAPTER 18

"Y ou're all going to die. I'm going to destroy the centaurs. I'm going to kill my family. The dogs—"

"Wolves."

"—and that poor gray mare." Tears now flowed freely. "And she just lost her son!"

Caid got on the floor beside Keeley. He needed her to keep her voice down and he needed her to stay calm. But he also sensed that telling her that now would only make her louder and more panicked.

He did the only thing he could think of . . . he took her hand in his, holding it loosely.

She gazed at their hands until she asked, "What are you doing?"

"Uhhh . . . comforting you?"

"Something you're not good at?"

"Not really."

Keeley turned over her hand, so that Caid's lay on top, and interlaced their fingers.

"Like this," she said.

"Thank you."

"And when you die," Keeley said on a new flood of tears, "your mother will miss you greatly. Because, even though you seem to never look happy, you are so very kind."

"You have to stop crying."

"I can't. All I can see is death and despair, and it's all my fault."

"If anything, Keeley, it's the fault of your sister."

"That does not make me feel better. How am I supposed to tell my parents that their love created a monster?"

"Well, after ten thousand children, one had to be bad."

Despite the tears, Keeley gave a short laugh. "My mother did not have ten thousand children."

"I've sat at dinner with all of them . . . it *felt* like ten thousand."

She laughed a little harder. "Stop trying to make me feel better."

"I should let you wallow?"

"Yes. That's what I'm asking for. Wallowing rights."

"We can't afford to have you wallow, Your Majesty."

She visibly shuddered and looked away. "Don't call me that."

"If all goes well, I won't be the only one calling you that. You might as well get used to it."

"I can't be queen, Caid. Not really."

"You can and will be." He gripped her hand a little tighter. "I hate to say this . . . but you really have no choice, Keeley. Without you—"

"Without me, what? My younger sister becomes queen? And before you say it, I know. I *know* what she did. I was there." She pressed her free hand against her stomach. "These scars will remain for the rest of my life. So I'll never be able to forget. But is what she's done any worse or different than past Old Kings that ruled these lands?"

"Not these lands, Keeley. Never these mountains. The Amichai Mountains have been the lands of the Amichai centaurs, the dwarves, the wood elves, and the barbarian tribes for eons. Only once has any Old King attempted to control these lands and that happened so long ago, I can only say my 'ancestors' were there because the use of 'great-great-great' would go on for so long you'd get bored and wander away."

"And what would change any of that now?"

"Your sister." Caid blew out a long breath and decided to barrel forward with the truth. Keeley had been lied to enough. "We have our own seers. We've never just relied on the Witches of Amhuinn with their math and science, because we are one with our gods and nature. Those things combined with our own witches keep us safe."

"They warned you about Beatrix?"

"No. They told us a queen would be the only thing that stopped the advancement of enemies into our territories and the complete and utter destruction of our mountains. We thought that meant Beatrix . . . we know now that our seers meant you."

"But why?" Keeley finally had to ask when she found her voice again; she was so stunned that her tears were no longer flowing. "Wouldn't Gemma be a better option? She's a War Monk. She has battle skills. She's actually been somewhere besides our farm."

"And she loathes Beatrix with all her heart. That rage and hatred blinds her in a way it does not blind you. It also matters that you *weren't* gone for over a decade. You probably know Beatrix better than anyone else. Can guess what her next move will be. Figure out where she'll strike next."

"That's easy enough," Keeley replied without really thinking. "She'll want to lock down the security of the royal palace and surrounding lands, and then she's going to focus on Marius's brothers . . . and why are you staring at me like that?" she abruptly asked.

"Do I actually have to say? Or can you figure it out on your own?"

She rubbed her forehead. "What if despite all this vast knowledge of Beatrix, I still fail?"

"We all die."

Eyes wide, Keeley turned her head to look at the Amichai. He gazed back . . . blankly.

"You are such a rude bastard!" she said on a laugh, bumping him with her elbow.

"You were clearly waiting for me to say something like that," he actually laughed with her, "and I hate disappointing you."

Exhausted but not in the mood to sleep yet, Keeley rested her head against his shoulder. They sat like that for a long time, neither saying anything. Caid just allowing her time to make up her own mind. But Keeley knew that he was right. She really didn't have a choice. Whatever happened from here on out would be her sister's . . . no, not her sister. Beatrix. It would *Beatrix's* doing.

"I'll do it," she finally said.

"I know. And I will be with you while you do."

Keeley shook her head and sat up. "No. You and your sister have done enough for—"

"Don't even bother to argue with me. It'll be useless. Because we both know that I'll only do what I want and so will my sister. She's infamous around here for doing what she wants."

"Look at that . . . my queenly orders are already being ignored."

"They are, but for good reason. You'll need us by your side when you meet with each group. They are *not* friendly to strangers. Especially human ones."

"Who will be the hardest to deal with?" she asked, getting to her feet, Caid right beside her.

"The barbarian tribes. Definitely."

"I thought maybe I'd start with the dwarves first but now I think the barbarians should be first."

"No," Caid said with gruff determination. "We will *not* start with them."

"I like to get the hardest thing out of the way."

"And that's excellent logic when one is creating a great sword. Not when you're attempting your first alliance. For your first alliance, you should definitely start with the dwarves. But, and I mean this sincerely, Keeley, I'd stay away from discussing your being a blacksmith."

Keeley gasped. She couldn't help it! "Why wouldn't I discuss that? I love discussing that!"

"They're dwarves. You can't compete with dwarves."

"I don't plan to compete with them. But we're fellow blacksmiths. We should be learning from each other. Discussing the wonders of steel and iron!"

"I can't express to you how badly that's going to work with the dwarves. Trust me on this, Keeley. You go to them as a human queen looking for an alliance because your sister is a worse choice. That's it. That's the card you play."

"But if they like me—"

"*No.* I can't say that strongly enough. Just no."

Caid could tell by Keeley's expression she wanted to argue, but he also knew that would be a bad idea. The dwarves, like most of the mountain races, were not to be challenged. And the dwarves took their blacksmithing so seriously, they would only see Keeley as another pathetic human who *thought* she was a decent blacksmith. And it didn't help how perky she was. Dwarves weren't naturally perky.

"Trust me," he practically begged. "Please."

She took a moment, staring at the ground. Then she looked directly at him and said, "I will do my best to follow your counsel."

Caid frowned. "Huh?"

"I'm trying to sound like a queen here."

"Is that what you're doing?"

She hissed at him a little, which he found a bit off-putting, and walked to her bed. She sat down on it and Caid, assuming they were done, headed toward the tent flap.

"Wait," she called out.

Caid stopped, faced her. "Something else?"

"There's something I'd like to do before I get some sleep. If you don't mind."

"You want me for sex?"

Keeley's eyes grew wider than Caid had ever seen. "Pardon?"

"Isn't that what you want? Human women always seem to want to have sex with centaurs."

"Actually . . . I was . . . um . . . hoping to meet your father? Not to have sex with him, though," she quickly added. "Or you. No offense."

"No. I'm sorry." Caid moved a little closer. "The few humans I've met who know what we are usually want to have sex with us."

"Even the men?" she asked, appearing confused. "They want to have sex with female centaurs?" Caid was about to get insulted for the females of his race when Keeley added, "I mean . . . don't they feel insecure? There's no *way* they could possibly live up to what I've seen trotting around your camps."

Caid turned away, attempting to stop his laughter by rubbing his nose with his fist.

"Come on," he choked out. "I'll take you to my father."

Keeley followed Caid through the camps. It was easy to tell the difference between the more peace-loving centaurs and the ones who were bred to be warriors. The soldier centaurs had antlers or horns and lots of scars from past battles. They were always strapped with weapons and their eyes were the eyes of predators, not prey.

But they lived easily among their kin because they didn't use their power and strength against their own. Instead, they were there to put the others at ease. To make everyone feel safe. Something that, to Keeley's mind anyway, was what power was for. To protect those who weren't meant to carry a sword or kill on command. Not everyone had the desire and very few were good at it. So why force them when it wasn't their skill?

They reached an open field with a herd of horses racing around it. The gray mare was in their midst and the sight made Keeley smile. Seeing the horse doing what she did best. Run free.

Caid put two fingers to his mouth and whistled. One of the horses split off from the herd and raced toward them. As it neared, Keeley realized that it wasn't a horse; it was a centaur. He hadn't shifted either. He'd simply blended into the herd, and it wasn't until he was on his own that one could see what he was.

How he managed to hide those antlers, though . . . ? She'd never know. They were enormous. Bigger than Caid's. *They must get bigger the older a centaur lives*, Keeley thought, which she found fascinating.

He came to a stop in front of Caid and Keeley.

"Father, this is Queen Keeley of the Hill Lands."

Keeley blinked, shocked to hear herself given such a title.

"Keeley, this is my father, Hearn, chief of our clan."

Hearn nodded at her but that was all.

But when Keeley didn't say anything—she was still staring at his antlers. Did he sleep with those? Were they uncomfortable to sleep in? Did he hit low-hanging things often with those things?—Caid said, "Keeley would like to speak with you, Father."

With a scowl as fierce as his son's, Hearn looked down at Keeley. "Yes?" he asked, sounding mostly annoyed.

Keeley cleared her throat and began, "Many years ago, you saved a young soldier you found in the lower mountains. That young soldier was my father and I just wanted to say thank you."

Then Keeley did what her father had always told her to do if she was ever lucky enough to meet the centaur who'd saved his life . . .

she wrapped her arms around his lower waist—the last bit of him that was humanlike when he was in his natural form—and hugged him.

Caid watched his father's confused expression turn downright panicked; his hands flailed a bit as he tried to figure out where to put them. Caid could almost guess the stallion's questions: Should he hug her back? Should he push her away? Should he wipe her from the face of the earth?

So many questions right there on his father's face.

Caid's father usually knew *exactly* what to do in any given situation. That's how he'd lived as long as he had. By being smart and determined. But Keeley had a way of confusing even the most confident of males.

"Uh . . . uh . . . you're welcome . . . ?"

Oh, good. He'd settled on *not* wiping her from the face of the earth. Caid was sure that had been hard for his father to go with.

Smiling, Keeley stepped back. "My father also wanted me to send his best. He's never forgotten what you did for him."

What happened that day, so many seasons ago, was not something their father discussed much. The other protector clans had thought it was stupid for Hearn to bring a human to their camp and have him nursed back to health. A soldier of the Old King, no less. Not some lost child. The clan leaders at the time had all felt the soldier should have been put down where he lay among the rocks he'd fallen into with six human-made arrows still in his neck, chest, and hip. But Hearn hadn't agreed for some reason. He'd gone against everything he'd been taught and brought the soldier to safety.

The move had secured Hearn's place in Gaira's heart, though. He'd already had a son from the future leader of the centaur clans but there had been other stallions sniffing around Gaira, and she had seemed uncertain about claiming Hearn as a long-life mate. That would mean in times of incredible danger, Hearn would lead the centaur and mountain tribe armies into war. She'd worried that the scowling, mostly cranky, snarling male would hunger for war and the death of humans, and Gaira was not one to go to war because she was bored or had an axe to grind.

All these years, Caid had assumed his father's decision to help the human soldier had been a calculated one. Hearn knew that Gaira had a soft spot for all living things, including humans and, in his own way, he had loved Gaira for a very long time. Caid didn't actually approve of such a calculating move, but he understood it. And he was grateful that Laila was his sister, if nothing else.

But now, watching his father as he had to deal with one of the soldier's grateful offspring, Caid realized his original belief might have been wrong. Very wrong.

"How is your father?" Hearn asked Keeley.

"Fine, I hope. I had to leave him and the family at my uncle Archie's."

"Crazy Archie?" He smirked. "You sure that was wise?"

"We were out of choices, but I made him promise to behave himself."

"Especially with your mother."

"Yes! Still clinging, he is."

"Your father's love of the Blacksmith Maiden is legendary. He'll give her up to no one, but especially not his brother."

"The Blacksmith Maiden?"

"That's what your father called her. He kept telling me he needed to get back to his Blacksmith Maiden. Even when he was suffering the worst fever from his wounds, he talked about her. He already had plans for his farm and the raising of his . . . three children, I think."

Keeley laughed. "Three?"

"She's had ten thousand," Caid said.

"She has *not* had ten thousand," Keeley quickly corrected. "There are twelve of us."

"With another nine thousand on the way."

Keeley dismissed Caid with a flick of her hand that almost hit him in the nose.

"Now," Keeley began, "I wanted to give you this." She pulled a beautiful battle dagger from the sheath attached to the belt around her waist.

"That's not nec—"

"I know." She placed the weapon in his hand. "But my mother would want you to have this. To thank you."

She hugged Hearn again and, to Caid's eternal shock, Hearn hugged her back.

Keeley pulled away first, walking back to camp before Hearn could see the tears in her eyes. Caid started to follow, but his father yanked him back by his hair.

"Ow! I wish you wouldn't do that!" Caid snapped.

"Don't do anything stupid," his father told him.

"What are you talking about?"

"You know exactly what I'm talking about. Keep your kilt down and forelimbs on the ground. Understand me?"

"Sadly, yes," Caid sighed as he moved away from his father so the mean bastard couldn't grab Caid's hair again.

Hearn watched his son and the future queen walk back into camp. When they disappeared behind tents, he looked down at the blade he held in his hands. He was amazed at the workmanship. It was not the work of some average blacksmith one could find in any town, but of someone with real love in their heart for the art of it.

He remembered the sword the young soldier had possessed. It had been forged by the soldier's "Blacksmith Maiden." Hearn still had it and often used it when necessary. He and the young soldier had exchanged swords before Angus had headed out of the mountains and back to his battalion. Hearn had become friends with that young soldier, despite their being so different in every way. And, unbeknownst to many, they'd kept in contact over the decades. Sending each other books and letters. Keeley Smythe was exactly as her father had described her. Beautiful, bold, and caring. She looked more like her mum, based on the way Hearn's friend had described the Blacksmith Maiden, but his War Monk daughter resembled him. Especially around the eyes.

Hearn had to admit, he'd been worrying about his old friends since Laila and the others had arrived with Keeley. He doubted that Angus knew what had happened to his eldest daughter and what his middle child had done. The betrayal. And the true danger he and his entire family were currently in. Angus wanted to believe the best of everyone but that's what had nearly got him killed all those years ago.

"Are you all right?" his mate asked, nuzzling the back of his neck.

"I . . . I think I need to take a platoon of our best and go get my friend. Take him and his family someplace truly safe. Here. Among us."

She put her arms around his neck and rested her head against his jaw. "You'll hear about it," she warned. "From the other tribal chiefs."

Gaira ruled over all the clans—especially during times of strife—which was why she had the title Chieftain. But each centaur clan had its own chief and each of those leaders had a say in how day-to-day things worked.

"Until he talks with Keeley, Angus will never know the real danger he and his family are in. But we can't wait for her to go get him. We need to move now. And she needs her allies."

She kissed his cheek. "I think you're right. That woman loves her kin. If something happens to them . . . it may break her. We can't afford that right now."

Gaira took the blade from his hand, nodding in appreciation at its quality. "Take what you need. Kill our enemies. Come back to me."

He nodded at her orders before kissing her throat.

"As you command," he murmured against her skin.

CHAPTER 19

Keeley woke up, buried under fur, with a centaur standing over her, glaring.

"What? What's wrong?"

Caid didn't answer, just waited for her to realize that she was in bed with two of the demon wolves.

"It's not what it looks like," she argued, trying to sit up, but neither animal seemed to be in the mood to move yet.

"Uh-huh."

"It was cold last night and the fur covering wasn't doing much." She pushed against the wolves again. But when they still didn't move, she ordered, "Off! Now!"

They scrambled from the bed and Keeley quickly slipped out as well.

"Notice they were on *top* of the fur covering . . . just keeping me warm. Like good friends."

"This is a disturbing conversation," Caid said. "I'm walking away now."

And he did.

"We're almost ready to go, Your Majesty," he sarcastically tossed at her before walking out.

"You almost got me in trouble!" she whisper-yelled at the wolves. "Not everyone understands our relationship!"

The wolves responded by rolling around on their backs or digging into her travel bag for something to eat or playing tug with one of her leather sheaths.

Keeley found a new set of clothes waiting for her, but they were just like her old clothes. A sleeveless leather tunic, leather leggings, and leather boots. There were also bindings for her ample breasts, short braies, and warm socks. Under all that was a leather breastplate with matching pauldrons.

Creating leather armor wasn't her strength as much as chainmail and plate armor, but Keeley knew good work when she saw it. Especially when she held it.

Grinning, she put everything on and took a quick look in the mirror. What she loved? More than anything? Her crest. A black hammer and anvil burned into the brown leather.

Love, love, love!

Slipping her hammer into a leather holster that allowed her to strap it to her back for travel, she headed outside and was delighted to see the gray mare waiting for her. Keeley had assumed that the horse would stay with the herd she'd been running with last night, but no. She still wanted her revenge and Keeley was fine with that. She wanted her revenge too.

Keeley saddled up the mare and took the additional travel bags handed to her by helpful centaurs. Bags filled with bread, hard cheese, and dried meats. As well as containers for water and another for ale.

"Morning," Gemma grumbled as she watched Samuel saddle up her stallion.

"Sister."

Laila and Caid, in their natural forms, arrived with their mother.

"Such a beautiful day!" Gaira cheered, reaching down and patting Keeley's shoulder.

"Thank you for the armor and holster for my hammer. I adore them all!"

"They look very good on you. We took a chance on the crest. Figured you could change it when you're ready."

"Why would I change it?" she asked. "It's perfect!"

Gaira faced her children. "Be careful. And take care of each other." She kissed each on their cheeks and was about to move away when she saw something behind Keeley and her eyes grew wide.

Keeley turned and immediately reached over her shoulder for

the handle of her hammer, watching Quinn stalk toward her as human, pulling his long sword as he did.

Without saying a word, Gemma stepped in front of Keeley, her own two short swords out. Laila and Caid moved quickly toward their brother, but before they could reach him, he abruptly dropped to one knee and slammed the tip of his sword into the ground.

"Oy!" Keeley barked, cringing. "That's no way to treat such a fine weapon! And when will I be near a hot enough fire so I can fix it for ya? Eh? Tell me that!"

"Is that really your main concern here?" Gemma asked, her tone typically annoyed.

"I pledge my sword to you, Blacksmith Queen," Quinn announced loudly. The statement had Keeley's and Gemma's heads snapping around to gaze down at him.

"You do?" Keeley asked Quinn.

"You do?" Laila also asked.

"I do!"

"Why?" Caid coldly questioned his brother.

Gaira pushed Caid away and lifted her eldest son's chin with her hand. "Quinn, are you sure about this?"

"I don't do anything I'm not sure about. And I'm sure about this."

"Well, I won't stop you . . ."

Quinn stood tall; then, with a slight shake of his head, he stood even taller as he shifted. He put his blade back into the sheath strapped across his back.

He kissed his mother.

"Safe travels," she said to them all.

Keeley mounted her horse and walked it over to Quinn. "Why have you committed your sword to me?"

"If I want to be leader of the Scarred Earth Clan one day, I need to have more battle experience. And you seem like a mad cow that'll get us into a war faster than your demon wolves can take down a wild boar and eat it. Add in that you have a War Monk sister at your side who is absolutely *chewing* at the bit to sink her sword into something warm and blood-filled, and I can't ask for a better way to secure my future. Can you?"

He winked and moved away from her, heading out of the camp.

"What did my brother say to you?" Caid asked, stepping in next to her.

"Oh . . . nothing." She glanced over at him. "Do you think I'm a mad cow?"

"Well . . ." Caid began, but Keeley immediately waved away his answer.

"Forget I asked."

Their group started off, now filled out with another unit of centaur warriors keeping them company. But they'd only gotten a few feet before Keeley called a halt and yelled out, "Keran! Godsdammit, *wake up!*"

It took Beatrix little time to realize something very important. Her husband could barely read. She'd discovered that when the Dowager Queen's Follower of Her Word—his true name was Agathon—handed Marius a parchment with the words he was to speak during the nuptials. His reaction was so violent and angry that she knew immediately he could read but a few words.

It should have appalled her. A king's son who couldn't read? But it was beyond perfection. She had closely and silently watched as Marius's mother quickly jumped in. Not only to protect the Follower of Her Word from getting beaten to death by her son, but also to hide her son's lack of basic capabilities.

Maila taught her son the words by reading them to him . . . twice. Under the guise that he didn't like how it sounded the first time around, so he wanted to "hear the words" again. After the second reading, he could repeat them back perfectly. It meant he was definitely smart, so Beatrix would have to be careful. But she could—and would—use this discovery to her advantage.

What Beatrix desperately needed now was an ally within the palace walls. The Queen Dowager would never fully trust her. She'd always known that. Especially since Maila trusted no woman fully. The few consorts of the Old King who'd managed to survive the massacre were not simply killed on Maila's orders immediately upon their return to the castle. They were burned at the stake, which had seemed excessive to Beatrix. What point did it make?

And all the screaming . . . ? She'd been trying to read several important dispatches intercepted between Marius's twin brothers and Cyrus the Honored when she'd been completely distracted by all that damn screaming! And it went on for ages since they burned each woman separately. Another waste of time and done simply for show.

Beatrix couldn't wait to get control, so she could stop that sort of excess and waste. It needed to be reined in, used only when a message needed to be sent to all.

Sitting in her wedding gown, waiting for the time when she would walk down the aisle and lock her life to that of a petulant man-child who couldn't read and relied too much on his mother, Beatrix looked up from the parchments she was studying.

The Follower of Her Word . . . er . . . Agathon, walked into Prince Marius's privy chamber but froze at the entrance. They both knew she shouldn't be here.

"My Lady Beatrix?"

"Agathon." She lifted her hand and gestured at him with two fingers. "Come in. We should talk."

He didn't move, his eyes wide in near panic. Poor thing. He'd been so abused by Marius and his kin that Agathon didn't realize when there was a hand being held out with a treat.

"Come, Agathon."

He let out a breath and took several steps in.

"Close the door behind you."

He did. "My lady, I think your time to—"

"I know. Don't worry. I'll be there to take my place beside my husband and declare my never-ending love." Beatrix gestured to the chair across the table from her. "Sit."

He did.

"Do you enjoy what you do for the Dowager Queen?" Beatrix asked, removing her spectacles so she could clean the fragile glass with a soft cloth.

"Of course, my lady. She is kind and fair and—"

"Dear gods, man, you don't have to lie to me." She carefully put the spectacles back on. "It does nothing but irritate me and set my teeth on edge and you're very bad at it."

Agathon fell silent, gazing down at the table.

"I understand that choices are hard. Especially when you've been given so few. But you must understand that there are those who will take you far into the future and those who will do nothing but drag you down until they dispose of you. When you are no longer useful. I've watched you—I see great potential."

"My lady, I say this with *great* deference, but . . . you do not know the strength of will of Prince Marius and his mother. I say this to you as a warning and a—"

Beatrix held up her hand to halt his words and rested her arms on the table. She leaned in and said, "Look into my eyes, Agathon. Look deep. And you tell me, using the instincts that have allowed you to survive this long . . . what do you see?"

When Agathon hesitated to meet her eyes, she urged, "It's all right. Look. And tell me what you see."

He finally did, meeting her gaze, staring. And, the longer he stared, the whiter he became. All the blood left his worn, much-too-young-to-look-so-old face, his tongue swiping his suddenly dry lips, the lump in the front of his throat bobbing as he attempted to swallow.

That's when Beatrix allowed herself a smile.

"Now you see, don't you, Agathon? Now you see."

Beatrix pushed back from the table and stood. "They'll be coming for me soon," she said, stepping around the table. "To take me to my future husband. Such a grand wedding created in such a short amount of time. Maila really should be proud." She placed her hand on his shoulder, enjoying the way it tensed at her touch. "You and I could do great work together, Agathon. If you would just . . . trust me."

"Do I have a choice, my lady?"

"Sadly . . . no. But neither do I." She patted his shoulder and walked toward the door. "Keep in mind, though, Agathon . . . I have no time for petty cruelties and random acts of abuse. I have grand ambitions. Wouldn't you enjoy being part of something like that? Rather than groveling to a former whore and her bastard son?"

Agathon wisely didn't answer that specific question, and she didn't blame him. She wouldn't have answered it either.

But, as Beatrix put her hand on the door handle, he said, "There is a rumor, my lady . . ."

"A rumor?"

He nodded. Barely. "That your sister, the blacksmith . . . she's not dead."

Beatrix looked back at Agathon. "What?"

"There are rumors coming from those who live near the Amichai Mountains that she lives. Prince Marius does not know this . . . but the Dowager Queen does."

Beatrix made a fist with her left hand, letting her small nails bite into the skin of her palm. She did it to clear her mind. This information had surprised her more than she would have expected.

"Thank you, Agathon," she finally got out.

"Yes, my la—" He cleared his throat. "My queen."

Pushing the thought of her eldest sister out of her mind, determined to deal with this news at a later time, she opened the door but stopped. Realized she couldn't just ignore the fact of her sister still being alive.

"Agathon?"

"Yes, Your Majesty?"

"Can you get a message"—she faced Agathon again—"to Straton the Devourer?"

"I'm sure I can. I'm assuming you don't want it to be from you."

"Exactly. Not from me."

"What kind of message?"

"The location of my family."

Agathon frowned. "My lady?"

Beatrix shrugged. "A sacrifice, I know. But if I can't kill my sister . . . I definitely need to distract her. Don't you think?"

"Uh . . ."

"And I'm assuming the death of her entire family will do just that. Don't you agree?"

"Yes. I'm sure that tragedy will . . . distract her."

"Exactly. So see me after we say our vows and all that. I'll want the message to go out immediately. Understand?"

"Yes . . . Your Majesty."

"Excellent. Now, tell me honestly, Agathon . . ." She grabbed the skirt of her gown and held it out, away from her body. "What do you think of my dress? Maila picked it out herself. It's not really to my taste."

Agathon's mouth briefly dropped open but he recovered quickly. "You look amazing in it, Your Majesty."

"Hhmmh. I guess." She took another look down at the gown. "The color white is fine, but I've never been a true fan of lace."

CHAPTER 20

It was when Keran brought out the ale that things got bad. The way the Smythe sisters had been bickering all day, Caid had assumed he'd have to separate them at some point during the night, but it was Gemma and Keran who got into it. It probably had to do with the fact that Gemma's order had a vow of sobriety while Keran had never made and, according to her, never would make that vow.

Keran drank heartily and expected everyone to join her. Quinn had a few sips but as soon as his eyes watered, Caid and Laila waved the offer away.

Keeley hadn't bothered. Instead, she sketched with a piece of coal on parchment she kept in her travel bag. After they ate and began to get ready to sleep, Caid noticed what she was doing.

"What is that?" he asked.

"A hammer-axe combination weapon. It'll be all steel. Nice, isn't it?"

He had no idea how to tell her that the days of her being a full-time blacksmith were probably over. He'd assumed she already knew this but now . . . he wasn't sure she'd ever get it. As a queen, she'd have much more important things to do with her time than work a forge, but he didn't want to get into that at the moment. He might not even be the one she should "get into that" with.

Then Gemma had declined the offer of ale from her cousin. But she hadn't simply waved the offer away like Caid and Laila. She'd been a bit judgey about it all. With pursed lips and a disappointed frown, she'd asked Keran, "How much do you drink a day anyway, Cousin?"

It was downhill from there.

Before Caid could suggest that they all get some sleep, the first punch was thrown.

At Quinn.

For once, though, his brother hadn't started anything; he'd simply made the mistake of physically placing himself between the arguing cousins. Quinn would never do that if mares were involved, but he didn't have as much experience around humans. He especially didn't have much experience around the Smythe clan.

Unfortunately for Quinn, it was Keran's fist that rammed into his cheek. As a former fighter, she had power behind that move that perhaps the War Monk lacked. Quinn went down hard and, for several long minutes, did not get back up. He wasn't even conscious.

"You idiot!" Gemma screamed after a few shakes didn't wake Caid's brother. "You killed him!"

"Oh, he's fine!" Keran snapped back. "And is it my fault he has a face made of glass?"

"Are you going to help your brother?" Keeley asked Caid.

"You heard Keran . . . he'll be fine."

She snorted and went back to her sketch.

When Gemma and Keran began pushing each other, Caid became worried the argument would escalate. He nudged Keeley with his elbow.

"Hhmhh?"

"You may want to stop them," he suggested.

Keeley glanced up at her kin. "Oy! You two! Stop it."

"Shut up, Keeley!" Gemma snarled back.

Keeley shrugged and went back to her work. "I tried."

Laila leaned around Caid. "Seriously?"

"What?" Keeley asked, oblivious.

"You're going to let them get away with talking to you like that?"

Keeley frowned. "Like what?"

They both stared at her, waiting for her to understand on her own. She needed to learn this sort of thing and they might as well start now.

And . . . it did take a bit. Longer than Caid would have hoped, but when she got it, her grin was wide as she handed him her sketch.

"What's that?" Laila asked, gazing at the drawing.

"Hammer-axe combination weapon. All steel."

"Nice."

Keeley pushed her cousin and sister apart. "That's enough! And you'll do what I tell you."

Keran glanced at Gemma and they both smirked. "We will?"

"You will. Do you know why?"

"You're delusional?" Gemma suggested.

"No, bitch. It's because I'm queen. Me. Keeley! I'm queen. And that means you two slags have to do what I say. So when I give you twats an order, you have to listen to me. Understand?"

"Well . . ."

"Actually . . ."

"Samuel!" Keeley barked.

The boy had been off tending to the humans' horses, but as soon as he heard Keeley, he ran to her and dropped to one knee before her.

"Yes, my queen?" he asked, his head bowed.

Laila quickly covered her mouth with her hand to stop from laughing, but Caid was too impressed to laugh.

Keeley dramatically pointed at Samuel for the benefit of her sister and cousin before she asked him, "Did you take care of the gray mare?"

"Yes, Your Majesty. She lets me take off her saddle now and didn't try to kick me this time when I brushed her coat. She didn't want any of the grain we have for the other horses, though. She'd rather graze."

"Excellent. Thank you, Samuel. When we have a more secure situation, I will reward you with something like a title. Would you like to be an . . . earl . . . or whatever?"

"As you wish, Your Majesty."

"Thank you, Samuel. You may go."

He got to his feet, bowed to her, and ran back to the horses, where he seemed most comfortable.

"See?" Keeley asked Gemma and Keran. "The benefit of following my orders?"

"We'll get to kneel to you—"

"—and brush your horse?"

"Yes! And you'll be happy to do it. Do you know why?"

"Because you're queen?" Gemma asked.

"Yes! Now, if you'll excuse me . . . I'll take first watch."

Laila's head dropped as Keeley proudly marched off.

"She doesn't realize she doesn't have to take first watch?" Laila asked him. "You know . . . because she's queen."

"We'll have to ease her into this."

"You're right. You're right." Laila pointed at Gemma and Keran. "And you two," she called to them, "at least when we're around outsiders, attempt to treat her like the queen she literally is. Think you can do that?"

"We can do it," Gemma admitted. "We just won't like it."

Keeley nocked an arrow and pulled back the bowstring. She wasn't hunting anything, she just wanted to get used to using Laila's bow. The centaurs made amazing bows and she wanted to make her own. Woodworking wasn't one of her specialties but every Smythe knew how to make bows and arrows. It was a good part of her business. But there was always a way to do even better. . . .

Keeley lowered the weapon, dropped the arrow to the ground, and pressed her free hand to her chest.

It was like waves crashing over her. The despair. The pain. The memories.

"It's gone," she heard herself whisper, not feeling as if she was actually talking but knowing that she was. "It's all gone."

"Keeley?"

Caid came toward her. He saw her bent over at the waist and quickly shifted to his human form. He went to her. She felt his hands on her shoulders.

"Keeley, what is it? What's wrong?"

"It's gone," she repeated. "Everything's gone."

"What are you talking about?"

"The town. My business. It's all—"

He closed his eyes. "I assumed you just didn't want to talk about it."

"When I woke up, all I thought about was Beatrix. I couldn't think past her and worrying about my parents and the children ... and Beatrix. And Gemma only told me what had happened *after* I'd been stabbed. But it is, isn't it? The Witch Queen told me. The town. My business. All of it. It's gone."

"I'm so sorry, Keeley." Caid stroked her back with one hand.

Keeley held up one finger and pulled away from him. She walked behind a tree and vomited. Everything she'd eaten in the last hour came out of her in one big rush. When she was done, she was sweating and shaking, but her head was a bit clearer.

She came from around the tree and Caid waited for her with his water flask. Laila now stood beside him.

"You all right, Keeley?"

She didn't want to answer Laila. She wasn't in the mood to discuss this with her. Or Gemma. Or Keran.

And those feelings must have been on her face because Caid grabbed Keeley's hand. "Take first watch," he ordered his sister, dragging Keeley behind him.

He took her deeper into the trees until he found an ancient one with an extremely large trunk. He pulled Keeley around it and sat down, tugging her until she sat next to him. He gave her his flask and she poured some water into her mouth without drinking from it. She swished it around and then spit it out. Next she took a long drink.

"Thank you," she said when she was done. "How could I forget what the Witch Queen told me? How could I forget any of that?"

"Your mind handled what it could at the time. Waking up remembering that your sister had attempted to kill you would have been more than most could handle. The rest came when you were ready."

"All those people. Everyone in town. Their homes, their businesses, all gone. And it's all my fault—"

"It's not your fault!" Caid snapped, surprising her. He'd never snapped at her before. At least not that she could remember. "It's Beatrix's fault. She started this, Keeley. All of it. The only thing you can do now is attempt to fix it, but you can't keep blaming yourself."

"But—"

"I won't *let* you blame yourself. Is that better?"

Keeley raised her knees and rested her elbows on them. She lowered her head so she could rub her forehead with her fingers.

"Maybe Gemma's right," Keeley wondered. "Maybe I do need to kill Beatrix."

"We both know you can't do that."

"I can't do that." Keeley smiled, realizing they'd said those sentences at the same time.

"And I understand it," Caid continued. "She's your sister. You love her, even if she doesn't deserve it. But as queen . . . you won't have to kill her. You can have her exiled to one of the strict religious orders. Let her become the nun you thought Gemma was."

Keeley let her head fall back, resting it against the tree's giant trunk. She blew out a breath and said, "You're right."

"I know."

She smiled again. "Are all centaurs as confident as you?"

"Yes. We're centaurs. We're amazing."

They sat silent until Keeley asked, "Do you have to go back to camp yet?"

"To what?" Caid asked. "To a whining Quinn? Your vicious demon wolves that are, last I looked, brutally ripping apart an ox for their dinner . . . and entertainment? Your bickering cousin and sister? Or perhaps I should get back to the needy Samuel?"

"Don't pick on Samuel. He performed just like I needed him to."

"Excellent point."

Keeley placed her head on his shoulder. She was starting to enjoy this particular move too much. It comforted her as little else did.

Keeley let out a long breath. "I'm going to rebuild the town," she promised.

"I know." And she heard no doubt in his words. No placating. "You could have Archibald design it."

"What?"

"He can manage the building of it. He's mad, but he is talented."

"That's such a good idea. Giving him something to focus on actually helps with his crazy. It quiets his mind."

"See? All easily fixed."

Eventually, after a long, comfortable silence, she felt Caid's shoulder move beneath her and she thought he was trying to get away or get comfortable . . . but then she felt his arm slip around her shoulders and he pulled her closer into his body.

Shockingly happy about this new position, Keeley snuggled closer to him. She rested her head on his chainmail-covered chest and he rested his jaw on the top of her head. And they stayed like that until Keeley fell asleep.

Caid woke up to find the face of the War Monk close to his.

"What are you doing?" Caid asked.

"You need to get up. We need to get on the road."

"You couldn't tell me that from over there?"

"Could have. Didn't."

"Anything else?"

"You need to wake up my sister."

Now he was annoyed. "Wake her up yourself."

"Okay." Gemma stretched her arm across Caid and tapped her sister. He hadn't realized Keeley had been asleep on his chest.

Her head snapped up. "What?" she demanded. "What's wrong?"

"Nothing," Gemma replied. "We just need to get moving." She stood, hands on her hips. "Time to face the day, my friends!"

Caid glared up at her. "I hate you and your cheery personality."

"So does Keran. That reminds me! I think I'll go sing her awake!"

Keeley pressed her hands against Caid's chest and levered herself up. She smiled down at him. "Sorry."

"For what?"

"Trapping you here."

"I'm never trapped where I don't want to be." He sat up, pushed her hair off her shoulder. "Feel better?"

"I do." Keeley sat on the ground, facing him. "It was Straton the Devourer who came for Beatrix, yes?"

"Yes."

"And the one who destroyed my town?"

"Yes."

"Okay." She stood. "Caid?"

"Mhmm?" he replied, also standing.

"Thank you so much for being kind when I needed it," she said with great sincerity, her suddenly shy gaze on the ground. "It's meant a lot to me."

"Despite the fact it's all your fault and we're all going to die?"

Her head snapped up, her gaze wide. They stared at each other until her eyes narrowed and her lips pursed.

"I hate you," she said, walking back toward camp. "Can't even give me five seconds of wallowing!"

"We don't have time for your wallowing, Your Majesty."

"Stop calling me that!"

He chuckled but the sound faded when the demon wolves appeared all around the tree Caid and Keeley had been sleeping against, trotting after the new queen. They'd been there all night, he was guessing, watching out for Keeley.

And, in no uncertain terms, *freaking* Caid the unholy hells out!

CHAPTER 21

They stood in front of a large cave and Keeley couldn't help but gawk at the stone barrier blocking their entry. She wished her uncle Archie was here to see it. They weren't double doors that could be opened by large men pulling them. They weren't boulders that went to the roof to prevent entrance. It was simply one stone door with no design or markings to let one know what lay beyond.

Laila, in her centaur form, which she'd stayed in for most of their few days traveling here, moved forward and yelled out, "I am Laila of the Scarred Earth Clan! I demand entry to see your king!"

In silence their small traveling party watched as that stone door rolled up and back! Keeley's mouth dropped.

"How . . . ?"

"Dwarves are not just good with iron and fire," Caid replied. "At least half their population are stonemasons instead of blacksmiths."

"I really do wish Uncle Archie was here to see this."

The gigantic door—taller than hundred-year-old trees that reached the sky—opened completely and they rode inside. Once they were all in, the door rolled back down, slamming shut behind them.

They were briefly in total darkness before a few of the centaurs lit torches and they all began their long march deep into the mountains.

Keeley couldn't say she felt comfortable. The darkness around them made the ceilings feel closer than they probably were, stretching her nerves. Making her want to see the sky and the trees and grass. Not so much rock and, ahead of them where the torches' light did not reach, blackness.

Even worse, the loyal wolves had to stay behind, unable to cross some barrier the dwarves had put up. As they had tried to run past her toward the mountain entrance, they'd suddenly disappeared, reappearing a few seconds later one hundred or so feet behind them all.

"See this?" Gemma had asked pointing at some blood-covered totems built around the entrance. "These are to protect this area from pure evil." Gemma gazed at her. "And your wolves could not get beyond this point. Does that tell you anything?"

Keeley had smiled and replied, "No!" before riding on.

But now, deep in this dark place, she wished her wolves were with her. She'd gotten used to their presence. Caid, however, did walk beside her in his centaur form. Always near but never crowding her. She appreciated that.

Finally, the centaurs stopped and Laila called out again, "I am Laila of the Scarred Earth Clan! I demand entry to see your king!"

When the door opened this time, Keeley couldn't help but grin. The light was bright, there was plenty of activity inside, and she no longer felt lost in the dark.

"Dismount," Laila ordered the humans on horses, and the centaurs shifted to their human forms.

"Dwarves find our true selves a hostile challenge," Caid whispered to her.

"Being yourselves is a hostile challenge?"

"Apparently yes."

"Huh." Keeley placed the reins around the pommel of her saddle and started walking, the gray mare following behind her without needing to be led.

"You trust her not to run?" Quinn asked.

"She can do what she wants," Keeley replied. "She's not my horse."

Quinn studied the gray mare and the saddle on her back. "If she's not your horse, then what is she?"

"A mother looking for justice."

They were in a city. A city filled with dwarves and the homes and businesses of dwarves. They weren't the only humans or centaurs inside the city walls but none of the humans there looked like they were from the Hill Lands. They appeared to be more like traveling merchants looking for dwarven iron or steel to sell. Not that Keeley blamed them. Dwarven steel was worth plenty, and weapons or other items already made with dwarven steel cost a lot of gold.

Keeley had only been lucky enough to work with dwarven iron a few times and it had always been a bloody delight. But there were few who could afford such weapons. She'd actually only done such work when royals had come to her with the dwarven iron already purchased, asking her to make them a sword or spear.

She wondered if these people knew another, easier way into the dwarf stronghold. She envied them . . . being able to avoid that road into darkness.

Eventually, they made their way through the city and to the massive front steps that led to the Dwarf King's castle.

They stood at the bottom of the steps and, yet again, Laila called out, "I am Laila of the Scarred Earth Clan! I demand entry to see your king!"

Keran rubbed her forehead. "How many times are we going to have to hear her yell that?"

"Perhaps, Cousin," Gemma softly suggested, "you shouldn't drink so much in the evenings."

"And maybe you should shut the fuck up, bastard monk!"

"That's enough," Keeley growled, finding her growls worked better on Keran and Gemma than her higher-pitched, snappy voice. "Let's just get through this."

Her kin nodded and fell silent, allowing Keeley to focus on her sudden onset of panic.

She'd be meeting the Dwarf King. Her. Keeley Smythe. She didn't know how to think about that. She'd never thought she'd meet a dwarf, much less their king. But here she was. About to be introduced to him as Queen Keeley.

She'd laugh if she wasn't afraid she'd end up vomiting.

Three loud bangs rang out from inside the castle. Caid swiped his hand over Keeley's back before he joined his sister and the pair headed up the stairs. The rest fell in behind them, Keeley doing her best not to start panting. She sometimes panted when she was excited and/or terrified.

They made it up the stairs, and there they met three armored and armed dwarf warriors.

The one in the middle rammed the end of his steel spear against the floor.

Laila nodded at him. "Unroch."

"Laila of the Scarred Earth," Unroch growled back, his voice lower than Keeley had ever heard. "Good to see you again." He glanced at Caid but didn't speak to him. Keeley sensed they had a past.

He turned and headed inside; their travel party followed. The throne room was filled with dwarves. Almost all of them attired either in stunning armor or exquisite chainmail. Keeley wanted to run around and touch each piece of metalwork, getting a closer look so she could see how it was made. Could she buy her own? For her size? A queen needed stunning armor, did she not?

Gods, Keeley had so much more to learn when it came to being a blacksmith.

They walked down a long stretch of black cloth until they reached the throne of King Mundric. He sat upon his metal throne and Keeley wanted nothing more than to shove him out of the way so she could take a long look at it. How had they made it? It appeared to be built from a single sheet of steel but she knew better. The seams were just invisible. But she wanted to find them, look at them, then ask a thousand questions about how the dwarves did that and what kind of iron they used and—

"You need to pay attention," Gemma snarled low against her ear, "and stop staring at their bloody throne!"

Keeley cringed, knowing her sister was right. She didn't realize she'd already been introduced to the king until Laila cleared her throat.

She looked away from that amazing throne and saw that Caid and Laila were staring right at her, waiting for her. Actually . . . so was everyone in the throne room.

"King Mundric," she said, nodding at him.

Now Keeley noticed that King Mundric had vicious scars all along his right side. Burn scars, starting from the right side of his head, all the way down and disappearing under his armor. But she guessed that those scars kept going since his badly burned right hand was wrapped tightly around a steel walking stick.

He sat on the edge of his throne, gazing at her with his left eye since his right was damaged, his left arm resting on his knee.

Mundric was an extremely wide dwarf. Wide. And despite the scars, muscular. His neck was like that tree trunk she and Caid had slept against their first night of this trip.

After gazing at her, he motioned to Laila and Caid with his left hand. Just a small wave, but they seemed to understand. They gestured to the others, who all moved off to the side so Keeley stood alone in front of the king—and everyone else.

Now she really did want to vomit.

Before she could choke down the bile building in the back of her throat, the king rammed the end of his walking stick against the floor and his dwarven guard moved in front of her entire travel party and locked their spears in such a way that none of them could get to Keeley if she needed help.

"Dammit, Mundric! What are you doing?" Laila demanded, shifting back to her centaur form and causing all the dwarves behind her to make a mad run for it before she could start kicking them with her back legs.

"Quiet, woman!" Mundric barked, his voice low like Unroch's.

"I'm not a woman, I'm a centaur! And if you betray our alliance, the tribal lords will find out about it."

Mundric ignored Laila, who was pushing against the spears that blocked her, and motioned Keeley to move closer.

She didn't get too close, making sure not to go up the few stairs to his throne. He had armed guards on either side of him.

"So . . . you're the Blacksmith Queen."

That confused Keeley a bit. "Well . . . I'm a blacksmith and now a queen. But Blacksmith Queen implies that I'm queen of all the blacksmiths, which I'm not. But yes."

Now the king appeared confused and he glanced to his left at Unroch, who could only shrug.

With a quick shake, the king focused on her again. "You brought a War Monk with you? Was that to threaten us?"

"No. She's my sister. That's Gemma. And be glad. I thought she was a nun. Can you imagine any woman giving up her life to—"

"*Do not start that again!*" Gemma bellowed at her.

Caid briefly closed his eyes. They were all going to die, but at least they'd die in such a way that the tale would be told for ages.

A dwarf guard pressed the tip of his endlessly sharp spear against Laila's throat and warned, "Go back to your human form, horsey, or I'll run ya through."

Caid heard Quinn growl, always defensive when their sister was even looked at the wrong way, much less actively threatened. But he caught Quinn by his hair and kept control of him before he could shift.

"Stop. Think. For once, Brother."

Caid's words calmed Quinn down but the way he sucked his tongue against his teeth told Caid that with even a tiny bit more provocation Quinn might start causing more damage to the dwarf-centaur alliance than anyone could imagine.

Laila shifted to her human form and the spear returned to its locked position with another spear, no longer close to her throat. Caid let out a breath and moved his attention back to the king and Keeley.

"So, you *are* a blacksmith," the king was saying to Keeley.

"I am."

"Have you made anything legendary?"

"Not that I know of." She pulled her hammer from the leather holder strapped to her back. "Made this hammer, though. Love me hammer."

The king studied it from where he sat on the throne. "It's cute," he finally said.

Caid grimaced and Gemma let out an "Uh-oh."

Keeley slammed the head into the floor—the sound ringing around the stone throne room—and leaned her weight on the handle.

"What's that supposed to mean?" she snapped.

"I think," the king said, "you're just tellin' everyone you're a blacksmith, so you can claim to be one of the people. Humans are stupid like that. They'll believe anything."

"I don't lie, King Mundric. I have no reason to. I'm from a long line of blacksmiths. Some of the best blacksmiths in history."

When the entire room erupted into laughter, Caid whispered to his brother, "Get ready to move. Preferably before she starts killing everybody."

Because Keeley took her blacksmithing more seriously than almost anything. Anything except her family, of course.

"I don't see what's so funny!" Keeley barked out, looking around the room.

"If you're such a mighty blacksmith family," Unroch annoyingly suggested, "you should know the Old Songs."

"Old Songs?" Laila desperately whispered at them. "What bloody Old Songs?"

"The songs we were taught as children," Gemma whispered back. "They're blacksmith songs."

"Of course I do," Keeley replied, with way more confidence than Caid was feeling. Just because her family of human blacksmiths had their "old songs" didn't mean they were the same Old Songs as the dwarves'. Especially when the dwarves had their own gods-damn language.

Mundric grinned and it was not pretty.

"Then sing one," he ordered.

Keeley frowned and Caid felt his heart drop into his stomach.

"I'm not much of a singer," she confessed. "How about if I recite the words?"

"Anyone can learn the words. The question is whether you know the words *and* the tune. So *sing*."

Keeley let out a breath, bent her neck one way, then the other. Both times her body making loud cracking noises.

She cleared her throat. Once. Twice.

"In times long by when blood did pourrrr!"

And . . . oy. She hadn't been joking. She had a *terrible* singing voice. And the song was not made for bad singers. Because it was slow and a bit boring. But Keeley, gods bless her. She kept going.

"A hammer and anvil, I did score.
A hammer and anvil, I did roar!
To bless the gods, the gods, the war gods
I'm covered in blood from war gods!
For the blood of war is our way!"

"Ow," Laila muttered, sticking her finger in her ear and wiggling it around after Keeley had hit that last high note.

Caid thought it was over. But it wasn't. Because the tempo changed. Abruptly. Into a fast-moving jig that didn't sound any better than the earlier dirge.

"I used my hammer
To beat that iron, finesse that steel
Make that spear, craft that bow
For the blood of war is our way!"

The king rammed his spear against the floor again and Keeley stopped singing—thank the gods!—as he struggled to get to his feet. Unroch attempted to help but the king angrily waved him off.

Once he stood, he made his slow way down the three stairs to the black cloth and walked along it until he reached Keeley. While she stood much taller than the Dwarf King, he was definitely wider. Caid couldn't figure out if he *wanted* to see them in a fight or not. If nothing else, a fight between those two would definitely be interesting.

When Mundric only stared at her, not speaking, Keeley cleared her throat once more and reminded him, "I told you I was not the best singer."

The king raised his walking stick and Caid readied himself to attack. Because he looked as if he was about to strike her.

But he didn't. Instead, he sang out, "In times long by when blood did pourrrr!"

"Oh, gods," Laila gasped. "We're going to have to hear that thing again." Only this time, it was two equally bad voices singing.

And they did. From the very beginning, they both sang that stupid song. Only now, the king's musicians joined in and the other dwarves sang along. It was a nightmare!

But only in the sense that none of their group wanted to hear that gods-damn song again. Other than that, the whole thing couldn't have gone better. Especially when the king and Keeley began to dance with each other, hooking arms, and moving around to the "old song." The king couldn't move well but Keeley kept that in mind, giving him ample time and keeping things loose.

"Huh," Quinn said to them, sounding shocked. "I did *not* see that coming."

CHAPTER 22

They were released and Laila had to fight her urge to slap Mundric's face.

Rude bastard. To take her and her brothers prisoner while rudely "testing" their choice of queen.

Laila knew her mother would have handled things brilliantly—as she would no doubt remind Laila as soon as she heard about this affront—but Laila wasn't sure what to do. She felt repercussions were necessary, but she also knew they needed armies at their back or they'd have no chance against Marius and Beatrix.

So, when Laila saw Quinn reaching out to grab one of the dwarves to slam him into the wall, she slapped his arm down.

"Not until I give you my signal. And if I were you, Brother, I wouldn't expect that anytime soon."

Quinn gave an annoyed growl. "They dare treat our guests this way? After we've promised Keeley and the others safe passage?"

"Keeley wasn't the one in danger. We were."

"Meaning what?"

"That our job is simply to keep her alive. The rest are expendable. And trust me . . . they all know it."

Mundric took them to his favorite forge for a tour. A tour Caid didn't need or want, but the fascination and joy on Keeley's face made it all worth it. At least for him.

The forge was, to say the least, immense. Giant chains and cuffs were currently being made from dwarven steel by several of the king's best blacksmiths.

Keeley grabbed one of the enormous cuffs and lifted it, studying the entire thing, which was at least four times the size of her head.

"What, exactly, is this for?" she asked.

"I don't know," the king admitted. "The wood elves ordered them. I do know they sometimes have to deal with trolls, which is probably why they constantly need new sets."

"Interesting latch mech—"

"My wife," the king cut in and Keeley dropped the cuff back on the steel table. It wasn't until the metal piece landed that Caid realized how heavy it was. It landed with a brutal clang and shook the entire thick table.

Keeley faced Mundric and ended up gawking at a dwarf female.

The two females walked around each other, their heads tilting from one side to the other. They sized each other up until Mundric said, "Queen Keeley of the Hill Lands, this is my wife, Queen Vulfegundis."

Keeley gazed down at the short but powerfully built dwarf female who wore a sleeveless leather tunic, leather leggings, leather boots, the brand of the dwarven blacksmith guild on her shoulder, and had a hammer strapped to her back. A much *bigger* hammer than Keeley wielded.

Matching grins spread across the faces of both females and they nodded at each other.

"You two hungry?" the king asked.

And, completely by coincidence, they said together, "I could eat."

The feast was a little off-putting only because the roasted meats that were brought out still had their heads and not all of them were animals Keeley knew. But she was grateful nothing appeared to have once been human. So that was good.

Keeley sat to the right of the king and his wife sat on his left, across from her. And they spent the entire meal discussing blacksmith techniques and blacksmith history. Dwarven history that even Keeley didn't know. It was, in Keeley's estimation, the most splendid dining experience she'd ever had with those who were not family.

Once the meal was finished, the king demanded more Old Songs. But this time, he pointed at Gemma, who had not spoken once during the meal. And Keeley knew why—she didn't trust anyone.

"You. War Monk. You two are sisters, so you should know the Old Songs too."

Gemma looked up from her steel cup of water. "I do. But I have no desire to sing on command."

"I thought you wanted our help, Monk," Vulfegundis said, pushing her short black hair off her face.

"Yes."

"And yet you expect us to hand over our armies to people we don't know, of a race we don't particularly like?"

"*Our* armies?"

"We rule together. And it's together we choose who we help. And my husband knows I'm not much a fan of . . . monks."

"It's true," the king said, smiling lovingly at his wife. "So if I were you, Monk . . . I'd sing."

Keeley thought for sure her sister would have long forgotten all those songs their mother had sung to them since they were in their cribs. But then, Gemma sang one of the saddest Old Songs ever, about the death of a blacksmith's loyal hound. Her voice was crystal clear and beautiful and by the time she was done, Keeley, the king, his wife, and every dwarf in the throne room was openly sobbing. The centaurs, however, were not. Although they did look disturbed. Samuel, of course, was crying. And Keran was asleep, most likely waiting for the dinner wine to turn into hearty dwarven ale.

"That was beautiful, War Monk," the king said to Gemma with great respect, using his fist to wipe his wet eyes.

"Thank you, Your Majesty." She turned to Keeley, her mouth opening to say something, but when she saw the tears, she stopped. "Woman . . . are you crying?"

"I love that song," Keeley sobbed out.

With a wave of her hand, Gemma started to stand, but Keeley asked through her tears, "Do you remember Butch?"

Gemma froze. "Keeley, stop."

"He was our mother's dog," she explained to the king. "He

went with her to her forge every day. And walked her home every night."

Gemma leaned back in her chair, her own eyes now filled with tears. "Keeley, I said stop."

"He took care of us and watched out for all us kids—and then one day . . . one day!"

Keeley looked at Gemma and together they cried out, "*Butch!*"

Caid watched with his mouth open as a battle-ready blacksmith and her murderous War Monk sister sobbed over a dead dog. It wasn't just sobbing either. It was hysterical sobbing. The kind of sobbing one saves for finding one's father dead. Not because of a dog.

Next to him, Laila rubbed her nose and immediately Caid barked, "You better not be—"

"Are you kidding?" she demanded, eyes dry. "My nose is itchy."

A short time after the sobbing finally stopped, the dwarves brought out their ale. That's when Keran snapped awake and, out of nowhere, began to sing another Old Song. This one was a jig from the start and all the way through. The sisters and cousin started off the dancing and the dwarves happily joined in. Now, all of them were singing.

That went on for quite a few hours until almost everyone passed out except the on-duty guards—who didn't drink at all—the king, Queen Vulfegundis, Laila, Quinn, Keeley, and Gemma.

They didn't head off to bed, though; instead all of them sat down at the dining table once again.

"If I give you my armies," the king haggled with Keeley, "what will you give me?"

"My armies—"

"Which you don't currently have," Queen Vulfegundis tossed in.

"—will be there for your wars, of course. And we protect the Amichai Mountains from any raiders. Human or otherwise. All this territory will belong only to the tribes. I'll make it a royal edict. And if anyone disobeys it . . . they'll be beheaded."

"Is that it?"

"You're getting a royal edict out of this—what more do you want?"

"That's a nice hammer," the king noted.

"You're not getting my hammer," Keeley quickly said, making the king laugh. "And you said it was cute."

"I thought my granddaughter would like it. She's nearly eight seasons now."

"Oh, that's very nice," Keeley coldly replied.

"I want something," the queen suddenly interjected, her gaze locked on Keeley.

"And what's that?"

When the queen smirked, Caid's ears twitched and Laila sat up a little straighter in her chair.

"I want gold," she finally announced.

Keeley's eyes rolled and she sarcastically replied, "I'm a little low on gold at the moment. New queen and all that."

"Sichar's gold."

Keeley's mouth fell open and Gemma abruptly leaned forward, her arms slamming down on the table. Both sisters openly gawked at the queen. Even Keran reacted . . . a little. She sat up from her spot on the floor where she'd passed out an hour before, yelled "Sichar!" then dropped back down and started snoring.

"You can't be serious," Keeley hissed.

"More serious than you know. You come to us," Vulfegundis barked, her mood suddenly changing, "you make demands—"

"I asked nicely!"

"—bring your blood-soaked War Monk sister—"

"*She sang for you!*"

"—and you offer us nothing except an army you don't have and that worthless hammer!"

"I didn't offer my hammer," Keeley growled out.

"You want our armies, bitch, you get us Sichar's gold."

Keeley looked at her sister and lifted her arms, as if she was showing the king and queen their own throne room. "Where?" she demanded. "Where's Sichar's gold? Because if I had Sichar's gold, *I'd be making Sichar's weapons!*" she ended on a powerful bellow that brought the king's guard closer to the table.

"I know where there's Sichar's gold."

As one, they all looked down to the end of the table where Quinn sat. He scratched his head. "At least, I've heard rumors."

"Oh, it's no rumor, centaur," Mundric said. "They have Sichar's gold."

Fed up, Caid demanded, "What is Sichar's gold?"

Keeley looked at him now with mouth agape.

"What?" he demanded.

"I'm so disappointed in you right now," she replied. And he knew she was very serious.

"Sichar is one of our most powerful gods," Mundric explained. "And, many centuries ago, he gave us a special kind of gold. We and specially trained blacksmiths of other races are the only ones who can use it to create weapons."

"And?" Caid pushed.

"The last of it was stolen from us and we want it back."

"And you want *me* to get it for you?" Keeley asked.

"You're going there anyway."

"I am?"

"The rumor," Quinn said, "is that Sichar's gold is with the wood elves."

Keeley tossed her hands in the air. "I don't even know the wood elves. Have never met them. Know nothing about them. Why in hells would they give the gold to me?"

"And why can't you get it yourself?" Gemma asked. "Don't you all have an alliance with the elves?"

"They say they don't have it," the king replied.

"They're lying," the queen snarled.

"But unless the dwarves want to start a war," Caid explained for Keeley's benefit, "they can't search the wood elf territory to find it."

"Exactly," Vulfegundis said on a sigh, before pushing back from the table. "If you get us the gold, Blacksmith Queen . . . you get our army."

"I was also hoping to get the wood elf army, though," Keeley reminded them.

The king and queen laughed at that, Vulfegundis taking her husband's arm before they headed toward their royal bedrooms.

"Yeah," the queen said, still laughing, "good luck with that, human."

Once they were gone, Keeley cracked her neck, a sure sign to Caid that she was ridiculously stressed.

"Well?" Keeley pushed, looking at Laila.

"You have two choices, my friend. Try to get the elf army *or* find the fucking gold." Laila shook her head. "Sadly . . . there are no other options."

Keeley rubbed her eyes. "And they were both so nice to me all night! I thought they liked me."

"They definitely liked you," Quinn said, standing up from the table.

"How do you figure?"

"You and your sister yelled at the king and queen of the Amichai dwarves . . . and you're *still* breathing. Trust me, blacksmith. They *liked* you."

When Keeley looked at Caid for confirmation, he shrugged and admitted, "He's absolutely right. I thought we'd be rolling your head out of here."

CHAPTER 23

Straton the Devourer attacked their town before the suns had risen above the distant horizon. Such a sudden, brutal attack—the mercenary army they'd all been hearing about for weeks yanking their gate doors open and riding in—that the town's guards didn't have time to do anything but be immediately slaughtered.

She just happened to be up so early because she and her sister Efa had to set up the stall where they sold eggs and whole chickens from their farm.

Most of the other sellers had panicked when those mercenaries came riding in, hacking away and shooting down good, honest people with their arrows. But for some reason, she didn't panic. She simply grabbed her younger-by-a-year sister and they ran until they found a good hiding place.

Once, ages ago, these lands were ruled over by rulers called "jarls" rather than kings. The old jarl's longhouse still stood despite the fact that the rest of the town had been made over into something much more modern to accommodate the travelers and traders who came in off the river behind them. This was a port town and, she now realized, a perfect place for the Devourer to set up a new home base since Prince Marius still had control over the Old King's castle. But the lord who ruled this town and his advisors thought they'd be safe from an attack by Straton because they were "friends" of the former Old King.

She assumed they quickly learned that wasn't true when they

were dragged from their homes and immediately hung from scaffolds until they were dead.

The raid was short but devastating. Afterward, all the town's inhabitants were dragged into its center. Straton stood in front of them, informed them that this was now *his* town and all would be well as long as they were "nice" to him and his men. While he gave this speech, the bodies of their town leaders swayed from the scaffolding.

He also promised that things would remain "normal" but soon after, many of the younger women were separated from their families and forced to one of the pubs to "work." She knew what that work would entail. Something she didn't want for her sisters or herself.

Yet the most horrifying thing that she and Efa saw from the safety of their hiding place was when one of the Ó Broin sisters was dragged kicking and screaming before Straton.

"Here she is, my lord," one of the mercenaries said. "The local witch."

It was true. She was a local witch, but she wasn't the only one. All of the Ó Broin sisters were witches. But they weren't like witches in the big covens. They were just nature witches who made basic potions and healing balms from herbs and small spells. They were not witches with enough power to take down a whole city or even a small battle unit. They just helped locals with their basic aches and pains and births. That was it.

But it seemed Straton was expecting more. Perhaps the loss of the Amhuinn Witches was a bigger issue for him than it was for the rest of the Old King's sons. If he thought that one of the Ó Broins could help him with his battle for the throne . . . he was sure to be disappointed.

Unfortunately for his captive, he probably wouldn't know that for a long time.

Frightening-looking cuffs were placed on the witch's wrists and Straton dragged her off to the longhouse where he planned to live until he became the Old King.

"What should we do?" Efa whispered to her. But what could they do? Nothing. Nothing but hide.

When she saw their chance, she grabbed her sister and led her to the hidden tunnels under the town and prayed that this occupation would end soon. But she had the feeling that the gods weren't listening. Not anymore.

Beatrix sat in the smaller throne and waited for this waste of her precious time to end.

She was trapped under a fur cape that felt as if it weighed ten thousand pounds while a priest walked around her in a circle, swinging that gold jar from its long chain so blasted incense slid into her nose. She'd already sneezed twelve times since this ridiculousness had begun.

Initially she'd amused herself by staring into the audience of royals watching the proceedings and wondering how many of them were planning to betray her. When that grew tiresome, she tried to guess which she'd end up beheading for some little infraction she'd come up with.

But soon she had to stop because her gaze kept falling on the Dowager Queen, who insisted on indicating to Beatrix that she should smile. But Beatrix hadn't worked this hard to be here so she could smile when she didn't feel like it.

After at least two hours—two hours of this dreck!—they put the gold and gem-encrusted crown on her head, a scepter in one hand and an orb in the other.

There were words spoken and she repeated them. And as the suns set, Beatrix was finally announced "the undoubted queen of the Hill Lands."

She was then forced into another gown chosen by the Dowager Queen and the festivities began. King Marius—thankfully—found himself a pretty young virgin to amuse himself with and Beatrix was about to slip away from the revelers in the main hall so she could go to her room and get some much-needed work done.

But before she could—and as the royal attendants became more and more drunk and outrageous—Duke Gennadius decided to yell across the room to Marius, "And what about your remaining brothers, my *king?*"

It wasn't the question that caught her attention. It was the way he'd said "king." There was a tone to it she didn't like. A sarcasm.

Of course, Marius, drunk as well and deep into the mortified virgin's cleavage, was completely oblivious.

"They will be hunted down and killed, one by one, my friend!" Marius yelled back to the delight and cheers of the court.

"And the other queen?"

There it was. Proving to Beatrix that the duke wasn't drunk at all and that her sister had already become a problem. Just as she'd always known she would be.

Beatrix glanced behind her at Agathon and gave a small nod. He lowered his gaze and quickly disappeared behind the satin curtains that hid the hallway exit.

"There is no other queen!" Marius replied, still oblivious. "The only queen of these lands sits by my side."

Marius gestured to his left but quickly realized it was his mother who sat next to him. Squinting, he looked down the length of the table until he spied Beatrix.

"I mean . . . there she is! My beau—" He cleared his throat. "My very handsome bride and your undoubted Queen Beatrix."

"But the Witches of Amhuinn also named her sister as queen. Will she be queen of other territories? Perhaps you'll share the Hill Lands with her."

"She will be queen of her gravesite," Marius shot back. "That pretender will never wear the crown; she will never sit on the throne."

"Rumor has it that she has already gotten the backing of the Amichai tribes. What if they come from the mountains to be her army?"

Marius gazed drunkenly at Duke Gennadius and managed only to repeat, "But *I* am king."

Panic and insubordination. Beatrix watched it spread among the royals in the hall like a fast-moving plague.

The Dowager Queen was quickly on her feet, attempting to soothe with words. But Beatrix knew better. She'd been preparing for all this since she'd read her first scroll on the early Old Kings. She'd only been three at the time and her mother had thought she was merely playing with the parchment, so she kept taking it from

Beatrix's grasp. It had been Keeley who'd realized that Beatrix could read and returned the scroll to her. Then brought her more. Then brought her books.

She'd always be grateful to Keeley for that.

Slowly, Beatrix pushed her chair back and stood.

"My lords," she began, happily cutting off the Dowager Queen's useless speech. "Duke Gennadius. I understand your concerns and I've already put plans into place to address any trouble that may come from the Amichai."

The Dowager Queen's gaze quickly snapped to her but it was Marius who asked, "You have?"

Beatrix moved away from the table and across the floor so that she stood before the table where the duke and his wife sat.

"My lords and ladies, I need all of you to understand that my main concern as your queen is the safety of these lands and of your persons. I, and of course your king, are already ensuring the protection of this great kingdom by increasing our armies. But I wasn't sure that was enough. Your safety and the safety of your families are all that matter to both the king and me."

Beatrix held out her arms and Agathon quickly walked over to her. His head down, hair covering his face and his delightful shame. He handed her the child. A toddler. Duke Gennadius's youngest.

The duke started to stand, but one of the lords beside him caught his arm. The duke's wife covered her mouth, eyes wide over her hands.

"*This* is our true concern," Beatrix announced, holding the babe close. "This innocent, defenseless child is all we care about. Protecting our children from outsiders. From those who don't care about them at all."

Beatrix walked in front of all the tables so that each royal could see the duke's child in her arms and understand the full meaning of her act.

"And to ensure the safety of your children, I had all of them brought here to the castle while you've been attending the coronation." She smiled; not because she had to but because she wanted to when she saw all the panicked looks and heard the terrified gasps. "I just wanted to make sure each child was truly safe, and I knew they'd be perfectly safe here. With us. Your king and queen.

And while our war is going on," she told the lords and ladies who would provide the resources, gold, and soldiers she and Marius would need, "your children will be safe inside these castle walls with us and our *many* soldiers. All of them willing to do anything, absolutely anything to protect these perfect, precious children. They'll have everything they need. Food. Education. And, of course ... love."

She returned to the middle of the hall, between the tables, the child still in her arms.

"So please, everyone, enjoy this wondrous night. Eat, drink, dance! And know that your king and queen are here for you ... and your entire family. Musicians!" she called out. "Play!"

The music began and Beatrix walked out of the hall ... still holding the duke's child.

Once she was out of the view of everyone in the hall, she returned the child to Agathon. "Put it back with the others," she said, brushing her hands against her dress. That child's hands had been sticky. Why had they been so sticky?

"If you need me, I'll be in my privy chamber getting some work done."

"Yes, my queen."

"And Agathon?"

He stopped; faced her.

"Keep an eye on Gennadius. I don't trust him."

"But ..." He glanced down at the child he held. "Do you think he'd really risk—"

"Maybe he's not as attached to the girl since he has a first-born son. It's best not to risk it."

Agathon nodded and rushed off, clutching the child to his breast.

Beatrix cringed a bit. He seemed strangely attached to the child. She might have to get Agathon a wife soon so he could have his own family one day. It was best to give good people the simple things so that they could stay mostly satisfied. She'd hate to have to replace Agathon anytime soon.

That idiot Gennadius, however ... if he kept asking questions about Keeley and whatever she was doing in the Amichai Mountains, Beatrix would find out exactly how attached to his children he truly was.

"What have you done?" Marius demanded from behind her.

Beatrix faced him calmly. "I'm protecting us."

"By holding royal children hostage?"

"Who said they were hostages? They are merely your guests, my king. That's all. Now if you'll excuse me—"

He grabbed her arm and Beatrix slowly looked down at his hand, then—just as slowly—moved her gaze to his face.

She didn't do anything. Beatrix merely waited. And despite his drunkenness, Marius released her rather than push his luck.

Now free to walk away, Beatrix didn't, but said instead, "Everything I do, my lord, I do for the good of this mighty kingdom and for you. Our undoubted king. So please, don't worry. You focus on getting your men ready for battle and I'll focus on the boring day-to-day details. Let *me* take some of that pressure off your back."

With one more smile, Beatrix walked to her privy chamber and the many hours of work ahead.

CHAPTER 24

B ecause the Amichai dwarves lived inside the mountain range, traveling to the Amichai wood elves' territories didn't take long; their home was just a few leagues away in the forests outside the mountains.

But in the end, it didn't matter how long the trip took. Because, much to Laila's surprise, the king absolutely refused to meet with them.

She didn't understand why. The king usually met with centaurs as long as it wasn't Laila's mother. And that was only because Gaira was still friends with the king's former wife. She'd left the king and their children to be with her lover, a dark elven lord. A decision that had made her a hated enemy of the wood elves and their tribal king.

Gaira, however, refused to let anyone—king or peasant—tell her who she could or could not be friends with. Not when she'd known the former elf queen for years before the royal marriage.

So, when the centaurs needed to communicate with the elves, they just didn't involve Gaira. But for some reason the king was making some sort of stand here. Laila simply didn't know why.

While Laila argued with the king's long-eared emissary, Lord Elouan, Keeley and Gemma stood nearby. Keeley examined everything she could see. Ever since they'd entered the elven forest, she'd looked at all around her in wonder and fascination; the very sight of the elven city built directly above them making Keeley smile. Then Laila had told Keeley that the elves had built their kingly city *from* the ancient trees of the forest. That nothing had been cut or torn down, but merely enhanced with old magicks and elven care. The joy that brought to the human had amazed Laila.

Perhaps her friend's enjoyment amazed her because Gemma's reaction was nearly the exact opposite. She seemed unimpressed with everything in the elven city and suspicious of everyone. And the more Elouan spoke, the more suspicious Gemma seemed to become. True, she hadn't said a word, but there were some beings in the world who got their point across with silence. Gemma was definitely one of those beings.

"I simply don't understand," Laila continued to argue with Lord Elouan. "Why does he object to seeing us? Could you at least make that clear?"

Elouan tossed his silky white hair over his shoulder before snidely replying, "I don't have to make anything clear to you. My king has made his decision and he doesn't have to explain to you or anyone else."

"So he didn't tell you either?"

The elf's eyes narrowed the slightest bit. "Watch your tone with me, centaur."

Keeley tugged on Laila's arm. "Let's just go."

But Laila wasn't done. She pointed a finger at Elouan. "Do not forget to whom you speak, elf. I am my mother's heir and—"

"And nothing. You are not your mother, and therefore do not have any of her power here in our lands. As for being her heir . . ." He shrugged. "Life changes."

That's when Gemma cracked her knuckles. Again, she didn't say anything, but the elven royal guards abruptly appeared, standing behind Elouan, their weapons gripped tight.

The emissary glared at Gemma but spoke to Laila. "Is that why you brought this one here? To threaten us?"

Gemma blinked in surprise. "I'm just standing here."

"Like hells you are, human. You're a War Monk, everyone knows what that means."

A small smile curled the corners of Gemma's mouth. "If you truly knew what that meant . . . you'd be much nicer to my friend."

"Or we can just go!" Keeley suddenly announced, motioning with her head. "Really. Let's just go."

"Fine," Laila snapped. "But this, Lord Elouan, will not be forgotten."

They turned to depart, Keeley leading the way back out, but Gemma suddenly tossed over her shoulder, "Give Beatrix our best."

"Oh . . . I will."

Laila and the sisters stopped, Laila spinning around to gawk at the elf. And she saw the truth on his face.

Slamming down her front hoof, she barked, *"You motherfucker!"*

Keeley pressed her hand against Laila's hip. "It's all right," she soothed.

"It is *not* all right."

"It is, Laila. It is. A mistake," Keeley added, glancing at Elouan, "but their right to make it."

"You're threatening me too?" he questioned, smirking. "Like your War Monk sister?"

"My sister didn't threaten you, and neither have I. But an alliance with Beatrix is, in my opinion, a questionable choice on your part. But at the end of the day, also none of our concern. So good luck to you."

Without waiting a moment more, Keeley headed back the way they'd come with her sister beside her; and, after a withering glare in Lord Elouan's direction, Laila followed.

When they reached the rest of their travel party outside the forest, Laila was absolutely livid.

"How dare the king and Elouan take sides with Beatrix without speaking to my mother first!" she angrily announced before either of her brothers could ask her how everything had gone.

"Isn't that what you did with me?" Keeley asked.

"What?"

"You sided with me without speaking to the elves first."

"We don't have to talk to them! We're centaurs!"

"Isn't that what they think about themselves?"

Now, even angrier, Laila slammed her front hoof again and demanded, *"Why are you being so bloody calm about all this?"*

"I guess I just don't see the point of getting upset. Besides, we can still get the dwarf army if we find Sichar's gold."

Laila dropped her arms to her sides. "And how do you suggest we do *that*? If the elves do have it, I doubt they'll give it to us now."

Keeley didn't have a chance to respond because the gray mare was bumping her in the back with her muzzle.

"Did they find it?" she asked the horse, which was when Laila and Gemma glanced at each other. Gods, had Keeley finally lost all reason? Was that why she was so calm? Because of insanity? Not all insane people began tearing their clothes and crying to the heavens. Some became very calm . . . just before they started destroying everything.

The horse didn't seem to respond to Keeley in any way that Laila could see, but Keeley then asked her, "Do you know where they are? Good. Take me to them."

Keeley mounted the gray mare and rode off, forcing the rest to rush after her.

They followed Keeley for miles until she reached a cave opening in a mountainside. The demon wolves stood outside that opening, obviously waiting for her.

She dismounted from her horse and crouched in front of the lead wolf, her hand stroking his neck and shoulders.

"Did you find it?" she asked.

The wolf nodded its head, his eyes leaving a brief—and disturbing—trail of flame as he did so.

"Thank the gods. Show me."

"What the hells is going on?" Laila demanded before Keeley could run off.

"Are you talking to those things now?" Gemma wanted to know.

"I've always talked to them. They're my friends. Now come on."

"We're not going anywhere with you until you tell us what's going on."

"Sichar's gold."

"What about it?" Keran asked, surprising them all because she was actually paying attention for once.

"The wolves found it for me. That's what they were doing while we were talking to the elf lord."

"In other words," Gemma reasoned, "you sent them on a mission?"

"Yes!" Keeley cheered.

"And that doesn't bother you at all? That they understood exactly what you wanted?"

"Why should it?"

"Gods, Keeley!"

Keeley quickly held up her hand. "I'm not having this conversation with you yet again. We don't have time for it. How long before the elves figure out we've found this place?"

"I'm guessing not long," Keran put in before yawning; she was already looking for a place to sit down and get more sleep. The woman slept a lot.

"We are *not* following demons into a dark cave that could have all sorts of traps and spells ready to eviscerate us!"

Laila had to admit . . . Gemma had a point. The wood elves had strong magicks. It was doubtful they would just bury something as precious as Sichar's gold in the middle of a cave and then leave it without any protection.

"Look, just stay here," Keeley told her sister. "I'll be right out."

"Then I'm going with you," Caid piped up but Laila immediately grabbed his arm.

"You," she said, looking at him long and hard, "are not going anywhere near the inside of that cave."

"I'm not letting her go in there alone, Laila."

"And I'm not going back to our mother and telling her that you were killed inside a cave because of demon wolves."

"Laila—"

"Stop," Gemma ordered. "I'll go with her. You lot stay here and make sure to keep the elves off our backs if they show up. Understand, *Keran?*"

Keran, who'd already sat down with her back against a boulder, and her eyes about to close, pointed at herself. "*What are you coming after me for?*"

"Because you can't really keep watch when you're asleep!"

"I'm tired!"

Quinn shook his head and laughed. "Just go. We'll watch your back."

Laila couldn't help but cringe a little. "You sure about this?"

"*No.*" Gemma glanced after her sister, who'd already disappeared into the darkness. "But it's not like I have much choice."

* * *

Keeley already had two torches lit by the time Gemma found her sister. She took the one offered and together they followed the wolves, heading deep into the cave.

They traveled down dark tunnels and through dark caverns; carefully inching through tight crevices until the wolves led them to a very large but seemingly empty chamber.

Keeley, trusting as always, started to go right inside, but Gemma grabbed her arm and yanked her back.

"What are you doing?" Keeley snapped.

"Give me a minute, would you?"

Gemma let out a breath, closed her eyes. She tried to push all worries and distractions from her mind so that she could focus on one thing: whether there were any magickal traps protecting this space. She searched desperately, assuming the elves must have left something. If this was, in fact, where they'd buried their gold. Yet the more she searched . . .

"There are magicks here, but I can't find anything inherently dangerous."

"Like what?"

"Traps, you idiot. I have a hard time believing the elves have *no* protection on the gold."

"Except you can't find anything, yes?"

"Not anything that's obviously—"

"Great!"

"Keeley!"

But she'd already entered the chamber, using her torch to light a few others that had been affixed to the walls.

Examining the sconces, Gemma could tell they'd been left by elves.

Once those few torches were lit, Keeley began searching the cave while the wolves watched her.

"This is crazy, Keeley."

"This is our only chance to get King Mundric's army. Unless you have money somewhere that I am unaware of so we can buy our own army."

"What are we going to do here? Just start digging? That could take a century."

"Stop being so negative. Why are you always so negative?"

Gemma cracked her neck. "Maybe because our baby sister already has an alliance with the elves. That's a reason to be negative."

Keeley stopped in the middle of the cavern. She stood still in the light when she looked back at Gemma. "How did you know? About Elouan and all that?"

"Because that elf was being such an asshole to us. I had a feeling he'd only act that way if he thought he had some kind of protection. Beatrix protection." Gemma shook her head. "I have to admit . . . I really underestimated her. She's good."

"I didn't underestimate her." Keeley blankly stared off into the dark part of the chamber. "But I tried so hard, Gemma. I tried so hard to . . . I don't know . . . fix her?"

"I know you did. But sometimes there's no fixing—"

Gemma's words faded off and the sisters slowly locked gazes. They both heard it. Coming from that dark part of the chamber.

Keeley raised the torch, trying to look farther ahead. That's when Gemma could see that the ground they stood on abruptly ended a dozen or so feet away, leaving a gap between the ground and the chamber wall. It wasn't the opening that had their attention, though. It was the sound coming up from that opening.

Gemma pulled out one of her swords and raised it, carefully moving backward. But not Keeley. No. Never Keeley. She walked forward, pausing briefly to light a few more torches near the crevice, curious as always.

"Keeley Smythe, you get your fat ass over here!" Gemma urgently whispered.

"I just want to see what's making that noise."

Gemma snarled and darted forward, grabbing the collar of her sister's leather armor. She started to yank Keeley back, but her sister fought her. Refusing to stop leaning over the crevice and gazing into the blackness below.

"Keeley! Come on!"

"All right, all rig—"

Both sisters fell back, hitting the ground hard when a claw exploded from the crevice and landed on the ground, talons digging into the stone floor. Another claw followed. Both were covered in black scales with dark red sliding in and around the scales' seams.

Each claw also had a steel cuff on the wrist and chains hung from them, disappearing into the crevice where the rest of the monster resided.

The claws were so large, Gemma didn't *want* to see the rest of that thing. She wanted to go. She wanted to flee. And she had to get her sister out of there. To safety.

"We have to go," she told Keeley, pulling at her collar.

The demon wolves stood near the crevice, barking at what was pulling itself out.

Without thinking, Gemma accused, "They brought us here to die!"

"They wouldn't do that," Keeley argued, attempting to pull away from Gemma's grip. "They brought me here for a reason."

"Don't be an idiot! Let's get out of here!"

The wolves backed away, still barking as that thing rose from the pit. Eyes. Black eyes glared at them from over the crevice before the entire head made its appearance, followed by the body.

Scrambling, Gemma and Keeley crab-walked backward, trying to get away from it. The wolves continued to bark and howl, moving back but never running away.

Gemma felt fear. A fear she could never remember feeling before. It took all her strength and training to stop herself from running away and leaving her sister to her own stupidity.

Breathing heavily, the creature pulled itself from the pit and Gemma cringed at the look of it. Wisps of sad gray hair grew at the top of its head, as if it had been shorn and just never grew back. The head and claws implied a bigger animal but the beast's torso was narrow. She could make out the ribs. Had it not been fed?

And gods, if it hadn't been fed . . . how the sisters must look to that thing!

The chains from the wrist cuffs linked to a steel collar around its throat and more chains disappeared into the crevice. Perhaps it was also cuffed on its back claws.

Keeley was on her hands and knees now. "Gemma?"

"Yes?"

"I don't think we're going to get the gold."

"I know. I do think we should run, though."

Keeley nodded and they both jumped to their feet and ran toward the exit. But a scaled tail with a sharp tip lashed out and slammed into them, sending them flying back toward the beast.

Gemma rolled over seconds before one massive claw came down to crush her. She tried for the exit again, but she heard Keeley scream and saw that the thing had her wrapped in its tail. With her arms pinned at her side, Keeley couldn't reach her weapon or even use her hands to defend herself.

Still running, Gemma curved away from the exit and back toward the thing that held her sister. It made its claw into a fist and tried its best to slam her into the ground. She zigged and zagged to avoid that rampaging fist, finally reaching the part of the thing's tail that rested against the ground. She climbed onto it, glancing at her sister. Keeley was still alive but her face was starting to turn blue. It was crushing her with that blasted tail.

Once on top of the tail, Gemma started to run up its back. The beast started to move around, trying to reach one forearm behind it. That's when the wolves attacked, barking and leaping up to bite its underbelly. The thing stood and started to use its back claws to stomp on the wolves. She heard the unmistakable sound of wounded canine but she had to ignore it and keep running.

She reached the back of its neck and pulled both her swords. She went up a little farther until she began to slide back down. That's when she raised her weapons and, with a scream, brought them both down in the middle of its neck.

Rising up on its hind legs, the monster threw its head back and roared. The sound shook the chamber and rocks began to fall from the ceiling.

Yanking out the blades from the thing's back, Gemma raised her arms to protect herself but she lost her balance and tumbled back along the beast's spine until she hit the ground hard, knocking herself out.

When Gemma opened her eyes again, the tail had unwrapped from around Keeley and her sister was lying on the ground, out cold. The beast, however, was stumbling around. Gemma, at first, didn't know why. Then she realized blood poured from a gaping wound on its forehead.

Assuming one of the rocks had hit it, Gemma forced herself up and ran to her sister. She re-sheathed her weapons and grabbed her, trying to drag Keeley over to a safe corner. But as she moved, she felt her strength waning.

Then the wolves were there and they grabbed Keeley on different parts of her armor. Together, they dragged her through the beast's twisting legs. They'd just gotten her outside the cavern when it finally dropped to the ground with an impact that shook everything around them.

Gemma fell beside her sister. She panted and rubbed the back of her head where she'd taken the brunt of her fall.

The wolves were panting next to them, a few either bleeding from rips in their flesh left by the thing's talons or nursing broken bones from getting hit with its fist.

"Thank you," she said to them. "For helping me."

Keeley gasped awake, arms swinging, eyes wide and panicked.

"You're okay," Gemma said, patting her shoulder. "You're okay."

"What . . . what happened?"

"It's dead, I think. I don't hear it breathing anymore. But we shouldn't wait to be sure."

Keeley sat up and nodded. "Yes. You're right."

But the lead wolf ran up and barked at the thing.

"If you wake that fucking thing up . . ." Gemma warned.

But apparently that wasn't its purpose. Because her sister was suddenly crawling over to the wolf.

"Keeley Smythe, I swear to all the gods!"

"Give me a minute!"

Keeley went over to the thing's side and ran her hands over the scales, stopping where the wolf's nose briefly rested.

"Holy shit."

"What?"

Keeley glanced at her, grinning. Then she pulled one of her knives out of its sheath and began cutting away at the thing's scales. It took a few minutes but finally Keeley faced Gemma and held open her blood-covered hand.

Gemma leaned in and took a look. "That can't be all of it," Gemma complained in disbelief about the flat, circular disk of gold in her sister's palm. "Tell me I didn't risk my life for *that*?"

"Tell *me*," Keeley shot back, "that a sister of mine doesn't remember how Sichar's gold works." Gemma's head hurt and she could feel that bits of her were becoming decidedly sore. So she wasn't really in the mood for any of this. When she didn't answer, her sister said, "With this amount of Sichar's gold, a true blacksmith can outfit an entire army from helmet to boots and all the armor and weapons in between. *This* is a fortune in Sichar's gold."

"Ohhhhh. Now I rememb—"

"No," Keeley cut in, waving her free hand. "I can't. You've disappointed me greatly."

"Oh, shut up." Gemma stood, but not too quickly. "You know," she reasoned, "if that's really a fortune—"

"*If?*"

"Maybe you should keep it and fund your own army."

Keeley got to her feet. "But we promised them. We promised to get this *for* the dwarves."

"We almost died for this."

"I don't care. I'm not going to go back on my word."

"Keeley . . . for all we know, the elves aren't the only ones that have a deal with Beatrix."

"If there's one thing I *do* know about our sister . . . she has never cared about anything that has to do with blacksmithing. And that's *all* the Amichai dwarves care about. Besides, Beatrix's word may mean nothing at the end of the day, but mine does. I'm taking this back to them. Like I promised."

"It's foolish."

"Fine. It's foolish," Keeley muttered as she turned to look down at the thing that had tried to kill them.

With her back turned, Gemma couldn't help but smile a little. Yes, it was definitely foolish that Keeley would return something so valuable to the dwarves when they had done nothing to get it themselves, but she loved that her sister was true to her word. It would probably get her killed one day, but you know . . . everything had a downside.

"I feel so bad for him," Keeley said, still gazing at the thing on the floor.

"Are you kidding?" Gemma asked. "It tried to kill us."

"He saw us as a threat."

"It saw us as dinner."

"Because he was being starved. Look at these chains. They were using him for something." She shook her head. "It's just cruel."

"Keeley . . . I know what you're thinking. And don't you dare—*gods-dammit, Keeley!*" Gemma exploded when the cuff around the thing's neck fell to the ground.

Only the best blacksmiths—and the daughters they taught—knew that all dwarven cuffs had a secret release mechanism. It was a way for dwarves to ensure they never got trapped in their own chains.

"You are ridiculous!" Gemma yelled.

"Don't be so dramatic," Keeley sighed out as she walked toward the exit. "It was just the neck cuff. If he truly isn't dead, he still has the leg cuffs binding him. But now he has a chance to be free."

"All that sounds great, Sister, except that the neck cuff was the only one imbued with protective magicks." Gemma pointed at the runes burned into the collar. "The others aren't."

Keeley stopped, looked at her sister. "What kind of protective magicks?"

Gemma shrugged. "I don't know. I'm sure something that helps to keep it bound here."

"See? That's just cruel. He shouldn't be bound anywhere. He should be—"

"Keeley, I don't want to hear it."

"Fine." They again started toward the exit but Keeley abruptly stopped and looked down.

"What's that?" she asked.

"What's what?"

"What we're walking on." Keeley bent over and lifted something up. "What the hells is this?"

Gemma leaned close to see what Keeley had spread all over her hand. "That's hair." Very lush. Very black with some red streaks hair.

As one, the sisters' gazes lifted and they stared at each other.

"Or maybe," Gemma said with dread, "it wasn't a protective spell but a binding spell."

"A binding spell?"

"That can prevent something from being at, shall we say, full strength."

"And once that binding spell is removed?"

Gemma didn't answer. She really couldn't at the moment. Not when she heard that . . . breathing behind her. The loud breathing of a very large, very pissed-off animal.

Without turning around, Gemma screamed, "*Run!*"

Caid continued to pace in front of the cave entrance.

"Where the fuck are they?" he finally asked his sister.

"I don't know. But I'm not waiting any longer." She pulled out her steel spear, hitting a latch that caused the weapon to extend several more feet. "We're going in and we're going to find—"

The roar that exploded from inside the cave caught them all off guard, but only Quinn was crazy enough to immediately move in closer. Then he laughed.

"I *love* these women!" he crowed, oblivious to any danger. As always.

Caid grabbed his brother by the hair and yanked him back, seconds before the Smythe sisters charged from the darkness of the cave, the demon wolves right behind them.

"It's not my fault!" Keeley chanted as she ran by him. "It's not my fault! It's not my fault!"

Gemma was right behind her sister until she spun around to face the entrance.

"*Move back! All of you!*" she roared.

Then Caid heard it again. They all did. That angry, ball-shrinking roar. One Caid had never heard before and prayed never to hear again.

A few seconds after that he heard horses and turned to see Lord Elouan riding toward them, leading a well-armed company of elven soldiers. Nearly a hundred, if he were to guess. A much larger force than their small travel group. Even with the extra centaurs they'd brought with them.

"*What have you done, woman?*" Elouan bellowed at Keeley as soon as they were close enough to hear.

"Don't blame me for this!" Keeley argued. "You're the one who had him chained up in there!"

"That *thing* is not a 'him.' It is an 'it' and you let it free!"

"I thought it was dead!"

"All of you shut up!" Gemma yelled, her arms raised high, palms out. She closed her eyes, lowered her head, and unleashed a spell that shook the ground. The top of the cave entrance crumbled and stones crashed down until there was no way in or out.

Gemma dropped to one knee and Keeley rushed to her sister's side. She helped her back up.

"You all right?"

"I'm fine."

"Here." Keran handed her a flask. "Drink this. Get your legs back."

Gemma tipped her head back and took a long drink, but when she was done, her eyes grew wide and the arm not resting against her sister dropped to her side.

Caid and Laila turned to see what had her attention. It was the elves. They'd all unsheathed their weapons.

"What the fuck do you think you're doing?" Laila demanded. Caid now stood on one side of her and Quinn on the other. Their small band of centaurs were arrayed behind them, ready for whatever came next.

What should have the elves concerned, though, was Quinn. He was no longer smiling and laughing. He was no longer delighted by the situation. Some wild animal attacking them was just good-hearted fun. But elves unleashing weapons near their sister . . . ? That was literally a call to war.

"I just realized what a wonderful opportunity this stupid human has given me," Elouan said. "Sad, though, how devastated your mother will be when she finds out that you, your brothers, and all your human friends were killed by that thing." He smiled. "It will be such a sorry tale I'll tell."

Before Caid could move, Keeley stepped in front of all the centaurs. Right by her side were Gemma and Keran. She had her hammer out and she was so angry, her entire body was shaking. So angry, she couldn't even speak. So angry, she could do nothing but point her massive hammer at the elven lord.

"Ahhhh, *Queen* Keeley," Elouan said with great sarcasm. "You're as pathetic as your sister said you were, and you deserve what she's happily planning for you and anyone idiot enough to foll—"

Caid and everyone else stumbled back when Elouan's blood

splattered a good number of them as giant jaws slammed shut around the elf and bit down, cutting off his words and the top half of his body. His horse galloped off with the lord's legs and waist still attached; the feet in the stirrups. His hands were twitching on the ground.

The top half of Elouan, however, was still screaming as he was swallowed down. A few seconds after that, his sword and shield were spit onto the ground.

Caid raised his gaze to what now stood atop the damaged cave with its black horns on its massive head and long black and red hair blowing in the wind. Its black scales appeared to pulsate because of the glowing red line running between each one. But it was the wings that had them all gaping silently. Those massive black wings that stood spread out from its back.

In that instant, everything changed.

"*Kill it!*" one of the elves screamed and the bombardment of arrows began. Not just from the elves but the centaurs as well.

The dragon stumbled back a bit, swiping at the projectiles fired at him. A few hit their mark but not enough to take the creature down. Now he just seemed pissed.

He took in a deep breath and Caid lowered his bow.

"Fuck," he heard Laila gasp because their instincts were warning them. Those instincts all horses had. Even those only half horse.

Caid grabbed Keeley, and his siblings grabbed her kin and they started running. Running as fast and hard as they could.

As he ran, Caid looked over his shoulder. The dragon's long neck snaked down and it opened its maw. That's when it released . . .

"Holy gods!" Caid cried out.

Because the dragon didn't unleash fire. It was lava. A violent spray of lava that soaked the remaining elves. He could hear their dying screams as the elves burst into flame or simply melted from the lava that covered them.

"It's not a fire dragon!" Caid yelled to his sister. "It's—"

Elf bodies were tossed in front of them, forcing them to turn or jump over them. More flew at them, hitting some of their comrades and knocking them to the ground.

Caid pushed Keeley to his back. "Hold on!"

"Caid! Wait!"

Caid would have ignored her, but big back claws slammed hard onto the ground right in front of them, forcing the centaurs to rear up on their back legs to prevent them from running directly into the beast. The horses running with them, one of which carried poor Samuel, darted around the dragon and kept going.

"Stop! Stop!" Samuel yelled. "I need to go back!" But the horse—and now Caid realized it was the gray mare that Samuel was riding—kept going.

He honestly did not blame her.

With a screaming, half-eaten elf hanging from one of his fangs, the dragon leaned down a bit. Caid was ready to rear up again in hopes of protecting Keeley from the lava it would spew. But it didn't spew anything. No. It simply growled out, "And where do you think you're going?"

And instead of Keeley screaming and attempting to run away, she leaned around Caid so she could ask with surprise and what sounded like delight, "You can speak!"

"*Really?*" Gemma screeched. "*That's what you have to say?*"

And for once, Caid really had to agree with the War Monk.

"Why are you yelling at me?" Keeley wanted to know.

"Maybe," Gemma growled, "because he's going to kill us and you're worried about whether he can speak or not."

"Kill us? But I saved him."

Gemma, sitting on Quinn's back, leaned in a bit and loudly announced, "I don't think he gives a fuck."

"He should." Keeley looked at the dragon. "You should. I saved your life! If it wasn't for me, you'd still be trapped in that cave!"

The dragon gazed down at Keeley as he picked the screaming elf off his fang, stripped the elven armor off with a talon, and placed him fully into his mouth. He chewed. The screaming stopped but the crunching began. When he swallowed, he said, "You took my gold."

Laila's head dropped. "You stole his gold?"

"We need the gold for the dwarves. I had to take it." She looked up at the dragon. "You understand that, don't you?"

"No."

Keeley slid off Caid's back and walked closer to the dragon, shaking off Caid's hand when he attempted to grab her.

"*We* didn't trap you in there," she reminded the dragon. "And if you hadn't attacked us, we wouldn't have fought back. We did what we had to do to survive. But after it was over, *I* was the one who removed the cuff. I could have left it on you."

"You thought I was dead."

"I wasn't sure, actually."

"So you expect me to be grateful?"

"*Yes.*"

He glanced at the centaurs. "She doesn't know about dragons, does she?"

"We don't have dragons in these lands," Laila explained. "Which makes me wonder why you're here at all."

"The elves found me when I was returning to my homelands from the dwarf cities. I was taking the underground tunnels and had stopped one night to sleep. When I awoke I was chained like some human slave and trapped in that cave. They would occasionally feed me with convicts or anyone who'd annoyed their king. But otherwise, they let me starve."

"And the gold?"

"They buried it near me. And it was pretty. So I took it."

"None of that matters. Keeley's right," Laila pointed out. "She did save you."

The dragon looked off, but that didn't stop Laila.

"She saved you, dragon. Let her go."

"No," Keeley cut in. "Let us all go. They're my friends. They're with me."

The dragon didn't answer; he was still glaring off into the distance.

"Hey!" Keeley yelled up at him, ignoring the startled gasps behind her when she grabbed a rock and threw it at the dragon's chest to get his attention. "I'm speaking to you!"

Eyes wide, the dragon slowly looked down at her. "Did you just throw a rock at me?"

"Yes. I'm trying to talk to you."

"I could melt your face off and eat your friends. I always did like the taste of horse."

"Do dragons not have honor? Because it seems to me a being of honor should—"

"Honor?" He motioned to the wolves. "Do those things have honor? Your little demon dogs?"

"They're wolves," Caid corrected. "What?" he asked when everyone stared at him. "They are wolves."

"They're loyal to me, but they protect my friends," Keeley explained "So yes, they have honor. More honor than you seem to have."

"Well, it was nice knowing everyone," Keran announced, waving at the centaurs. "Since it looks like we're all going to die together."

The tip of the dragon's tail was suddenly right in Keeley's face. Not touching her but so close she saw that it could easily be used as a weapon. It was pointed, like a very large metal arrowhead.

"I don't like you," he said, his voice low.

"I have to admit . . . it's mutual. But you can't say that I'm wrong."

He didn't say anything, simply moved around them all. Keeley thought he was just going to unleash his wings and fly away. Or, if he was really determined to see her dead, he'd unleash his lava and actually melt her face off. Just as he'd threatened.

But with his back to her, he finally crouched down and buried his claws directly into the dirt.

Confused, Keeley moved closer to see what he was doing.

"Keeley, stop," Gemma warned.

"But—"

"Trust me." Her sister reached out and grabbed her arm, yanking her back beside the centaurs. "He's a mage."

"So?"

Her sister didn't answer because the dragon had closed his eyes, bowed his head, and started to chant.

"What's he doing?"

"I'm guessing . . . he's getting revenge on those who have truly harmed him."

Keeley didn't understand. Well, she understood revenge but she didn't understand what putting one's hand in the dirt was supposed to do. The dragon was a mage, so maybe he was poisoning the ground or something . . . ? Or calling up ghosts? Or whatever mages do. What did they do?

To answer, the ground beneath them began to shake and buckle and then that shaking and buckling shot across the land, heading right for the forest of the elves.

And once it reached the forest, the rumbling became worse and the screaming began.

"Stop!" Keeley yelled. "What are you doing?"

She moved toward the dragon but her sister's grip on her arm was iron.

"Leave him be, Keeley!"

"But there are children there! Old people! It isn't fair to do this to all of them!"

"He doesn't care," Gemma said. "Just let him have his revenge."

But what kind of revenge? Keeley heard the screaming and the ground was still shaking but she didn't know what was hap . . .

"Oh, by the gods," Laila gasped out.

It grew up and out of the ground in the middle of the elves' forest. It just grew and grew and grew, destroying everything in its way until it was all Keeley could see.

"Is that a . . . volcano?" Keran asked.

It was. Keeley knew that as soon as it began to spew lava and big orange balls of fire.

And just like that . . . the wood elves lost their home.

The dragon pulled his claws out of the ground and looked down at Keeley. "Consider yourself lucky, human. You and your friends. We're now even."

Without another word, the dragon unleashed his wings and took off into the air. But he didn't fly away; instead he turned over and dove toward the ground. Their entire travel party scrambled out of the way as the dragon hit the ground and dug into the earth in seconds. He vanished, leaving a giant hole behind for them to stand around and stare into it until an explosion had them spinning away to face the elves' forest again.

Keeley only had a second to see the volcanic fireball screaming toward them before Caid picked her up and took off running once more.

Keeley watched over Caid's shoulder as the boulder landed hard, and the world around them exploded, sending the centaurs and the humans they were helping tumble hooves over head.

When they finally stopped rolling, Keeley pulled herself out of Caid's arms and stood. She gazed at exactly *where* the red-hot boulder had landed... in the hole that the dragon had left. He'd blocked his exit so no elves could follow him home.

Gemma stood beside her and sneered, "I'm so glad you released that dragon, Keeley."

"Oh, *shut up*."

CHAPTER 25

The two brothers were in the middle of another one of their arguments when Emma slammed down a carafe of ale and three steel mugs.

"It's late," she said, also slamming a wooden platter of bread, cheese, and dried meats on the table next to the wine. "And you two nattering bitches haven't stopped fighting once!"

Grumbling, the brothers leaned back in their chairs and refused to look at each other.

Fed up, Emma reminded both men, "Our babies are out there, risking their lives, and you two are just going at each other. I can't stand it another second!"

"He took what was mine!" Archie accused.

Emma finished pouring out some ale, shoving the cups in front of each man. She picked up her own and dropped into a chair, putting one leg up on the table.

"If you're talking about me—"

"I am!"

"—I was never interested in you."

"How could you say that to me?" Archie asked, pressing his hand to his chest. "You loved me."

"No. I didn't. But I do care for you as my husband's brother. That's why you're still breathing."

Angus laughed as Archie's eyes narrowed on her. "You're a cruel woman, Emma Smythe."

"I am. Now let's eat and drink and not annoy me anymore."

"Then what fun will we have?" Archie asked.

Emma chuckled, bringing her cup to her lips. But she stopped before drinking and gazed at Endelyon. Her young daughter. She held the little hammer Keeley had given her tucked into her elbow, both hands rubbing her eyes.

Placing the cup down, Emma asked, "What are you doing up, little bit?"

"Can't sleep. Too many horses coming. Is Keeley back?"

Emma looked at her husband and his brother.

"Farlan? Cadell?" she called out to their protector centaurs. "Where are you two?"

"Under the stairs, getting ready for night watch. Why?" Farlan shot back.

"You need to get out here now," she told the centaurs as she swung her legs off the table and tore off her skirt. She'd been wearing it to hide her chainmail leggings and all her weapons from the younger children, not wanting to panic them.

She went to her daughter and picked her up. "Let's go get your brothers and sisters up, yes?"

The attack started as soon as Emma disappeared up the stairs to round up the children. The attackers had a battering ram and were banging at the door.

Archie tossed Angus a sword and shield. They'd already blocked the door when they'd settled in for the night.

"How long do you think?" Angus asked.

"Before they take the door down? Not sure. But they're coming."

Brothers faced the blocked door together, shields and swords raised.

"You know," Archie said as they waited, "I built this place out of stone so they couldn't set fire to it and trap me inside."

Angus glanced at him. "Do you worry often about people trying to kill you with fire?"

"Yes."

Deciding they didn't have time to debate that, Angus continued to wait. After a few minutes, his wife and children rushed down the stairs with the centaurs. The eldest ones helped the younger ones, and Emma with the very youngest tucked against her breast in a sturdy leather sling he'd built for her. The centaurs had their weapons out and were keeping everyone moving quickly toward the tunnels Archie had built under his home.

"Let's go, gentlemen!" Emma ordered.

"You go," Angus replied. "We'll catch up."

"*Angus Farmerson!*"

His wife's bellow had Archie pushing him toward her. "Just go, Brother. Before she tears both our balls off!"

"Come with us."

"They'll not make me leave my home, Angus. No one will make me leave my—"

Angus dragged his brother toward the tunnels as the front door was finally battered open.

The two brothers ran into the hallway, where the door to the tunnel was still open, but Angus heard men behind them.

He turned, brought down his sword. His brother used his shield to slam another into the closest wall and finish him off with a sword slash to the throat.

More soldiers poured in, wearing the colors and crest of Prince Straton.

"Come on!" Emma yelled from the stairs.

"Go!" Angus ordered. "Now!"

"Angus—"

"*Go!*"

He heard the door behind them slam and the brothers continued to fight until three arrows hit Angus in the right part of his chest. He stumbled back, and his brother stepped in front of him.

Angus worked to ignore the pain and the way it became harder to breathe. He stepped back up to the line and pushed at his brother.

"Go to them, Archie. Take care of my family."

"*I'll not leave you, Brother!*" Archie bellowed. "I'll kill them all!"

"Archie, no!"

But it was too late—his brother waded into the charging men, swinging his sword and shield; screaming like a crazy man.

Angus snatched open the tunnel door with his good arm. "Archie!"

"Go, Brother! Go!"

Archie swung his shield, knocking the unit of men back. Then he stopped, stared.

"Huh," he muttered, shocked at what he saw. "Horses are in my house," he got out before the horses were trampling poor Archie into the ground.

"Owwww!" his brother cried out. "You bastards!"

"Get up, idiot!" one of the horses demanded and that's when Angus saw a human arm reach down and grab hold of Archie, pulling him back to his feet.

"Hearn," Angus said before he realized he was on his knees and bleeding out onto the ground.

"Oh, no you don't, you old bastard." Hearn helped Angus up. "I'll not face that daughter of yours and tell her I lost her da."

Hearn took a quick look around until his gaze stopped at the stone entryway leading to the hallway. "Your brother's not that big an idiot." He pointed his sword. "Kel! The ceiling!"

The biggest of the battling centaurs, a massive stallion, pulled the war hammer he had strapped to his back. He swung it left and right, knocking the soldiers out of his way, and then up. He struck the ceiling once, twice . . . and stones began to drop. The centaurs shifted to their human forms and dashed into the hallway. The soldiers that followed were hit by the falling boulders that now blocked the hallway off from the front of Archie's house.

"Move! Down the stairs!" Hearn yanked the door open. He jerked back as a sword-wielding blacksmith came at him from the stairway.

"Emma, no!" Angus yelled. His wife immediately stopped when she saw him. "He's a friend. Now go, go, go!"

Emma ran down the stairs, the centaurs following. Hearn still had his arm around Angus's waist.

Archie moved in front of them. "This way!"

It took them little time to catch up to the children. That's when the centaurs shifted back to their natural forms, lifting the screaming children and placing them on their backs.

Once the older ones realized they were being rescued and not massacred, they calmed the others, who were now just excited to be riding on the centaurs.

"So you really do have centaur friends," Emma said, moving

while simultaneously trying to stop the bleeding from Angus's wounds.

"Told you. And Hearn's not just a centaur either. He's a chief."

"Well, who knew you were so important."

"You just never listen, woman."

She chuckled a little before barking, "Hold." Hearn stopped so she could break the ends of the arrows off. "We'll leave the tips in for now. Go!"

Hearn helped Angus onto the back of the big stallion with the war hammer. "Hold on, old friend. Don't let go."

Angus grinned as he watched Hearn place his wife on his back. No, he wouldn't let go. Not now. Now when he could finally tell his wife, "Told you so!"

"Let's move!" Hearn called out. Then he motioned to Archie. "Come on, idiot."

Archie snarled as he ran after them; Angus's brother refusing to mount one of the centaurs. "Stop calling me that!"

Caid dropped several rabbits by the fire and looked around. "Where's Keeley?"

"She went off that way." Laila pointed toward a small group of trees. Much too small to be a forest, but it was near the lake they'd found a few hours earlier.

"She's in a mood," Gemma muttered while sharpening her steel weapons.

"Maybe because you kept starting slap fights with her all the way here."

"She started it!"

"How old are you?" Caid wanted to know.

"Here." Laila handed him a thick blanket with some dried meat, bread, and a bottle of ale. "Take this to Keeley. Make sure she eats."

Caid started to walk off, but his sister briefly pulled him back to whisper in his ear, "Maybe if she spends the night away from her sister, we'll *all* get some sleep."

"I'll see what I can do."

"Don't keep her away on my account," Gemma snapped, apparently hearing Laila's words. "I can ignore the whiny bitch forever if I have to!" she yelled out toward the trees.

"She hasn't said a word since we left elf territory," Laila reminded her.

"It doesn't matter. I can see her whining through her eyes!"

Quinn laughed at that bizarre statement and Gemma's snarling at him to "Shut the fuck up!" did not help the matter.

Caid shifted to human and followed Keeley's scent until he found her sitting with her back against a large tree.

He sat down next to her, spread the blanket in front of them, and put the food out.

"Here. You should eat."

"I'm not sure I'm hungry," she said, still continuing to stare off.

"Keeley . . . this wasn't your fault."

She shrugged, her gaze still locked on some far-off space. "I did unleash him, but I didn't put him there. And I didn't make him mad."

"If you know that then why are you gazing despondently into the distance?"

"I'm not despondent, I'm thinking. It's just something you said."

"Before or after the dragon brought up that volcano?"

"Before. You said he was *not* a fire breather."

"Yes. That's right."

"So there are others like that one? The dragon we faced today. But that breathe fire?"

"Well . . . not exactly like him. He's kind of small."

"What?"

"Based on what we've learned from our cousins, the Dark Plains centaurs, there are all kinds of dragons, in all kinds of very large sizes. From what I understand there are no truly small dragons. Just small for a dragon."

"Tell me you're joking."

"The Dark Plains dragons are a well-organized, lethal, family-based group of giant beings with sharp tails and horns on their heads. The one we dealt with was a volcano dragon but there are others."

"Others?"

"Some breathe fire. Some lightning. Some sand. I've also heard about acid—"

"*Acid?*"

"I believe those are rare, though."

"Oh," she said, closing her eyes. "How nice. And what else?"

"They have armies."

"Not just one army but *armies*. As in plural?"

"Well, you need to understand that there are dragons all over that side of the world. And they don't all get along. The sand dragons are ruled by a king in the Desert Lands. The fire breathers and volcano dragons are ruled by the Dragon Queen."

"There's a Dragon Queen?"

"Of course there's a Dragon Queen. But there are also Northland dragons—"

"Northland dragons?"

"The Lightnings. They're actually very interesting."

Her gaze flickered over to him. "Are they?"

"Yes. At one time they lived in hordes."

"Hordes? There are hordes of these things?"

"Uh-huh. Small, clannish groups made mostly of sons, nephews, and brothers of their leaders. Although I've heard that they now have one leader for all the Northland dragons but I have no idea who that is or what that title is. I just know it's a male."

"Fascinating."

"What's the matter?" he asked, pouring them each some ale in their travel cups. "I thought you'd find all this very interesting."

"Interesting, yes. But how am I supposed to fight them?"

Shocked by Keeley's response, Caid accidentally poured some ale onto the blanket. He quickly put the stopper in.

"Why in the world would you even think about fighting the dragons?"

Keeley stood and began pacing. "What if we have no choice?"

"Gods, you're not planning a strike on them, are you? Tell me you're not planning a strike."

She spun around to face him, her eyes wide. "*Why in the hells would you ask me that?*"

Confused, he pointed out, "Because you specifically asked how you could fight them. You'd only have to fight them if you struck first."

"Not necessarily."

Still confused, he asked, "What are you talking about?"

"Beatrix already has an alliance with the elves."

"Yes, Laila told me."

"But not only that; she's made deals with the Dowager Queen and Prince Marius. For all we know, she's done the same with the Dark Plains dragons, allowing them to run roughshod over the Hill Lands." Keeley scowled. "What is so funny?"

"That you'd think the dragons would need to run roughshod over anything. They could have come to our territories anytime they wanted over the centuries, but they haven't bothered. Because they're too busy fighting each other and the humans right in front of them. And none of that has changed in eons. I doubt it will change now. Even for your very ambitious little sister."

"But she seems to have a way. With *everyone*."

"Not with the dragons."

"But how do you know—"

"Keeley . . . they eat humans."

Keeley froze. "What?" she finally asked.

"They eat people. You saw what that dragon did to some of those elves."

"He was fighting for his life."

"No. If he was doing that, he would have just used his tail. Or one of his spells. He was a mage. He ate them because he was hungry. Humans, to the dragons, are nothing but two-legged cattle. They're a staple of their diet. So unless your sister is willing to hand her power over to a force much more deadly than she is—and, based on what I've heard from others, even more insane than your uncle Archie—I doubt she'll attempt to get the dragons on her side, much less manage to do so. You know, without becoming a scrumptious appetizer in the process."

"So I have no reason to panic?"

"Not about that, no."

"*What does that mean?*" Keeley demanded, not appreciating when Caid began laughing at her. Again.

"Can I make a suggestion?" he asked.

"Fine. Make a suggestion."

"Relax. For the night. Please."

Caid was right, of course. There was nothing she could do this night. And she'd had an exhausting and weird day. She might as well eat and get some sleep. She could panic about dragons and her sister and everything else in the morning.

Keeley sat down next to Caid, their shoulders touching. He handed her a piece of bread and she gratefully accepted it. She hadn't realized until now how hungry she was.

"Those centaur travelers we met on the road . . ."

He nodded. "What about them?"

"They said Straton had attacked a town. Another town that sounds like mine."

"He didn't burn it down at least."

"Yes, thankfully. But all those people trapped there now. I don't even want to think about what's happening to the women—"

"Then don't. Don't think about that *right now*."

"You're right, of course. It's not like I can help at this moment."

"Exactly."

Keeley ate a piece of cheese. "Do you think I need a castle?"

"What now?"

"That's why Straton raided that town. So he could have a base of operations for his army. I don't have a base of operations. I can't wander the land picking up troops as I go along."

"That's how the Daughters of the Steppes do it."

"The what?"

"Never mind." He took a breath. "Are you planning to raid a town to take it over?"

"Of course not! I'd never do that."

"Exactly. So why are we even discussing this? *Now?*"

"Yes, yes. You're right. I'll just relax and eat."

"Good."

Keeley sipped the ale Caid had poured for her earlier. "Think I'll have to buy my army?" When Caid stared at her, she added, "I can't expect the dwarves to do all the fighting for me. I'll be leading humans, so I'll need humans to fight for my cause."

"I don't disagree," Caid said slowly, speaking around the food he had in his mouth. "I'm just not sure why you're worrying about that *now*."

"Excellent point," she agreed. "I just need to relax."

"Yes. Relax."

"Take the night off!"

"Take the night off."

Keeley leaned back against the tree and ate more of the food Caid had provided.

"Maybe," she began, "we should see the barbarians *before* we head back to the dwarves. What do you—"

"You *really* can't relax, can you?" Caid demanded, gawking at her.

"I have a lot on my mind," she argued.

"You're going to make yourself sick. My grandfather had what a healer called a hole in his stomach. She said it was from all the worry he had. It was like he was being eaten from the inside out. You don't want that, do you?"

"No! Why would you tell me that story? Now I'm going to worry that I'm going to get a hole in my stomach."

"You need to find ways to distract yourself."

"But I don't have a forge."

"What?" Caid asked on a laugh.

"That's how I relax. I go to my forge and work. But, at the moment, I don't have that." She leaned forward, tried to look through the trees. "Unless there's a forge around here that you know about?"

"Keeley . . . I don't even know how to respond to that."

"I thought you knew this area."

"*Keeley.*"

"Fine. Forget it." She leaned back but one of them must have moved because she was now half on Caid's shoulder and left side. "Is your kilt magickal?"

The ale Caid had been drinking suddenly sprayed across the ground. "What?"

"Is it magickal? It turns into a bridle when you shift to centaur."

"I am centaur. I shift to *human*. And yes, there is a bit of spell-enhancement involved in the making of our kilts."

"Interesting."

"Is it?"

"It is. I work with leather, but I never thought about enhancing it with spells to make it better."

"Not sure you can. We have witches and mages who work with our armorer."

"Oh. I see. I don't have magick skills." She snapped her fingers. "But Gemma does!"

"She's a War Monk. Her skills are limited and she's only to use them in battle."

Keeley frowned. "How do you know all that?"

"I looked into being a War Monk when I was younger."

"Oh."

"But the thought of human men telling me what to do set my teeth on edge, so . . . you know . . ."

"As a human woman, I have to admit, I feel the same way."

Cross-legged beside him, Keeley picked up the bottom of his kilt and felt the material. "This is really excellent workmanship."

"Thank you."

"Did you make this?"

"No."

"That's disappointing."

"Not for me."

Instead of verbally responding, Keeley just looked up at him and briefly flicked her hands into the air and sucked her tongue against her teeth, letting him know she was now disappointed with his response.

The slight physical move and expression on her face made Caid laugh. Keeley always made him laugh. Always made him . . . comfortable. There weren't many who did. He did fine around his family but strangers bothered him. He hated chatting. Hated idiotic conversations about nothing, but not as much as he hated conversations about what some random being thought was important. Honestly, Caid was most happy when he was by himself, in an open field with horses. Not centaurs, but actual horses, because they didn't bore him with constant conversation either.

Keeley was the only being he could think of whose conversation didn't make him homicidal. Even when she was panicking, pacing and prattling on, he didn't want to get away from her. Instead, he wanted to help. To calm her down. Even if calming her down meant letting her prattle on and on until she'd worn herself out.

It was a price he was willing to pay. For her.

Keeley finished examining his kilt, released it, and put her hands in her lap. She looked at him then.

"What?" she asked when she saw his face.

He didn't know what to say to her. Didn't even know how to begin. So he said nothing. Silence had always been his friend; he'd assume the same thing now. It was safer.

Safer to keep his mouth shut. Safer not to say what he was thinking and feeling. Safer not to push too hard and lose everything.

But he should have remembered . . . Keeley never played it safe. She never did anything that anyone expected. That's what would make her such a powerful queen one day.

One moment she was gazing at him, and the next . . .

Her lips touched his. Soft. Gentle. Hesitant. No doubt she hadn't forgotten his earlier reaction to an innocent request. She was probably worried he'd push her away this time too; assume she was just another human female wanting to "try out" a centaur. But he knew now that wasn't Keeley. She didn't see any being as something that was simply for her own entertainment. An object to be used. If Keeley was kissing him, it was because she truly desired *him*. Caid.

Wanting to show her that the interest was mutual, he slid a hand behind her neck. Tugged her in closer; pressed his lips harder.

It happened all at once then. Their mutual desire exploded. It was all so fluid, Caid didn't even know when it happened. Sitting next to each other; calmly chatting. Then they were on their knees and facing each other. Hands on each other. Caid with his hands dug into Keeley's hair; Keeley with her hands on his shoulders and neck.

They seemed to open their mouths at the same time and their tongues touched, played. Their breaths mingled and Keeley groaned. Caid felt it as much as heard it. It went up his spine, spread to his shoulders, down his arms, and out his fingertips.

Keeley abruptly pulled out of their kiss.

"What?" he asked. "What's wrong?"

"Nothing." She looked to her left. "Go," she ordered . . . the air? Who was she talking to?

Then he saw them. They appeared from behind the other trees that surrounded them, their flame eyes watching Keeley and Caid. As they all trotted off, the leader moved the slowest, his glare for Caid and Caid alone.

Once the wolves had left them, Keeley leaned back and pulled her chainmail shirt up and over her head, tossing it aside. Caid did the same and once he cleared his chainmail away from his face, he saw that Keeley already had her breast bindings off.

She leaned in again, sliding her arms around his neck. Caid gripped her waist, pulled her in close so her breasts were flush against his chest. They kissed again, this time even more urgently.

Knowing that Keeley wanted him as much as he wanted her made Caid unbelievably hard, his cock pressing against her, the kilt barely keeping them apart.

He moved in closer and they somehow slipped, Keeley falling back; Caid going with her. When they landed, they were both laughing, but they still held each other tight. In fact, the laughter only made it better. More relaxed. More perfect, if that were possible.

"We need to get you a kilt," Caid complained as he tried to pull down her leggings with one hand while still holding her with the other. "This is taking too long."

Keeley silently agreed by moving his hand away and pulling her legs into her chest. She lifted her hips and brought the leggings down as far as her arm could reach. Then she tried to push them off the rest of the way by moving her feet and legs.

Caid grabbed the chainmail and tugged it off one foot. But he didn't get it the rest of the way because Keeley was already pulling him back on top of her.

They were kissing again and he didn't even know when it happened. It was just so natural, it all seemed to flow seamlessly.

So when Caid entered her, his cock pressing into her, Keeley was ready for him. Her hips lifted and her muscles pulled him in deep.

Her pussy was hot and wet and her groans against his ear nearly too much for him.

One leg wrapped around his waist, but the other was weighed down by the chainmail still hanging from her foot. That chainmail scratched the back of his leg, teasing him.

Her hands gripped his back; nails digging into his flesh, urging him on.

Caid rocked into her, his lips pressed against the side of her neck. He dug his hands into her hair and just enjoyed the feel of her. The sounds she made. The way she made *him* feel.

Keeley's entire body tightened around him, gripping him. Unwilling to release him. A climax shuddering through her that was so strong it took him with her when her pussy clenched onto his cock and squeezed everything out of him.

His own climax wiped his mind clean and had him shaking and panting, staring down at the human woman he'd just lost his heart to.

Keeley kept her eyes closed. Not wanting this moment ruined by that expression men often got after sex. That look that said, "That was great, luv. Thanks," before they rode off to another war or to meet up with their regiment. She didn't want to see that same expression on Caid's face. Not Caid's.

So she kept her eyes closed and just enjoyed how she felt, which was very good. She felt *very* good.

But Caid didn't leave. He didn't give her a friendly punch on the shoulder and walk away. He just curled his arms around her and rolled to his back, bringing her with him.

He let out what sounded—and felt—like a happy sigh, holding her against his big chest.

"I'm still wearing my kilt," he finally said.

"Yes, you are. And if I hadn't mentioned it before . . . I've become a big fan of the kilt."

CHAPTER 26

Caid woke up the next morning with his arms around Keeley, the pair facing each other as they slept, and his brother staring down at them.

"What are you doing?" Caid whispered desperately, not wanting Keeley to wake up and find Mad Quinn of the Scarred Earth Clan glaring down at her.

"I'm wondering what you're doing," Quinn whispered back.

"What does it look like? Now fuck off!"

"I can tell you it doesn't look right, Brother. Not right at all."

Assuming his brother was talking about Keeley, Caid was about to get up and beat the bastard into the ground with his front hooves, until he felt something resting against his hip. Something . . . furry.

He glared down at the wolf sleeping on him like he was nothing but a pillow. He growled at the lead demon wolf and one lid opened, its flame-covered orb gazing at him.

"Fuck off," he whispered at the beast, but it ignored him. He attempted to slap the demon away but Caid nearly got his hand snapped off.

"Keeley," he finally said.

"Hhhm?"

"*Keeley.*"

Startled, she sat up and threw her sword. Quinn barely ducked in time, the weapon impaling a tree right behind him.

"*What the hells was that?*"

Keeley opened her eyes and looked at Caid's brother. "Oh. Sorry."

Snarling, Quinn stalked back to camp and Keeley motioned to the wolf still resting on Caid.

"Piss off with you," she said sweetly. "You're making Caid uncomfortable."

Those disturbing eyes of some hell flickered over to him, then away. With a loud, dramatic sigh, the creature rose to its feet and trotted off after Quinn.

Caid kissed Keeley's forehead and asked, "You knew that was Quinn when you threw the blade at him, didn't you?"

"Oh, yes. I knew."

Dressed with her weapons strapped to her back and around her hips, Keeley began to walk to camp, but Caid caught her around the waist and pulled her in close.

"Is this over before it's barely begun?" he asked.

"Not for me, but . . ."

"But what?"

"Can't speak for you, can I?"

He frowned, appearing confused. "Keeley . . . do you expect me to be like human men?"

"I guess I do."

"Except I'm not human."

"Which means what? To me, I mean."

"That, like it or not, my heart belongs to you. So if your interest was only in one night—"

More excited than she could say, Keeley didn't let him finish his grand speech but instead threw herself into his arms and kissed him.

"Are you sure this is what you want?" he asked, laughing, when she pulled away.

"Why wouldn't it be?"

"Because . . . I'm not human. You have to remember that, Keeley, because trust me when I say . . . everyone else will remember it for you."

Gemma had just watched Samuel saddle her horse when her sister returned with Caid. The pair said nothing to each other and weren't even holding hands, but Gemma knew that things had changed between them.

She'd rather that hadn't happened. She'd rather things were simple and clear-cut. At least until they got Keeley onto her throne, but that was just not how life worked. At least not for her family.

"You and Laila," Quinn muttered to her, "such looks of disapproval between the two of you."

Gemma glanced up at the big blond centaur. "Stop talking to me," she ordered.

"But I find you fascinating."

"No, you don't."

"No," he agreed with his mad grin and little laugh. "I really don't. But you do entertain."

Gemma mounted her horse and waited for the others. They were heading back to the dwarves to give them their gold and, hopefully, get an army in return. It wasn't nearly enough of what they needed, but it would be a healthy start. Gemma just hoped the dwarves were as true to their word as her mother and the Smythe clan believed them to be.

Keeley mounted the gray mare, which had returned in the night with Samuel, and looked around at them all. "Let's move out," she ordered, and set off. Everyone followed.

After just a few feet, Keeley called a halt and suddenly yelled out, "*Gods-dammit, Keran!*"

"Coming, coming," their cousin returned, stumbling around the boulder she'd passed out behind the night before.

When they'd run from the wood elves' territory and that angry volcano, they'd simply taken off. Not really caring where they were going. Unfortunately, to get back to dwarf territory, they had to circle around until they could get to another mountain entrance that would lead them back to the dwarf city.

But in making this move, they were forced to cross from elf territory into barbarian. A small section that Caid and hundreds of other centaurs had crossed on many occasions. From the elves' woods into an open plain.

Only this time, instead of just moving right through and back into dwarf territory, they had to stop.

"What the hells is this?" Quinn asked, gazing out at hundreds of silent barbarians. Barbarians that had clearly been waiting for them.

They weren't attacking or making their battle cries, but they were armed with their flint weapons and had on their war woad, the blue markings clearly visible even from this distance. The barbarians were also blocking them from moving out of their territory and into the dwarves', so Quinn's question was legitimate. What the hells were the barbarians doing?

Keeley dismounted and came to stand between Caid and Laila. "What's happening?"

"We're not sure," Caid replied.

"Do they want something from us?"

"I think I know what this is!"

Surprised by the speaker's identity, they all turned and looked at Keran.

"What?" she asked.

"You know?" Keeley raised an eyebrow. "*You?*"

"I know things."

"Do you?"

"We've had barbarians in my fighter's guild. I learned from them. So I think I know what this is." Keran nodded when they just stared at her. "I do," she insisted. "I know."

"So what is it?" Gemma asked, now standing behind Keeley and sounding as disbelieving as her sister.

Keran began to answer but she turned abruptly pale, raised one finger at them, then quickly walked a few feet away so she could vomit in peace.

Keeley rolled her eyes. "Anyway," she said, dismissing her cousin and focusing on Laila, "what do you lot suggest?"

"We've never seen them like this," Laila admitted. "We either see them attacking like crazed animals. Or ignoring the world completely. This is"—she gestured toward them—"just strange."

"Then I'll go talk to them," Keeley said.

"No!" the rest of them all said together.

"They are *not* friendly, Keeley," Laila explained, "and those are their warriors. For all we know, they may want to capture you and force you into marrying their leader."

Quinn pointed. "That's their leader there. Torin-sa."

"How tall is he?" Keeley asked, eyes wide.

"Seven and a half feet . . . or so," Quinn guessed. "Maybe eight."

"You are not helping," Laila softly chided him.

Keeley shook her head, horrified. "I'm not marrying him!"

"Of course not." Laila patted her shoulder as the barbarian leader strode purposefully into the center of the open field, between the two groups. "I'll speak with him."

"We'll go with you," Caid said.

"No. Both of you stay here with Keeley. I'll be fine."

Laila made her way across the open field until she reached Torin-sa. They began to speak and though Laila attempted to keep things calm, the barbarian leader continued to gesture in Keeley's direction.

"Do you think this has to do with Beatrix?" Gemma asked.

"No," Keeley replied with a slow head shake. "I think it has to do with the wood elves. I think they blame me for what happened to them."

Gemma glanced at Caid in disbelief before asking her sister, "What in the world makes you think that?"

She pointed. "Because their troops are holding some of the half-melted bodies."

"Oh, shit." Gemma began to push Keeley back. "Caid, Quinn. We need to get her out of here now and—*Keran, nooooo!*"

But it was too late. Keeley's still-drunk cousin had looped around and was now charging straight at the side of the barbarian leader.

He turned his head toward her just as she launched herself off the ground and slammed her sword directly into his neck.

"*Oh, shit!*" Quinn exclaimed, saying what everyone else was thinking. Poor Laila, blood splattered across her face and chainmail, was forced to turn and dash back to their side.

Torin-sa dropped to his knees and Keran yanked out her sword. When the barbarian fell over on his side, she stood in front of him, chopped off his head with one blow of her blade, and grabbed it by its hair.

She held it up toward the barbarian horde and screamed at

them. No words. Just screaming. Then she threw the head at the horde and sauntered back to her kin.

When Keran finally reached them, she smiled. "All done."

"You've killed us," Laila softly accused. "You've killed us all."

"Gods, don't be so dramatic." She looked at her cousin. "Go on, Keeley. Take your horse. And walk right through."

"What?"

"They won't attack."

"How do you know?"

"Do you trust me or not?"

"Not!" Gemma barked.

"I wasn't asking you, trifling cow. Go on, Keels. Give it a go."

"Give it a go?"

"I'm sure about this, Cousin."

So Keeley started walking. Caid reached out to grab her, to stop her, but Keran caught his arm and held him with a strength that continued to surprise.

The gray mare fell in right beside Keeley and together they walked the distance between their group and the barbarians. When Keeley was no more than a few feet from the horde, they suddenly separated into two groups, allowing her to walk straight down the middle. When she'd made it halfway and no one had attacked, the rest of them followed.

They moved through the silent barbarians and all was fine until Keran herself stepped onto dwarf territory. That's when the barbarians began to make a loud noise. Kind of like communal humming. It was disconcerting and Caid rested his hand on the pommel of his sword, ready for an attack even though they were no longer on barbarian lands.

But Keran looked at the leaderless warriors and snapped, "Stop that!" They did.

Putting her hands to her head, Keran complained, "Got such a headache." She looked at Keeley. "I may have to throw up again."

"Wait a minute." Gemma gestured at the barbarians. They were just standing there . . . waiting. "What's happening with them?"

"I'm not positive," Keran admitted, "but I may now be their leader."

Keeley lowered her head, but Caid got the feeling it was so she could stifle her laughter.

"What do you mean, *may be*?" Gemma demanded.

"I don't remember all of the conversation I had with that barbarian back when I was in the guild, but it had been a long night, a bloody fight, and there was some drinking—"

"Och!" Gemma marched toward her cousin. "You barely remember this conversation and you put us all at risk?"

"I remember the conversation," Keran insisted. "I just don't remember exactly what it meant. What the final outcome was. Or the barbarian's name. Or whether I fucked him."

"I'm sure you fucked him," Keeley muttered.

Keran laughed. "Yeah, probably."

Gemma had her fist pulled back, ready to strike her cousin, but Keeley caught her sister's arms and pinned them to her sides.

"What?" Keran wanted to know. "You can't say I didn't help!"

"You could have killed us all!" Gemma insisted.

Keran sighed sadly. "Must you always be so negative?"

At that point, Keeley just wrapped her arms around the screaming-and-threatening Gemma, picked her up, and carried her away.

CHAPTER 27

Caid knew something was wrong as soon as they entered the Dwarf King's throne room.

Keeley had been smiling, holding Sichar's gold, ready to hand it over to the king and queen. But their expressions were so dour it was obvious something had happened. And standing beside their throne and General Unroch was Hearn's personal messenger, Henok.

Caid and the others held back while Keeley spoke with the royals and Henok.

"What do you think is going on?" Quinn asked him.

"How would I know?"

"Just asking."

They stood in silence for a bit as Keeley's expression grew darker and darker while she listened to Henok.

Then Quinn wanted to know, "So you attached to this one, or what?"

"None of your business."

"Father won't be happy. And who knows how long she'll be queen before she loses her head in battle?" He thought a moment, then asked, "And are you planning to breed with her? That could be strange. What if the offspring have horse back legs but everything else is human? And they can't shift? Or they have front forelegs instead of arms but human legs? What if they just have a horse's head on a human body? Can she even marry you? She's a queen, you know, and you're nothing, so she may leave you for a human prince. Would that bother you? Especially if they have normal babies and banish your horse-headed baby from the territory."

Laila, by this point, was pacing in front of her brothers; her gaze worriedly locked on Keeley. Gemma had her hands on the hilts of her two swords, her back straight, her body tense. Ready for anything.

Keran was asleep at the table, her feet up. She was snoring.

They'd left the horses, the demon wolves, and Samuel outside the mountain entrance. A good plan for many reasons, Caid was guessing.

"Do you think Dad would be happy with your horse-headed baby?" Quinn asked, either pretending he didn't see how things were turning or truly oblivious. Caid seriously didn't know which was worse. "I'm sure Mum would. She'd like to have a horse-headed grandchild. She'd be happy with that. So that's good."

His brother smiled at him and Caid was seriously considering pulling out all those pearly white teeth with his bare hands when the sound of metal ramming into metal snatched Caid's attention away from his brother. Keeley was no longer standing by the dwarf king and queen but they appeared duly concerned. He followed their shocked gazes across the room until he saw Keeley standing over a massive steel anvil. Something he knew was not used for any blacksmithing tasks but, instead, as a symbol for all the Amichai dwarves. It even had a plaque on it, dedicating it to one of the top dwarf gods. Despite that, it was definitely solid metal and Keeley was currently battering at it with her hammer. Over and over. Her current rage focused on nothing but hitting.

Laila quickly made her way over to Henok and returned just as quickly. She motioned Gemma closer and told them, "Well ... I found out what's wrong."

Keeley continued her assault on the anvil until she couldn't lift her weapon anymore. Then she dropped it, threw her head back, and roared out.

She finally dropped to her knees before the roar could even finish echoing throughout the dwarves' stone home.

Devastated and panting, she stayed on her knees, ignoring the sweat pouring from her brow and neck and pooling under her clothes.

"Keeley?"

Keeley quickly held up her hand, stopping Laila from coming any closer. And she did keep her distance but she continued to speak, which Keeley didn't want.

"Your father is okay," Laila said. "He's going to survive. My father has the best healer taking care of him."

"And I'm grateful, but . . ."

Keeley couldn't finish. Of course she was worried about her father. About her family. But that wasn't what had her raging. That wasn't what made her want to tear this castle down stone by gods-damn stone. Not because the dwarves had done anything wrong—they absolutely hadn't—but simply because she wanted to destroy.

"Then what's wrong, Keeley? Tell me," Laila gently pushed.

Keeley couldn't say it out loud, though. She simply couldn't.

But when she looked at Gemma . . .

"How did Straton's men know where our family was?" Gemma asked Laila.

"Oh, uh . . . I'm not sure. Perhaps Archie told a friend—"

"Uncle Archibald has no friends. He trusts no one. He told no one."

"So what are you saying?"

Keeley and Gemma stared at each other a long moment before Gemma finally said, "It was Beatrix. She did this. She sent that bastard after her own family."

Laila gave a little shake of her head. "We don't know that."

"We don't?" Gemma asked. "Then how did Straton's men find them? Only Beatrix knew where the family was."

"Trackers?"

"With you centaurs getting us there? Doing everything you could to ensure that trackers couldn't follow us to Archie's? You really believe that?"

"But . . . do you really think she'd do that? To her own family? Even to the little ones? The baby . . . ?"

When Keeley and Gemma did nothing but stare at her—silent, accepting the truth of what they believed—the centaur could do nothing more but fold her arms over her chest and look away.

But Keeley couldn't look away. She had to face this. She had to make a decision.

"So what do we do now?" Keran asked.

"I think it's finally obvious to all of us," Gemma said. "We kill Beatrix." Gemma looked at the centaurs they'd grown to trust and at Keran. And, each one in turn, nodded in agreement.

"Anyone who would do this to their own family..." Laila shook her head again as she still struggled to believe the truth. "She has to die."

Gemma looked at Caid, undoubtedly thinking his support was the most important right now.

Caid gave a small shrug. "It would be hard but... it's what I would do."

Quinn simply nodded when Gemma turned to him.

And Keran growled, "Kin or not, the evil bitch has to go."

Gemma finally faced Keeley. "Now are you ready to do this, Sister?"

Keeley gawked at Gemma for a few seconds before she said, "I was ready after she stabbed me."

"Good!" Gemma turned toward the others. "Let's all get what we need and—"

"But that's not what we're going to do," Keeley added, slamming the head of her hammer against the floor and using the handle to help her get back to her feet.

By the time she was standing again, Gemma was scowling at her. "What do you mean it's not what we're going to do?"

"What part of that did you not understand?"

Gemma stomped toward her. "You can't seriously be thinking of letting that little slit live!"

"What I'm *not* going to do is let her dictate my plans."

"What the fuck does that mean?"

"Why do you think she did this?" Keeley demanded. "She sent Straton after Mum and Da to distract me. To make me crazed!"

"And because you want to prove what a queenly woman you've become *you're going to let that vainglorious cunt live?*"

"I'm going to do what I need to do!" Keeley yelled back, now staring down at her smaller sister. "And if that's a problem for you, *fucking leave!*" She waved toward the castle exit. "There's the fucking door!"

Determined, fed up, and crushed by everything that had happened, Gemma grabbed her travel bag and stormed out of the throne room.

"You're really leaving?" Quinn said from behind her.

"I am." She'd return to the protective gates where she'd left Samuel and her horses and those damn demon wolves and she'd head to the Old King's castle. "Beatrix has to die and clearly Keeley doesn't have the guts to do it."

"Really?" he sneered. "You really think that?"

"If nothing else, it's clear my queen sister doesn't need me anymore. She has your brother and sister—"

"And Keran."

Gemma stopped on the last step and looked back at the centaur.

Smirking down at her, he said, "You know, the one who may or may not have started a war with the barbarians due to a drunken conversation she had with one that she may or may not have fucked over a decade ago." He came slowly down the steps toward her. "And of course there's your mother and father who will always be by her side. I'm sure they can take time out from watching your siblings to risk their lives in battle to keep the queen safe." He reached the step just above the one she stood on. "I'm sure servants can raise the children, should all three be lost."

"So you're assuming I'll fail to kill Beatrix?"

"Yes," he said with a wide grin. "Because she's expecting either one or both of you to come and she'll crush you before you can get near her. And then she'll laugh and laugh! Or," he added, leaning down so they were eye to eye, "you can stop being a spoiled little nightmare and fight by your sister's side to secure her crown and the safety of your family. Of course, that means you'll need to start trusting her judgment. As hard as that may be for you."

"But as long as Beatrix lives—"

"She will keep coming for you and your family. I do not deny that. For some reason she's trying to wipe all of you out. The memory of you . . . offends her, I guess. I'm not sure why, but Keeley knows. But to go after Beatrix right now? Keeley knows better. She's learning to play the game. Beatrix's game. Because Prince Marius's army will be waiting for you with open arms if you make this very predictable move. And even a War Monk can't fight an entire army by herself."

Gemma hated that he was right and that he felt the need to pat her on the head like a dog.

As he patted, he noted, "You are surprisingly short considering the size of your sister."

Gemma jerked away from his hand and started back up the stairs, punching him in the side as she passed.

"Owwww! Evil viper!"

Unroch watched the Smythe sister return to the throne room, the centaur Quinn behind her, rubbing his side and wincing.

Making sure to catch the attention of his head guard, Unroch motioned to the human females. Keeley Smythe might have been made queen by the Witches of Amhuinn but anyone who could batter away at Soiffart's Anvil and not destroy her arms in the process was someone to be feared. And her sister? Well . . . she was a War Monk. Nothing else needed to be said about that.

So Unroch wanted his men ready for anything should the sisters decide to turn on the king and queen.

At first, the sisters did not speak. Queen Keeley kept her back to her sibling. The War Monk dropped her travel bag to the floor and leaned against the table. The cousin was eating.

Finally, the War Monk seemed unable to take any more of the silence and asked, "So, what do you want from us . . . my queen?"

Queen Keeley glanced over her shoulder at her sister. They stared at each other until the War Monk silently mouthed, *Bitch.*

Unroch tensed, ready for the fight that would ensue. But the human queen merely mouthed back, *Asshole.*

And when the queen looked away from her sister, there was a small smile on her face.

"Well, Sister," the queen said for all to hear, "I have been thinking that I need a place to live. I mean, as queen."

The War Monk frowned so harshly that Unroch thought she'd explode and storm out yet again.

But, when the queen faced her and added, "Perhaps a chunky *nun* can help me secure such a place," the frown faded, replaced by a small smile. Then a much bigger smile.

"A queen *does* need a place to live," the War Monk practically purred.

"Then, my friends," Queen Keeley announced, "let us get ready."

King Mundric did offer his army to Queen Keeley, but the human only said, "Not yet, my friend," and then handed him the most important resource the gods had ever given Unroch's people: Sichar's gold.

After that, the centaurs and humans moved quickly to gather up what they needed for whatever they were going to do next. The human queen paused only to yell, "*Keran!*"

"I'm awake!" the guild fighter barked, jumping up from the royal dining table. "I'm awake! What are we doing? What's happening?"

Once they'd all left the throne room, Unroch examined Soiffart's Anvil.

"By my cock!" he exclaimed to his king and queen, smoothing his hand across the metal. "She dented the fucking thing!"

"That's not possible," the king argued; he and the queen now stood over the anvil and gawked at it along with their general and several of the shocked guards.

"My ancestors made this themselves," the queen gasped. "With the best of our steel given to us by the gods . . . it's *indestructible.* This should not be possible."

"It's a *dent,* my lady. A small dent, but it's a dent. That human dented it with that hammer she made herself."

"He's right," Mundric said. "That . . . *woman* dented it with her pathetic little hammer."

Unroch blew out a breath. "I do not envy her enemies, my liege."

CHAPTER 28

Lars watched the chunky nun approach the closed gates with her two mules.

"My lords," she called up to them. "I beg you in the name of my merciful god to allow me to enter so that I may bring the words of love and care of the god Simon to those who are within."

Lars glanced at his men and asked, "Simon? You lot ever heard of a god named Simon?"

After getting nothing but head shakes, Lars returned his gaze to the nun, who had moved closer. All two thousand pounds of her. Well, she wasn't *that* big but still . . .

"Sorry, Sister. You'll have to take your words of love and whatever to someone else. We don't need them here." Grinning, he glanced at his men. "We wouldn't want the ladies of this lovely town to change their ways toward us."

The nun's eyes narrowed a bit. "Yes. I'm sure they've all happily welcomed you into their town."

"What?"

Her soft smile returned. "I asked that you please allow me inside so I may bless this place in the name of my god."

Lars shook his head. "No, Sister. No one in or out."

She disappeared for a moment as she moved her bulk, covered in white robes, closer to the gates; and Lars heard a loud, panicked screech. A moment later, the nun reappeared. There was blood splattered across her face and on her white robes.

"Woman, what have you done?" Lars demanded with a startled laugh.

"Cursed you!" she said dramatically. "My god will come down upon you! And you will know true suffering. Because you're all bad men! Bad, bad, bad!"

"Your god Simon will come for us?" he asked with great sarcasm. "Yes, I shiver in fear. Now go." He motioned to his bowmen. "Or we'll leave your body as warning to others."

"Bad men!" she said, shaking her finger. "Bad!" One of his bowmen leaned forward and the nun ran off screaming, hands above her head.

"Where are her mules?" one of the men asked.

"She left them, I guess."

"Should we bring them in?"

"We're not opening the gates for anyone. So no. They'll wander off on their own."

Lars motioned to one of the young boys they'd recruited from among the locals as squires. With a few words, he sent the boy to the other side of town to alert the bowmen on the back gates. He wanted them to keep a lookout for the nun.

But as the boy took off running, there was a banging at the front gates. Hard, brutal banging that didn't stop.

"What is that?" he demanded, looking over the battlements in an attempt to see below. "*What is that?*"

His men and bowmen also leaned over the wall, trying to see below. That's when he heard the sound, slicing through the air. He'd been a mercenary for decades and instinctively ducked. But he had many younger, less experienced men under his command and they were hit with arrows to the head, neck, and chests. Those who weren't killed outright died when they fell from the wall and landed hard inside the city.

"Blow the horn!" Lars yelled to the men below. "We're under attack!"

She heard the horn blow and knew that someone was attacking her town. She looked at her sister and Efa nodded. They'd be losing their hiding place but they couldn't live like this much longer.

Every time they had to steal food or get water, they put themselves—and the few who'd managed to make it into the safety of the tunnels under the town—at risk of being caught and killed by Straton's men. Or worse. For the younger girls, there was always the promise of much worse.

Of course, who knew what horrors lay on the other side of that gate? It could be Prince Marius's army trying to get in, and that royal was no better than his brother. But he had a queen now. Perhaps she would bring a bit of humanity to the men of the prince's army.

As she gripped her sister's hand one last time, the pair charged out of their hidden position toward the big wooden gates.

"Stop them!" someone yelled as she and Efa grabbed the wood pieces blocking the doors and lifted, tossing them aside.

Hands grabbed her, but she swung her arms, hitting the men, and lunged for the third and last piece of wood. She and Efa tossed it aside together as the soldiers caught her and her sister and dragged them away.

The doors banged open and . . . two mules ran in.

Two mules. Mules!

The soldiers laughed and one said to her, "I guess your great rescuers aren't coming, whore!"

Foolish! How could she have done something so foolish?

The soldiers started to bind her and her sister's wrists, to drag them to the brothel.

But before the men could tie those bindings tight, one of the mules lifted its head and that's when she realized the animal's throat had been cut. Its eyes were also red from blood and it . . . it was dead.

It was dead!

The mule swung its head toward her and her abductor and the man's grip on her loosened as her captor went for his sword.

She yanked Efa away from the soldiers as the second—also dead—mule charged the men.

Both animals turned and began kicking at the men with their back legs, apparently still possessing that instinct even in their dead state.

She dragged Efa back toward the safety of the tunnels and shoved her sister inside. As she was about to follow, she stopped and looked over her shoulder. The attackers came in on horseback... she thought. But no. They weren't on horseback. They were horses... and human.

Centaurs! Centaurs with bows and swords and deadly intent.

Grinning for the first time in ages, she followed her sister back into the tunnels.

Laila rammed her spear into one soldier, yanked it out, spun, speared another. She sensed a soldier behind her, and she kicked out her back legs, sending the man flying.

Caid leaped over her, tackling another soldier coming from her right. Quinn cut off the head of a mercenary to her left. The rest of her battle squad took down soldiers running in from the barracks.

Laila took off toward the longhouse where she assumed Straton was staying and where Keeley was headed to confront him. But a small unit of soldiers came at her from the side, startling her. She reared up on her back legs. One of the soldiers attacked her there with a spear, so she shifted to human, diving over the weapon. When she landed on the ground, she again shifted to centaur and kicked out with her back legs. Bones cracked and a body flew.

She tried again to get to the longhouse but more soldiers cut her off, blocking her from reaching Keeley.

"Gemma!" she called out. "Get to your sister!"

Keran swung her axe and took another head before she ran into the town behind Gemma. But she wasn't meant to be fighting by the War Monk's side. Keeley had given Keran very specific orders after they'd talked to those who lived outside of town and discovered what had been happening since Straton and his men had taken over. And Keeley needed *that* dealt with in case none of them made it out of here alive.

Samuel tried to follow Gemma, but Keran grabbed his arm and yanked him with her.

Together, they quickly ran down the streets but kept close to the buildings, hoping to avoid running into any soldiers. They reached their destination and Keran pulled out the axe given to her by the dwarves. She ran up the stairs to a front door and kicked it in, but she immediately stopped.

The soldiers assigned to keep an eye on the brothel were standing in the main room. All the women who'd been trapped there cowered behind them. And one of the soldiers, a big blond, had a blade to the throat of a sobbing young girl.

Samuel started to dart forward but Keran blocked him with her body and put down the axe. She held up her hands and said, "It's all right, lads. No problem here. Everyone can stay calm."

The blond nodded to one of his men and he came toward Keran. He pointed a sword at her belly with one hand and reached for the rest of her weapons with the other.

As he leaned in a bit, Keran looked over the shorter man's shoulder at the girl currently being held hostage. She didn't say anything. Didn't even smile. Keran just stared and waited.

The girl's gaze slid away, then back.

That was all Keran needed.

Straton stormed from his bedroom, putting on his chainmail as he walked.

"What is going on?" he demanded, hearing the warning calls and screams from outside the walls.

"We're under attack, my prince," one of the mercenaries announced.

Straton smiled. "My brother is finally here to face me."

"No, my lord. Something else."

Allowing his squire to finish putting on his clothes and bits of armor, Straton stared at the mercenary. "What are you talking about?"

"It's not Prince Marius," the man repeated. "But I did see Amichai."

"Amichai? What are Amichai doing..." Straton's words faded out. "That mad bitch." He laughed. "That mad, wondrous bitch! The false queen is here attacking *me!*"

Loving the very idea, Straton adjusted his armor and stalked through the feasting hall toward the front doors but abruptly stopped midway.

And without even turning around, he knew the false queen was already behind him.

Keeley pushed her way through the small door that led into the jarl's bedroom. She hadn't been acquainted with this type of royal home; the jarls of the past had faded to mere memory ages ago. But these stone buildings had held up well and the dwarves knew about the ways those rulers would get their young children and wives to safety during wartime.

Once she was halfway out of the escape tunnel door, she paused to take a quick look around the bedroom. She didn't see anyone, but she could hear . . . sobbing. Muffled sobbing.

Dragging herself completely out, Keeley stayed in a crouch and inched quickly across the dark bedroom. She froze when she reached the bed, spotting the bruised and obviously battered naked woman chained to the bedpost. Keeley went to her quickly. She knew she shouldn't. She had one goal. To sneak up behind Straton and slit his throat. That was it. That was all she was supposed to do. But how could she just leave this woman here? Suffering. The answer was, she couldn't.

Keeley grasped the cuffs that kept the woman trapped.

"Don't bother," the woman whispered through her tears. "They're dwarven made. You can't—"

One cuff fell away; then the other.

Shocked, the woman gawked at her. "How did you . . . ?"

"Blacksmith secrets," Keeley whispered back. "Now go. Through the tunnel on the other side of the bed. I left the door open. Go before he comes back."

"He'll kill you," she warned.

"Maybe. But at least you'll be gone. Go someplace safe; don't look back." Keeley started to go but stopped, grasped the woman's bruised but now free hands, and added, "I am so sorry for what's happened to you. So sorry."

Determined to keep Straton off this woman's back, Keeley would no longer lure him to his bedroom for a quick blindside attack, which was what she and Gemma had planned. Instead, Keeley went to the big open doors that led out into the feasting hall.

No longer crouching, she walked away from the safety of that bedroom and into the hall. She waited until he turned and spotted her.

"Come to face me, bitch?" Straton taunted.

She was surprised to find that he was actually quite handsome. She'd assumed he'd be horrific looking. A living monster. But no.

It was amazing how someone so handsome could be so unbelievably cruel.

"Want revenge, do you?" he asked. "For your family?"

Keeley pulled her hammer from its sheath, letting the head slap hard into her opposite palm.

The prince laughed. "Oh, dear girl . . ."

He made a motion with two fingers and soldiers appeared from dark corners around the room. Weapons out, advancing on her.

The prince, however, spun around and again started toward the exit.

Samuel was busy trying to figure out how he could get the poor girl away from her captor and get the rest of the women out of the brothel without being harmed by these brutes, when Keran suddenly slapped both her hands onto the face of the man in front of her and leaned in as if to kiss him. But the man started screaming as Keran forced him to the ground.

Startled, most of the soldiers simply watched the attack, but a few attempted to rescue their comrade. The captive girl tried to drop down so she could get away from the blond man holding her but he was quick and yanked her back. But then the other women threw themselves at the soldiers standing with him. The soldiers who'd kept them here against their will. With just fists and feet and their bodies, they assaulted the men.

Samuel jumped over Keran and the soldier she still had pinned to the floor and went right for the young girl. The blond man started to drag the blade across her throat, but Samuel followed Keran's example and tackled the man to the ground with the poor girl stuck between them. He grabbed the man's hand and pulled with all his strength to get the blade away. The girl took her chance and slipped out from between them.

The soldier used his leg to flip Samuel over him. When Samuel landed, he rolled over, expecting to see the man going after the girl. But he didn't have the chance.

Keran was standing in front of him, blocking his way out.

Her face covered in blood, she gazed up at the man until she finally spit at him. Samuel thought she'd only spit blood to blind him but then something fell to the floor and Samuel quickly realized that it was a tongue. She'd bitten that first soldier's tongue off.

Keran slapped the blade out of the blond man's hand, hooked her leg around his, and yanked him to the ground. Then she grabbed him by the collar and began hitting him in the head. Blow after blow from her fist. Over and over until she'd destroyed the man's face.

Another soldier attacked her from behind but Samuel got to his feet and pulled his sword. He blocked that soldier's blow at Keran's back and pushed him away. He then went on the offensive, striking at the soldier again and again until he'd backed him out the door and kicked him down the stairs.

Turning, he grabbed Keran's axe.

"Here," he said, forcing the weapon into her hand. He had to do it in order to get her to stop hitting the blond man, who was clearly no longer breathing. "Take this. There are more."

"Oh." Keran smiled at him as if her face and hands weren't covered in other men's blood. "Okay!"

Some of the soldiers attempted to escape with a few screaming girls through the hallway.

"Take the women to safety, Samuel," Keran ordered. "I'll get the rest."

Samuel probably shouldn't leave her alone to fight but when he looked down at the blond man with the crushed-in face and the other soldier choking to death on his own blood and without his tongue . . . he assumed she'd be fine.

Gemma paused in the middle of the town to watch her centaur compatriots fight the mercenaries. Rapidly shifting from human to centaur and back again so they could confuse their opponents, they avoided direct assaults to important body parts. But as fascinating as that was, Gemma had to move. She grabbed an abandoned sword from the ground and pointed it at a group of soldiers attempting to drag off some women who'd been trying to use the sudden battle to escape.

"Leave them!" she ordered and a few of the men snickered at her. "I said leave them!"

"Or what?" one of them demanded, facing her. "What will you do, *nun?*"

Burying the tip of the sword into the ground, Gemma grabbed the collar of the white robes she wore and ripped out and down.

The man stumbled back. "*War Monk!*" he screamed. "WAR MONK!"

Quinn heard the soldier's scream and turned to see a battle unit release the women they'd been dragging away and run. From Gemma Smythe.

"You really love doing that, don't you?" he had to ask, briefly ignoring the fighting going on around him. "Scaring the unholy shit out of them when they see what you really are?"

She looked at him over her shoulder, the smile on her face pure sin. Which was kind of strange since she was a monk and all.

Yet it wasn't that she simply scared her opponents away. He saw that now when she caught the handle of a war hammer aimed at her head—one not nearly as large as her sister's hammer—without even looking at her attacker.

Yanking the war hammer and its wielder close, she rammed one of her short swords into the soldier's belly, then slashed him across the throat before shoving him to the ground.

"Are you fighting, Brother?" Laila called out to him. "Or watching the woman?"

"Can't I do both?"

"*No!*" his kin yelled at him.

Surprised by his siblings' intensity, he twisted around to see more mercenaries—a lot more—racing into the town on horseback.

Quinn's stomach dropped. "Oh, shit."

* * *

Keeley lowered her head and readied her weapon. The prince had walked out of the hall but with a cry, he tumbled back in. The lead demon wolf knocked him to the ground.

"Get it off me!" Straton screamed. "Get it off me!"

One of the men ran to Straton's side and kicked the wolf off. He rolled across the floor but, as Keeley would expect, righted himself quickly enough and charged back. Straton stood and pulled his sword. He slashed down, hitting the animal in the head.

"*No!*" Keeley screamed out, hitting two of the soldiers that stood closest to her and running. But another soldier caught her and held on.

The prince studied her with cold eyes. "A pet of yours?" he asked. "This *thing?*"

"Leave him!" she ordered, watching her friend stumble from the blow, leaving a trail of blood as he moved.

"I'll end this thing," Straton swore, raising his sword above his head, "and then I'll end you."

Keeley yanked her arm free and rammed her elbow into one soldier's face. She pulled away from the other and brought the head of her hammer down on his foot, crushing it.

As the soldier howled in pain, Keeley charged forward but she stopped when the demon wolf's blood abruptly disappeared into the ground and a crevice opened up in the stone floor. The soldiers and Keeley moved away from that opening when paws appeared, and then wolf heads . . . their eyes made of flames.

Keeley looked at her old friend and watched the wound to his head heal, leaving a raw scar from the top to under his jaw. Then he flashed his fangs at her. Not in warning, but a smile.

A brutal, merciless smile.

That's when they came tearing up from the crevice. Ten. Twenty. More.

Full-grown. Eyes full of flame and rage for one of theirs who'd been harmed by a human.

They charged at Straton and the bastard dragged one of his own men in front of him before running back toward the bedroom.

Keeley ran after him. "*Straton!*" Keeley barked to stop him before he could go back into the room. She didn't know if his captive had made it out yet and she didn't want to risk it.

He came to a stop.

"Afraid of me, are you?" she taunted.

"Afraid of *you?* A farmer's daughter? You're nothing," he said, walking toward her, his bloodied sword still clutched in his hand. "You're no one. *And you will never be queen!*" he bellowed.

"Then come for me, prince. Or are you afraid of a woman who can fight back?"

"Cunt," he hissed.

"Right here," Keeley agreed. "And waiting."

Straton now held his sword with both hands and raised it over his shoulder.

Keeley readied her hammer, smirking as she heard the sounds of the soldiers behind her being torn apart by the wolves.

That smirk was too much for the prince. He ran at her first and Keeley raised her weapon to block the downstroke of his sword. But he abruptly stopped, removing one hand from his weapon and reaching behind his back. As he did, he turned, and Keeley spotted the knife that had been rammed into his spine.

Straton fell to his knees; his sword fell from his hand. As he dropped, Keeley saw the woman who'd been chained in his room. Still naked, her hand covered in the blood of the prince; but the woman hadn't killed him. Straton wasn't dead. Her strike had been precise, Keeley guessed, to keep him alive but leave him unable to fight.

"You need his head," she calmly said to Keeley, walking past her. "Feel free to take it at your leisure."

Keeley watched the woman walk out of the longhouse, and Keeley sucked her tongue against her teeth. She motioned to the lead demon wolf and then the woman. He sent several of his original pack to follow her. They'd help her get to safety.

With the woman cared for, Keeley looked down at Straton. She sheathed her hammer and pulled the long sword hanging from her side.

"As I told the first contingent of mercenaries you sent to kill my kin . . . you chose the wrong family."

"You'll never be queen, peasant!" he desperately gasped out. "You'll never—"

The head came off swiftly and cleanly, bouncing a few feet away.

Done with that bit of unpleasantness, Keeley switched back to her hammer and headed out to join the fray.

"Bring the head along, would you?" she asked the lead demon wolf. "The rest of you can have the body."

Keeley met Gemma outside the doors. Her sister looked in, then glared at her. "Where did all those extra demon wolves come from?"

"Why do you ask me questions when we both know the answers will only upset you?"

"Pull back!" Caid ordered the centaurs. "Pull back!"

Caid knew not asking the dwarves to send a battalion or two with them was a danger but he also agreed with Keeley that they would need the king's dwarf armies far more when they took on Prince Marius and Beatrix. It would be foolish to waste their good favor for such a small battle.

Of course, they hadn't expected fresh mercenaries would be arriving during their attack and now they had to contend with the new arrivals. They were holding their own but Caid didn't know how much longer they could.

Although, he had to admit, his brother was enjoying the melee.

Dragging two soldiers off their steeds, Quinn threw them to the ground. He used his front hooves to batter one to mush while he bashed his sword into the other's head, bellowing like a madman as he did.

"Pull back!" Caid ordered again, hoping this time his brother would hear him. Maybe even obey.

A hand pressed against his hindquarter and he recognized Keeley's touch.

"Is it done?" he asked.

"It's done. Quinn!"

Quinn stopped bellowing and looked at Keeley. "Yes, my lady?" he asked calmly.

"Your brother said to pull back."

"But he's not my queen."

"Do it anyway. I have a greeting for those reinforcements."

Quinn moved quickly, joining the others, and Keeley stepped in front of them. The lead mercenaries came to a stop and stared down from horseback at Keeley.

"Turn back," she called out. "It's over. Straton is dead and the town is ours."

One of them moved his horse closer to Keeley. "So what? It's a nice town." He glanced at a few of the buildings. "Maybe we'd like to stay a bit. Have some fun."

Keeley glanced at Caid and the others over her shoulder. "We like fun. Don't we, lads? Don't we all like fun?"

Caid thought she was talking to him and their team . . . but no. She was talking to her demon wolves.

The wolves appeared beside them, around them, and above them. Standing on the tops of buildings and growling down at the men. Growling with their bloody drool pooling in the dirt.

And there were more of them. Not a few more. An army more. An army of angry demon wolves with eyes of flame and drool made of blood.

"Come on, my beauties!" Keeley called out to her "friends," raising her arms in the air. "*Go have some fun!*"

The demon wolves had the first half of the reinforcements torn off their mounts and dying in the dirt within seconds. Then they chased the soldiers who made a mad run for it.

Keeley faced Caid and the others, smiling. "That went well, yeah?"

Laila pointed down. "What happened to its head?"

Keeley looked down at the now-scarred lead wolf standing beside her, with Prince Straton's head hanging from his mouth.

"What do you think happened?" Keeley asked, confused. "It got cuff off."

CHAPTER 29

Keeley sat next to Gemma on the stoop that led into the longhouse.

"I can't believe how tired I am," she said, watching as the bodies of the mercenaries were dragged off to a burning pit outside town. The local men had happily taken on the duty, offering Keeley their services for nothing.

"I didn't think one could be this tired without being dead."

"Hhhm."

"Where's Keran?"

"After she got the girls from the brothel to safety, she took Samuel to the pub."

"That, Sister, might be a plan."

Keeley heard the startled screams of the locals and she knew the demon wolves were returning to her. When they arrived, they had a dark-haired woman with them.

"Are you Keeley Smythe, the Blacksmith Queen?"

Despite her exhaustion, Keeley couldn't help but smile a little at the title. "I guess I am."

"You returned our sister to us. She was a captive of Prince Straton and I wanted to thank you myself."

Keeley combed her hair off her face. "Does she need anything? We don't have much right now, but the women ... who were ... I mean ..."

"Me, my sisters ... we're witches. It wasn't sex that Straton wanted from my sister, but her magicks to advance his cause. She refused simply because she didn't have the skill, but she could have done little things. Little things to appease him, to give a bit of help in his war. But my sister wasn't blind to the kind of leader he would be. That he was not a leader she could allow in the world. So he beat her, every day. And we were unable to rescue her because we lacked the power to do so." She shrugged. "Perhaps we should have joined an order, but it's too late for that now."

"I have some healing skills—"

"No, thank you, War Monk." The woman cut off Gemma not only with her words but a brutal look.

Gemma flicked her hands. "As you like."

"Are you two sisters?"

Keeley nodded. "Yes."

"You fight together then?"

"We do."

"That's nice." She gestured at the longhouse. "And you will stay here?"

"Once we get the stench of Prince Straton and his men from this place," Gemma said.

"Actually, my plan is to reinforce the town walls first," Keeley explained. "My family will be arriving soon and I want everything to be secure for them as well." She thought a moment. "Or maybe we shouldn't stay here at all. I don't want these poor people to be put through any more—"

"You do understand that you can't save her?" the woman interrupted Keeley.

Keeley glanced at Gemma. Was the woman speaking of Straton's former captive?

Unsure, she said, "Pardon?"

"Beatrix. You can't save Beatrix. She was never yours to save. I know that hurts you and I'm sorry, but you shouldn't continue to hope. She'll only destroy you with it."

Keeley shook her head, a little confused. "I must admit, I haven't had that hope since she stabbed me."

"I wasn't talking to you, blacksmith. I was speaking to the War Monk."

Shocked, Keeley again looked at Gemma and there were tears in her sister's bright blue eyes. "Gemma?"

"You were right," Gemma admitted. "I shouldn't have left the family. I should never have left."

Keeley put her arm around Gemma's shoulders. "Gemma, come on. You have to know that whether you had left or stayed, Beatrix would have done all this. But you had to go. I see that now. So should you. Because now I have a much-feared War Monk by my side. To fight with me."

Keeley wiped the tear that rolled down her sister's blood-covered cheek. "And you are with me now . . . yes?"

Gemma nodded. "Always. Of course, that doesn't mean I won't punch you in the face should you deserve it."

Keeley kissed Gemma's temple. "I'd expect no less."

"I have to get back to my sisters," the woman said, turning away from Keeley and Gemma. But she stopped and added, "You know, the old jarl had a throne in there. Straton was a fan. He'd sit in it, feeling all proud of himself. As if he thought he was already the Old King. If I were you," she said, moving away from them, "I'd get rid of the bloody thing. Tear it from the ground." She glanced at them one last time over her shoulder. "Just a suggestion."

The sisters watched the woman until she disappeared into the crowd of workers removing the bodies; then they jumped up and ran into the longhouse.

The centaurs were sitting at the long tables, eating and drinking ale.

"What's wrong?" Caid asked as Keeley and Gemma rushed over to the throne.

"It's bolted into the stone floor," Gemma noted.

"So?"

"We're both exhausted." When Keeley stared at her, Gemma rolled her eyes. "Get the tools."

The local blacksmith, apparently delighted to be free again, gave Keeley whatever she requested and she quickly returned to the longhouse.

Caid watched her and her sister start working on prying the throne from its moorings.

"What are they doing?" Laila asked. She was so tired, her face nearly dropped into her plate of food.

"They're trying to pry up the jarl's throne."

"Why?"

"Why do they do anything?" Caid just wanted to get into bed. With Keeley. And sleep for the next ten weeks or so. He'd assumed she'd want to do the same thing until she started obsessing over that bloody throne.

But the Smythe women were not to be dissuaded by something as simple as exhaustion and hunger.

They worked hard, ignoring Caid's offers of help. Finally, though, when they'd nearly gotten the thing up, Caid and Quinn joined in to heave the ridiculous throne off its moorings and away from the floor—

Gasping in shock, they all shoved the throne back into place.

Laila jerked awake again, sitting up straight. "What? What's wrong?"

She frowned, watching their expressions, and pushed away from the table.

"What is it?" she asked.

"Something the jarl left, I guess."

"What was that?" Together, the four of them moved the throne again.

Laila gazed down into the hole built beneath it. "Holy shit!"

"Yeah," Keeley said, grinning.

"Is it all gold?"

"I think I see some gems in there. Look at those rubies."

"How did you know about this?" Laila asked.

"Someone told us."

"It's been here all this time?"

Keeley shrugged. "I guess. But it belongs to the town, yes?" When they all just stared at her, she asked, "What?"

"You're the queen, dumbass," Gemma sighed out. "It's *your* gold."

"Oh. Well . . . that's good." She blinked and stared off, forcing Caid to look away before he started laughing. Because he kind of knew what was coming next. "But what do I do with it?"

"Run your kingdom?" Laila asked.

"Build your army?" Quinn suggested.

"Reinforce the town and this longhouse to protect yourself and all those within?" Caid offered.

Keeley smiled. "Oh, those are lovely ideas!"

That's when the War Monk slapped the new queen in the back of the head. "Idiot."

It took a few days, but Keeley knew as soon as they arrived. Running out of the longhouse, she threw herself into her father's good arm; the other still trapped in a sling so he could heal from his arrow wounds.

They burst into mutual tears, hugging each other tight while her mother and sister hugged and rolled their eyes at the emotional outburst.

"That's not the way for a proper queen to act," her mother softly chastised.

"Are you going to start shoving *that* in my face now?"

"If I have to."

"Come on, you lot. No bickering between me girls." Her father set Keeley on the ground and kissed her forehead.

"Da," she began, "about Beatrix—"

"No," he said quickly, shaking his head. "We won't be talking about that now. Maybe not ever," he added before he turned to hug Gemma. Understanding how her father felt and not wanting to upset him, Keeley went ahead and hugged her mother. Then, of course, came all the children.

The whole ordeal went on for a bit. The hugging and kissing and occasional sobbing. And started all over again when Keran came running over.

While that was going on, Keeley went to Hearn. He'd also accompanied her family and Keeley would be eternally grateful for his care and protection of them. Although he didn't appreciate when she hugged him and kissed his face several times while his offspring watched.

Of course, that only made Keeley do it more.

"Stop it, woman!" Hearn ordered, pushing her away. But when he thought it was over, Gemma threw herself at him. Then Keran, both of them kissing and hugging him too.

It was official now, Caid realized, when Keeley winked at him as she tortured his father with affection and then got her sister and cousin to join in. It was official that he loved her. How could he not love a woman who purposely tortured his father?

"Stop it!" Hearn bellowed, pulling away from the human women. "I'll not stand for this!"

"Father," Laila suggested, taking his hand, "come. Let's go to the pub and get you some ale."

"Can I come, Father?" Quinn asked.

"*No.*"

"Excellent! I'm coming anyway!"

Caid knew he had to go as well, but he stopped long enough to slip his arm around Keeley's waist and kiss her cheek. "I'll be back later."

"Good. We're having a feast in honor of my family and your father."

Caid gave her another kiss and followed his own kin. But before he could catch up, Angus was by his side. Caid smiled at him. "It's good to see you again, sir—ack!"

Angus's very strong arm trapped his neck as the farmer growled, "I'll only say this once, *boy*. You break my daughter's heart and I'll strip the skin from your bones. Do we understand each other?"

"Yes, sir," Caid gasped out. "I understand."

"Good!" Angus released him. "And welcome to the family!"

Keeley sat on the stoop in front of the longhouse, the lead demon wolf asleep at her feet. She'd thought he and his friends would have left her by now, but no. The newer ones had left, wanting to return to their underworld, but the lead wolf and his pack, they'd stayed. As had the gray mare. Although the mare refused the stables and instead stayed in the nearby forest. But she did come when Keeley called for her, which was very nice.

"You wanted to see me, niece?" Archibald asked.

"Yes. I have a job for you."

"And do you have an axe for me?"

"You'll get your axe, but I've been busy."

"Too busy for the forge?"

"Are you *trying* to make me cry?" she demanded.

"Sorry, sorry," he quickly replied, appearing ashamed. "I forgot who I was dealing with. So what do you need?"

"A stonemason."

"To make your longhouse here fancy?"

"No. Not to make anything fancy. I need the battlements and house walls rebuilt. The escape tunnels need to be reinforced. A moat and traps set for any enemies that may attack our new home. I need all of that. You up for the challenge?"

His head tilted, his expression a little confused. "So I can stay here? With you lot?"

"Did you think I'd throw me own uncle out on the street?"

"Yes."

Keeley laughed. "Go find Gemma, you crazy bastard. She has drawn up the plans. And no beating your workers," she yelled after him.

"I only beat them when they deserve it!"

Keeley was about to argue about that, but she was in no mood. She still had so much to do.

About to get to her feet, Keeley stopped when her mother came out of the longhouse and sat beside her.

"How are you doing?" her mother asked.

"A lot on my mind. The children—"

"They're settling. Stop worrying about them. They're fine. Just glad to be back with you."

"I still need to rebuild our old town. So you lot can go home."

"Keeley, you are our home. We go with you. And you can worry about our old town later. And stop feeling like it's your fault. This was Beatrix's work. We all know that."

"Yes. I know you do. Da still won't talk about it, though. He doesn't even want Beatrix's name mentioned."

"We were staying with the centaurs before we came here. Gaira and Hearn told us what Beatrix did to you." She shook her head. "There's nothing else to know. Not for us."

"Mum, I'm sor—"

"Stop. I don't want to hear it. Ever. Understand?"

Keeley gave a quick nod.

"Now, I have something for you."

Her mother reached into a bag she had hanging from her shoulder and pulled something out.

"I made this for you at a centaur's forge. It helped me work out my rage at what Straton's men did to your father."

"Just so you know, Straton got his due."

"I know. I saw his head outside the town walls. Nice touch by the way. Reminds me of me old gran." She bumped Keeley's shoulder with her own. "Here. Take this."

Keeley looked down at what her mother held out for her and she blinked in surprise.

"A crown?"

"Fit for a Blacksmith Queen. That is what they're calling you, you know? The Blacksmith Queen. A perfect name, I think, for one of the Smythe clan."

Keeley held the crown in her hands. It was beautiful. Made of the finest steel with rubies inset into it every few inches. Perhaps her mother's finest work.

"Put it on," her mother urged.

"I won't look silly?"

"You think it's ugly?"

"No! I've just never worn anything fancy before, Mum. You know me. I never look right in jewelry or anything."

"Give it a try anyway. For me."

With a deep breath, Keeley put the crown on her head. Her mother stood in front of her, adjusted the crown a bit. She stepped back to take a long look.

"Yes. That works nicely. I'll also make you a helmet so you can wear the crown into battle."

"All right."

Her mother leaned in and adjusted the crown a bit more.

"All right," she said when she finished. "Now we're all done."

"All done?"

"You just had your coronation, luv," her mother said wryly. "Welcome to the world, Queen Keeley."

With a pat on her shoulder, her mother headed back into the longhouse.

"Aren't I supposed to get a stick or scepter or something at my coronation?"

"Just use your bloody hammer!" her mother yelled back. "What do you think this is?"

Keeley shrugged at that. "Well . . . it *is* an awesome hammer."